DUNGEON
DIVING 104

CONTENTS

THE STORY THUS FAR:

Ken and his party did some wild training with his grandparents, becoming a little more assassin in the process. Afterwards, they returned to Haylon College—the school for adventurers to learn to dive the dungeon—to finish out their second semester. During their studies, they farmed an event on the seventh floor until they were level ten, and pushed into the next zone, waiting for the end of the school year.

They went much farther than most first years, but they weren't alone. Everyone at the big four was pushing themselves to new limits.

Crimson changed up the classes so that the top five parties would now be in her class. This rotated Felicity's party and Penelope's into Class 1-A. Candice and Kendra's parties made the cut with Ken's from the original Class 1-A.

The adventures continued on the eleventh floor, a realm of bouncy clouds.

But all good things come to an end. As their class wrapped up the year with a maid cafe, and most of the class joined Ken's family guild, the Silver Fangs, the capstone event of the festivities was for the elite adventurers and their guests only.

In the dungeon's safe zone, what was meant to be a simple demonstration turned deadly.

Lysandra, one of the upperclassmen, betrayed them all. She changed the portal destination and opened up a portal to a safe zone near the naga world before trying to carry the scientist responsible for the new technology off to the Kaiming. Those present fought hard, but it was a messy and gruesome battle.

Red naga had poured through the portal, fighting the top adventurers that humanity had to offer while Crimson battled a powerful naga matriarch. Barely holding on to her control, Crimson defeated the matriarch before entering the portal and going on a rampage among the naga.

Ken, in an accident, absorbed the synthetic spellbook which had created the portal and he was able to use the restricted ability to close the portal, attracting the attention of the Harem Queen among other elites. But to Ken's grief, Crimson was stuck on the other side, and he could not figure out how to use the spell to reopen the portal.

Neldra—protecting Fayeth's Adrel and the best chance her princess had at truly becoming a Trelican—wasn't going to let anything happen to Ken. Grabbing him and the powerful new skill he'd developed, Neldra charged out of the dungeon with Fayeth and Ken in tow.

CHAPTER 1

The world rushed by as I held on to Fayeth. Both of us were tucked under one of Neldra's arms while her sword was out in the other hand. For all the trouble Kaiming went to in order to trap us, they weren't showing a huge presence as we exited.

As if reading my mind, Neldra spoke, "Did you forget about your grandparents? They stayed on the floors below to make sure that no one could run away with anything."

Neldra jumped across sand dunes, passing right by the monsters before they'd even fully realized she was near.

"Unhand him!" The Harem Queen exploded in a column of blue fire and shot ahead of us with a flourish as she tore the side of her dress so that she could move more freely.

Helen's mother had the same fiery red hair as her daughter, and she did look wickedly intimidating as she leveled her flaming blue sword at us. Even though she was the wet dream of many teens in high school, I had zero interest in her at that moment. Instead, I saw her as a tyrant.

"Hold on." Neldra squeezed us tight to her side as she sped up even more as she covered the last several platforms. Her sword flashed out in a blur of attacks that drove the Harem Queen back for just a split second. That moment was all Neldra needed to slip into the seventh floor.

The floor was typically another floor of endless sand and bright light. But as we entered, the entire space shone red, and gore covered the ground.

My grandfather flicked his blade as he turned with Neldra's sudden arrival. "Haha! Come to join us for the fu—" He noticed our expression and his laughter died.

One second he stood in front of us, the next he exploded in a maelstrom of blades aimed at whoever was behind us. He didn't hesitate or even care who was coming; our expressions had apparently told my grandfather everything that he needed to know.

The Harem Queen blocked his attack, both of them coming to a sudden stop. Grandpa flipped back out of her reach as she swung her huge sword around.

"I've got them." Hemi appeared by our side, taking us out of Censor Neldra's arm.

"Good. I have a score to settle." Neldra dropped us off and shot back, her sword arcing straight for the Harem Queen's head.

A clear shield sprang into being around Helen's mother that cracked a second later, but it gave the Harem Queen enough time to get mostly out of the way of the hit. The very edge of the blade caught her face, a red cut opening on her otherwise pristine face.

"The elves shouldn't be running off with our prize." Two more adventurers appeared. One of them held his hand up, clearly the creator of the shield.

"Oh. I'm just following Crimson's orders and keeping him safe. Didn't seem to me like you had his best interests at heart." Neldra took a step back as my grandmothers arrayed out behind her, ready to enter the fight.

"Crimson is gone. Even she won't make it out of a dungeon teeming with those naga." The Harem Queen spat and stood in a relaxed pose. "Why don't we ask the boy?" She gave me a half-lidded look and pursed her lips. "Want to come with me?"

I crossed my arms to make an X. "Nope. Not one bit. Bye. Hard pass."

Grandpa shook his head. "If it becomes necessary, I will sacrifice myself for my grandson." He took a deep breath and puffed himself up.

The Harem Queen gave him a droll glance. "Your grandson is the one I want. He absorbed the synthetic spellbook and even used it to close the portal." Her eyes shined. "An ability like that is worth quite a bit. I could remove one of my top four and make a spot for you at the top of my harem." She licked her lips.

"I already declined. Besides, imagine when Crimson gets back and finds us." I shook my head sadly. "I'd just be sealing your fate."

"Shut up, kid," one of the men chuckled. He wasn't one of the Harem Queen's but from another guild, he flexed his muscles as he talked. "Are you implying that you and Crimson have something? Crimson doesn't date anyone."

Grandma Sakura kept her bow drawn and shifted it to the man who had spoken. "Let's focus on the matter at hand. If you try to touch my grandson, I will put an arrow through your eye socket."

The muscular one chuckled, but the caster took a step back. "They are the Silver Fangs. I would treat that as a promise, not a boast. The Harem Queen might walk out of here alive if we fight, but the two of us won't."

I decided he was 'Smart One' and the muscle-bound man was 'Dumb One'.

Dumb One snorted. "Has beens."

"Then think about the elf," Smart One said. "She fought the Harem Queen while holding on to two young adventurers. Now she's not burdened."

"Shame. Would really like you both to have been dumb enough to keep this going." Neldra had her sword poised with a lopsided smile. "What about you, Tits?" she addressed the Harem Queen.

Helen's mother's eyes were reflecting the blue fire of her sword as she focused back on Neldra. "I'm going to make you regret that little nickname." She exploded forward.

Everyone else stood still as the two of them fought, exchanging blows powerful enough to make gusts of wind. The battle would have shaken me to my core when I was an early adventurer, but after seeing Crimson fight the naga matriarch, it didn't seem quite as impressive.

"Adrel. She'll win," Fayeth tried to comfort me. Neldra was one of the strongest elves in their world, and the elves were a step ahead of humanity.

I watched the two of them and already saw Neldra taking the advantage and pushing the Harem Queen back. "I know."

"Don't worry. We could kill her if necessary," Grandma Hemi promised, still standing beside me. "We'd just have to have Akari protect both of you for a moment until Grandpa kills the other two."

I looked over at Akari. My blood-covered grandmother positioned herself in front of us, dropping a heavy tower shield into the ground and standing stalwartly behind it to protect us.

The other two adventurers were still staring at the fight, and I could tell that they also saw the outcome long before it happened. Smart One pulled Dumb One back to the sixth floor.

Grandpa zipped over to me, his eyes like two giant stars. "The Harem Queen and Censor Neldra are fighting over you, you lucky dog. Tell me your secrets."

Yui knocked him over the back of the head. "Cut it out. It seems while we were playing with Kaiming, something disastrous happened to our grandson."

"Crimson got portaled to the naga area of the dungeon," I told them. "I got a portal ability, but it says restricted at the moment."

Grandpa rubbed his chin. "Odd. We'll figure it out. So, then Neldra carried you two off when the Harem Queen fell in love with you."

"Pretty much." I glanced around at my grandparents. "It might be in my best interest to go with her to the Elven world for the summer. There will be many after my ability, and without Crimson, it will be a lot for us to take on. Going will give Crimson some time to get back here; I refuse to believe she's gone."

Grandpa nodded. "Yes. Take lots of pictures. We men of Earth need to know what we are up against."

"Yes. I'll help, Grandpa," Fayeth added with a chipper tone.

Grandpa abandoned me to grab her hand. "Please. If you could take some pictures of the ladies, especially wh—"

Thwack.

Grandma Akari cut him off with a knock to the head. "Don't corrupt the girl. But I do have a request. Ami, come out."

The girl from the Nagato clan unstealthed not ten feet away. She stood in her black suit and pants with a mask over her face and long, white hair dancing from the wind of the fight not that far away.

"We brought her to get some experience, but seeing that you are without the rest of your harem, I would feel much more comfortable if you had an ally with you," Akari told me.

Fayeth puffed out her cheeks. "I'm his ally. He is my Adrel."

Akari gave her an amused smile. "Then you two should work together to keep him safe. I know there are politics at play in your world, and I wouldn't want you in a tight spot without recourse."

"Deal. But while I'm gone, you'll look out for my party?" I asked.

Grandpa nodded. "I think the new recruits of the Silver Fangs deserve an intensive summer training. Except that damned rabbit. Little bugger keeps getting into the garden. Lucky for him, Charlotte is so cute that I'll still let him in."

"You are gracious, Grandpa." I bowed at the waist.

There was a final explosive clash, bringing my attention back to the fight. Neldra was relatively unharmed, a few scrapes to her armor and some of her hair loose from her ponytail. The other side was the Harem Queen who had chunks taken out of her dress and cuts all over her body.

Grandma Yui waved her hands, and a healing mist washed over Neldra, putting her back in top form.

"You would require aid to match me." The Harem Queen held her head aloft before glancing my way. "You will come to me eventually. There's no need to rush things." She twirled her sword before putting it back in her CID. "Have a good trip." She blew me a kiss. "I'll be waiting for you to come back." She put on a seductively sweet smile and turned away.

"She has even bigger tits than Des," Fayeth blurted.

"Yes, she does." Grandpa nodded. "17.3% larger than even Akari."

"What was that, old man?"

"Critically evaluating your opponent in every way is a vital skill for battle." Grandpa's eyes shone before dipping down to Grandma Akari's chest.

"Alright, let's go, Neldra. I don't need to see this. Oh, and Ami is coming with us, if that is all right?" I waved at the woman to my right.

Neldra frowned slightly.

"If it is acceptable, I'll help you all down to the fifties." Grandma Yui nodded at Neldra.

"I'll never turn down a healer." Neldra nodded before glancing my way. "You sure you want to come home with the two of us?"

I glanced at Grandpa. "Make sure the president of the UG knows where we are going. I have a feeling that if Crimson makes it back and can't find me, there's going to be trouble."

Grandpa clicked his tongue. "You rapscallion. Got her hooked nice and deep? It's okay, she'll make a wonderful granddaughter. I'll let her know when she returns. I don't think a few naga are going to keep her from getting back."

"Of course. Otherwise, why would my first thought be to make sure people are safe from her?" I grinned at him. "Let's go."

Grandma Yui waved her arms. Neldra, Fayeth, Ami and I exploded into mist that shot up the path for the dungeon. I watched with wide eyes as my future dive through the dungeon rushed past, leaving the sandy wasteland behind.

Cloud platforms were replaced by a hellscape with green fire and then by a jungle. More and more views flashed by for an instant before we were moving on to the next floor.

***

Des stood with her and Charlotte's parents. The families had blocked off any remaining adventurers who had tried to rush after Ken.

Marcus DuVell leaned on his giant sword and was decked out in bulky green armor. "I know the ability Ken Nagato got has many of you drooling, but it is in everyone's best interest not to go after the grandson of the Silver Fangs."

"You just want him for yourself!" Javier of the White Tigers stepped forward.

"No, my daughter is dating him." Marcus laughed. "I want him for the next generation. If today taught me anything, it is that the next generation already has a leg up from the rest of us. Who here was level eleven after your first semester?"

While he paused, no one raised their hands.

"That's what I thought. Today we lost many great adventurers. Tomorrow we might lose more if we don't let the next generation step up and grow stronger than us. So, I will plant my sword here and stop you from touching the next generation for your own greed. Instead, I'd ask what we are going to do to answer for the naga threat. Will we weaken ourselves by fighting amongst us?"

Arthur Renard, Des' father, rubbed his beard. "It would be best if we accelerated our kids' growth."

"What?" someone shouted. "We'd be better off leveling ourselves."

Arthur shrugged. "I could go dive the dungeon, and in two months do what? Maybe push a level and get a few stats. But my daughter, I could get her to level twenty before the second year..."

Candice's mother stepped forward with her hands on Candice's shoulders. "I agree. It also seems our daughters have all joined the same guild. Maybe we could coordinate?"

Arthur chuckled and glanced back at Des, his eyes flashing red. "Yes, hellish training always goes better in a group. They push each other that way."

"We'll see how your 'hellish' training compares to an average day with Crimson," Des taunted her father, only making the situation worse.

Her mother gave her a knowing look and pursed her lips to hold back a smile.

Ken was no doubt going to get a crash course in Elven training. Hopefully, he'd come back far stronger. Des was certain that if she didn't push herself as hard as she could, she'd be left behind when he returned, and she was not going to let that happen.

Charlotte grabbed Des' hand. The shy girl showed a strong vein of courage standing in front of all the other adventurers. "Dad, I want to join them. See how hard we can push ourselves. This year's class is going to blow everyone away."

Two adventurers rushed out from behind the DuVells, and Charlotte's mother spun, blasting hurricane level winds at them and pinning them to the dungeon wall.

Des could feel her hair start to stand on end as the older woman gathered enough lightning in her hands that the two would be toast.

The President of the UG stepped between her and the two adventurers. "Stop this. We are already suffering losses from this attack. You wish to self-inflict more?"

"I warned them not to chase after my son-in-law." Charlotte's mother wasn't backing down, but she put one hand on Charlotte while the other held what felt like an entire storm's worth of lightning. "They attacked my family."

"Mom." Charlotte's eyes were watering.

Des couldn't keep the smile off her face. She knew that Charlotte struggled with her relationship with her mother. Charlotte had once confided in Des, and Des knew Charlotte's mother's acceptance of Ken was also an acceptance of Charlotte diving the dungeon.

"Yes, daughter? If you want to leave enemies at your back, you must be stronger."

"I will be. Anything you deem necessary as training for the summer." Charlotte nodded hard enough that Bun-bun had to grab tightly to her hair to hold on.

"Fine." Her mother dismissed the lightning, her expression not changing the slightest in the whole interaction. "They can live."

The Harem Queen chose that moment to emerge too, but she was in a new dress. A few cuts marred her face. "Helen. We are leaving."

"No, mother." Helen stepped closer to Des. "I won't be going with you."

"Excuse me?" The Harem Queen stopped dead in her tracks and turned slowly towards her daughter. "I don't think I heard you correctly."

Helen grabbed the patch and ripped it off Des' jacket before pressing it to her own. "I have guild practice all summer. Won't be home before the school year."

The Harem Queen stood tall and looked down her nose at Helen. "You will come home, and you will be training with me."

Marcus DuVell interposed between the two. "I think the little lady has made herself clear."

"Are you going to step into a family matter?" The Harem Queen put her hands on her hips and raised an eyebrow.

Des nudged Helen and glared at her. There was an obvious solution. Helen frowned, her eyes working quickly to try to decipher the nudge, but she didn't seem to be putting it together. Des made a motion of scribbling in a book below her waist where the others couldn't see.

Helen closed her eyes and cursed under her breath. "Mother. I am in love with Ken. I write smut about him online called 74 wives."

Des was having trouble keeping from laughing as joy flooded through her at the admission even if it wasn't true.

"I am joining the Silver Fangs, and I will be here for him when he gets back," Helen finished the statement as Ken's grandfather walked in.

"Oh, really? Well, welcome to the guild. My grandson has a way with recruiting people." The old coot chuckled and came up behind Helen, holding her shoulders.

The paladin sighed and spoke through her teeth. "Yep. I'm joining the Silver Fangs, and one day, I'll be his wife. So lay the fuck off, mom. You already almost ruined my chances."

Ken's grandfather chuckled. "Oh. But you are just as beautiful as your mother. I'm sure you could turn his head easily."

The Harem Queen was quiet, watching her daughter with searching eyes. "Fine." She directed her attention to Ken's grandfather. "I would request that I be able to supervise and assist my daughter with her training, even if she's under your banner."

"Of course. Of course." Ken's grandfather pecked his head like a chicken. "We'd happily welcome the Harem Queen into our home. You'll find that the Silver Fangs training is remarkable, but an adventurer of your esteem must have carefully trained your own daughter. We'll need to work together to make sure she's the best she can be for next year's school."

The Harem Queen gave a light smile, and the tension around the group fell. Des released a breath she didn't know she was holding.

"Oh, and Ken asked for everyone to pass the word around. He'll be in the Elven world. We are a little worried Crimson is going to resurface and be a little cranky that she can't find him."

"Does he have the ability to portal her out?" someone asked.

"No. But she's been working with the Nagato Clan on my grandson's training, and we are fully aware of her capabilities. She'll be back." Ken's grandfather seemed completely confident in his statement.

Des wondered if his feelings had to do with the electric red mana that Crimson had given off during the fight with the matriarch. Ken had clearly understood more of the situation, but now he was gone. "Mom. I'd like to start training as soon as we can." Des turned to her mother.

"Yes. Let's go." Des' father took a step forward and the crowd parted for him. "We can't let you all fall behind. Silver Fangs, join me. I'll carry you all to the Nagato Estate." He glanced at Ken's grandfather. "Don't suppose you'd extend your offer to the Harem Queen to me as well?"

Ken's grandfather looked around at the many eyes focused on him. "We'll rent out all the nice hotels and make sure we have space for everyone." He was all smiles.

The Silver Fangs were about to be surrounded by powerful adventurers while training the best and brightest in the new class. Seeing his old guild revived brought him more joy than he'd imagined was possible, especially with his grandson set to take over.

CHAPTER 2

The boss of the forty-fifth floor—a giant triceratops that would have pulverized me—turned into black smoke as Censor Neldra sheathed her sword. "Let's get going and find a place to rest in the next safe zone."

Neldra swept the loot into her CID as was her right. She did all of the work with just a few heals from Grandma Yui which really just saved her on potions.

Meanwhile, Fayeth, Ami, and I were just huddling in the corner making sure we survived. None of us being carried this far deserved any of the loot. Plus, I was already getting something out of the fights: experience.

I checked my CID.

Ken Nagato
Class: Emperor
Secondary Class: Demon Lord
Level: 15
Experience: 45198/84000
Strength: 25 (+6)
Agility: 65 (+14)
Stamina: 50 (+2)
Magic: 44 (+4)
Mana: 39 (+4)
Skills:
Dark Strike, Earth Stomp, Charm, Metamorphosis, Sprint, Absorb, Discharge, Dark Blades, Shadow Arm, Camouflage, Shadow Ambush, Elemental Shield, Portal [Special] [Restricted]

I had gained two levels from our trip down through the dungeon to be able to connect to the Elven dungeon. Neldra hadn't been holding back. She'd cut through entire floors like she was trying to show off as we moved.

It occurred to me that she might be trying to power-level me as well. She had wanted me to return with her to Lady Rendral when I was level twenty. While I was thankful, I couldn't help but compare the amount of stats I was getting moving through the dungeon to fighting on my own. While I was leveling from Neldra's efforts, my stat gain was minimal.

Why adventurers avoided power-leveling the younger generations was making even more sense the more I experienced it for myself. If I leveled too much this way, I'd be critically weak against monsters my own level, and if I went too much lower than my level to farm, I'd gain experience at a far slower rate.

I came out of my contemplation to see the safe zone ahead of us. It was far more compact than the ones I had seen on the fifth and tenth floors previously. The buildings were also far less refined. Yet it all had a pressure that spoke of power.

"That's the gathering of powerful adventurers," Grandma Yui spoke up. "Besides you two, most will be the appropriate level to be here. That means that, while they may not be the very elite of humanity, they are all powerful adventurers in their own rights."

Using my CID, I checked the group around us. Everyone I saw was at least level forty.

Neldra marched straight up to a classic tavern. It seemed that, even this deep in the dungeon, people still fell back on the classics. She kicked the door in and strode through with a hand on the hilt of her sword.

Her arrival made heads turn. Most of the heads turned back to what they were doing when they saw the elf. I thought for sure there would be some gawking.

"Censor." A party of elves jumped to their feet.

"Relax." Neldra waved them off and led us to a table in the corner.

My eyes scanned the crowd. Off in the corner, I noticed a table of Nekorians. The other race varied widely, but they all had cat ears sticking up through their hair. When one turned my direction, their eyes were vertical slits on otherwise human faces.

The ladies were kind of cute until they opened their mouths. The set of tiger-like teeth in their mouths gave me pause.

"Don't stare. The Nekorians will take offense. They prefer to keep to themselves, but this deep in the dungeon, they don't have a choice." Grandma Yui scooted in next to Neldra. "If you want more detail, I'm sure your grandfather has porn you could watch."

I snorted, and could have sworn I saw one of the Nekorians' ears twitch our direction from across the place. I paused, wondering if their hearing could reach as far as we were sitting.

"They are very adept at stealth. You could learn a few tricks from them," Neldra spoke up before staring down a server until he came over to check on us.

"What can I do for you?" He was polite enough to Neldra

I took a peek at my CID and realized he was level twenty. Someone must have helped him reach the safe zone, which meant he wasn't going back up without help too.

"You still have that hydra meat?" Neldra asked.

"You bet. It comes from the forty-sixth floor; we are always flush with it," he answered.

"Is it good?" I asked Neldra.

"Actually, it's very tender, a bit of a buttery flavor to it."

"Then I'll do one too," I told the man.

"Me too," Fayeth added while Ami just nodded at the server.

Yui was looking over a menu. "I'll do the demonic stew." She had a sweet, grandmotherly smile as she spoke.

"It's very spicy, ma'am," the server cautioned my grandmother.

"Nonsense. It is what I ordered, isn't it?" Grandma Yui went from being a sweet grandmother to a dangerous adventurer.

"R-right," the server stammered. Thankfully, Ami had gathered the menus and handed them over to prod him back into action.

I glanced over at Yui. "Was that necessary?"

"No. But it was fun. There are some perks to being a powerful adventurer." Yui stuck her chin up. "On that note, how much deeper do you want me to assist you?" She shifted her focus to Neldra.

"Your ability to travel with them as a mist has made today very easy. The bigger question for me is how far you can go before you can't get back on your own?" Neldra asked.

"I can go to the fiftieth floor boss. But I'll turn back from there." Yui gave a firm nod. "If I'm on my own, I can sneak back to the 40th easily and then just race back up from there."

Neldra dipped her head. "I would appreciate your help."

"Then we'll travel together briefly tomorrow." Yui smiled. "What are your plans for Ken? I do feel the need to remind you that he should be returned for the next school year."

"It will happen," Neldra promised. "Besides, I'd be shocked if it takes all summer for Crimson to pry herself from the naga. That... ability she used at the end was terrifying."

Yui thoughtfully nodded but didn't speak before she threw a side glance my way. "Your teacher has a few secrets, doesn't she?"

"Probably." I didn't feel comfortable telling Crimson's secrets. A subject change was in order. "Beyond that, I'm excited to see the Elven world."

"It is beautiful. You'll love it." Fayeth grabbed my hand and bounced in her seat. "Are we going to stay in the palace? I know I can, but I'm not sure about him." She looked over to Neldra.

"He's going to be treated as a guest of honor." Neldra was glaring at the server, likely because he hadn't even come back and given us water. "Better service than we are getting here. Lady Rendral will put him up in her personal guest suites. After all..." Neldra blushed slightly. "Never mind."

"She wants my Trelican powers," I filled in. "Before, you had wanted me to be level twenty before coming. Does that level hold significance?"

Neldra's green eyes broke away from staring at the server and back to me. "She or I will likely participate in power-leveling you."

"No," I answered firmly. "I don't want to be power-leveled; I'll become relatively weak."

Neldra's gaze sharpened. "You are already ahead of comparably leveled adventurers. That lead can be reclaimed. But the time that you can be here is limited."

"I'm aware. But if you want me to level, it needs to be from training." I held my ground, even as the powerful elf continued to stare me down.

"Fine," Neldra grumbled, turning away. "Don't let Crimson say that I didn't treat you well."

A smile curled up on my face. "What about you, Fayeth, and you, Ami? Are you both going to join me in this training?"

Neldra's eye twitched at me inviting them to join.

"Of course!" Fayeth said with gusto. "We are Adrel—I won't be left behind."

Less enthusiastically, Ami just nodded.

Fayeth grabbed the quiet woman by the shoulder and squeezed her in a side hug while swaying back and forth. "It is going to be great. We are going to get along wonderfully, Ami. You are so beautiful. And your hair is so pretty, like snow."

I smiled at seeing the two of them get along. "Do you even see snow on the Elven world?"

"Nope!" Fayeth giggled. "But it was in many of the Christmas Romance books that I read to practice my language. You took me on that date this winter in the snow. It was... beautiful." She breathed the word.

I shook my head. "Next year, tell me these things and I'll make a bigger deal of it."

Fayeth stuck out her tongue.

I turned the tables and my fingers found her tender sides as I tickled her before calmly turning to Ami. "Help me next year plan a few snow dates with Fayeth here?"

"Affirmative." Ami nodded.

"No—hehe—Ami, you are supposed to be on my side." Fayeth tried to get words out in between the giggles.

"Negative," Ami answered. "I am Ken's butler." That was the strongest statement I had heard her speak.

"Not a maid?" Grandma Yui pushed.

"Maids keep the dust off shelves. Butlers fix everything," Ami spoke proudly.

Yui shook her head. "But you are a girl. We should get you into some frilly…"

Ami turned to my grandmother with a fire in her eyes, something I had never seen in the quiet girl. "I wear suits because I am a butler." There was a forcefulness in her tone, so I gave her my full support.

"Yeah, Grandma. Are you blind? Ami is my butler, because of course butlers are far superior to maids." I promised myself that I'd never make the mistake again. "Did the maid cafe make you uncomfortable?" I asked Ami.

"No?" She tilted her head like an innocent kitten. "Just because I don't want to be a maid doesn't mean that others can't be. Even if I had to participate, I'd have worn my suit and served customers properly as a butler."

Yui was glaring daggers at me for siding with Ami instead of her. But I was also sure that I was earning points with my butler which would come in handy later. Yui would always be a sadistic grandmother. That was just a part of her nature.

"Your dinners." The server came back with a platter balanced on one hand and swiftly laid out our plates before hurrying away from Neldra.

"Wait." Neldra's voice froze him. "Waters, please."

"Y-yes, ma'am." He hurried away.

Neldra frowned. "I'm not that old, am I? He doesn't even call your grandmother 'ma'am.'"

"It's the silver hair." I pointed with my fork at her hair that was pulled back tight enough to pull her brows upward.

Neldra played with her silver ponytail for a moment. "It is a good color among elves."

"It is very pretty," I agreed. "It does look a little odd with your tan skin for a human, though."

With her hair pulled back, her pointed ears were on display and she touched one gingerly. "Someone would have to be blind to make that mistake."

"Agreed." I nodded, turning to my plate and focusing on the piece of hydra before me. It was still giving off a little steam, and the plate was hot enough that the oil that came out of the meat was boiled a little to the ceramic. Taking my knife, I went to cut the meat. It parted around the blade easily like a piece of slow cooked prime rib.

"This is good," Fayeth hummed as she took her first bite.

I joined her, my tongue quickly agreeing. The meat fell apart in my mouth like butter with a rich, meaty, buttery flavor. It reminded me of fancy steaks that were cooked in a pound of butter.

Yet the first time I swallowed, the meat hit my stomach like a brick. "Oh. This is heavy."

"You are eating high-level meat. It is probably going to restore more health than you even have." Neldra dug into her hydra like a starving bear. "If you can't finish it, I'll take the rest."

I wrinkled my nose and instead ate slowly, with a purpose. My whole attention was so consumed by eating that I didn't notice the group that had come over to our table until they spoke.

"You like leering at us?" A big Nekorian with coloration like a leopard was standing next to our table. His arms had scars that looked more like they were a marking on purpose rather than from an old injury.

While the big guy had distracted us all, a soft weight pressed itself onto my shoulders.

"No, Grr'ish." A female Nekorian was behind me, leaning on my shoulders.

I got a good look at her hands. They had a light layer of fuzz on the back of them, and I could see retractable claws peeking out between the webbing of her fingers. Never would I think a Nekorian was unarmed again. Those claws would make a wicked fist weapon if she closed her fist and let them out.

Her current position also had the effect of vaguely threatening me.

Neldra tensed and her hand was on her sword as she focused on the one leaning on me. "I wouldn't do that if I were you."

Grandma Yui was continuing to eat as if nothing was happening. "Come now. Can't we behave, little kitties?"

"What did you call us?" Grr'ish snapped.

Yet, despite his distraction, Neldra didn't move. She was paying attention to the one leaning on me.

I could feel her hot breath on the back of my neck.

"Grr'ish. This is the first group we've seen that is so... varied. Besides, I like this human. He smells good, smells like potential."

I could feel my hair pull as she breathed in my scent.

"Why don't you go and sit back down, Grr'ish. I don't need your protection. This one won't touch a little hair on my head, will you?" She rubbed her face against the side of my head and purred.

18

"She's in no danger as long as you calm down," I spoke for my group. "Neldra could kill this whole place without blinking an eye, and she would if you attacked me." I nodded towards Neldra, who was still poised to strike.

"See? What an interesting group. A human with lots of potential that smells like this little elf here, but he's the one with a high-level elf guard." The Nekorian leaning on my shoulders clicked her tongue. "I'm very curious about you. Can I join you for the meal?"

I was surprised at the question. I'd expected a lot more antagonism from the group, and I was happy to help de-escalate whatever was happening. "Sure."

The Nekorian pulled a chair up next to mine such that it clacked and flipped gracefully into it. Somehow, she moved with disturbingly little sound into the chair next to me.

I got a good look at her as I turned. "Whoa," I blurted.

Her eyes pinched in happiness, and she let out a chuckle that sounded oddly like soft little meows. "Do you like?"

If I had to describe her expression, I'd call it curiosity.

"Sha—" Grr'ish tried to say something, but one look from my new neighbor shut him down.

"I'm Felin." The oddly colored tiger girl held out her hand.

I shook it gently, and her slit pupils widened slightly at the touch.

It was hard to tell what was normal and what was strange for the Nekorian. She had tiger patterns, but the colors were all wrong. Her hair was white, with two prominent blue streaks through it. Some of the blue stripes carried down into her otherwise human body, giving her a very tribal appearance.

Her chest was bound by a tight piece of leather armor that pushed her chest up. The armor rose up and wrapped around her neck, leaving her stomach exposed where her abs rippled with every movement she made, outlined by her tiger stripes.

Below that, she wore a pair of incredibly tight, blue, scaled pants with a tail that flicked out through the gap in the chair and was currently playing with my thigh.

I wondered what her feet were like, but they were stuffed into a pair of boots.

"Hi Felin, I'm Ken. This is Fayeth, my Adrel. Ami, my butler. Yui my grandmother and Neldra—"

"The Royal Censor to the young Empress." Felin smiled and leaned on the table while gazing directly at me. "Which is why I say again, your little group has sparked my curiosity."

"So, you come say 'hi' merely out of curiosity?" I asked.

"If we don't let our claws sink into curiosity, how are we going to learn anything?" Felin smiled and her large incisors caught my attention.

"Want some of this? I'm having trouble finishing." I pointed at the hydra.

Felin licked her lips and just waited. I stabbed a piece and held it up for her.

She moved quickly, with a bite that could remove a human neck as she removed the meat from the fork without scraping her teeth. "Tasty." She licked her lips.

My hand shook where I was holding the fork as I kept wavering between finding her cute and finding her terrifying.

"Shaman. I must insist that we head out." Grr'ish was still at our table, clearly uncomfortable.

Felin snapped towards him. Her tail pattern changed from the gentle playful flicking of my thigh to a rigid curl. "No. I am going to talk with my new friend. Isn't that right, Ken?"

"I would love to learn more about your people," I admitted.

"Good, good. See, Grr'ish? Everything is fine. You can wander off. I'll find you tomorrow." She waved him away.

I had to wonder how powerful she was to order him around. I tried to check my CID, but her tail curled around my wrist as I tried to look at it.

"These things. I always see humans with them. They are how you interface with the dungeon?" Felin asked.

"Yes. It's a CID." I looked her over, but I didn't see anything comparable on her body. "What do your people use? And how are you so good at English?"

Felin chuckled and tried to pull her chair closer, but it was already as close as it could be, so she ended up half in my chair when she threw her weight to the side.

I wondered if the move was on purpose.

"We don't use devices. Our people don't use technology like humans, elves or the short ones."

"Dwarves," I suggested.

"Yes. Them. We don't much like them." She shrugged.

"No one does," Fayeth answered. "I heard that they believe that the entire dungeon belongs to them, because the dwarves think this is all a giant mine under their land."

Felin snorted and waved her hand. "They are pests. But strong. Are you all going to the elves? I've never seen a human going that way before."

I couldn't help but notice that she avoided the question about how she interfaced with the dungeon.

"As for your language, for those of us that wander far from the tribes to hunt, it is necessary for us to pick it up. Even the elves speak in human tongue when they are in human territory."

CHAPTER 3

The night in the tavern had gone long, but I couldn't say that the experience wasn't entertaining.

Felin had guarded information about her people closely, but she asked us plenty of questions. We'd chatted late until Neldra had stood up and announced that we had to go to sleep if we were to be rested for the next day.

Neldra's announcement had made the Nekorian pout and try to weasel her way into coming with me.

"I can't believe that I had to shoo her away three times," Fayeth muttered, curled up with me in a tent that Ami had insisted on putting up. Fayeth sniffed. "You smell like cat."

"Not surprising with how much she was rubbing against me." I sniffed at myself but couldn't pick up any of the scent. "It'll wear off."

"I don't think it is supposed to wear off easily," Fayeth sighed, wiggling against me to get comfortable. She perfectly fit against my body as the little spoon, pulling the covers over both of us. "It's been a long day." She let out a cute yawn and continued to snuggle in like she was going to eventually burrow into me.

"Maybe you are right." I wiggled my nose, wondering at just what had made the Nekorian so interested in me. She was a very curious woman, or maybe I was putting cat traits on the race of cat people.

My mind only wandered for a minute before the day and its excitement weighed down on me, letting me drift off into a deep sleep.

***

Ami came out of her tent in the middle of the group's rest and drew a blade in the dim light. She sensed someone by Ken's tent.

"Nya~!" The Nekorian from before made an oddly cute noise when startled. "Oh. It's the servant."

"Butler," Ami corrected, narrowing her eyes. "Why are you here?"

With her eyes adjusting, Ami could see Felin better as the woman returned a wide, pleading expression. "I was hoping to get his clothes."

"His clothes?" Ami asked, not expecting that answer.

Felin bobbed her head. "Yes. I'll even trade for them. You both are hunters, yes?"

"Assassins," Ami corrected.

The Nekorian's wide grin couldn't be seen as anything but predatory with those large teeth. "My English isn't perfect, but I think those are the same thing." She flipped a skillbook in her hand. "I'll trade you."

Ami didn't even know what was on the skillbook. But any skillbook would likely be worth far more than a set of clothes. "Why?"

"I like his scent. Tell me, who is he really?" Felin cozied up next to Ami, but Ami was still fully on guard. "Censor Neldra has been passing through this way multiple times and is known. But for her to be guarding him..." Felin left the statement open.

Ami had noticed that Ken had been dodging quite a few questions earlier that night, just as Felin had been protecting her own information. Ami wasn't about to give up more of his information. "He is just a member of the Nagato Clan, as he said before."

Felin's nose twitched before she went still. Her ears pinned to the back of her head. "Does it have something to do with Crimson?"

Ami froze and cursed herself for the tell.

Felin's tail flicked behind her. "It does. I knew it. She and the Censor have been seen traveling together."

"Is that why you've approached him? Crimson?" Ami wondered if it would make more or less trouble for her master if she killed the Nekorian. Ami wasn't positive she could win, but she wasn't weak either.

"No. He really smells that good." Felin sniffed his tent. "Really, really good. Did I hear his grandmother say he had porn of my people?"

"My master is a pervert. According to his grandfather, he nearly bought out an entire porn shop at the end of the semester," Ami replied. "If it exists, he likely has porn of it, or his grandfather does. There is a room... that I am forbidden by the grandmothers to enter."

Felin blinked at Ami's frank admission.

Truthfully, Ami had hoped to drive off the Nekorian with such knowledge.

"Interesting," Felin finally spoke after a brief bout of stunned silence as her tail curled back and forth. "I will go get some sleep now." The Nekorian turned to Ami's master's tent and started to undo the zipper.

"What are you doing?" Ami stepped forward.

"Going to sleep." Felin put a finger over her lips and slipped into the tent in an instant.

Ami closed the distance in a flash, but the Nekorian was still too fast and had already laid down behind Ken and started to cuddle him. If she had meant Ken harm, she would have already attacked. Ami was not sure of the Nekorian's level, but she was likely more advanced than Ken by a decent margin. But likely weaker than Censor Neldra.

"Out," Ami hissed.

Felin ignored her, nuzzling closer.

After a moment, Ami let out a deep breath and pulled a long sword from her CID before stepping forward to poke the Nekorian.

The cat girl swatted the blade away, shattering it silently and curled back up against Ken.

Ami picked up the skillbook from the ground and rubbed at her forehead. This cat was going to be bothersome. But so far, she wasn't doing anything that Ami really had to defend Ken against.

"Bad, kitty," Ami spat and closed the tent.

Whatever the cat was up to, Ami would leave it to Neldra or Yui to deal with her. If the woman had nefarious intentions, one of them likely would have woken to deal with the situation.

After all, Yui would probably love to make mittens from those cute cat ears.

***

I woke up the next morning feeling overly warm.

"Still sleepy," Fayeth murmured.

I stretched my back and shook my head as I sniffed the air. Now I definitely smelled Felin on me. It wasn't an unpleasant smell, but it was powerful. "Fayeth, you need to get out of bed before people call you lazy."

"Sleep is better than people. What do I care about their opinions?" She pressed herself into the pillow and cracked an eye open. "Must we get up?"

"Would you rather wait for Neldra or Yui to be the one waking you up?" I asked.

That question got her to sit up and rub her eyes. "Neldra is not gentle when she wakes someone. I doubt that Yui would be much better."

"Where is she?" a voice growled outside our tent, and I burst out, my weapons ready.

Grr'ish stood over everyone, glaring at Neldra who sat calmly drinking something out of a steaming mug. When I burst out of the tent, he spun to me and his nostrils flared. "You reek of her."

"You draw a weapon, kitty, and I'll cut you down before you take a step towards him." Neldra closed her eyes to enjoy another sip of her drink.

Grandma Yui wasn't far off, watching the whole show with barely concealed glee. The woman was hoping for something to happen.

"Where is she? I cannot allow for the Shaman to go missing." Grr'ish turned to me with anger still in his eyes, but there was a small plea in his voice.

"She's here." Ami came back; Felin was with her.

Grr'ish fell to his knees. "Please return with me. I cannot go back without you."

Felin cast a glance towards me and bit her lip then glanced at Ami.

My butler sighed. "May I have your dirty clothing, Ken? It is to remove a feline problem."

Felin's tail flicked back and forth excitedly. I knew something was up, but I allowed Ami to take care of the situation.

"Sure." I tapped several times on my CID before giving the clothes to Ami. Ignoring Grr'ish, I headed over to sit down by Neldra.

"You bring a lot of excitement." Neldra glanced at Felin. "Not worried about what'll come of it?"

"What level is she?" I asked.

"Twenty-five. Might be a year or two older than you," Neldra answered.

I was surprised. I'd expected a higher level given how deep we were in the dungeon. But it seemed that I wasn't the only one being brought around.

"It will be what it will be." I shrugged and pulled out some rations.

Out of the corner of my eye, Felin danced away from Ami and followed after a much-relieved Grr'ish.

"She's trouble." Fayeth sat down next to me. "Ami, I hope you got something out of that little exchange."

"I did." Ami didn't elaborate, and I didn't care. "She is trouble, though. Snuck into your tent last night."

Fayeth rubbed her brows. "I know my Adrel is incredible, but I did not expect him to be catnip."

Neldra clapped her hands together loudly. "Regardless, we have progress to make." Neldra seemed annoyed at the Nekorians more than anything. "Ken. Since you are so energized this early in the morning, you can take down the tents."

I scratched the back of my head, not quite sure what I had done wrong and got to work.

***

Neldra, Fayeth, Ami, and I said goodbye to my grandmother. From that point forward, the three of us lower-level adventurers made progress more difficult for Neldra.

But one thing was certain. I was getting more practice in stealth than I particularly cared to get. If discovered, I wouldn't just have to deal with a fight. I'd likely be stuck in a battle that would lead to my death.

But Neldra wasn't holding back as we moved, working to eliminate any threats. She cleaved through monsters left and right, rapidly accumulating experience for all of us along the way.

Rather than skip over them as we had with Grandma Yui present, she was clearing a wide area to ensure we didn't run into any danger. Probably wider than she needed.

I was starting to think that she was upping my experience on purpose. She knew that I wouldn't let her power-level me once we got to Lady Rendral, and I had a feeling she was now doubling down on seeing how far she could get me before we arrived.

"I'm just clearing the path for your safety." Neldra flicked her blade to the side as a large stone giant crumbled and shook the dungeon floor beneath us and broke down from boulders to rocks and finally to black smoke as loot appeared amidst it all.

"This seems rather slow for you." Fayeth joined me.

"Well, it is for your safety. There are three of you; I can't carry all of you. So this is the safest way to travel." Neldra argued before flashing forward her sword cutting through two more stone giants.

"It is fine. Maybe this will be good?" Fayeth tried to find the positive. "We might be caught up a little with Lady Rendral and unable to dive as much as the others. But we will focus on our exercise."

I nodded. Controlling my [Shadow Arm] skill, I grabbed several of the pieces of loot that Neldra had left behind and dragged them across the floor with a bit of concentration before stuffing them in my CID.

"You are getting better with that skill." Fayeth watched.

"That's the hope. The goal of this thing is to train my magical abilities, after all." After dragging back the armor, I quickly snatched up the mana crystal. We were coming back down and in the 30's, and this crystal was several orders of magnitude more valuable than the ones we normally collected.

Neldra returned and puffed out a breath. "Just keep moving."

I nodded and hurried after her, grabbing the loot of the two she'd just killed with my [Shadow Arm]. Ami was a sort of quiet shadow to me, always behind me. She seemed capable of moving quietly even at these speeds.

"Ami, what sort of stats do you have?" I asked.

"Agility," Ami answered.

Fayeth turned. "Wait, all of it?"

"Being fast means you won't get hit. Being fast means you can complete tasks on time, and cut where it hurts. Agility is without a doubt the best stat. That... and I like to be quick." Ami's eyes shone for a moment as she shot forward, her long, white hair flapping behind her before she returned.

I shook my head. "You should balance out your stats better. Strength and agility work together to deal greater damage."

"Thank you for your advice," she answered dutifully, yet I was sure she wasn't going to take it. "About the skillbook..."

"Is it useful for you?" I asked.

Ami nodded rapidly, her white hair swishing with the motion.

"Then use it. I really don't want to accept a gift from Felin if I'm honest. She is trouble, and I'd rather not owe her anything." I continued after Neldra, using my [Shadow Arm] to grab as much loot as I could.

All the while, I was working on silently casting abilities. While running, I was sporadically casting [Sprint] as we moved, but my success rate was not great yet.

"Thank you." Ami tapped on her CID, and the sparkle of her learning an ability wrapped around her. "I have learned Silent Paws."

"You don't have paws." Fayeth frowned.

"Doesn't matter." I nodded at Ami. "It works?"

Ami muttered under her breath, and her running became silent behind me. "Yes." Her footsteps came back. "Very low mana cost, too. It will help me in my duties so that I can traverse places unseen, and swiftly strike down tasks without my master knowing."

I shook my head. She was really into this ninja butler thing.

While the two of us were talking, Fayeth was huffing and puffing, trying not to slow us down. The petite elf was all strength and magic for her stat distribution.

Compared to me who was more evenly distributed but focused on agility, and Ami who apparently went all agility, Fayeth was having trouble with the run to keep up with Neldra.

But my Adrel didn't complain at all. Instead, she appeared more determined to not slow down. Because of her tank abilities, she had a sound foundation of stamina.

Neldra zipped back and saw us. "The floor thirty safe zone is up ahead. We'll take a break and let you all catch your breath."

Fayeth huffed. "Do you think the others are catching their breaths?"

Her words made me think of Desmonda and Charlotte, likely training hard this summer. I missed them already.

"They are all working hard, I am sure." Neldra nodded, a look of respect crossing her face.

"We can spare enough time to eat," I agreed. "Then we get back to the journey. Once we hit the seventeenth floor, I'd like to try my hand at fighting some monsters solo to see how I stack up."

Neldra nodded with a smile. "That we can do. Hurry up."

True to Neldra's words, we left the rocky hills and Fayeth breathed a sigh of relief as we stepped out into the peaceful planes of a safe zone.

"That was some good training." Fayeth wiped at her brow. "I still hate hills."

"No one likes hills," I chuckled. "Come on. Let's see what sort of Elven food there is here."

The idea of the familiar foods cheered Fayeth up as she took the lead. Returning to a familiar environment really perked her up. It made me smile.

The safe zones had changed as we'd headed more into the Elven territory. All of them had an enormous tree in the center shading most of the safe zone and the buildings. And instead of squares braced with sharp triangle architecture, the buildings were rolling curves.

I wasn't an engineer, but I knew there was a lot of strength in circular designs. It just wasn't what we used. It seemed that the elves had taken to that design and built lower, rolling buildings. Many of them connected to each other to keep the waving design constant. The tallest building was three stories, and there were only a few of those.

But as I considered their design, I understood. If they built under trees, that meant they were always conscious of building too high and hitting the canopy of the tree. And living under a tree probably had its fair share of maintenance clearing off limbs and leaves.

The rounded buildings probably weathered an impact from above far better than a square.

"Here. Let's go get some genuine Elven cuisine." Fayeth pulled me into a building. "You are going to love it."

I didn't say anything, just following along as she sat down first.

Neldra trailed behind us, and I noticed that many of the elves did a double take when they saw her before moving to the side to create a clear path for her to pass.

An elf with bright blue hair came up next to our table and trilled in the Elven language excitedly, her focus on the Censor and a broad smile on her face. I had some knowledge of the language, but she spoke fast, and I realized my grasp of it was still quite weak.

"Mind if I order for you?" Fayeth asked, she must have sensed my hesitation.

"You know me well enough, Adrel." I kissed her cheek.

My action made the server turn to me and realize that I wasn't an elf. "Human?!" The one word stuck out before she asked Neldra several questions.

I shrugged and glanced at the older woman. "Am I going to cause issues?" I spoke in clipped Elvish.

"No." Neldra turned away from the server to answer me. "We just don't have humans venturing this far into our territory of the dungeon. But you are with me. You are safe."

I wasn't sure how much I needed protection, but I wasn't looking to cause trouble. I was just on a trip for the summer or however long it took for Crimson to return.

"It's fine," Fayeth whispered. "She's just asking a lot of benign questions. Censor Neldra is well known among our people as the personal Royal Censor of Lady Rendral and as one of the top adventurers. The server is mostly asking for gossip about Lady Rendral and a little about why you'd be, she presumes, going to meet with the Lady."

The server noticed Fayeth and turned to speak to her for a moment as I assumed Fayeth ordered for Ami and me.

"What did we get?" I hadn't understood the dish names.

"We don't eat as much meat as humans seem to eat. So, it's like a sandwich wrap with a little meat and mostly cooked beans and some vegetables," Fayeth explained.

"Less meat?" I asked as the server wandered off, and Neldra shifted her focus back to us.

"Grass doesn't grow well under the great trees. Too much shade. So grazing animals are difficult to raise. We have Diodecs, kind of like a chicken, but they are scaled and they don't fly. They eat bugs and some grains grown at the edge of the tree."

I nodded. The harsher environment in their homeland would make food far more difficult. "So, there are farms outside the tree's shade?" I asked.

"Yes. The area around the tree is often broken up into that which always has shade, that which has shade for some of the day, and then beyond that the area that doesn't have any shade." Fayeth tapped her lips and explained. "People live in the fully shaded area. The partially shaded area we grow lots of root vegetables. Out in the full sun, we grow grains. But people can't last long out in the full sun, so many of those systems are automatic now."

"Is water a concern?" I asked, thinking the harsh weather would make gathering water more difficult.

"There are a few dungeon opportunities to get things like water sacks or other mostly water liquids," Neldra answered. "They are heavily farmed and protected by the Empire. Most of the great trees have access to a large well underneath them. Those are heavily monitored, and water from the dungeon is dumped on the land to restore them if necessary."

I thought about just how reliant the elves were on the dungeon, and it made me wonder if the dungeon had a sense of their specific needs. It seemed like the dungeon was going out of its way to help them.

And after I'd felt the attention of the dungeon when I'd absorbed the synthetic spellbook, there was no doubt in my mind that it was sentient and fully capable within its domain. For all I know, it listened to what people needed.

My ponderings were quickly interrupted as the elf came back with platters.

"Smells amazing." I poked at the burrito-shaped wrap before picking it up and taking a bite. The meat was scarce, but the vegetables had a rich, almost oily flavor.

Fayeth had a big grin on her face, biting into real Elven cuisine. Even if it wasn't what I was used to, seeing Fayeth smile at the flavors made me like the food a little more.

CHAPTER 4

Charlotte walked away with her mother while the rest of the class was getting acquainted with the Nagato Estate.

"I want to start training." She stood up straight and was ready to prove to her mother that she could handle it.

Her mother's face turned sad. "You chose the path of a healer. None of the roles are more important than the others, but a healer is a particularly vital role. Your ability to keep healing and stay standing is the most important for the party's survival. You see, as long as the healer stands, the rest of the party will too."

Charlotte nodded, missing the familiar weight of Bun-bun on her head. Bun-bun had gone with Grandpa Nagato to train. The two of them fought like children, but Charlotte knew that Grandpa would train her companion well. Bun-bun could use some tough love, she spoiled him too much.

"Pay attention. Do not let your mind wander," Charlotte's mother chided her. "In order to be a top-tier healer, you must endure. Can you do that?"

Charlotte puffed herself up. "For my party and Ken, I'll endure anything. If you can train me to be a stronger healer, please, mother. I want to be my best."

Her mother's face softened from its normal impassiveness and she touched Charlotte's cheek. "I derive no joy from this."

Then her mother held up a finger and pointed it at Charlotte as wind whipped around her. Her two braids smacked the sides of her head and her clothes threatened to rip off as the wind continued to pick up.

"Heal yourself or you'll pass out from the damage. Stay focused and don't let up. When you can heal no more, we'll take a break for your mana to restore. Then we'll start again." Electricity built up around the storm.

Charlotte didn't hesitate. "Heal!" She felt the soothing magic as minor scrapes and bruises healed on her body.

The storm picked up intensity, yet she was at the center of it. The winds were so strong that she was picked up off her feet and slammed to the side. It didn't stop though, while battered around, she didn't fly out. Instead, she was trapped in this small storm with her mother watching her.

"Heal!" Charlotte shouted defiantly, making her mother's eyes sparkle before a bolt of lightning hit her in the chest and stopped her next healing spell.

Charlotte had to grit her teeth and shout the next spell as bolts of lightning tried to break her concentration and prevent her from healing herself. That wouldn't be enough to stop her.

"That's it," her mother encouraged her. "This is how a healer should be trained. Focus on stamina, mana, and magic. Without the healer, the group fails. You must be the strongest link, my little Char. I love you and I will forge you into an adventurer that returns to me!"

Three bolts of lightning hit Charlotte this time. She cried out in pain, falling to the ground. The wind didn't disappear, instead tossing her around.

"Get up!" her mother yelled, her tone was that of a drill sergeant to a lacking cadet.

Charlotte pushed off the ground with one arm, then the other. As soon as she had a knee under her, she grit her teeth. "Heal!"

The small buff gave her just enough strength to get back to her feet.

Her mother stared down at her with a smile. "Good. We will continue."

***

Des followed along with the rest of the crowd after Charlotte had broken off to go train.

"Here's another available house." Grandma Akari gestured to the side.

"We'll take that one." Desmonda's mother flashed a charming smile.

"Oh no. You'll stay with us in the center of the compound. Des knows the way." Akari waved away the comment. "The Harem Queen can stay here, though you may not be able to stuff your whole harem inside."

Helen's mother laughed the barb off, now ever the noble lady. "No need. They can make themselves comfortable. After this tour, we'll start the training, yes?"

32

"Yes, we will." Akari smiled back at Des. "The Nagato Clan would be happy to pass along some of our stat training methods to everyone. We also have our own personal dungeon entrance. I would recommend going on a large-scale excursion together this summer."

Many of the high-level adventurers were nodding along with her words.

Des's mother's attention, however, was on her daughter. "Are you going to follow our family's training?"

"The grimoire?" Des asked.

Her mother nodded. "You asked to become stronger. We would like to offer our help in obtaining high-level demon blood."

"I thought I had to collect it myself." Des stared back at her mother. Her parents had never let her take the easy route in her entire life.

Her mother pouted. "Nonsense. Crimson cheated and gave Ken the blood of a level forty-five. While I'm not Crimson, I can't help but feel a bit of competitiveness. Besides, your power will grow nicely with powerful blood. Your father and I found some demons in the fifties."

Des thought about her mother's offer for a moment. Part of her wanted to claim the demon blood for herself, but in the same breath, she couldn't pass up such an opportunity. "I accept."

"Good. We'll work on the ritual later." Her mother grinned. "In the meantime, we should prepare for you to crush the competition here. Can't have your man come back to see you slacking now, can we?"

***

Grandpa cackled like a madman as he sat across from Bun-bun, both of them on reed mats. "Did you think I'd just feed you the carrots from the dungeon? I know your weakness."

Bun-bun had several lumps on his head, and his eyes kept darting over to the giant pile of magical ingredients behind Grandpa before he started squeaking loudly at the old man.

"Ha! An ungrateful, long-eared rat doesn't get to tell me what to do. Dodge a hundred swords in a row, and I'll give you... one." Grandpa drew his blade slowly, staring over the edge of it at Bun-bun.

Grandpa smiled. He planned to dice the rabbit into pieces in the name of practice. Despite the old man's aura washing over

Bun-bun, the rabbit didn't back down. Instead, he pinned his ears back and glared right back.

"Squeak," Bun-bun complained.

"It isn't like I want to train you either!" Grandpa lashed out, hitting Bun-bun with all three strikes. Grandpa made sure to turn his blade to not draw blood, but he continued to attack. "I'm stuck training a f-ing long-eared rat when I should be training my grandson and his beautiful brides! The sweat, the glistening curves! You are making me miss out on all of it!"

***

I sneezed three times in a row and rubbed at my nose. "Huh. Didn't think adventurers got sick."

"Maybe it was the smoke." Fayeth wiped at her brow as we finished up with the monsters that Neldra had brought to us. "It doesn't smell that great."

Ami reappeared behind me. "Two more."

Fayeth shifted slightly, but roots spread out below her feet, stopping her from taking a step. Without a healer, we were relying on her self-healing far more than ever before.

A moment later, two level-fifteen lizard men came rushing out of the jungle at us.

Fayeth crouched down in her defensive stance with her shield up, gripping her spear towards the top, and the butt of it pushed into the ground behind her.

Both lizard men had huge machetes, which Fayeth took on her shield, staying rooted to the ground.

"Agitating Spores." She blew a cloud over both of the lizard men which would help her keep them focused on her.

And that ability was the signal for me to start. Jumping around her side, I cut into the first. "Dark Strike."

With my previous manacles broken, there wasn't a sudden weight on my wrists, and my strike fluidly tore through the lizard-man's hamstring. Though I had Crimson's replacements in my inventory, I wasn't using them at present. Even for the sake of training, I had taken them off during this trip. No need to make it harder than it had to be.

Ami appeared beside me, going for the other lizardman. Her blades crisscrossed the back of the monster, leaving shallow, bleeding wounds all over it.

"Switch," Fayeth grunted, slashing at both of the lizardmen. Her hits weren't as strong, hampered by her need to keep on blocking.

Without a healer, it was troublesome to let her have the time to build up too much aggro. Thus, we opened up on one and then switched when she thought that she was close to losing the focus of one of the monsters.

I spun around Ami and tore into the other lizard man with my short blade and my dagger. Unfortunately, they weren't magically inclined, and I didn't get to show off a part of my class's toolkit. But our current approach was enough.

My lizard man went down in a puff of smoke, and I jumped on the other, striking it down a few seconds later.

Fayeth picked up the mana crystals and then threw the few pieces of loot in her CID. "More junk, but sellable junk." She shrugged.

"Not bad." Neldra stood nearby, watching us. "For your level, you guys could fight alongside the Elven guards. Ami, you do need a little more punch behind your attacks. And Ken, do you only have that one attack?"

"I... well, I have more, but not a lot of things I can use for just hammering away at monsters. Earth Stomp, I save for a situation where Fayeth is in danger, same with Metamorphosis," I thought through my usage. "I have a buff on my blades as well. If the target were magic, I'd have absorbed and discharged."

Neldra was unamused. "You need more abilities. Preferably, as a melee fighter, you need something that can build as you fight and then a finisher." She paused and tapped her lips. "But either way, we are going to hurry the rest of the way so that we can be back for dinner."

"I'm going to meet Lady Rendral today?" I picked at my clothes.

"If we go faster, we can have time for you to shower." Neldra seemed to have the same opinion on my current state and attire.

I glanced at Fayeth then back at Neldra. "Can you carry Fayeth? Ami and I can run faster then."

"Hey!" Fayeth puffed out her cheeks. "I am not slow."

"You are a fantastic tank." I dodged the subject. "Meanwhile, Ami puts too many points in agility."

"Speed is king," Ami answered without any apology.

"Let's hurry." Neldra picked up Fayeth and shot forward. Her blade lashed out at any nearby monsters, and Ami picked up some of the loot if she could spare the moment and keep up.

I was sure that Neldra had intended to power-level us a bit, but in the end, I accepted the help. We had progressed significantly on our levels. Now my mind was focusing forward at the idea of Lady Rendral, and the questions swirling in my mind about how I'd even be able to help her.

The prior information I had received suggested that I'd have to marry the Lady for her to get my Absorb power. Which meant harmonizing in the Elven culture.

Those thoughts occupied my mind.

We charged forward, the dungeon growing more crowded as we moved. Soon, elves were everywhere. It was humans that were the oddity, and our group got a number of stares as we passed through the dungeon.

"We can't go through the royal dungeon entrance, but we'll exit from the closest public dungeon entrance."

"Whatever you think is best." I nodded, letting the Royal Censor guide us. Our self-interests aligned perfectly, so I knew I could trust her. We both wanted me alive and stronger. More information about the Trelican and how he gave his powers out would also be nice.

Time flew by as we headed out of the dungeon until... we were there.

I stepped out of the dungeon with Neldra, who had slowed down by that point to avoid running into anyone. Glancing over my shoulder, I took in the dungeon entrance. The entrance was a rock face with decorations hanging down over the lip of the cave that would turn into the dungeon a hundred paces inside.

"They were originally treated as shrines. We still decorate them as such," Fayeth answered the question in my eyes. "Keep moving though."

Elven heads kept turning my way and then fixating on me. Whispers seemed to burble up around me.

"Ignore them," Neldra muttered. "We have to keep moving."

People parted away from her, but they recoiled from me.

"Sorry." I scratched the back of my head, uncomfortable with how the elves were reacting. "Are elves afraid of humans?"

"The most popular stories are those of Crimson." Fayeth blushed. "And they are horror stories."

"Fair." I nodded. "Crimson is terrifying. She'd probably love the fact that she's the boogeyman." Talking of Crimson made me look off into the distance, wondering what she was up to. Was she all right? More likely, I wondered how large the piles of naga corpses around her had become.

Pulling my mind off of Crimson, I looked up and saw a tree larger than even my imagination had been capable of conceptualizing. "Whoa."

"That is the Holy Great Tree." Fayeth grinned. "Pretty incredible, isn't it?"

The thing was... massive. I couldn't see the sky. Instead, there were just leaves with pale green bottoms that went on forever. The leaves got darker close to the center of the tree, where I guessed they were reflecting some of the light from the edges back at us.

"Even with all this shade, it is still pretty warm." The air held a dry heat, like early summers.

"This is cool. It'll be cooler the closer you get to the tree. The tree provides a cooling effect that radiates from it with all the water evaporating from it," Fayeth explained.

"Are you all arborists?" I teased.

Fayeth stuck out her tongue. "We learn a lot about Great Trees in school. Anyway, to compare to your temperatures, it's around 70 degrees Fahrenheit next to the tree. Just outside the tree, it is more in the 90's or 100's. But once you get far enough from the tree's cooling effects, the world is easily 140 or hotter."

I blew out a breath. "That's... not livable."

Fayeth gestured at the Holy Great Tree with no small amount of pride. "Thus, the trees."

"While we walk, I need to make sure you are aware that you need to behave while you are here," Neldra cautioned. "We are a civilized people. Basic laws about theft, murder, and assault are in place for egregious actions, so you don't have to be too concerned. But beyond that, you need to know that the nobles can be prickly. Censors will probably take their side, or that of the royals, if the opportunity arises. So please, do not go anywhere without Fayeth, me, or another royal you trust." She said the last bit with a hint of a smile.

"I can do that," I answered distractedly, casting glances all around the city as Neldra marched forward, parting the crowds.

Outside the dungeon stood an open-air market, where it appeared that Elven adventurers bought and sold their most recent goods. The market extended and then bled away to buildings and warehouses that seemed to feed the market itself.

Given everything, I could only imagine that we were heading closer to the trunk of the tree, where the palace stood like a grand monument to the tree.

"Does the tree still grow?" I wondered, noting how close buildings were situated to the trunk.

"Of course it grows." Neldra gave me an odd frown. "We get all the wood from trimming the limbs." She pointed up. "As for the trunk growing larger, at this stage in the Great Tree's life, it doesn't grow enough to be a concern when city planning."

I nodded along, my mind filled with plenty of questions as I saw the elves for the first time.

Fayeth grabbed my hand and squeezed it as we walked at a brisk pace towards the tree. "It'll be great. You'll love it here, and then we'll head home for the next year of school."

I squeezed her hand back. "I'm sure I will."

"Come on, love birds. We are going to pick up the pace." Neldra continued charging forward.

***

I stepped out of the bath. Rather than showers or baths, the elves had more of a steamy sauna with a bucket of hot water.

Fayeth came out behind me, her face flush, and not just from the heat.

"Your clothes." Ami had laid out a dress for Fayeth and an interesting-looking suit for me. The outfit was made of very thin material. "Is there an undershirt?" I asked.

"There was not one provided." Ami bowed and stepped back.

"We don't normally wear multiple layers. Just put it on as is, please?" Fayeth dropped her towel and worked to get the dress on. It had far too many straps to be practical, in my opinion. Yet despite the tangle, she got it on in quick order.

I ignored that Ami was present as I dropped my towel, putting on a pair of boxers and then the pants that had slits that started at my calves and opened up the legs for more air. The top was a little longer than I was used to, covering my butt completely. The shoulders weren't as square as what I was used to. Instead, they sort of pinched and left my chest partially exposed.

"You look so good!" Fayeth squealed as she turned to see me dressed.

"Well, if I knew your people's clothes would make you smile so much, I'd have had some made," I teased. There was nothing better than seeing my woman this happy.

Ami bowed. "Would you like for me to procure some? Or at least take measurements?"

"Don't wander off on your own. I don't need you to get into any trouble," I warned Ami.

"The Censor has introduced me to the staff here. I will use their assistance." Ami bowed and used her speed to disappear.

Fayeth looked me over hungrily and bit her pink lips.

"Down." I booped her nose before replacing my finger with a kiss to her lips. "Unfortunately, we don't have time. Besides, I thought I just satisfied you in the bath?"

She stuck her tongue out at me. "I like seeing you in my people's clothes." She eyed me a little more before she held her arm out and I took it, walking out of the room arm in arm with her. "But I suppose I can wait until tonight."

Fayeth was holding on to me a little more tightly than usual as we walked through the palace, and I wondered if she was feeling some trepidation about our meeting with Lady Rendral.

"You know, you are the best elf in my eyes, right?" I teased her.

She blushed all the way to her ear tips. "It's not that. Just... just... promise me that you won't let Lady Rendral sweep you away?"

"Never. We are Adrel. I'm more concerned about her fitting in with our existing Adrel. I think, without the rest of the party here, it sort of becomes difficult, does it not?"

Fayeth blinked several times, and I could see her reorienting how she viewed the upcoming interaction. After a moment, she nodded. "Yes. She will have an uphill battle, as you say." She held my arm tightly again, but she managed to stand a little taller as we came to a set of double doors.

The servant opened the doors, announcing our entrance. I only caught Fayeth's last name, Lyntean, and mine, Nagato, amid the rapidly spoken Elvish.

CHAPTER 5

The room on the other side of the door was opulent, but not with gold.

Instead, it contained what I assumed were pieces from the Great Holy Tree, polished to mirror shine. The sconces with magical light came from the dungeon, and so did a floating chandelier. The pieces of wood were often unadorned, just polished within an inch of their lives with intricate carvings, and then magic items from the dungeon added light and color in contrast.

"Welcome." The only seated occupant stood up.

She was in a strappy dress much in the style of Fayeth, but it was bright blue with gold trim. It went well with her brilliant red hair that was done up, holding most of it behind her head, while two strands fell down around her face, making you focus there.

Her azure eyes matched the dress, and a single blue gem necklace that seemed to be almost ready to fall into her cleavage.

"Thank you for having us." I bowed. "Wasn't sure if you spoke English."

"We've been preparing to accept you and Crimson this summer." She gave me a bright smile.

I stopped at the other end of the long table and glanced down at the chairs.

"Please. I arranged for a more private dinner on your first night. Come sit next to me so that we can get to know each other." Lady Rendral gestured to the chairs on either side of us.

Fayeth tensed.

I wasn't sure what that meant, but I held Fayeth's arm and pulled her with me.

The motion of both of us coming to the same side made some of the warmth fade from Lady Rendral's face, but it didn't become unpleasant. Instead, she just seemed disappointed.

It was too quiet for Fayeth to explain, so instead I glanced at her and raised an eyebrow asking her what she wanted. Fayeth let go of my arm and nodded to step around Lady Rendral to the other side.

Two Censors pulled the chairs out for us while Neldra positioned herself behind the Lady and we all sat together.

"Fay-fay. It's so nice to have dinner with you again. It has been so long, and you've become Adrel." Lady Rendral gushed and grabbed Fayeth's hands with a genuine smile. "Dear cousin, I'm so happy for you."

Fayeth couldn't quite meet her eyes. "Lady— I..." Instead, she glanced at the five Royal Censors in the room.

I didn't blame her, the four of them were putting out oppressive auras that blanketed the room. From what I understood, they were judge, jury, and executioner to the nobles like Fayeth. She didn't feel comfortable calling Lady Rendral anything but her title.

Lady Rendral's jovial mood vanished in an instant. "I see. The Censors make you uncomfortable." She held on to Fayeth's hands but glanced around the room. "You four." She met the eyes of the Censors besides Neldra. "Understand that these two and their aide are to be treated like my family. I only want to hear how you've made them feel welcome, protected, and cared for within the palace and in our world at large." Lady Rendral motioned to me with her chin. "This is..." She spoke something in Elvish that made all of them stand up a little straighter. "Understand?"

"Yes. Lady," one spoke in stilted English.

"Wonderful, please leave and reflect that you've made my cousin uncomfortable enough that she didn't dare use my name." Lady Rendral held a bearing that shattered any oppressive feeling that the Censors were giving off with her own.

Fitting for a woman that would become Empress one day.

The Censors left with the speed that only high-level adventurers could.

"There." Lady Rendral pat Fayeth's hands. "I know you know my name."

"Elysara," Fayeth said before blushing. "Ely. Life has been good. I'm happy to be able to show my home to my Adrel."

Elysara Rendral's smile returned and bloomed in her eyes.

"Though, we have to explain 'cousin' to him or he'll misunderstand," Fayeth said.

"Ah. Yes." Elysara focused on me. "It's the apt word. But we are very distant, at least eighth cousins, though I'd have to consult the archives to be certain. All nobility are family of the Royal Line and greet each other with familial terms. In my research of humanity, I was unsure how that would play out. Romantic relations with relatives is both broadly proclaimed as bad, yet privately it seems to be ideal?"

I laughed. I couldn't help it. "No. Yes? I don't know. It is fetishized, but not really common."

The Lady frowned and turned to Fayeth, who translated something into Elvish. Upon hearing the answer, Elysara's cheeks turned as red as her hair. "I see. I will have to be more careful when reading about human culture."

"We are weird like that. Sex and a lot of things around it are privately exciting, but publicly shameful. Don't ask why that's become the norm, but do keep that in mind," I said.

"Ah. But you two are Adrel, you must have already been privately quite excited?" Elysara teased Fayeth who didn't even blush.

"Yes, we have. We are very compatible. I am part of his dungeon party, and two others are part of our Adrel."

"But you didn't travel with them?" Elysara sat back as someone knocked on the door and a servant came out with three plates of food.

"There was a situation with the naga," I said.

Elysara glanced at Neldra for a moment before turning back to me. "I've heard some of your exploits and of Crimson, but I'd love to hear the tales from your own mouth. Sadly, I don't get out much besides for lessons and to train. The tales of the next Trelican should be recorded." She beamed at me with genuine interest.

I wasn't sure where to start, so I started at the beginning when I took the entrance exam and came up an Aberrant and nearly didn't get accepted.

Elysara nearly threw a fit. "They almost passed up the next Trelican!" she shouted. "The fools, just because they didn't understand, they... they almost did the unspeakable. But at least Crimson had sense."

Then I got on to the stories of class, and she snorted several times, enjoying the stories of us interacting with our classmates with a gleam in her eyes. Meanwhile, the stories of Fayeth exploring things like sushi made her giggle and promise to let Fayeth be there when she tried them for the first time.

Through the whole thing, she was genuine and excited to hear the stories. Meanwhile, Neldra was a strange mix of happiness and sadness watching all of this.

I got the deep sense that Elysara's reclusive life had been tough on the young woman. The way she drank up my stories spoke quite plainly.

She had no friends.

The Censors were her close subordinates, and she was public in controlled settings regarding management of the kingdom, but she couldn't be anywhere with people privately for fear of exposing her lie.

She wasn't the Trelican that her father had presented her to the world as. Since then, she had been almost entirely isolated.

"She killed a naga matriarch?!" Elysara sat back. "But what of the portal, is humanity engaged in open war with them now?"

"No. My Adrel used Absorb on the synthetic spellbook and gained partial access to the skill, enough to close it with Crimson on the other side. After that, several powerful adventurers tried to capture Ken, so Neldra swept us away," Fayeth over simplified it, but the meal was already done and our wine glasses had been refilled multiple times.

Elysara gasped. "Then Crimson? Is this why she didn't come?"

"Oh, she's still alive and she'll be back," I chuckled. "Few know the true extent of her strength, but I'm aware of it and know that she was holding back against the matriarch for fear of injuring the other humans present. Now that the restriction is gone, the naga are in for a world of hurt."

Crimson's [Limit Break] was almost too powerful. Though, the drawback of her losing control was quite the cost. That and her lack of control in activating it had caused her to step down from diving the dungeon as much as she used to.

"Incredible." Elysara sat back with her glass of wine, the stiff formalities of her were partially lost, but some of them were so ingrained in her that, even with a light flush on her face, she still stayed straight and daintily held the wineglass with her other arm crossed under her chest.

She took a long drink. "I am impressed that you guys fought a naga warrior like that."

"I don't know if 'fought' is the correct word," I chuckled. "Maybe 'survived' is a more apt term. Besides, Charlotte's mother did the real fighting."

Elysara shrugged as if it didn't make a difference. "That you stood up to it is worthy of note."

"What about you and your stories? We can't take up the whole night talking about ourselves," I teased, the atmosphere having relaxed significantly.

"Oh. My life is boring. I do several daily, weekly, and monthly events at my father's side, and then the rest of my time is consumed with training both for the dungeon and to cram every ounce of knowledge I can in my head to be a better ruler when the day comes." Elysara waved away the question.

"Oh, come on. You have some stories. Those events can't be completely boring. Anything funny happen?" Fayeth goaded her cousin. "I remember a few farmers coming to ask for help with their pigs not having sex once," she snorted.

"They are more controlled than you remember, Fay-fay. The guards take and screen them before they step into court now. My father is growing older and is... streamlining things more, as he has less patience."

"Boo." Fayeth slumped back into her chair. "That pig sex moment had the entire court covering their mouths and trying not to laugh. Even your father was still as a statue while he tried to contain himself."

"I remember that time." Elysara smiled. "Didn't my father offer to trade his duds for some young boars?"

"I think so." Fayeth smiled at the memory. "People really do love the Royal Family." She said that mostly to me, missing the brief moment of Elysara's smile fading. "I know that in your land people have a negative connotation with royalty in governments, but it works for us."

"Oh?" Elysara perked up. "What do your people have?"

"The world isn't united like yours. I think with how harsh your world is and how early in your culture the dungeons appeared changed things. But most of the major countries are led by a large body of representatives, much of them elected, some appointed. Each of your cities are so isolated though."

Elysara shook her head. "The dungeon is how we travel between them, mostly. There's a regent for each Great Tree that serves in the Royal Family's stead. They get audited every five years."

"Seems healthy. I see a little of Earth's changes here. Our focus is shifting downwards rather than to our neighbors," I said.

"The dungeon is rich with resources," Elysara sighed. "But you are diving with your party. I like this Desmonda, it feels like each of them are a sort of their own royalty on Earth?" She sought to understand my existing party better.

"They have powerful adventurer families..." I tried to think of an equivalent. "It would be like they were the daughters of Royal Censors here."

"Oh. Powerful and connected people." Elysara nodded. "But back to Desmonda, do you really think there is demon blood in her family?"

"A little," I admitted, thinking of the secondary class she could obtain. "But what about you, we don't even know what class you are?"

"I'm a Trelic— Fuck. I have said it so many times, even I am starting to believe it." She rubbed at her face. "We even modified my equipment to say it on my character details. But before that change, I was a..." She checked her CID for a translation. "Eidolon Priest."

"Interesting. I am not familiar with it," I said.

Fayeth jumped in. "It's a broad-spectrum class. They have summons that merge with their bodies. They can take on aspects of monsters from the dungeon."

"Right. So since Fayeth is a tank and you are DPS, if we wanted to go into the dungeon, I could summon my current max of four Eidolons and focus on ones that have healing capabilities. Right now, I do two tank, one DPS and a healer. Basically, I'm my own party, which is nice because I dive alone with a Royal Censor or two watching over me," she explained.

"Well, if you dive with us, you can be our Charlotte." Fayeth's eyes pinched closed with her smile. "Everyone loves the healer."

"Speaking of Charlotte, I would love to meet Bun-bun one day." Elysara's eyes gleamed at the idea of the cantankerous rabbit. He was everyone's favorite.

"You'll have to come visit sometime," Fayeth laughed over her drink.

"That I may." Elysara gave me a partially lidded look over her own glass of wine. "I sincerely enjoyed this. Would you two be willing to do meals with me while you are here?"

I shrugged and glanced at Neldra before looking back at the Lady. "We are in your hands while we are here. Happy to participate in anything you'd like us along for and we'd love to do some training while we are here."

Elysara sighed. "More training?" She glanced at Neldra.

"They are hard workers, or else they wouldn't have survived what they have," Neldra spoke for the first time the whole dinner. "You might enjoy training more with people."

"Yes." Fayeth put down her glass and leaned over to grab one of Elysara's hands. My Adrel was very drunk. "It's great. Especially when fighting in a party and knowing that the better you are, the more you can help the rest of the party should an incident happen. It makes training an act of love, passion, and family. It brings you more in harmony with your Adrel."

At the mention of bringing in line with your Adrel, Elysara smiled. "Then you'll both join me tomorrow for training? We have conditioning in the morning after my father holds court."

"We would be honored," I answered for Fayeth. "If I'm to get her up in the morning, we had best stop for the night."

Elysara snickered. "Apologies, I didn't mean to push her so far."

"Huh?" Fayeth completely missed us talking about how far she had gone into the wine. My adrel was a lightweight, more in line with her stature than her role as a tank.

"It's fine. But I better get her to bed. Once the excitement winds down, she'll pass out." I stuck my tongue out at Fayeth who was squinting as she tried to process what we were saying.

"Yes then. Have a good night. We have plenty more, and I find myself looking forward to them." She put her glass down.

I gave her a big smile and scooted back to stand and go grab Fayeth.

Who only as we were getting up suddenly shouted, "I'm not drunk!"

"If it took you that long, then you are indeed, cousin," Elysara chuckled. "Enjoy your night, you two."

I held Fayeth and helped her walk out of the room. One censor from before fell in behind us and helped me find our way back.

"Thank you for being a guide," I said.

The Censor bowed at the waist so low that her forehead nearly touched the ground. "The smile on our Lady's face when I opened the door made me understand my folly. Please continue to visit her while you are here and if anything makes you uncomfortable or wish to leave, please allow me to take care of it." The woman raised herself to meet my eyes.

The sincerity in them moved me.

These Censors, while it certainly seemed like a position that might abuse its power, they genuinely cared for Lady Rendral a great deal and were decent to us.

"We'll do our best, but we are only here for a few months," I said, nodding to the Censor and helping a Fayeth that was already lightly snoring into the room.

Getting her undressed, I slid her into the bed, and the second I laid down with her, I was asleep, the fatigue from the trip here catching up with me in an instant.

***

"What do you think?" Elysara leaned back in her chair with just Neldra in the room.

"That you were smiling far more than I had seen in a long time." Neldra avoided the question she knew her Lady was asking.

Elysara sighed and met her eyes. "Are you aware of the current situation?"

"The others have informed me of some details that I missed in my absence. It seems that you asked them to keep much of it from me when I came to give you updates?" Neldra didn't appreciate being kept in the dark.

"We were already planning on them visiting this summer. Just with Crimson in tow. Without her, it might even be easier. She may not even return," Elysara said.

"Don't underestimate her," Neldra cautioned. "We've crossed blades many times, and I can confirm what Ken said, she was holding back against the matriarch."

Elysara slowly shook her head. "Unbelievable. But she fought the reds, they are strong, but nothing compared to the whites. We need to keep an eye on the reports of naga attacks. Major changes might give us an idea on if she's alive."

"You still kept me in the dark. When were you going to tell me about it?" Neldra was concerned for her Lady. Things had not been going well while she'd been watching over Ken.

"When you returned with him." Elysara smiled. "I didn't want to worry you until there was something that could be done." Her smile grew more and more tired. Things were going to be more difficult.

Neldra kept her face impassive, lest she show just how worried she was for her Lady. The girl had so much placed on her shoulders at a young age, only to be isolated from any support.

Of course she had her Censors, but they were all older women who she couldn't relate to. Not in the way she had just spent the night drinking, laughing, and chatting with Ken and Fayeth. This was good for her and Neldra would do her best to keep other things from ruining the small joy that Elysara had found.

"With your leave, I'll go check on a few things." Neldra had work to do. She would protect her Lady from the dangers that had crept up since she had been away.

CHAPTER 6

"So, this is where you train?" I asked, finding the gym both different and familiar. The room was lined with mirrors and flooring that was made out of some sort of rubber material.

Fayeth was next to me wearing a sports bra and tight yoga pants. Elysara was staring at her outfit while I was taking in the gym.

The machines and the motions they did were the same, but there were no heavy irons; instead, there were hooks on the floor and heavy elastic bands hanging up around the equipment. I guess, when you lived under a tree, mining wasn't that viable. But some bars were still made of metal, likely from the dungeon for the heavier lifts.

"What is that outfit?" Elysara was wearing some gauzy material that looked like it probably breathed well and was showing plenty of skin.

"Oh. This?" Fayeth pulled at the material over her thighs and let it snap back. "Workout clothes from Earth. They are actually super comfortable."

"Huh." Elysara bounded over to Fayeth and pulled at the yoga pants before touching at her sports bra. "It seems like it would feel tight and pinch?"

"Not at all." Fayeth quickly went through a small stretch routine. "Want to try a pair?"

"Yes!" Elysara's bright red hair shook and threatened to come loose from her excitement, but managed to stay put.

"Can I pull out a sword over here for warm up?" I glanced at the Censors who were watching.

"You may," one said quickly before Elysara had to order them.

Then again, it probably wasn't a prominent concern. With all of them here, Elysara was perfectly safe.

Finding an open space, I pulled out a low-level sword and started through the motions of the Nagato Clan's form. First it was slow, focusing on all the little details, where my hips and elbows were and making sure my form was as perfect as I could make it before I sped up. Once, twice, and then a third time at full speed, practicing with the image of a large monster in front of me and I would land multiple deep blows as I flowed through.

When I finished two rounds at full speed, I stepped back feeling a faint sheen of sweat on my forehead.

Elysara started clapping. "That looked fantastic. What do you think, Tish?"

"It is a powerful form. Viable for monsters, but if he pulled his elbows in and did it, I believe it would hit many human vitals. He was trained by an assassin." The Censor who had bowed to me last night reviewed my fighting.

Elysara raised an eyebrow at me in challenge. She was wearing a set of tight, electric blue workout clothes. Standing next to Fayeth, I could compare the two. She was a good three inches taller, but like all the elves, she was lean. Even if she was destined to be an Empress, she clearly still paid attention to working out. Toned muscles lined her body.

"She's right on. My family was once assassins before the dungeons appeared, and afterwards we've shifted our focus into diving." I nodded to Tish for guessing correctly.

"Wonderful, let's get to exercising." Elysara clapped her hands. "If you don't mind, we can run through my routine and swap around on the equipment?"

"We can do that." I smiled, both ladies were excited and worked up enough that they probably didn't need too much warm up.

"Squats first." Elysara moved over to a machine that looked vaguely like a squat rack with those hooks in the ground and the ceiling. "Two of the black ones and one red on each side please and don't judge me, I don't use my Eidolons during workouts."

"We don't use skills either," I teased. "That would be a waste."

"Ah. But you have some passive strength, do you not?" She glanced at me a little strange.

I blinked, because I did. My Demon Lord secondary class gave me substantial bonuses. "Yeah, sometimes I forget about it. It is a secondary class that I got through one of my other Adrels." I scratched the back of my head.

"Tell me all about it!" Elysara said excitedly.

I wasn't sure if I should, but then again, the only reason I had kept it quiet was to hide it from Headmistress Marlow who would absolutely assume the worst. That charm ability wasn't something I used much.

"First come spot me while you make up your mind. I understand some secrets are best kept that way for adventurers' safety." Elysara got her shoulders under the bar and waited for me to step up behind her.

She stood up, and I kept my arms out to the side while keeping a polite distance behind her and tried my best to keep my eyes up. Mirrors lined the place, so I focused on her eyes in the mirror.

"So, my Adrel, who is a warlock, her family most likely has demon blood. When I didn't have a class in our system, I couldn't use my stat points, so she used her family knowledge to seal a demon in me and give me a demonic secondary class."

Elysara gasped, and her eyes gleamed. "A powerful demon?"

"Yes. A level forty-five demon lord. A named boss from a deeper floor," I explained.

She took one more small step back and dropped into her squat. The change in her position made her rear pop out farther than expected and she pressed her tight rear into my crotch as she breathed hard and focused on the exercise.

It was quiet except for her heavy breathing as she went through twenty reps, each one rubbing against me enough that I felt my vigor rising.

"Ah." She finished and racked the bar. "That's so cool. What kind of bonuses do you get from it?"

I hesitated, thinking about the [Charm] ability.

Fayeth giggled. "It doesn't have the same connotation to us that it does humans. Just tell her." Yet she respected me and didn't say it herself.

"It was an incubus, so focus on stamina and magic, but some nice all-around bonuses for our level given how powerful of a demon it is. I have a Charm ability and Metamorphosis." My cheeks turned a little warm telling the princess that.

"Oh." She glanced around me to Fayeth and gave an exaggerated wink. "Must be fun."

"Very." Fayeth didn't back down. The two had history and had reconnected like two peas in a pod.

"Here, we'll rotate, I'll spot Fayeth, you can watch." Elysara scooted back, bumping into me again as she took the spotter position.

What was happening? Normally, I would be far quicker on these things and avoid her, but she was getting me multiple times, and she wasn't even reacting to it.

That left me confused, was this on purpose or did it just not mean anything to the elves?

Fayeth went up to the rack, and Elysara held the bands so that she could quickly move the bar down and set it for her height before getting underneath.

"I might need a little more weight, let me do a few." The shorter elf easily pumped the weights and asked for two more black bands.

"By the way, Ely, I didn't say it last night... but I'm sorry." Fayeth said as she added the new bands.

"For what, dear Fay-fay? For not knowing my situation? For letting me push you, along with everyone else, away?" Elysara laughed. "That was on me and necessary. I'm just so relieved that because of your Adrel's situation that I get to tell you and we get to be friends again."

Fayeth threw herself into Elysara's arms and squeezed her tight for a moment. "Thank you, Ely."

Watching the two made me rub my nose and look away. Right, all I could see were reflections and Censors around the room.

"Alright, you got this, Fay-fay. Crush these weights," Elysara cheered Fayeth on as the smaller elf dipped into her first set.

We were doing higher reps when lifting; unlike many people whose goals were to show off their exercise, we were more concerned with performance. The dungeon didn't let up, and we needed not only strength, but the endurance to fight fights that lasted several minutes.

Fayeth in her lime-green workout clothes was followed by Elysara in her electric blue ones, the bright colors on their tan skin kept making my eyes track back to them as they went up and down, pushing their rears out.

"Enjoy watching?" Neldra whispered from behind me.

I nearly jumped out of my skin. "What?" I didn't know what to say as I turned to Neldra to avoid staring. "When did you get those?"

The silver-haired Censor had on a pair of white workout clothes that were similar to the other two, only her top crisscrossed over her chest, and her legs had more supporting seams. It went very well with her tan skin.

"Fayeth wasn't the only one who was trying new things. These are very nice." She ran her hands over her sides and down to her hips. "We exercise too. Training doesn't stop just because you hit a high level."

My Adrel finished her reps and turned to me. "You too, Neldra?"

"How do you like them?" Neldra did a small spin. "I thought I'd be the one to get to show them off to Lady Rendral. But I brought back a few styles and gave them to your tailor this morning, Lady."

"Perfect." Elysara was all smiles. "I'll have to check them out..." She paused, clearly going through her schedule. "We'll squeeze it in before dinner. Proper clothing is important."

Even Elven women liked new clothes. Some things transcended worlds.

"Your turn." Fayeth undid one of the black straps but left the rest. "I think this should be about right."

I slid under the bar while Elysara and Neldra chattered behind me. It gave me and Fayeth a moment of privacy.

Fayeth's hand cupped my hips, and she spoke quietly. "So what do you think of Ely?"

I sank into a squat to test the weights; it was a little light, but I'd add a smaller band on the next one. This was fine for the first set. "She's being a wonderful host."

My eyes were on the mirror, watching the room and Fayeth. So I saw it when she rolled her eyes.

"You know what I meant." She wanted to know what I thought of Elysara as a potential for our Adrel. How quickly things had changed.

"What happened to that bit of jealousy yesterday?" I teased her.

She at least had the sense to blush. "Well, I was expecting a soon-to-be Empress, not my old best friend," she admitted.

That made sense.

I kept my mouth closed as I pushed through a few of the reps, the bands challenged me a little differently than the weights, and I had to lean into the weight to avoid any pull backwards.

Fayeth was growing concerned as I was silent.

"Thinking," I said, making her face bloom into a smile. "This isn't just as simple as saying we'll add one. There are responsibilities, and we still don't know how this works."

Fayeth nodded rapidly, but stayed quiet as Neldra and Elysara shifted their focus back to the workout as I finished my reps and put the weight back. "That wasn't a no." She said at the end.

Ignoring her comment with the other two watching, I focused on the workout. "I'll do another of the smaller bands for the next one."

"Good. We should push ourselves." Neldra stepped up and pulled an object from her CID before putting it over her shoulders making her biceps flex as she moved it deliberately. "Eight black and one blue, please." She got into position under the bar, resting it on the clearly very heavy object.

"How much does that thing weigh?" I asked.

"A lot," Neldra answered. "Want to spot me? One of you on each side, please."

"The high-level adventurers get some metals or stones from deep in the dungeon. That material is much denser," Elysara clarified. "If she tried to get up to her full weight on bands alone, she'd pull the anchors out of the ground. So putting on that makes up the difference and she can use bands to fine tune to her desired weight."

I nodded along, it all made sense as I positioned myself to the side of the bar and Neldra took a few careful steps back, before sinking into a squat and grunting as she pushed her way back up.

Those white yoga pants were a little thin and some of her skin tone showed through at the bottom of her squat, making me look away.

"Hey. Focus if you are spotting," Elysara reminded me.

"Sorry." I was quick to focus back in.

Neldra pushed through the last few and racked the bar before quickly changing out the bands. "While these are wonderful clothes, he finds them a little stimulating," she told Elysara.

"Is that so? Then can you come back here and spot me?" She grinned as she leaned on the bar.

This was entirely on purpose, wasn't it?

I shook my head and stepped up behind her.

"Take a step closer; otherwise how are you supposed to have your center of gravity below the weight to help?" Elysara took the weight on her shoulders and stepped back into me again. "Come with me," she breathed as she started her first rep.

I sank down with her, having her shapely rear in my crotch, and those words, her smell. All of it together caused a reaction and I couldn't help but poke into her.

Yet, if it bothered her, she didn't say anything during the set.

When she racked the weights, she turned around. "Well, at least we know you are a very healthy male." She was all smiles. "Don't feel awkward, that's natural and shows you are healthy. It doesn't offend me or any of my Censors."

"It's a little awkward for me." I scratched the back of my head.

"Well, there is a human phrase. 'When in Rome?' Did I get that right?" she asked.

I nodded with her.

"Well then. When under the Holy Great Tree, do as the elves do. I want to know if we are compatible as Adrel. Because, frankly, there is no other man for me," she said.

I frowned. "It isn't flattering for me to be the only option."

The fiery-haired elf frowned. "Then that phrasing didn't translate well. I mean to say that you and I are destined."

"Because I am a Trelican and you are stuck in a lie," I said.

"A lie perpetrated by my father." She grew slightly angry. "I am stuck in this reclusive life as a result, only showing up in very controlled public spaces and not even keeping regular meetings with my peerage."

I shook my head. "Still, that isn't affection, it isn't love. That's what we need to harmonize and become Adrel, isn't it? How can that come to be if you are forcing yourself?"

She stopped short of whatever she had planned to say next and stared at me. As the moment stretched on, I felt some pressure from the Censors around me.

"You aren't wrong because you cannot be wrong about your own sense of romance and affection. I can't force anything on you." Elysara took a step back.

Censor Tish spoke out, "Any man would be lucky to try to harmonize with you, Princess!"

"Silence!" Elysara snapped. "Do not pressure him. He has made it clear: the more we pressure him, the more he'll resist, right?"

I thought about it for a second, and she was right. The more they pushed, the more I would push back if nothing else than to stay steady.

"No pressure is to be applied to him, understood?" Elysara glanced around the room at the Censors.

Tish looked like she had swallowed a fly and Neldra was contemplative as she watched the whole interaction.

"Lady, but wh—"

"Leave." Elysara's tone was deathly calm as she stared at the Censor in question who ducked her head and left immediately. "There, no pressure. But I still want to be sure we are physically compatible. That and while you are here, I would like to continue to be your guide and host."

Fayeth had finished her set and was watching this interaction carefully. "Ely, you went too hard and too fast for him. It took me months."

Elysara shook her head. "But I only get him here for maybe two months? Can you blame me for trying to accelerate things?" She turned her focus back to me. "I was told a skilled human was the Trelican—Neldra has shared many things about you with me. Given your relation to Crimson, I was worried you'd be some sort of overbearing monster. Instead, I find a man who's gentle to my best friend, careful with his words, and very observant. If it isn't too forward of me, I think you are also quite empathetic picking up on people's emotions from small gestures. Then what do you get from me?"

I blinked at how forward she was being and a little embarrassed at how she thought about me. "Well. If you can't read people, how can you see danger coming?" I asked rhetorically. "As for my impression of you... Since you are politically inclined, I worry that everything you show me is a facade."

One of the Censors' swords clacked as she shifted.

Elysara didn't speak. Instead, Neldra moved like the wind behind me, and I had no doubt that the Censor was being removed.

I continued. "So, instead I watch the actions of those around you. The Royal Censors all seem very protective of you, to the point that they'd want to threaten me and push me into a situation with you. I'm to assume that we need to become Adrel for you to receive the Trelican's Absorb?"

"That would be correct." Elysara didn't hide that. "In fact, I'll grant Fayeth access to any private documents about the Trelican while she's here. Sorry, but letting you in would cause a stir."

I nodded. "So far, you seem like a good leader. You are an attractive woman who desperately wants out of her situation. It is that desperation and your political expertise that concerns me about whether things are genuine."

Elysara laughed. "Harmonizing can't happen with lies, you can't fake it. Either you spend time with me and enjoy it, or you don't. It isn't like I could sleep with you, fake everything and still get the Trelican's Absorb. I have to put myself out here, expose myself entirely. You do realize that the knowledge you have could destroy my father for lying to the public about something this important and I would go down with him? Truthfully, that path would lead to me having to force myself to find love in some other noble family that would take the throne."

Fayeth came up next to me and held my arm. "Trust her, trust me? She's being genuine. There's no need to think there are layers to this."

My Adrel was so sweet, and sometimes, I worried that she was naïve. Yet this harmonizing had been real, and she had always been more intuitive about it than me.

"Fine." I kissed Fayeth and pressed my forehead to hers.

"Wonderful. I think that's long enough between sets. Come spot me again and don't be shy about getting so close," Elysara said before swaggering up to the weight rack again.

Fayeth gave me a thumbs up. "And don't worry about the rest of the party. We've talked a little about this and they are all aboard. Des wants to tie up an Empress at least once in her lifetime."

CHAPTER 7

I panted in bed while Fayeth curled up on me. I was spent.

She was giggling. "Maybe we should let Ely tease you more if it does that much to you."

"Not fair." I pulled her to my side. "Any man would become a beast after an hour of something like that."

Fayeth nuzzled my shoulder being sweet on me after a few rounds.

After the workout, there had been some meetings that Elysara had to attend, and we were welcome to go with her, but I begged off and punished Fayeth for all the teasing I had endured.

"Are you really that okay with her trying to steal your man?" I kissed her forehead.

"She's not stealing anything. I... I wasn't sure what I was going to find when I came back, and Neldra had thoughts of Lady Rendral marrying you." Fayeth blushed. "But I expected Lady Rendral, not my old friend Ely. My old friend Ely is different. I'd happily work towards becoming Adrel with her."

"Still. I get the feeling there is more going on that we don't understand yet." I blew out a breath and stared at the ceiling of our rather richly decorated room. "Bet there are two of her Censors right outside this room."

"Because you are the first human to come into the palace." Fayeth rolled on top of me. "And they already know you spent most of the afternoon making one elf scream."

I snorted. "Love you too. But Elysara is most certainly done with her task, and probably the next two. We should get out of bed." We didn't come here to enjoy each other all day. The feeling of missing the rest of our party and knowing that they'd be training hard, pushed me to get out and work on our own strength.

Fayeth laid on top of me. "Maybe we can just get a little bit of sleep." She pinched her fingers together with the cutest plea face she could muster.

"Oh, no you don't." I pulled her off of me as my sleepy Adrel tried to drag me back to bed.

"But sleep," Fayeth tried to lure me back once again.

"Begone, foul demon," I teased.

She laughed. "Says the one who has a seal down there." She tickled at my pelvis. "That's right. And Des says I'm supposed to keep track of it while she's away. Have you heard anything from the demon since you and Des gave it that big stack of magazines?"

"Nope. I can only assume he's happily busy with the smut, and I am thankful for that. The less I meet that pervert, the better." I pulled Fayeth out of bed and set her on her feet while I fished for some clean clothes. "By the way, where did Ami go?"

"She was with a Censor when we came into the room, but we'll have to figure out how to get a hold of her if you need her." Fayeth paused thoughtfully as she was pulling up her robe.

There was a knock at the door. "Reporting, Master," Ami spoke from the other side of the door.

I felt my cheeks warm up. "You were outside. That means you've heard all of that?"

"Yes. Do you need anything?" Ami asked.

"I was wondering if we could find Elysara." I paused as I glanced down at myself. "After a bath."

***

"This way." Ami opened a door for us and gestured us through. She was taking her butler role quite seriously and had made fast friends with Elysara's Censors.

Elysara was in the room we entered, talking with several other elves. She had a polite smile on her face, and if I hadn't spent hours the night before talking with her and seeing a very different smile, I would have told you the current smile was genuine.

Her ruby red hair was coiffed up beautifully. It was different from the night before, with the familiar two heavy locks framing her face.

She glanced up, noticing as Fayeth, and I entered.

"Ah. Hello." She switched to English. "We were just wrapping up." She switched back to Elvish and spoke to the two briefly before it was clear they were saying their goodbyes.

The other elves gave me the stink eye while Fayeth, and Elysara kept polite smiles on their faces.

Once they left, Fayeth plopped down on the couch. "Was that the Duke of Levifort? They came a long way." Fayeth seemed concerned for some reason.

Elysara waved away the concern. "They have business here, my father is putting on a thing. Anyone important that comes lately is trying to at least get to know me. Sadly, it is always in these controlled settings." She glanced around, and I noted the multiple Censors in the palace room. "What I'd kill for going out to a restaurant." She let herself sag a little into her seat.

"Anything you'd like can be catered in?" Tish offered. She seemed to be the number two of the Censors, coming in after Neldra.

"Yes, yes. I'm a very important person," Elysara sighed apparently having had this conversation before.

"It must be so difficult being a princess." I rolled my eyes in jest.

She froze for a moment before she burst out laughing. The Censors looked like they were about to cut me down for my statement.

"That's wonderful to hear." Elysara wiped at some tears that had squeezed their way out. "No one dares tease me these days. So, I hear you two were preoccupied this afternoon."

I couldn't meet her eyes. "Yeah. Fayeth and I were... uh... checking on our harmonization."

Fayeth kissed my cheek. "It went well."

"I bet it did. The Censors told me I might have the entire afternoon to myself." Elysara wasn't even blushing. "I'm jealous, Fayeth. It seems like the high stamina demon bonuses he has are getting put to good use."

"Stop," Fayeth responded half-heartedly. "You are embarrassing Ken. Besides, at this rate, the Censors might try and keep him from your morning workouts."

"Oh no. They were telling me all afternoon that I was in a particularly good mood and that I pushed myself well during workout this morning. It seems that having a man there to impress was helpful for me."

I wanted to blend into the room and disappear. I tried to cover up my inferno of a face with my hand.

"Maybe we should stop teasing him or he will be the one who stops going," Tish advised.

Elysara focused back on me and flashed me an apologetic smile. "Sorry. This is normal conversation for us, but I will do my best to dial it back."

"How has your day been?" I picked at the food that had been left out for the meeting, which was still mostly untouched. The afternoon with Fayeth had left me with quite an appetite.

"Oh, just boring things," Elysara tried to get out of talking about business, and I was left with the feeling that there was much she wasn't saying.

Fayeth's brows pinched together. She clearly noticed the same. "No. The Duke of Levifort would go straight to the Emperor with any matters. Not only is that right, but he's one of the most powerful people besides your father..." Fayeth's eyes went wide open. "Your father is stepping down soon, isn't he?"

Elysara sighed. "You were always smart in your own ways."

Fayeth stuck out her tongue. "Did you just call me stupid?"

"No. You are just selectively smart." Elysara made a teasing face back. "Yes, my father has made some choices in the last few years that have added up. He's considering taking all the burdens unto himself and stepping down to give me a clean slate, as it were."

"Like what?" I asked.

"He sealed off the sixty-first to the sixty-fifth floors. The connection to the naga is actually somewhere below that. So, those floors have essentially been turned into magical minefields while concealing the stairwells between them." Elysara leaned back. "That also means that they are closed off to the elves as well. Needless to say, it has become an unpopular move."

"The number of elves that venture that high are so few, though," Fayeth argued.

"But their influence isn't small. They feel stifled by him and have bandied about all sorts of excuses, like he doesn't want them to gain fame or that he's a coward for not wanting to confront the naga." Elysara shook her head. "Anyway, as a result, the dukes all want to meet me, the next Trelican, and ask how my training is going."

I felt for her. That was an incredible amount of pressure on her shoulders. She was living a lie that she was the next hero to save her people, while her father tried to prevent conflict knowing that the elves couldn't win should the attack come.

Everyone was looking to her to step up and become the Empress, not just the next body on the throne, but a true embodiment of power in a conquest to push back the naga.

Yet she was cut off from everyone while dealing with that pressure.

My heart went out to her.

"Don't give me such a sad look," Elysara pouted at me. "Thankfully, with the excuse of my training, I will be free for years to come. He still has years on the throne." She managed to smile even with all the pressure on her. That only made it more precious.

"Then can we sneak you away for some time in the dungeon?" Fayeth asked hopefully.

"Tish, think you could bring us down?" Elysara asked.

"It would be my honor." The Censor bowed and crossed an arm over her chest. "Which floor would you like?"

I raised an eyebrow in question.

"Tish has a powerful group movement ability. We can be down on any floor we'd like to train on in maybe twenty minutes." Elysara checked her CID for a moment. "I'm level twenty-three. But that's not nearly as impressive as the two of you. One year and you are both level seventeen. I'm a little jealous."

"Blame Crimson." Fayeth crossed her arms. "The woman is a sadistic trainer."

"My grandparents weren't much better," I grunted. "Besides, there was a recent jump when Neldra decided to slaughter her way here."

"Like when they threw you in the dungeon during the night?!" Elysara remembered the story from the night before and seemed to have latched onto it.

"Savages," I grunted. "Do you have any good events near our levels? Honestly, the one we did was incredible for leveling. It is just a matter of finding them." I glanced at Tish over the couch.

She shook her head. "Given the Lady's situation, we cannot use them. We'd have to close them off to the public, which would be an abuse of her station."

I went to say something, but then I found myself agreeing with her. Only then did I realize. "Then, do you prevent anyone from approaching her in the dungeon?!"

Elysara sighed. "They form a perimeter around where I train, and Tish carries me through any safe zones."

I sat stunned. "So, you've never crossed paths with anyone in the dungeon?" That must be beyond isolating.

Elysara shook her head. "Nope. Which is why your stories were so exciting!"

"Well, then if you are level twenty-three and we are seventeen, we'd all get experience from something on the twentieth floor. But..." I glanced at Fayeth, worried about her tanking monsters that level.

"Nonsense. I can solo things on that floor. We'll go and you two can do damage to speed things up while I tank and heal."

Fayeth's eyes glittered. "I get to do damage for a change?!"

I smiled to myself. It looked like Fayeth would be fine.

"You really are a one-woman party?" I asked the Lady.

"You'll see when we get down there." She checked her CID for the time, and I checked mine to see if I needed to restock on anything before we went down. "That and starting at lower levels for me will help focus on our coordination."

"Good point." I nodded along, already thinking about how we'd have to shift with Fayeth trying to deal damage rather than tank. "Can we bring my butler as well? I'd hate to deny her training."

"Excuse me." A Censor stuck her head in before Elysara could answer. "A Mrs. Lyntean is here for you three."

"Mom?" Fayeth jumped to her feet.

A woman who could have been Fayeth's sister burst past the Censor, trilling in the Elven language too rapid for me to understand and sweeping Fayeth off the couch.

"Ah. Mrs. Lyntean, could you speak English for our guest? I know your husband has practiced with you," Elysara asked politely.

I appreciated her efforts to keep me included in everything. Her Censors all speaking English to me was a little shocking. I needed to continue working on my Elvish though; I doubted everyone was going to be so accommodating.

"Mom. Let me go." Fayeth wiggled in the woman's arms only for them to tighten further. Her mother continued to trill.

I picked up a few words, but certainly not enough.

Whatever she was saying made Elysara chuckle. "You really shouldn't ignore your mother so much. I didn't know that you hadn't made time to visit her yet."

"Mom!" Fayeth finally broke her grip and dove behind me on the couch. "Mom, this is Ken my Adrel. Ken, this is my mother Fay."

"I started calling Fayeth, Fay-fay, because otherwise it would get confusing." Elysara was still coming down from her earlier laughter.

It didn't appear that Fay was even hearing Elysara's words as she looked me over head to toe very slowly. "How's the sex?" were the first English words out of her mouth.

I turned and smothered my head in the couch cushion.

Elysara fell over sideways on her couch with laughter.

"Mom. Humans don't ask questions like that," Fayeth coached her mother.

"Well, too bad. He's Adrel with my lovely daughter. He's going to have to get used to Elven customs. So, daughter, how is the sex since your adrel is too shy?"

"Great!" Fayeth chirped. "We talked about it from the romance books, but it is right. The clit on humans is on the outside."

"The outside?!" Elysara blurted out. "How do they stimulate it then?"

"They use their fingers while penetrating, or some toys."

"Strange." The Elven ladies all thought humans were the weird ones.

"It isn't that strange when you think about it," I mumbled into the pillow, finally standing back up.

"Ah, there he is." Fay was still watching me. "So, how is my daughter? Does she please you?"

I couldn't help but notice Elysara leaning in. "Well. All the ladies I'm involved with are a little different. She does her own thing quite well."

"Ah. More of a variety type than a fixed ideal. That's a good thing with a larger Adrel." Fay shook her finger at Fayeth. "You found a good one. A lot better than that ungrateful man I married. He is off in another world without me."

Fayeth bowed to her mother. "You are holding down the family, and he's been sending letters back with Neldra."

"Work letters!" Fay threw her hands in the air. "It's all mostly work. Though, Neldra did bring flowers with the last one."

"I'll make sure the next one he sends is better," Fayeth promised before her mother caught her head and rubbed her cheeks against her daughter.

"You have always been the sweetest little thing. I'm sure Ken here gobbles you up every chance he gets," her mother teased. "How long will you two be visiting?"

"The current plan is to be here for the summer, about two months. We'll head back to school after that. But there's a chance that my teacher will appear before then," I answered.

"Who's your teacher?" Fay asked.

Fayeth's eyes darted over to me, and I could tell that she'd rather I didn't answer that question.

But I didn't want to lie to my mother-in-law. "Crimson."

Fay's face lost blood immediately. "C-c-crimson? The woman who slaughters elves by the hundreds and kills entire floors of people to make thrones out of their finger bones?" My mother-in-law wobbled.

Elysara scratched at her cheek. "Those stories are a little exaggerated."

I had to admit I was a bit interested in hearing the stories. If nothing else, I could use them to tease Crimson, who likely would revel in them. But at the moment, I wanted to do some damage control for when Crimson did likely show up.

"No. She's not like that at all. While she can be a brutal teacher, it is done with the idea of preparing us for the dungeon so that we survive. That, and she's a very good teacher. Actually, she wants to join us as Adrel." I was grasping at straws and the final one made the room quiet.

Fay's jaw worked but she didn't make a sound for several moments. "The Crimson Terror wants to... to become Adrel with my Fayeth?"

"Really, she wants Ken. But she works hard, Mother. Crimson treats me very well. If someone bullies me, she'd just make them disappear." Fayeth tried to reassure her mother, but it clearly wasn't helping. "Ken, you know..."

"Crimson has an ability that she struggles to control," I admitted to the group. "Your horror stories are probably—"

"What if she loses control around my baby?!" Fay clutched onto Fayeth.

This woman was a worrier.

"She won't. Ken is helping her, right?" Fayeth nodded encouragingly.

"Yeah. What she said. Crimson is working on control, and I'm helping her. Who knows, by the time she kills her way through the naga, she might have a better handle on all of it," I scrambled to try and recover.

Fay let go of her daughter and snatched me up. She was surprisingly strong. I felt like a kid again as she grabbed me. "You are such a kind man." She put my head up into the crook of her neck and started to sway with me while stroking my back.

For a moment, I was stunned. Then a little choked up, and I pushed away in embarrassment. It felt so... so warm and motherly. Yet, she wasn't my mother.

"I think you embarrassed him, mom." Fayeth clicked her tongue.

"Nonsense. He's your Adrel, so he's my son. Come here, young man." She grabbed me again and planted me on her lap facing the rest of the room and hugged me from behind.

"So." Elysara had a giant grin as she continued to hold back her laughter. "Are we canceling the dungeon dive?"

"Absolutely not," I confirmed. "But apparently, I need to get held by my new mother for..." I trailed off, glancing over my shoulder at Fay.

"A few minutes." She agreed. "I need to get to know my new son."

"Mom, why don't you cook dinner for the three of us tonight and we'll talk over that?" Fayeth suggested.

"That's a wonderful idea, Fay," Elysara pitched in.

Fayeth's mother let out a sigh. "Fine. Fine. But only if we can eat with Elven customs. That means not holding back my topics of choice."

I cursed. I had no doubt that was going to be an awkward dinner, but there was no way to escape the situation. "Okay. I can agree to that."

"Perfect." Fay gave me a motherly kiss on the cheek and squeezed me one more time before letting me go. "I'm going to go start cooking ~~" She started trilling in the Elven language, laying out whatever details around cooking she was envisioning.

I was just going to have to be surprised.

CHAPTER 8

I had finally been freed from Fay's clutches and it was time to dive the dungeon.

"It's almost like you are escaping," Elysara laughed as we hurried down the palace halls after the time with Fay.

"Oh, he totally is." Fayeth was doing her best not to giggle.

Ami, Tish, and a few other Censors were with us as well.

I decided to change the topic. "So, does your mother know that I'm a Trelican or that...?" I trailed off, not even daring to voice the rest. "We need to have an official story, eventually."

Fayeth, instead of answering, turned to her friend.

"That is a good question. Hypothetically speaking, if you were to become Adrel with me, then I would gain Absorb. And that solves some issues, but marrying a human and joining his Adrel rather than forming my own is a little troublesome," Elysara talked as we walked.

One of her Censors made a motion and there was a shimmer in the air, I assumed to keep the conversation from leaking.

"But what if I'm the human Trelican? That would be notable enough for people to make an exception?" I asked. "Hypothetically, of course."

"Hypothetically," Elysara agreed. "Crimson's protégé, a human Trelican, would be a tremendous boon. At the very least, it would make the match far more acceptable. There will always be those that disagree with me if I were to become adrel with a human."

"Yet you are going to continue?" I asked.

Elysara looped her arm around mine. "Yes. But mostly because I find the man that I hoped to save me is actually a very incredible man himself. Then again, I should have expected that from the next Trelican." She beamed up at me with a smile so wide that her eyes pinched closed.

She was beautiful, and despite my over-thinking before coming and meeting her, after spending some time together, she was growing on me.

I leaned against the top of her head. "That's nice of you to say."

Her smile only got brighter. "Yes, now let me show you just how incredible I am in the dungeon."

The palace had grown quiet as we'd neared our current area. We passed a few more Censors, though their outfit was different, and then we entered a room that smelled of earth and iron.

A dungeon entrance was before us.

"Your own private dungeon entrance," I guessed.

"Technically, it is the Royal Family's and not just mine. But father doesn't dive anymore, and mother wouldn't go without him." Elysara shrugged. "So, that just leaves me. Though, I have days scheduled where the staff can use it."

"Grandparents?" I asked.

"Still alive, but they are retired from both politics and adventuring. They live under another tree very peacefully." She smiled.

"Famously, they left the palace to avoid all politics," Fayeth added.

I nodded. Long years of managing an entire world must be exhausting. Even with additional stats from being an adventurer anyone would be worn down from it.

"What does that mean for you? I can't stay here," I added, my thoughts jumping to a potential future with Elysara.

She waved away my words. "Nonsense. I don't expect you to stay here. But I do expect you to become strong enough to visit often."

I nodded, and we walked into the dungeon. Elysara, Fayeth and I were all shoulder to shoulder. The first floor of this one was a large grassland. Several two-headed deer perked up as we entered.

"The meat from those are considered a delicacy. I think it is just because they are sort of a royal-family only food." Elysara shrugged and turned to Tish. "Let's go."

Darkness enveloped me as Tish used her ability. We moved so quickly that it felt like my stomach got left behind.

***

The darkness peeled away, and our group was alone in the dungeon. The ground around us was mostly red, dusty rocks with a few patches of parched brown plants. Not far away, there was a small settlement of muscular green humanoids moving about.

"Fan out," Neldra commanded.

Tish and the other Censors zipped away to take up a moving perimeter around our party.

"A little intense," I muttered.

"Necessary," Neldra shot back. "All clear."

Elysara nodded and clasped her hands together before closing her eyes.

The image of a minotaur appeared behind her, and she swelled as horns grew out of her ruby red hair. After that, an image of a hydra appeared and patches of scales bloomed along her exposed skin. Next, an image of a plant humanoid became visible and a wreath of flowers bloomed along her shoulders. Finally, an image of a black fox had a tail sprout out behind her while her wrists grew tufts of thick fur.

"Whoa." I watched the transformation with interest. "That's your class?"

Elysara's voice was a little deeper, with a pleasant huskiness to it. "Do you like?" She did a small spin. "It is an interesting class and very adaptable."

"The minotaur and hydra are defensive?" I asked.

She nodded along. "I can use any monster that I've fought and killed. The Censors took me around to collect a nice sampling. Though, it is really just a type of monster. I cannot go find a specific type of hydra and get their specific abilities."

"Think of the combinations," Fayeth cheered excitedly.

Elysara winked at me, adding another meaning to the comment.

I smiled but waved the comment away, staying focused. After all, we were in a dungeon. Even with all the support around us, I couldn't let my guard down. "What about your actual skills?" I asked.

"Gone when I take on monstrous traits. Think of it this way. I have a summon that I wear. Together, we are significantly stronger, but that comes at the cost of my own abilities."

"But before you take on the monstrous traits, can you use your own abilities?"

"Yep," Elysara confirmed. "But if I'm honest, with the flexibility all of those monsters give me, I haven't actually spent that much effort in working to fight without them."

"And how do we explain this?" I gestured at her. "If we pull off a harmony and swap skills, how will your people continue to believe you are a Trelican?"

"Hypothetically?" she added with a grin. "Already thinking a lot down that direction are we?" She was easily seven feet tall with the monster powers grafted onto her form.

"I like to solve problems." I frowned and didn't want to admit that I could see it.

"Thank you for your concern. I don't know the answer, but we'll probably have to fudge things a little. Thankfully, little is known about Trelicans." She pulled out a large trident from her CID. "There are also combinations that don't make me look quite so odd."

"As long as you have Absorb and fight like one, they'll believe it." I realized what her goals were.

Elysara winked at me. "That's right, the abilities we share should work even when using my class' ability. Anyway, let's do this." She pointed her trident at an orc that had roamed out of the village.

It was about half a head taller than me, just a little shorter than Elysara with all her monstrous traits packed onto her body. The monster had a crude, but sharp-looking machete belted onto its loin cloth as it wandered our way.

Elysara shot off with more speed than I expected from her currently large frame. She shouted loud enough to get the orc's attention before slamming into it with her horns and knocking it back while it shook off its daze.

She rounded on the orc with several slashes with her trident before it had recovered. The orc got its machete out of its belt as I hurried to join her. Yet, before I could get there, its blade slashed a shallow wound in Elysara.

She barely even flinched at the hit. Instead, her blood sprayed out of the wound onto the orc, making it stagger back. The orc's skin bubbled where it was hit.

I reached the orc a moment later, tearing my blades into the monster as Fayeth came just after me, her spear held in two hands as she swung it in large wide arcs. Each hit was powerful, but slow.

Ami stayed back, watching and holding herself as if a butler ready for orders.

"Ami?" I asked.

"There's no space for me on the single orc. I shall follow your orders." The pretty butler kept herself aloof. Even with the mask over her face, I knew she wasn't joking around.

"One isn't much of a challenge," Elysara agreed, taking a step forward and blurred into the orc with her trident and three slashes hit the monster before it exploded into smoke.

"Impressive." I stepped back to stay out of the smoke.

Elysara flipped her hair. "Thank you. That means a lot from someone so focused on adventuring. This class is very versatile."

"This is your favorite?" I asked.

She shrugged. "The minotaur dulls damage taken, and the hydra has great regeneration and acidic blood. Those two are the core of what I use to solo."

"Passives, all of them?" I asked.

She shook her head. "That would be boring. I get three skills from each, but I don't need twelve active abilities, especially with strong passives. They let me focus on my trident work." She spun the weapon.

I knew it was the weapon of choice for the first Trelican that the elves so revered. It was only natural that she was practicing it to fill the same iconic class.

"So, how many can we take at once?" I asked.

Elysara flipped her trident around and grinned. "Why don't we find out?" She rushed towards the village of orcs.

The funny thing about humanoid populations in the dungeon was that there were never any children, and those that were doing 'work' often were just moving objects back and forth. It was like the dungeon only tried to create a surface level imagery for them.

"Do you want me to take some of them?" Fayeth asked.

"No. I think I can do it. Keeping aggro will be the hardest part." Elysara glanced down at herself, and I noticed all the damage from the first fight had already healed. "What's the point of this if I don't get to show off to the man I'm trying to impress?"

She rushed forward and Fayeth hurried to catch up.

"You are a lucky man," Ami whispered almost too quietly to hear.

I smiled and leaned forward before shooting off after the two elves.

Elysara rushed into the center of the orcs, swinging her trident as she went, catching them with small slashes just to get their attention. She kept picking up more until she had eight of them, and then she spun around before dragging the trident over her chest, flicking the blood over all of them, causing their skin to bubble.

"Shadow Ambush," I activated the ability and closed the remaining distance, rising out of an orc's shadow. "What was that?" I asked.

"A special technique." Elysara winked. "Regrowth. Stomp." She touched her chest and a green glow closed the wound on her chest before she stomped down hard and stunned the orcs. Swinging in wide arcs, she struck multiple with each swing.

"So, you just abused your hydra blood to create an AoE?" I asked.

"Pretty much." Elysara stuck her tongue out and started to take hits as she fought. But her defense was actually quite strong. The machetes scratched her, but didn't go deep enough to slow her down. With her throwing in the active heal from time to time, she wasn't going down anytime soon.

"Cleave." Fayeth arrived and swung her spear through the whole pack.

I focused on the one that Elysara was stabbing. Then I used [Earth Stomp] on cooldown to disrupt the orcs and deal some AoE damage.

Ami appeared within the mess and worked her way through the orcs, applying bleeds to them. I noted that she made up for her lack of physical might by using bleeds to deal damage. It wasn't a bad approach at all given how dedicated she was to agility.

Elysara fought like a wild beast, and not at all the way I'd expect a princess to battle. Her trident flashed back and forth. While she did block occasionally, most of the time, she used her body to take the blows if she wasn't dodging.

And if an orc got too close, she had no issue bringing the horns on her head to bear and goring them badly.

We quickly whittled down the orc pack, and Elysara let out a gigantic sigh. "For the record, I'm not a masochist."

"Never thought you were. Now, are we going to chitchat, or are we going to keep grinding?" I gave her a smile.

Elysara snorted. "Fay-fay said you were a dungeon head. Of course that would be your concern."

The elf moved quickly, using some sort of activated ability as she slammed into another orc before moving swiftly and started to collect another eight orcs. Ami was finishing collecting the drops from the first group as we moved to assist Elysara on the next pack.

An explosive clash of two high-level adventurers came from the side and we all turned our heads to the greater danger.

Neldra appeared next to our party, and the orcs were removed from existence a moment later. "Someone is forcing their way to us."

I jumped in front of Elysara. "Get back."

Elysara just laughed as the monstrous parts disappeared. "Ken, thank you for protecting me. But if they get past my Royal Censors, I will have to meet them."

I still braced myself as Neldra stood tall in front of us.

"What is this?" A voice rang out as one of Elysara's ladies were pushed back, skidding along the red dusty ground. A young Elven man and two ladies walked forward in large strides. It was clear that he was the adventurer in charge.

"This area is for the training of Lady Rendral." Neldra held herself tall as two other powerful adventurers loomed behind the young man.

"Ah. Wonderful. We can practice together, Lady Rendral." He did a little circle with his hand before bowing. "It would be my honor to assist you today."

"Thank you, but I already have companions that I'm training with." Elysara gestured to me. "Besides, you were rude to my Royal Censors."

I realized that most of the elves we had met had been overly kind to the Censors, but this guy was arrogant enough to have one of his followers attack.

I had a feeling he was a headache wrapped in a shit sandwich.

"Juitar just wanted to spar. You know how the really high levels have gotten bored since your father closed the upper end of the dungeon." He shrugged. "But I'm happy to have his assistance on days like today."

"I was just trading a few blows." One of the high-level elves walked out of the dust, a pair of golden gauntlets made his hands seem larger than they were. "Knocking the rust off, so to speak. Want to go a round, Neldra?"

"Depends. Do you mind if I accidentally kill you?" Neldra stared him down.

Juitar snorted and turned his head. "You make it sound like it would be easy."

This guy was arrogant enough to challenge Neldra so openly, I had to assume he was up there with Neldra as one of the strongest elves. No wonder the Royal Censors weren't lopping off heads at this display.

"Now that you've knocked your rust off, please leave, Duke Selmia." Elysara held herself arrogantly, but I knew that most of it was posturing.

When the other elves puffed themselves up, I guessed it was best to follow suit.

I watched the Duke's eyes slide off of Elysara and onto me. "What is a human doing with you?"

"I'm—"

There was a ring of steel. The second guard behind the duke froze me with some ability.

Neldra moved and severed its power. "You've done no harm. But you've attacked one of our guests. Be thankful his master isn't present right now."

Juitar snorted. "What are you doing guarding a human? Go soft on us while you were off?" The man was itching for a fight.

I held up my hand before Neldra could continue. "What matters is that I am here, invited by Elysara, and diving the dungeon with my Adrel." I gestured to Fayeth in case there were any misunderstandings. "You are interrupting, and we would all like you to leave, preferably before Neldra has to remove you."

"You have no idea who I am. As a human, you have no stance in Elven politics and should keep yourself clear of this conversation," the duke sneered at me. "You are also currently diving the dungeon with a woman who is soon to be my betrothed."

That was news to me.

Elysara rolled her eyes. "I've turned you down several times. I would rather not have to reject you again."

"Then accept." The Duke puffed himself up.

"No." She sighed. "There. Now I've done it again."

"You'll regret this." The Duke actually ground his teeth. The sound was more irritating than I had imagined.

He huffed, and I saw the moment where he thought to order his two guards to attack, but then he thought better of the decision and stormed off.

"Tish, let's get ready to head back up," Neldra spoke.

Elysara pouted. "But we can keep going. Can you make sure they really are gone? Then we can have you stick closer in case they try anything again."

Neldra frowned at the Lady, who smiled back, and there was some silent war between them. Eventually, Neldra sighed and nodded before reforming the perimeter.

"Sorry about that." Elysara put her hands together. "Some of these noble types, am I right?"

"I can't believe he'd actually dared to do that." Fayeth puffed her cheeks out. "The nerve! The Censors should have his head for it."

"That's an abuse of power. I'll not rule through fear. Besides, the Selmia family is rising again." Elysara frowned. "Honestly, if I wasn't hiding my class, he would make a good political marriage. Not necessarily a happy one for me, but I could see my father tempted by the option."

"Really?" Fayeth asked.

"Who is the Selmia family?" I asked as Elysara took on the monstrous attributes once again.

"A noble family. Once they were royalty as all nobles were, but that was many generations ago. Recently, they were regents for three Great Trees, but they lost two of them, twenty years or so. It was before I was born," Fayeth explained.

"Misuse of taxes," Elysara added. "The patriarch at the time took the blame and sheltered their last city in return for him being stripped of everything and retiring. His second son, and the grandson we just met, is quite skilled, though. They've managed to rebuild some of their reputation and have a second Great Tree under their family now."

"Oh wow," Fayeth gasped. "Which one?"

"Galia," she answered.

"Not very impressive. But it's a step in the direction they probably want." Fayeth nodded along.

"Does your family have anything like that?" I asked Fayeth.

"Oh no!" Fayeth chuckled as Elysara pulled more orcs. "My family is much lower. My mother controls a small sector of the city under the Great Holy tree. Think of her more like a knight. Bottom rung of royalty and mostly administrative."

Nodding, a new wave of orcs came towards us, and we focused into battle.

But even as I fought, my mind was still on Duke Selmia and his interruption. His boldness spoke less about his intelligence and was a clearer insight into just how weak Elysara's political position might be at the moment.

It seemed that the powerful elements in royalty felt they could push her without consequence.

CHAPTER 9

E lysara, Fayeth, Ami, and I were back in the palace after our trip into the dungeon. After the small situation with the pompous noble elf, the rest of our dungeon dive had been fairly relaxed.

"I thought it went well," Elysara spoke up as we stepped back into the private dining room. We had broken apart to all go take showers before we sat down to eat.

Yesterday, Elysara had dressed to match her blue eyes. Today she matched her fiery hair. My Adrel had dressed similarly, wearing yellow with green accents. I was in another of the Elven suits, this one a navy blue.

Fayeth took a deep breath the moment we entered. "Smell that?"

I sniffed; there was a delightful scent in the air. "Smells like your mother's cooking?"

"It is things like your mother's cooking that you'll recognize for the rest of your life. It's savory and sweet tuber with meat like bacon that comes from the dungeon in the city. You shred the tuber and then put the meat on top in strips with gravy before you bake it. All the salty, greasy goodness from the meat drips down into the shredded tuber."

"Sounds delightful," I told her.

"It is very good." Elysara took her seat and sat up straight waiting for the food. "Nothing quite hits the same as your mother's cooking."

"My darlings." Fayeth's mother Fay burst through the door with oven mitts and a circular dish, steam coming off the top. "I made your favorite, daughter. Now you get to share it with your Adrel, and he'll understand you further." She swept in and placed the dish down in front of Fayeth along with a large serving spoon.

Even elves made casseroles it seemed. Fayeth wasn't shy, heaping a large portion onto her plate.

"Leave some for the rest of us," Elysara teased.

"Oh. I put another in the oven. My Fayeth just loves this dish. Now that she's an adventurer, she should really have an appetite." Fay was all over her daughter, watching her take the first bite.

Fayeth put it in her mouth with a big smile. "As wonderful as ever."

Fay clapped excitedly to herself. "Perfect. Come, come. Both of you have some and welcome to the family. Lady, I haven't seen you and Fayeth together in so long. This makes my heart happy."

"Mine as well." Elysara scooped some of the food onto her plate. "I've been isolated by my duties for far too long. It is time for me to pursue happiness and join an Adrel myself."

Fay choked a little. "Excuse me?"

"Ah." Elysara sighed. "You see, I need to apologize to you. It is because of me that your husband's letters have been sparse. There has been a secret about your daughter's Adrel that we've been hiding."

Fay looked like she wanted to take the food off of Elysara's plate, but she just narrowed her eyes waiting for an explanation.

"Ken here is a human Trelican." Elysara gestured towards me. "And just as he stepped into his class, the humans have come into direct conflict with the naga. We've been in talks with his teacher Crimson. But to have the two Trelicans join forces and unite our peoples against the naga would change many things."

Fay gasped and sat down next to her daughter. "You've done very well, daughter," she whispered loud enough for all of us to hear.

Fayeth nodded. "Ken is an amazing person and fun in bed. The other two ladies are good company as well."

I held myself together, not letting myself be bothered by the open talk of sex.

"I bet he is. As a Trelican, he will one day have enough stamina to satisfy a large Adrel." Fay nodded to herself. "But to be a human Trelican." She put her head on her hand and watched me as Elysara passed the dish around and I scooped it onto my plate.

My mother-in-law watched with keen interest to see if I'd like the food.

Putting the dish aside, I took my first bite. It was very different from what I had expected. The flavor kind of tasted like someone had wrapped sweet potatoes in bacon. "This is wonderful. A delicate balance of sweet, savory, and salty."

"Two Trelicans enjoying my dish." Fay was on her feet in a heartbeat. "That's an honor that I don't think any other chef has earned yet. Let me go check on the second dish." She whistled to herself and moved out of the dining room.

Fayeth let out a small sigh. "Thank you for letting my mother know more."

"I always liked your mother. So many of the noble ladies don't relax around me." Elysara smiled.

My eyes drifted to Tish who had taken up a post in the corner. "I can't imagine what would make people nervous around you."

"Oh, Tish is harmless. She's one of the nicest among my Censors." Elysara argued.

"Tish, what level are you?" I asked.

"Sixty-three," she answered smoothly.

I hooked a thumb at her. "Pretty sure that makes her automatically intimidating." She was a higher level than every human. If Crimson wasn't a freak of nature, I would say Tish was stronger than every human.

"It doesn't seem to bother you," Elysara argued.

Fayeth laughed. "That's because of his grandparents."

"Yes, the assassins?!" Elysara was uniquely interested in them. "They move through the night and kill people for a living? Yet they have a code of honor for what jobs they take."

Fayeth held her hands up. "When they get mad, it is like you are dropped in a sea of boiling blood that somehow makes your blood also freeze. It comes and goes. One second, his grandmother is the friendliest old lady you've ever met. The next second, you are scared out of your mind and you see your life flash before your eyes. Then she's a kindly old grandmother again." Fayeth held herself with wide eyes.

Elysara paused and turned to me. "You failed to mention that part."

"That's because he's used to it!" Fayeth shook her head in amazement. "His grandpa attacks him at random in the name of training. We are just having tea and suddenly Ken is leaning back to avoid losing his head!"

Elysara blinked. "Do you think it's been helpful?"

"I handle stressful situations well." Taking a bite of my food, I didn't think my grandparents were *that* bad. "I mean, what's a hard test, or a broken possession compared to having blades swinging for your neck at random?"

"I still want to meet them," Elysara declared.

"Despite all of that, they can be lots of fun," Fayeth agreed while stuffing her face. "Charlotte's pet Bun-bun really gets under Grandpa's skin."

"There is no way that ungrateful rabbit is as polite as Charlotte pretends he is." I took a forceful scoop of my food.

"He's cute and fluffy, though. So that makes up for it." Fayeth's face gave away her soft spot for the rabbit.

Both Elysara and I paused and stared at her. I shook my head. Being cute and fluffy was not enough for the attitude I was convinced Bun-Bun displayed.

"So. I think today went well, but I need to get some AoE attacks," Elysara changed the topic.

Switching gears to talking tactically about the dungeon, I couldn't help but nod several times with her assessment. "I think I do too. Fayeth and Ami were doing more damage than me. Ami's approach with the multiple bleeds wasn't quite as effective as Fayeth's cleave, but it was certainly better than mine. With a lower number of targets like two or three, it would probably be more effective."

"Have you not had much need for AoE in the dungeon yet?" Elysara asked.

"Not really," I admitted. "There were these small monsters, we call fribbits, in the early floors. But between Fayeth and Des's AoE attacks, they disappeared very quickly."

"One of those monsters that are numerous but fragile." Elysara understood. "You haven't seen anything like those orc villages yet?"

"No. The other floor was scorpions, but we did an event with twenty-five total adventurers. The spacing was the harder part, and we pulled them all into the center where the tanks and adventurers with frost-type attacks killed them," I answered.

Elysara leaned back. "Tish, can you get me the ledger of my different forms and a ledger for the royal library?"

I blinked. "You don't need to do that."

"Nonsense." Elysara grinned. "What fun is it being a princess if I don't get to use some of the skillbooks we have? I only have used a small collection of defensive and protective skills. I need to be prepared if an ambush ever occurs. But I can take one or two out for you in the name of trying to impress you." She winked as Tish stepped out of the room for a moment before returning.

It was obvious that Elysara wasn't going to let me turn her offer down, at least not easily.

"If it makes you feel better, this is to help me as the DPS for the training this summer. Increasing your damage will help me level faster." Her eyes sparkled.

I gave her a knowing look. She had several arguments already lined up. I could see it in her eyes—this was just the tip of the iceberg.

"Fine. Let's look at them." I had to admit, I was definitely curious.

Elysara put her hands in her lap and gave me an innocent expression to hide what I imagined would have been a little gloating.

Fay came back. "It's done." She happily set down the second dish next to Fayeth, who didn't hold back and scooped herself seconds. "So, what are all of your plans for this summer?"

"Well, of course, I need to visit my mother-in-law sometimes." I smiled at her and clearly earned myself a mother-in-law point.

"Yes you do," she agreed.

"We have to train," Fayeth spoke up. "Maybe we can focus on training five days a week?"

"On weekends, I have a little more free time," Elysara offered. "So, if we could dedicate one of those to training?"

That made sense to me. "The other for seeing the city and my mother-in-law?"

"Perfect." Fayeth's mother was all smiles and pounced on the idea. "I would love to see my daughter more regularly, and her Adrel. Lady, if you intend to step into that Adrel, you'll have to make an effort."

Her statement sounded a little rude to me, but something must have been lost in translation because Elysara just smiled. "Of course I will. Being Adrel takes effort."

"You look a little lost," Fayeth commented.

"Sorry. I was just thrown by that statement. Do elves believe that joining an Adrel is difficult?" I asked.

The three elves frowned at me like my head was on wrong or something.

"I don't know if I'd say it is necessarily difficult," Elysara answered. "Yet becoming Adrel and maintaining it certainly requires active effort. It can be considered difficult when the Adrel is already large. Two people don't just 'fall' in love, despite the human saying making it sound almost accidental."

"Now that you mention it, all the romance novels do make it seem rather happenstance and easy." Fayeth tapped her chin.

"It's a little romanticized that way." I came to the realization as part of the conversation. "Yet I think I agree with the elves more. It takes effort and more effort for a larger Adrel."

The elves nodded along with my assessment.

"So. Tell me about yourself, Ken." Fay sat down next to her daughter and scooped some of her own dish before eating with an expectant look at me. She really did look just like her daughter, only a slightly longer face.

I went into much the same storytelling as I had for Elysara the night before. Though, the princess often added details or pushed me to embellish certain aspects.

She was trying to help me win over my new mother-in-law, which was actually kind of nice. I could tell that she was putting in an effort to try to join our Adrel, and it made me like her even more. She was so far from the princess I'd expected to meet.

Tish stepped out during the talk and came back holding two books, but she didn't interrupt. Instead, as the story telling dragged on, it was Elysara who had to leave.

"Sorry, Lady." Tish bowed, coming back into the room again. "There are urgent matters that need your attention." Tish was clearly being intentionally vague.

Elysara dabbed at her lips with a napkin. "I apologize. This probably won't be the last time I have to step out while you are here with me, Ken."

"No need to apologize." I held up my hands. "You are going to be the next ruler of the Elven people. I'm sure you have some very important tasks that cannot wait. Right now, I am talking with Fay, but in some of these instances, I'd like to be able to come with you."

My offer made Elysara's smile brighten considerably. "Yes. We'll plan on that." She dipped her head and walked out. Tish followed after her, leaving the rest of us alone.

Fay's mood shifted when the princess left and she slowly shook her head. "Poor woman."

I raised an eyebrow at the statement and turned to my mother-in-law for more. "There's something I don't know."

"There are many things you don't know." Fay gave me a wry grin. "But the closing of the upper dungeon floors has created considerable problems for her and her father."

"She made it seem like it wasn't that bad." I leaned back in my chair. "Is that not the case?"

"Several of the dukes have formed a political bloc, probably one of the largest in our history that's stood against the Emperor. It's given them... substantial protection from the Emperor breaking them up or trying to rein them in. Their main stance is to open the dungeon back up, and it has drawn a number of our highest-level adventurers to them. That support is not helping matters."

"Duke Selmia?" I asked, suddenly wondering if it was all connected.

She nodded slowly. "He and his son share the title, but, yes, they are at the center of the bloc."

Suddenly, Neldra and Tish's lack of severity in the dungeon made sense today. Striking out harshly against the younger Duke Selmia would be just the spark that someone could use to make a move.

"So. When the younger duke found us in the dungeon earlier today and asked for Elysara's hand, apparently not the first time, that was more a form of pressure from this bloc?"

While their hands were tied, the duke was mostly flaunting, or at least that's the way it seemed to me. I doubted a random proposal in the dungeon really had any expectation of working.

"He did what?" Fay's eyebrows shot up.

Fayeth attempted to calm her mother down. "We stumbled into him in the dungeon. He didn't like Ely being with a human, so he got a little confrontational. But Neldra and Tish were there and shooed them off."

Fay played with her daughter's hair and shook her head. "I didn't know that had been happening. In my position, I just see the larger scale issues. Giving the Selmia family a second Tree to manage was when a lot of us realized the bloc had formed. They pushed that power increase through despite the Emperor's dislike of the family. It was very telling."

"A small, but powerful group." I nodded, understanding the situation well enough. "So, they are clawing for more constantly. Meanwhile, the elves are under the threat of the naga, are they... threatening to not assist?"

Fay's mouth moved but sound didn't come out. She was shocked by my suggestion, but seemed to reconsider the immediate rebuke. "That's possible. You have to understand, the Royal Family isn't really that wealthy. Sure, they live under the Holy Great Tree and the palace, and a significant amount of infrastructure is 'theirs'. But they don't have any huge bank account somewhere. A lot of money flows through them, and they essentially use that rather than hoard it.

"It is these high-level adventurers and the dukes who actually have large sums of both monetary and physical power stored up. Really, they don't have our best interests at heart. They just found a weak spot in the new policy that they are going to push on with all they've got."

"Mom. Are things really that bad?" Fayeth asked.

"The Emperor is old, with only a single heir. It is a low point for the Royal Family," Fay said, her eyes shifting to her daughter in question. "You never really bothered with these things before."

Fayeth nodded and frowned down at her hands. "Still, I don't want to see Elysara go through something like that. Now that I've gained some strength, my first thought was to use it, but then I realized I really don't have enough to do anything in this situation."

Fay grabbed her daughter and hugged her. "That's okay. This is a conflict among my generation, not yours. Besides, Elysara is the

Trelican. If push comes to shove, she probably has more than a few cards to play."

My heart fell into my gut.

They really put a lot of weight on her class, and the truth was that Elysara didn't have it. With that in mind, she was in a real pickle.

While the political bloc could do some sort of hostile takeover, the better plan was to do exactly what the young duke had offered. Marrying Elysara was an easy way to take over the Royal Family, but what they didn't know was that it would expose her lie.

They were already her enemy. She likely couldn't trust them to protect her lie. Worst case, they could use the information like a leash to keep her under their thumb.

I ran my hand through my hair, not sure how to handle the situation. I leaned back and let out a heavy breath. Elysara was in a tough spot.

"What is it, Ken?" Fay asked.

"Just that she's been smiling so much around us, even with all of this." I offered a bit of the truth.

My mother-in-law tilted her head in confusion at the same time as my Adrel. It was adorable to see them both do the action at the same time.

"Just because she's having a bad time, doesn't mean she can't enjoy her time with us. I am upset as well that she hasn't shared this with us. We can help her by providing more things to smile about so that she can recover from dealing with all of this."

"That's my daughter." Fay squeezed Fayeth in another side hug.

Was that really all we could do?

Not that I needed to do more, but with the naga attacking humanity as they did, it would be nice for elves to have some stability so that they could become our ally when the time came.

"Have some more." Fay piled my now empty plate full again. "You should eat up so that you can become strong and protect my Fayeth."

"Thank you." I dug in. She was at least a little right. We were still too weak to get directly involved in the battle forming, but I was convinced there had to be some way to help.

CHAPTER 10

When Elysara finally returned from whatever business had pulled her away, dinner was long over. She took me for a walk in the palace while Fay kidnapped her daughter for a little mother and daughter time.

Honestly, I had a feeling Fayeth's mother wanted to give me some private time with the Lady after she learned she might join an Adrel with her daughter.

"I hope you didn't miss me too much at dinner." Elysara smiled up at me as Tish opened a pair of doors deep in the palace.

The Lady was dressed beautifully in a low-cut, red dress that matched her hair, but my eyes were drawn past her.

Row after row of three-story tall bookshelves greeted us. Each and every shelf was stuffed to the brim with books, and some held tubes that I knew would have old scrolls. The bookshelves were polished so smooth that the wood was almost reflective.

Further down on the ground level were just a few reading areas, and in the center, an enormous statue of an elf with a trident. I could guess who that was with the trident.

Any response I had was cut off with the sight. "Wow. They are all skillbooks?" I asked.

"Yes." Elysara held out her hand, and Tish gave her a large tome that she set down on a large, tilted platform for it. "I think we should find you an appropriate area attack."

While it felt too big for a gift, I wasn't sure it was smart to turn down her offer. She probably had a dozen arguments ready to go.

"Would people really be okay with you letting a human have his pick of these?" I hesitated.

"You agreed at dinner," Elysara pouted and pulled my hand to bring me over to the tome.

"Yeah. But then Fay told us about all the struggles you are having." I stared her in the eyes.

I expected her to shy away, but she surprised me by bursting out laughing.

"Oh, because you care about me. Don't worry. Ken, the truth is that I will never not have difficulties. The idea of being an Empress might seem grand, but ruling is a different kind of hard. No one truly has an easy life. Instead, those who are lucky just get to pick what kind of difficulty they face." She held on to my hand, and her blue eyes were like two pools to her soul as we stared at each other for a long moment.

Her lips ticked up into a smile. "So, spellbooks?"

I sighed in defeat, and she did a little dance.

"Wait, reading here is boring." She grabbed the book with one hand and brought me over to a lounge and sat me down before she sat on top of me.

I let out a grunt as she sat down.

The noise earned me a glare. "Am I heavy?"

"No, but that book is." I smiled.

She paused and nodded, deciding she liked that answer. "Let's see. The book is unfortunately in our language. While you are getting better at speaking, reading is probably beyond you."

"Correct. I couldn't make heads or tails of written Elvish. Most of the languages on Earth at least share the same symbols. Here I can barely tell the difference between this squiggle and this one." I pointed in the book.

"This is a tel, this is a roe. See this here? That's the difference," Elysara gave me a quick lesson.

"It would take a lot of practice for me to start seeing the difference fast enough to read," I admitted.

"Good. Then I'll just have to be your guide. Let's settle in." She wiggled herself against me.

Her back matched up with the open chest, exposing the bare skin of her back to my suit. Our skin touched as she leaned back. It felt nice as heat built up between the two of us.

"Don't be shy. Hold my hips. As you said, this is a heavy book. What if it pulls me off, and I hit my head?" She batted her eyelashes.

"Fine." I held her tight to my lap with one arm. "For the record, I know what you are doing."

"Really? That means your cooperation is an even better signal. For a minute, I was worried that humans wouldn't pick up on the flirtation." She winked. "Is it working?"

She wiggled again, and I felt my stiff reaction to her brush against her rear.

"A little." I blushed.

"Good. I'm glad you find me attractive. Now let's see if I can't impress you with the library, but we only get to pick one because

I'll not spoil you rotten. So it has to be perfect." She settled her weight against me and her head came to the top of my nose. A few of her stray ruby red hairs tickled at my face and brushed my nose as I breathed in her scent with each breath.

She wore a lovely flowery scent that I couldn't quite place. I took a few breaths, curious and wanting to identify the scent.

"Like this perfume that much?" she asked.

"It reminds me of something, but I can't quite figure out what it reminds me of," I told her honestly.

"Then I won't tell you. Keep trying to figure it out. I don't mind you focusing on me, even if it is just my scent," she teased and kept the book closed as she leaned back into me, enjoying the moment and humming a small tune.

Elvish was really a lovely language, even if I butchered it. The words almost felt like they were meant to be sung.

"Your scent... I thought you said perfume?" I asked after a minute.

"Well, I haven't put on anything to change my scent. So, I guess you would say natural perfume. Or is that an incorrect usage of the word?"

"No. That works." I was feeling particularly relaxed in the moment, yet I really wasn't the kind to sit still. "Elysara. Are you really not in trouble? Fay made it sound like there was no small amount of pressure on you."

"There's always pressure on me. I assume she talked about the political bloc that Duke Selmia is organizing against my father?" Elysara tried to get a clear picture before she continued.

I nodded.

"Then the event with his son in the dungeon made you wonder if it was far worse than she led on. Truthfully, I get an elf trying to court me at least three times a day. Even with how reclusive I am, they find a way to get in front of me and ask. For my age, to not even be pursuing someone is very rare."

She looked back to meet my eyes. "What they don't know is that I am pursuing someone." Her eyes stayed glued to mine. "Am I doing a good job?" she asked, some vulnerability entering her eyes.

"A little more aggressive than I'm used to. But I can't say it isn't effective." It was hard not to feel something for the gorgeous woman. So far, she'd shown intelligence, care, and a bond with Fayeth which I hadn't expected.

"Good." A giant smile split her face. "Then let us continue with the night." She opened the giant tome and started flipping through it, reading the index.

Her perusal gave me a moment to rethink the situation.

She was certainly putting in quite a bit of effort. It was hard to debate whether she wanted us to unite, but the thought that my Trelican class was her ultimate goal was hard to get out of my mind.

She was a princess who would become an emperor ruling her entire people. We might be diving the dungeon now, but I doubted she'd come back to me at Haylon, which raised questions about what we were even moving towards. Would we be a long-term, long-distance relationship? Those didn't have a history of going well.

"Would you two like something to drink while you peruse the library late at night?" Tish had a big grin on her face as she held out several bottles of wine.

Elysara tapped one of them. "We should do something light if we are going to be reading and making decisions. But a little wouldn't hurt, right, Ken?"

"Absolutely fine." I glanced at the Censor whose smile felt like she knew she was drawing me out of my doubts. After a second, I was sure that she had asked that question to stop me from brooding on the current situation.

I went with the gentle suggestion, pulling the woman in my lap a little closer and focusing more on the immediate moment.

"Much better." Elysara responded to me holding her tighter. "I think I've found the sections that we can use. Your magic is mostly dark attribute, right?"

"I have a little lightning, but yes, most of my damage is dark attribute."

"Then your stats are a mix of agility and magic for damage?" she confirmed.

I somewhat liked that she always confirmed her thoughts rather than make assumptions. "Yes."

"Then we should go to this section." She licked her finger and paged through to a certain part of the book.

The scrawling text of the Elvish language lined the page; it was clearly a name and then a concise description. Some of them were crossed out, and after three pages, there were blank pages awaiting new entries.

"Tish, could you help me break down some of these into better use cases? You are probably more familiar with each of these than me." Elysara handed the book to Tish after Tish had finished pouring two glasses of light wine.

Elysara picked up a glass and handed it to me while she took the other and sipped on it.

"Yes, I see," Tish murmured. "So, we can split these up in a number of categories. The first question is how big of an AoE do you want?"

"I'm not a tank, so anything I'm trying to damage should already be reasonably clustered. Tighter usually means more damage, so as tight as you think I can get away with. You're the seasoned adventurer," I told her honestly.

Tish smiled at my acknowledgement "Not going to worry that I dupe you?"

"I haven't known you long, but Elysara seems to put quite a bit of weight on your word, and you work well with Neldra. Even if my teacher and Neldra bicker, I think she holds a candle worth of respect for her," I explained.

Elysara ran a hand along my thigh in response, telling me that my answer was a good explanation.

"Thank you. Even if it is secondary, the respect of a warrior like Crimson is an honor. We'll go with something in the range of five to ten meters in diameter. That gives you good wiggle room depending on the monster size." Tish ran her finger down the list. "Next, since this is magic, you actually have a decision. Do you want damage over time or instant damage?"

That question made me ponder.

While I thought, Elysara spoke up, "Damage over time is going to generally do more damage, right?"

"If it's a spellbook worth the space on these shelves, then yes." Tish smirked. "There are benefits of instant damage if you are fighting a larger number of monsters weaker than you and just want to destroy them. It isn't a bad option if you don't have much already in your rotation for a single target, which you don't."

"Damage over time allows me to keep doing my single target focus anyway," I responded.

Tish shrugged. "Two different ways of doing the same thing."

I wasn't sure I entirely agreed. If I could fit one of my sword forms in between each need to apply the damage over time, that would be easier for me. "Let's say I prefer damage over time."

Tish nodded and ran her finger down the list. "Then there are other things that could go along with it. Do you want some bonuses for it? These are each going to reduce the damage or increase the cooldown so you can use it less."

"If I can't keep it up one hundred percent of the time, does the damage it deals make up for that downtime?" I asked.

Tish nodded at my question and pulled her lips to the side as she went through the list again. "I can remove those that don't."

"Please," I answered. "So what bonuses would be options?"

"A defensive buff, one that hinders vision, and then one that is just straight damage." She trailed her finger down the page as she scanned the spells.

I leaned back and glanced at Elysara, who seemed to be enjoying herself. "Hindering vision seems like a poor choice given that the current use is with you."

"Though, as a member of an assassin clan, that seems right up your alley," Elysara countered me.

I shook my head. "Smoke bombs work well enough if I need to obscure vision." I felt more confident in denying that bonus. "Yeah. Scratch that one off. The defensive buff is tempting. What's the cooldown on that one?"

"Two minutes."

I let out a whistle. "And the damage makes up for that down-time?"

"Sort of. I kept it on there with the thought that the fights would only last about thirty seconds. The damage lasts for eighteen," she admitted.

"How does it compare to an ability that is just a defensive ability?" Elysara asked.

"Mediocre," Tish admitted.

"Then you should avoid it, Ken. Get a skill that has a broader use for what you want this one for, and then get a dedicated defensive ability," Elysara offered.

"The Lady has a point." Tish bowed her head. "The dual purpose I thought would help fill in his current lack of range in his abilities."

I raised an eyebrow at her statement.

"You are still early in your adventure days, but single-target, multi-target and AoE are the three modes of damage. Along with that, to really balance out your kit, you need some sort of self-sustain or defensive ability to help protect you. High-level boss fights will have attacks that cannot be dodged and are quite powerful. To help your healer, you need one of those," Tish explained. "You already have a few movement abilities, but you need to focus on rounding out your kit if I'm honest."

I glanced at Elysara.

"She's right. Even if Tish kind of ripped the bandage off abruptly there." The princess held out her hands for the book. "Which one are we looking for?"

Tish gave her the tome and put a finger on one entry.

"Casts, Blades of Shadow. User fans out blades made of magic to hit each target within a ten-meter arc in front of them. Each blade will leave a damage over time effect for twelve seconds," Elysara translated the entry for me. "You're good with the arc range? Since you are in melee, it should be usable."

I nodded. "Yeah, I can manage that. It says it makes a blade for each?"

"The number of blades will be variable and only hit targets you see as enemies. Dungeon spells can be smart like that," Elysara explained, tapping a spot at the bottom of the description. "Now let's go find it."

She bounded out of my lap, grabbing my hand and pulling me along as we deposited our wine glasses.

Tish moved the tome back to its spot while I was dragged over to the bookshelves. Elysara read placards at the top of each row, muttering to herself.

"Here. Can you grab me that ladder?" She gestured to one that ran on a rail and had wheels on the bottom.

I thought for a second how we had the same type of structure in our libraries, but it made sense given that both of us had worked to find a suitable solution to a similar problem.

The only difference was that Elven ladders were more triangle shaped, tapering towards the top. But they were making them out of wood rather than metal, so maybe that gave it more structural support.

Elysara whistled a tune to herself and climbed the ladder, going slowly as she made sure to get the rungs right with her heels on.

I couldn't help but see her round butt pushing against her dress, and it brought me back to the gym and then to when she was just in my lap. She'd felt so soft sitting atop me.

She had stopped, and I realized she was looking down at me. "Stare all you want. I enjoy you watching. You can even shift to try to get a view around the cloth."

Her statement made me blush and look away.

"You went too far, Lady," Tish reported.

Elysara sighed. "Are humans all so prudish?"

"Many of us," I admitted.

"Well, can you look back here? I need you to shift the ladder. The spell is actually a section over." She pointed to the right.

"Of course." I grabbed the ladder and pulled her over a section, looking up at her and getting another view. If I shifted just a little, I could probably see up her skirt.

Elysara had a mischievous twinkle in her eye as she looked down at me. "Perfect, now if you'd hold that ladder to keep it steady." She leaned way over towards the section that she had just been positioned in front of.

I rolled my eyes. "You are a troublemaker."

"Am I making pleasant trouble?" she laughed and grabbed the book before pulling herself back onto the ladder.

"It's not so bad," I admitted.

She slid down the ladder with the spellbook in hand, and I caught her on reflex. My hand ended up back on her rear with how I had caught her. Yet she didn't complain. If anything, she seemed happy about being close to me.

"Can I kiss you? Or will that make you blush and run away?" She leaned forward and whispered in my ear.

The challenge worked, and I made the first move, pressing my lips to her and then pressing her to the shelf behind her.

The book hit the floor and neither of us cared as I lost myself in her lips, with my hands wandering down her waspish waist and cupping her rear. Her legs came up and wrapped around my hips as her arms wrapped around my shoulders.

Our lips were wet with wine and she tasted good as we reveled in each other for a moment as our breaths mingled. The soft heat of her body enveloped my chest, and I crushed myself to her, craving more. We were so pressed together that I could feel her heartbeat and feel it sync with mine.

Her lips slid off of mine one more time, and she stared into my eyes. The new flush on her face was prominent with all the red on her. When her legs slid off my hips with the slow grace of a dancer, I wanted to pull them back up. But in the end, I released her.

Her hands left me slowly, keeping my attention as our eyes were still locked. Elysara smiled and bent over, maintaining eye contact to pick up the book and handed it out to me.

"Consider it a gift, and with it, I'd like you to know that I intend to pursue your Adrel. I know you have doubts, questions as to my intentions. I want you to know that I prepared for your visit with nothing but information from Neldra. Yet, now that you are here, I couldn't be happier that the man who can help me in a multitude of ways is you." She put the book in my arms and gave me a light kiss to seal the deal.

"Thank you." I took the spellbook. "Becoming Adrel takes effort, and though I have my doubts, I will respect you and put in the effort from my end as well."

Elysara's smile was so brilliant at my statement, I got a little lost in it. It looked like I'd nailed my answer.

"Well then. We should send you back to Fayeth before I push you down on the couch here to see just how compatible we are. Let her take care of you." She glanced down at the tent in my pants.

I shook my head. I'd never expected that I'd have one woman wind me up only to hand me over to another.

Grandpa would be proud.

CHAPTER 11

"Lady?" Tish asked after Ken had left.

Elysara sat down on the closest chair and swung her foot back and forth with a radiant smile that felt like it would stay for a while. "That was a pleasant end to the evening. We didn't get to looking over my other forms, but maybe we'll play with them over the next few days."

"Indeed. I'm happy things are going well for you." Tish bowed.

Neldra entered the room and looked around. "I had hoped to come back to a large mess, with Ken being brought back to his room. His clothes didn't look nearly ruffled enough."

Elysara blushed and waved the Censor's comment away. "Far too fast, especially for him. But he's every bit the man you told me he was. Honestly, I thought you were talking him up so that I'd not hesitate when he came."

"Crimson took a liking to him. You know she's going to be part of his Adrel." Neldra found a seat, and Tish shrugged before joining both of them in her own chair.

"She still terrifies me a little, but you make it sound like she's a different person around him." Elysara was interested in more information about Crimson. Learning about the current and future members of her Adrel was vital.

"She should. But if you have Ken, she wouldn't dare touch a hair on your head." Neldra paused before continuing. "But if we put all of it aside, how do you feel about him?" Neldra always was good to her and wanted the heart of the matter.

Elysara twirled one of the locks that framed her face. People spent a lot of time on her hair every morning. "If he weren't the Trelican, and I weren't a princess, I think it would be lovely for us to make an Adrel. Yet, I'm a princess and there are political pressures. The Adrel that I join is not just something for my heart to decide. I have to use my head too."

Elysara smiled. "In that, I'm thankful that he's a Trelican, and that makes him viable for me as a princess. Far better than Duke

Selmia, that's for sure." The smile fell from her face and an expression that Ken hadn't seen appeared.

This look was darker, more thoughtful, and no small amount intimidating.

Elysara leaned forward and bridged her fingers before pressing them against her lips. "Duke Selmia is growing bolder. He interrupted our dive today, seeded doubt in my future Adrel, and embarrassed me. I want Relsh and Givia to find me something I can use to push back, painfully. My future Adrel is concerned about them, and it is time I took some action. Cutting off the next generation should send a message to this political bloc.

"Find the skeletons they've tried to hide among the roots. They are connected and wealthy enough that they no doubt have them. I want that option in my hand for my generation of every major figure in the bloc for when they push me again. My father may be content with his current position, but it is time I show my generation that I will be a force."

Neldra grinned while Tish laughed.

"You should show Ken this side of you," Neldra suggested.

Elysara blushed and started twirling her hair again. "You don't think he'd think I was some sort of tyrant?"

"He's a trained assassin. Pretty sure he left it out of some of his stories, but there was a time where apparently he lured away a higher-level adventurer party and lined the swamp with traps, outright killing several of them when he sprung the trap. He's more familiar with the dark side of humanity and of elves than you give him credit for. Hell, he might think it sexy that you can join him on the dark side from time to time," Neldra encouraged her.

Elysara knew that her Censor was trying to encourage her, yet... "Sometimes I enjoy being the pretty princess. The way Ken looks at me..." She trailed off, warring with strange desires. "Keep this quiet for now and find something small for me to slap the younger duke away with for today. I'll save going directly for his throat until next time."

Elysara paused. "Oh, and thank you both for helping. This was a wonderful idea, Tish, and I really enjoyed tonight." She smiled at the two Censors.

Neldra rubbed the top of Elysara's head like an older sister might. "Do not worry. We have your back."

"I'm just happy you enjoyed the time and made so much progress tonight." Tish shrugged as if it were casual, but a small smile peeked out the corner of her lips.

"Either way. I'm so thankful to both of you and all your support. That goes for all the Censors, but doubly so for both of you. With all this isolation, you two have always been there for me," Elysara spoke from the heart.

Neldra blushed. "Don't worry, my Lady. We are trying so hard because we see how hard you are trying. All of your Censors are in agreement: you'll do great things for the future of the elves. Let us handle the investigations. Focus on your time with Ken over the next few months."

Elysara gave the two older elves a sharp nod. "I'll do my best."

***

"How was your night?" Fayeth was brushing her hair as I sat with her back in our room.

"Interesting." I still held the skillbook, a grin still fixed on my face from the end to the evening.

Fayeth turned around to interpret that better and smiled back. "You look happy. That's what matters most to me. Do I need to help you wind down or are you already ready for bed?"

I stepped up behind Fayeth and pulled her into my arms for a moment. "I told Elysara that I'd return the effort towards becoming Adrel."

Fayeth let out a little happy noise and pulled my head down for a kiss. "I can taste her on your lips."

"Is that a good thing?" I asked and was answered by a long kiss from Fayeth as she backed up until she tumbled down onto the gigantic bed in our room.

Her hands wandered under my clothes and peeled them off one by one. "I should think that was answer enough. Now, let me reward you. I look forward to expanding our Adrel, especially with someone I already love like a sister. You make her happy, and I will never protest to more joy in our Adrel."

She rolled me over and sat on my hips.

"You're never this aggressive," I mentioned, curious at the change.

"That's because you haven't given me reason to be. I like it when you take me, but sometimes I have to be the one giving the reward." She pushed down my pants and sank down as my cock pointed to the heavens.

It was a tight fit, but I could feel how swollen she was and how we wouldn't be apart until one of us was exhausted.

My soul sang with the intimate contact as she leaned down to kiss me. I tried to hold myself back given what she'd said, letting her take the lead, but it was difficult not to just flip her over and take her.

***

Crimson's whip glowed red with crackling energy as she unleashed [Sever] on the group of naga that had been waiting for her on the floor.

After a week of near constant activation of [Limit Breaker], her mind surfaced back through the bloody mess she had made. She blinked, her mind clearing as she felt the skill dialing down and she breathed as if she hadn't done so in a long time.

"Fuck. Where am I?" Crimson checked her CID to find the device cracked and non-responsive. "Which way is the way back home?" she asked aloud as she activated [Eyes of Wisdom].

The dungeon entrance she had just gone through glowed blue.

Crimson cursed up a storm before she calmed down. "Stupid ability. Can't I stay focused long enough to find my way out?"

Talking aloud was helping. She was loath to admit it, but Ken had reawakened some of her desire for community. Diving alone didn't feel the same anymore. She missed having somebody to talk to, so talking to herself would have to do for the moment. The naga weren't exactly riveting conversation, and she didn't have a volleyball to name.

Stepping back through the entrance she had clearly just entered, she noticed the stairs were going down. That meant she had deeper to go. She got to the bottom of the stairs only to be assaulted with the tang of blood in the air.

Naga corpses were strewn everywhere, and a few crab dungeon monsters were already cleaning up. Still, the scene looked like a massacre.

This was what would happen if she unleashed [Limit Breaker] back home. She was a danger to everything.

There was a sinking feeling, a question in the back of her mind. Would everyone be better off if she just stayed away and slaughtered naga? She'd become a monster to hunt the monsters.

Yet, one image surfaced in her mind and refused to leave.

Ken Nagato.

She closed her eyes and just let herself savor the memories with him, the feel of him, the smell of him. She'd been using him along her journey to keep herself grounded and sane.

She would succeed and get back to him one way or another.

The thoughts calmed her, steadying her heart and helping her breathe evenly. She knew Ken would tease her about taking too long to get back, and she'd flick him in the forehead for it and downplay how grueling it had been getting through the naga territory.

She wondered what he was doing. If he wasn't training, she was going to hand him his ass when she returned. She expected him to progress quickly so that he could dive with her soon.

Just the idea had her heartbeat quicken and a spark of her ability danced along her arm.

"No. Damnit. I'm not ready to go again just yet." Her stomach growled. She checked her broken CID. Sure enough, it wasn't about to give her any of the items she had stored.

Glancing down at the naga, she thought about it for a split second before dismissing the idea, she couldn't eat something that smart. So she poked around to see if they had some sort of inventory on them.

Sadly, she found nothing.

Which only left the crab monsters that were cleaning up.

"Here, little crabs." She shot forward and killed three crabs with one blow. "Wonder what floor I'm on. Those were fairly easy, and they seemed like a defensive monster. Maybe somewhere in the high thirties?"

One crab had dropped a packet of meat, and she was quick to get a fire going so that she could cook up the food. Using one of the dead naga's swords, she held the meat over the fire while her stomach growled at her angrily.

"Yeah, yeah. Maybe you should remember this body when you keep me in Limit Break for so long," she scolded her own stomach.

Rather than focus on her surroundings, Crimson let her mind play with the idea of what Ken would say if he was with her. He'd probably try to make her feel better, play the entire naga fight all off as something less gruesome than it was and then tease her.

Crimson pressed her thighs together and rubbed them back and forth. "I'm going to get a few more magazines made when we get back and tease him with them. Then maybe he'll..."

Red energy crackled over her, and she put a damper on the idea of what he'd do to her. Instead, she fixed Ken in her mind and imagined him calming her down as she played with the choker on her neck.

She imagined him snapping it on her and telling her what to do. She licked her lips, savoring the idea. He'd tell her to do naughty, naughty things.

Crimson was about to push the thought away so that she didn't push herself into chaos, but then she realized that in her little fantasy of him telling her what to do that her heart was picking up, but her ability wasn't active.

Ken was telling her not to activate it. To be his good girl.

Crimson stabbed the butt of the sword into the ground. Food could wait. This was a golden opportunity she hadn't had for years. Crimson whimpered with need as she rubbed herself through her suit.

The entire time she touched herself, she was focused on the thought of Ken bossing her around, the only man who had ever teased her in recent years taking control of the situation.

Her release came almost instantly after five years of nothing, and the peak was so intense that Crimson forgot how to breathe for a moment. Crimson finally gasped, and her body shook as she fell down panting for breath.

A giant smile bloomed on her face as she picked up the cooked crab meat and bit off a huge chunk. Crimson hadn't felt so good in a long time, and she was even more excited to get back to Ken.

***

Time had flown by. I'd spent almost a week already in the Elven world.

I did a small turn for Elysara and Fayeth who had helped me get dressed for a formal event.

"I think he passes." Elysara looked me up and down with a fake criticality.

"Almost too well. I don't mind more in Adrel with us, but I don't want *every* lady in the palace to be pawing at him." Fayeth was all smiles.

It was infectious, and I found myself beaming right back at her.

The week of us spending time with Elysara had really brightened her up. I hadn't realized how much being home and being with a friend would let me see her even more bubbly.

"His chest looks a little more defined," Elysara commented, and Fayeth stepped forward to poke the cleft between my pecs which might have been a little deeper. "Working out with us really does you well."

"You two are a hell of an encouragement," I admitted. Every day in the gym with both of them was something to look forward to.

"He isn't shy about spotting you anymore," Fayeth added.

I had been getting far more comfortable with Elysara, even going as far as to tease her back from time to time. She had switched to the tight workout clothes that Fayeth had brought with her and had similar ones made in Elven fashion, which meant they were more sheer and had more cutouts to deal with the heat.

More than a few men would have died from nosebleeds if she worked out in that clothing back home.

"We have lost him to a daydream. Thinking about my ass? It's right here." Elysara slapped her rear and made me blush.

"You two are going to be the death of me. Don't we have to act with a little more propriety at this event?" I checked myself in the mirror. The three of us were matching. I matched primarily with Elysara, and while Fayeth's outfit went with both of ours, it was off enough that the two of them weren't wearing the same thing.

The faux pas of wearing the same outfit apparently transcended cultures.

"Yes. We are getting it out of our system now." Fayeth and Elysara had become two peas in a pod. I had a feeling they had moved into a similar bond like they'd had as children.

"Though, I would like to send a message to some of the younger generation during this," Elysara added, taking my hand in hers. "Please be a little touchy with me. Hands on my arm, put yours around my waist and more."

"Similar level of touching to what you'd do if you were hitting on a girl at a bar," Fayeth translated.

Elysara gestured that she agreed. "Then, I get to lean against you. Touch your hair, fix your clothes."

"This is to signal that we are harmonizing our souls?" I asked unsure of the purpose.

She nodded. "You did it with Fayeth."

"She was a little less rushed. But yes, I remember it." Holding her hand, I focused on the feeling I had with Fayeth when we were perfectly in harmony and touching.

It wasn't there with Elysara, but maybe there was a distant hum. Now that I had experienced it with Fayeth, I thought there was something to the concept.

"It's faint," Elysara agreed. "That you can even search for it makes me feel like you are half elf or something."

"No way." I laughed. "But if that counts for something, can I show it with Fayeth?"

Elysara pressed her lips together in thought. "Maybe. I'll think about it and ask the Censors. There might be a way to show, but normally the harmonization is a very personal thing."

"Alright then. I think I'm ready." The event would be the first time I met her father, stalling was only going to make me more nervous.

Elysara pulled my lips down and went up on her tiptoes even in her heels to give me a slow sensual kiss. "Thank you for supporting me."

"You're welcome." I smiled. Fayeth, who clearly wanted a kiss too, leaned forward. I picked her up, and she made a happy chirp as we kissed with far more familiarity and no less heat.

When I put her down the two ladies turned to each other and kissed.

I couldn't help but stare at where Elysara's darker pink lips met Fayeth's, and for a moment, there were two little tongues slipping between them. It was brief, but when they broke apart, my mind was still stuck on what I'd just seen.

"I think that broke him," Elysara laughed.

"It isn't that normal for humans." Fayeth hid her mouth, trying to cover that she was fighting a smile.

"Are you both bi?" I asked.

They glanced at each other and shrugged.

"That was pleasant, don't get me wrong," Elysara answered. "But the best part was how much you seemed to enjoy watching it. I could probably get worked up enough to do something with Fayeth if you were in bed with us."

"It's different. Soft for my tastes, but not unpleasant," Fayeth agreed. "I kind of imagined that with him between us."

"Oh. That would be wonderful," Elysara sighed. "One of these days, we should try it. I'm sure he won't mind." She grabbed Fayeth and pushed their faces together. "What do you think, Ken? Two on one?"

I pulled at my jacket to cool off. "This event." My voice cracked a little as I worked to focus. "We should get going now that you've both got it out of your systems."

Rather than let them work me up too much, I headed out of Elysara's changing room.

Both of them moved behind me, giggling like two conspirators as they followed me out the door.

"I assume everything went well?" Ami had a second suit draped over her arm as she stood nearby. "Do you need a second suit?"

I looked back at the giggling women who had clearly given Ami the instructions. "You are all lucky that we have places to be or I'd be dragging you back into the bedroom for punishment."

"Oh. I didn't know that was an option." Elysara perked up.

"Shall I keep a rope on hand?" Ami teased me with a deadpan expression. Elysara and Fayeth's laughter grew, pleased that Ami had joined their side.

I grumbled as I walked away. Now I really didn't stand a chance against all the teasing.

CHAPTER 12

Music played around us like tinkling crystals. The event was in one of the larger ballrooms of the palace. The space had been transformed, no longer looking anything like the room I'd been in for dinner.

Glittering lights now hung from above, and sheer strips of cloth ran back and forth underneath them, softening the lights and setting the mood of a highbrow affair.

The walls were decorated with a number of banners. Each one was a different, distant branch of the Royal Family that made up the nobility of the elves.

Interestingly enough, any close branches weren't given noble status. They needed to be far enough away from the Royal Family that they were acceptable to marry back into it to be given noble status. It was an odd buffer, but one that seemed to work for them.

My eyes drifted down to the people moving through the crowd, gathering in groups and enjoying fine wine along with little morsels, many of which seemed to be seafood.

That choice in cuisine was a sign of wealth poured into the event and even significant for an event at the palace.

"Lady Rendral," a passerby called out to her.

Thankfully, we'd been working on my Elvish, and I could understand most of what was being said around me.

Rather than any fancy announcement, people came and went from the event with just a verbal acknowledgment. Sometimes when someone like Elysara came into the room, the single call would turn into a buzz and ripple through the crowd like it was now.

Many heads turned our direction, and I knew what I had to do. Putting my arm around Elysara, I held her to my side. She leaned against me with a giant smile.

"Duke Treble, how goes Flasom?" she asked with a smile.

"Wonderful. I am very satisfied with my appointment, and my family is getting along well. I'm afraid, in a year or two, it might be as hard to uproot my daughter as it is a Great Tree." He gave a hearty belly laugh.

"That's wonderful. And how is the duchess? I heard there was some difficulty with the third little one." Elysara apparently knew the lives of the nobility in detail.

"She's recovered. Thank you for your concern, but the healing corps that the empire provides are top-notch." He bowed slightly. "I'm not one to forget their skill anytime soon."

"Nonsense. They work for all of us, and if I'm honest, I couldn't pry them out of Flasom if I tried. So you are doing many things right there." Elysara grinned at him.

Duke Treble dipped his head. "Thank you for your kind words. I look forward to the day that you sit on the throne."

Elysara playfully waved his words away. "I like my freedom far too much right now. Ah, have you met Ken Nagato yet?"

The Duke blinked, the only show of his surprise as he took me in. I noticed that his eyes lingered on my ears. "I heard about a human in the palace with you."

"This is Crimson's student and humanity's first Trelican." Elysara held on to me.

"Truly?" the duke asked, stalling for time, and clearly unsure what to say.

"It is true. His teacher is currently off fighting the naga. The naga staged a large-scale assault on humanity. Crimson wiped out hundreds of their warriors and a matriarch on her own before rushing into their section of the dungeon and leveling entire floors," Elysara played up the battle.

I smiled and spoke slowly so that I didn't mess up my words. "Crimson and Censor Neldra have found a small comradery. Neldra is assisting me this summer with my training, and I've gotten the opportunity to trade pointers with Ely— I mean— Lady Rendral here. After all, with such a rare class, it is a unique opportunity to learn from each other."

Elysara gave me a small look filled with mirth as I purposefully started to use her name rather than her title, showing off quite a bit of familiarity.

I knew that pairing that statement with the way we were touching each other should make it clear that we were fairly close, even with just a short time together.

"Incredible." Duke Treble smiled at me. "Your teacher is a bit of a legend among our people."

"She's a legend among our own too." I laughed, and the tension between the duke and me eased a little more.

"Your Elvish is so clean," he commented.

"Well, that is partially because of my Adrel." I searched behind me to find Fayeth and pulled her to my other side. "We harmonized for the first time six months or so ago."

Now Duke Treble was very interested. "Humans can harmonize their souls to an elf?"

Fayeth played along. "He was fairly blind to it at first, but eventually, he got it. And he even feels it when it is off."

"Yes and he's learning so much more now that he's visited." Elysara leaned against me. "We've found that the two of us have a lot in common. Not just our classes, but given his teacher's position among humanity, we are finding ourselves in similar positions in the conflict with the naga that is brewing here in the future."

Duke Treble made a noise of understanding that was more like a low chirp. "I can see you two cut a fine pair. Good luck to both of you. I was thinking of trying to find some time with you, Lady Rendral, in the near future?"

"Yes. I cleared my calendar for the next week before attending, wanting to take advantage of so many dukes being under our shade." Elysara politely smiled. "I'll have someone contact you tomorrow to set up some time."

"Thank you, Lady." The duke did a small dip of his head again and moved on, having gotten what he had wanted.

"How was that?" I asked Elysara, switching to English so that we could speak privately.

"Wonderfully done. The added bit of almost saying my first name really cinched it, I think. He is an easy one, though. He just wants to stay in Flasom and he'll be happy." She nodded to Neldra who was positioned along the wall. The Censor took a note down on her CID.

"Flasom is a nice city?"

"One of the best. It's a very popular tourist destination. Being in one of the cooler regions, you can comfortably walk outside the tree's shade for about a third of the year. And there are all sorts of excursions that people go on to see the wildlife that live further out, and a giant lake for them to swim in." She noticed another noble coming up towards us and nodded in acknowledgement before whispering to me. "Another easy one. Let's do the same."

Elysara switched back to Elvish and put on a big smile. "Duchess Critch, a pleasure to see you."

***

The event became a whirlwind of names, and we repeated the same general script several times. Elysara had prepared me, and I was ready to play my part.

One of the goals was to introduce me, but we tried to do it using as much Elven culture as we could. Having an Adrel, understanding harmonizing souls, and speaking clean Elvish were all clues to make them like me.

I didn't care, but it would make Elysara's life easier, so I put in my best effort.

"Thank you. I'll have my people come arrange some time after," Elysara dismissed another duke.

"I think I have this down." I smiled, having lost count of the number of nobility we'd met at that point.

They were all a little different as Elysara worked to assuage each of their desires in varied ways. Some wanted her attention, others just wanted a little praise, or to make sure she would keep certain aspects of their comfortable lives the same.

Those that wanted changes were harder, because Elysara couldn't give them those concessions directly.

"You do. We might be ready for some of the harder ones and..." Her eyes shifted to the other end of the ballroom, where a bulky elf with familiar red hair sat in a throne and received dukes, only with a much higher hand than Elysara. "He's asked to meet you."

I let out a breath. "The friendly ones are much better." I looked away before I drew the Emperor's attention.

"Yes, well, nothing gets done if you only take the easy routes," Elysara answered as she moved towards her father's half of the ballroom.

I felt a shift as we moved, realizing that those who weren't rushing to the Emperor's area were smaller families or more content with the current status quo. Those talking to the Emperor himself wanted change. It felt more like wandering among sharks. One drop of blood could set off a feeding frenzy.

"...do something about the dungeon."

"Can't believe it..."

"A human?!" one of them gasped as I walked with Elysara through the crowd.

Elysara ignored the comment, maintaining her smile with every step. I did notice she clung to me a little tighter, as if to rub our proximity in the last speaker's nose.

"Don't worry. Gossip is just a way to soften people up." Elysara rolled her eyes.

"Ah. Lady Rendral." An Elven woman whose age was just starting to show greeted Elysara. "What a pleasure to meet you and your pet human here." She leaned in conspiratorially. "Such a novelty. You've really outdone yourself."

"Duchess Hichi, what a pleasure to meet you. Let me formally introduce Ken Nagato, student of The Crimson and humanity's Trelican," Elysara pressed the conversation forward rather than respond to the earlier pet comment.

"Oh. So you are borrowing Crimson's pet." The Duchess covered her mouth while she laughed alone.

"I do understand you," I spoke in crystal clear Elvish.

"And you've proven to me that you've been taught to bark." The Duchess looked down her nose at me. "Where is The Crimson if you are here? Hmm?" She looked around, aimlessly. "Not here?"

"No. She's off slaughtering naga," Elysara replied sweetly, but there was a slight edge in her voice.

I wanted to strangle the duchess, but I doubted I'd get away with it in the current setting. Maybe if I tracked her back to where she was staying and waited...

"Well then. Until she gets back, he's just a low-level human. Even if he is a Trelican." The duchess seemed bored with the conversation. "Unless he can spin up some of the ore trade from here to Grestain?"

"Ah. You know that trade is heavily controlled." Elysara clicked her tongue and shook her head. "Those monsters are farmed regularly, yet there never seems to be enough."

"Is it that precious?" I feigned innocence. "Huh, humans basically have heaps and heaps of it just lying around."

That statement caught the duchess' attention, even if she was trying to hide the interest in her eyes.

"See. We even build our CIDs out of them." I showed her mine. "Wait, a second." I pulled out an aluminum canteen out of my CID. "Really, we build everything from it."

The duchess' eye betrayed her with a twitch. "Really now?" Her voice was stiffer than before.

"I might have some pictures in here..." I trailed off, swiping through some pictures until I saw one of the classroom and grinned. "Look at this. We even build our desks out of metal; most of it is aluminum alloys of some sort. But those hooks to hang our bags on in the back are probably cheap steel. And this is how most humans get around." I found a picture of a car.

"Truly?" The duchess was leaning in and staring at the pictures as I pointed out parts that were made of metal. "Where do you get all of this metal from?"

"Mine it from our world. I guess we probably use some from the dungeon, but I don't think it has much value." I shrugged, acting casual.

She was pursing her lips now, and Elysara had stepped back to give me the field. Never was I supposed to offer the resources to the woman, only show her the opportunity until she burst. That's how this worked, and I got her to step down off her high horse.

"That is very interesting. What do you do with the metal from the weapons and such?" the duchess asked.

"I think we dispose of them in giant pits on our planet to rust." I thought about the answer, not entirely sure if anyone was taking the time to melt them down. There was a pretty good chance that they were rusting away in landfills.

"Dispose." The duchess nearly choked on the word. "Humans really are stupid creatures."

We were so close to building some sort of bridge, but in the end, her prejudice won out.

"I suppose that the elves could probably take some of it off your hands." She gave me a high-handed expression and tried to goad me into making an offer.

"No. I think that would be too much work. Why run all the way to the fifties to sell a low-level iron sword when you could just throw it in a bin at your nearest convenience and the city will go put it in one of the pits for you." I shrugged.

It felt like I had her on the hook, so I decided to pull back the rod.

"Anyways, it was a pleasure to meet you," I said dryly. "Ely, should we continue towards your father?" I turned away from the duchess.

The duchess cleared her throat. "It seems that humans might have some differences that appear nonsensical on the surface, but are just merely a different way of living. Who am I to judge an entirely different world? This conversation has been illuminating. I would be very interested in some time later this week to discuss humanity, and where Elven and human strengths and weaknesses might cover for each other."

Elysara and I were standing so that we could see each other's faces, but they were partially hidden from the duchess. Elysara gave me a wink that I returned before turning back.

"Ah. I'm a guest here for the summer. Can you help me set it up?" I asked the woman on my arm.

"Of course. I can have one of my people talk to yours, duchess." Elysara glanced over at Neldra who confirmed with a nod.

"Actually, I don't know heads from tails about Elven negotiations or really much from what you've told me. Would you mind attending with me?" I asked, feigning as if the conversation wasn't going exactly to plan.

"Certainly, I'd be happy to spend more time with you. Duchess, it is so incredible that I've gotten to meet another Trelican to compare notes with. We have just been attached at the hip. Not to mention, he is the heir to a powerful human faction as well. So our situations have been similar in that regard as well," Elysara laid it on thick.

"How... wonderful." The duchess' smile was brittle and forced, but she was at least making an effort to look friendly "If you'll excuse me." The duchess practically ran away.

"That went well," Fayeth commented. "Missed my part, though."

"That's fine. At that rate, she might have asked where your leash was." Elysara rolled her eyes and we continued through the party towards her father. "Though, we should actually talk about what humans can offer. I know our early attempts at negotiation were scant, and even now, most of it is considering aid towards the naga. But we should look at resources."

"I am one hundred percent just going to use the Silver Fangs to gather the iron or whatever she wants to trade," I answered.

"Do you know the costs, though?" Elysara raised an eyebrow.

"Sort of." I waffled my hand.

"Just don't get burned providing them to her at any cost. These sorts of bulk deals can be profitable, but you need to be absolutely sure of the costs involved," Elysara warned me.

"You could turn it down or make a provisional deal," Fayeth added.

"It would make him appear weak," Elysara countered.

I nodded, it would be tricky to get the balance right, yet at the same time, it seemed that the metal was scarce enough in the Elven world that I might just be able to put enough buffer in the deal that it wouldn't matter.

Truthfully, my biggest hurdle would be the transporting of the goods. But we could worry about that later when we talked to her.

"Lady Rendral. It is so good to see you," a duke greeted Elysara.

She was about to respond, but a tidal wave of killing intent washed over us. Elysara fumbled her words.

I didn't think, just stepping between the source of the killing intent and her head on. My move helped, softening the impact as she started talking to the duke.

My eyes shifted around to find the source, locking on an older man present that had the most ridiculous mustache on his face. It was the first mustache I had seen in the Elven world.

Despite his attempt to rile up Elysara, the killing intent did little to me. Compared to Crimson or my grandparents, I'd go as far as to call him sheltered. Though, he was clearly a high level.

I was surprised that Elysara had been affected at all. Clearly, she was not conditioned to withstand the pressure. And I was also surprised that the man would dare unleash that kind of intent in a room with powerful dukes and the Emperor.

I gritted my teeth, wanting to be able to stand up to the mustached man, but I was not yet at a point where I could go toe to toe with somebody of his power.

CHAPTER 13

E lysara nodded her thanks and continued the conversation while I glared at the elf with the mustache. Yet after someone passed between us, he disappeared, along with his pressure. One second, he was there; the next, he was gone without a trace.

I shifted my focus back to the conversation Elysara was having.

"Yes. This is Ken Nagato. His family is of some renown in his world, and he's the student of The Crimson." Elysara pulled me closer, and I made sure to touch her openly.

The duke in question huffed. "A buffed-up rumor. I don't see her here."

"Oh. Don't worry. I expect her to show up before the end of the summer." I smiled at him. "She's off slaughtering naga at the moment. You see, they attacked Earth recently, and she decided to hit back, hard. That's just the kind of woman she is. We humans have a saying: an eye for an eye. But she would take a head for an eye and then still not be satisfied. She doesn't do subtlety very well. She'd rather just reduce the entire person to dust."

The duke stared at me angrily.

"Yes, but she is your teacher," Elysara tried to dial back the intensity of my statements.

"Oh, of course." I took the hint and softened my next statement. "And the elves have treated me so wonderfully. Crimson has even become friends with Censor Neldra, and that's who's helping me train this summer." I smiled.

"Yes. Because you have no human allies?" the man asked.

"No. Because..." I pulled Fayeth to my side. "We are Adrel, and I wanted to see her homeland."

The duke saw that I had a woman on each arm and frowned slightly. "Has the human air addled your brain?" he spoke to Fayeth, his tone rude enough that I wanted to introduce him to my fist.

But Fayeth just put on a bright smile. "We are in harmony. I'm sorry that you have struggled so much with that, Duke Relius.

You know, rumors are that you and your Adrel aren't in harmony. Some say that you've never been in harmony."

He snorted loudly, and his face contorted. For the first time, I got to see what apoplectic rage looked like on an elf as his tan skin turned nearly purple.

"You," he hissed out the word through his teeth.

"That is right," Elysara joined in with Fayeth. "There are some rumors going around that you don't respect the soul harmony. Seeing your reaction, I can only assume you are so upset because it is true?"

The duke was clearly trying to rein himself in, but he was struggling. "Good day." He pivoted quickly to turn and strode away.

"Fayeth," Elysara chided her.

"What? He asked for that. Duke Relius is just an angry old man who has never found true love and hates everyone else because they are happy," Fayeth spoke in English and softly so that others didn't hear.

"You aren't wrong." Elysara sighed. "But every enemy I make is an ally for Duke Selmia and Rikter. That was the mustached elf."

"Ah. Tell me more about him?" I asked.

"One of the top ten adventurers among the elves. Not nobility, but he stands with Duke Selmia's bloc and most likely is here as part of his protection," Elysara explained.

"How does his status compare to Neldra?" I asked, curious how exactly she stacked up.

"She's number six, and he's number eight. Yet I think that difference is quite slim and not made up in a quick exchange." Elysara made a face and looked around for Neldra before shaking her head. "His plan was to rile me and the duke up. I think it was effective in keeping us apart so that Selmia could approach Duke Relius later."

"Sorry." Fayeth twiddled her thumbs.

Elysara put a hand on her shoulder. "It's okay. The chances of me actually forming any positive relationship with Duke Relius were slim to none already. And you are right. He detests those that have truly formed Adrel; he's the jealous sort. I have other pressures I can apply to him to make sure he doesn't go entirely against me."

"Not a huge loss," I agreed, trying to comfort Fayeth. Though, I was slightly surprised that Elysara had contingencies in place. Elysara was really prepared.

"But I was impressed that you shrugged off Rikter's killing intent." Elysara stared at me with shining eyes like there was a secret.

"Blame it on me being taken care of by assassin grandparents. Killing intent like that is thrown around when Grandpa gets caught eating Grandma Hemi's cheesecake before it is set," I chuckled.

Elysara blinked. "That sounds like a very fun place to grow up." Her tone was stiff.

"My grandparents are wild. I can't wait for you to meet them one of these days." I thought of the idea of Grandpa meeting her and hesitated.

"Aww." Elysara held me tighter. "You want to bring me to meet your grandparents?" She grinned from ear to ear.

"Oh, that's right. Grandpa wants me to get pictures of the Elven ladies," Fayeth remembered.

"Let's say we forgot," I chuckled. "Or at least, let's not do it here."

Fayeth nodded in agreement. "Speaking of meeting the grandparents, or parents in this case." Her eyes wandered across the room.

Mine followed hers, and I found the Emperor. The man was staring straight at us, and now that we were closer, I could distinguish some gray in his red hair.

"Well. It seems your father would like to meet us," I told Elysara.

She made a strange noise before taking a deep breath. "Let's go."

Against all the dukes and duchesses, Elysara had been a bastion of confidence, but now that she needed to speak to her father, she was filled with hesitation. It must not be so easy being a princess.

We made our way through the party towards her father. The moment we started his way, he turned away to deal with someone else. The very hot and cold reception was already making me more nervous.

I held both ladies around the waist and moved slowly with our larger profile. By the time we reached him, the Emperor had finished with another duke and leaned back, narrowing his eyes on me. Then his eyes moved to lock on to the arm I currently had wrapped around Elysara's waist.

"Ken Nagato." The Emperor's eyes stayed on my arm a moment longer before moving to my eyes. "How has my palace been? You've stayed here over a week and this is the first time we've met."

I couldn't quite tell if he was disappointed, testing me, or something else.

He kept his face and tone perfectly neutral.

"Greetings, your majesty." I dipped my head. "There was no need for me to waste your valuable time with simple thanks. My time in the palace has been wonderful, and your daughter has been a perfect host."

"It seems she has been a very wonderful host." He only shifted slightly to put his daughter under the full focus of his gaze.

The Emperor was intense as fuck, and that was even after I'd gotten used to dealing with Crimson and my grandparents. I couldn't help but pity Elysara if he was like this in private too.

"You know the situation, father." Elysara didn't dip her head to him. Instead, she glared back. "My time with Ken has been wonderful. We have lots in common, especially our class and having demanding mentors."

"You still disagree with my actions. It was five years ago." He dismissed her glare.

"Each day it weighs on me more. Ken has been a wonderful relief, though." She leaned against me and kissed my cheek.

There was some noise behind us as she made the gesture. I had no doubt plenty of people were looking our way and watching the interaction closely, even if we were given polite space to talk privately with the Emperor.

"You are old enough to start making your own decisions." The Emperor eyed his daughter. "But are you prepared for the consequences? A human in a royal Adrel? Just make sure that none of his blood enters the royal line."

"Unfortunately, he's already Adrel with Fayeth Lyntean." Elysara smiled at her father. "So, I will be joining his Adrel, of which I think he is settled on being the only man."

Her father's knuckles turned white as he squeezed his throne harder. "You dare."

"Old enough for my own decisions," Elysara reminded him.

"While I sit on this throne, your actions will affect me. I forbid this." The Emperor's attention turned to me. And if looks could kill, I would have instantly turned into a red stain on the floor of the ballroom.

The older elves were clearly grasping tightly to tradition.

I squeezed Elysara tightly to me and kissed her cheek back. "It is a pity that you feel that way. I've come to know this woman and her situation. Not only do I wish to help, but she's made a strong case that we could harmonize. I feel it would go quite well."

Elysara blushed slightly and stood with me against her father. "I tend to agree."

Her father snorted. "You are nothing but the key to her cage. Do not think that once you help her that she won't discover the sky far more beautiful. It is the same with the daughter of the Lyntean family. While among your people, she had no other option. Now here among the elves, both of them will prefer an Elven man over a human every opportunity given."

His words stabbed at some doubts that I held about Elysara and her situation. Yet I could feel just how tightly I was bound to Fayeth, and that was enough for me to push his comment aside. If I could achieve something like that with Elysara, then I wouldn't have any doubt left.

"Father, you are being rude to potential allies," Elysara stood up for me.

"I have allowed your negotiations under the pretense of getting The Crimson's aid. It is already my understanding that she's been portaled to the naga section of the dungeon and is currently forced into combat with them. The likelihood of her coming back is slim. She may have fought the red naga and been successful, but they are a lower echelon of their race."

He studied Elysara. "So tell me daughter, what more does humanity have to give? They've thrown their best chit into the game without any concessions. Their hand is open, and they have nothing left of value to give us. As the future ruler of our people, your hand should be used to bind the wounds that the naga have opened in our people rather than create strife."

I had to keep from grinding my teeth at how callously he evaluated the situation, as if Crimson's combat with the naga was a penny dropped on the street.

"Duke Selmia's son?" Elysara asked.

"Indeed," her father answered with a smile. "I knew you had it on your mind. You have always been quite smart and scheming." He shifted his attention back to me. "You've seen it? Her scheming side? Where she plans on how to tie up her enemies with false smiles and soft touches until they are entirely hers. Behind it all, she always holds a card to ensure she could crush any enemy."

My brows furrowed at the Emperor's words.

"Ah. Just think about the conversations you've had here. Each and every one she's been prepared with the water and the salt." The Emperor knew that he had found an insecurity of mine, and was going to apply a verbal wedge.

Yet I couldn't help but look at Elysara differently.

With the last duke we'd spoken to, she had said she had other pressures she could apply. If I turned her down, she might have such pressures prepared for me.

Elysara was waiting for me to say something.

But the Emperor spoke first, his attention still on me. "You know it as well as I do. I can see it plainly on your face. You've watched her expertly handle powerful dukes. What are you compared to them?"

"Father, that's enough," Elysara snapped. "Stop trying to poison the roots. Besides, your idea of Duke Selmia is already rotten. His son is a fool. He would just use the secret that you created against me."

"You could easily control the fool." The Emperor was ready with that quip back. "It would be but a small effort for you to turn around and take control of that bloc. I know you are capable of such."

My mind was already picking and pulling at my interactions with Elysara. She really was a consummate politician, handling everyone so well. Given what I'd seen thus far, it was hard to trust that she was being truthful with me.

Elysara held on to my arm like she was worried I would run.

I squeezed out a smile. "From what I've seen, you could step in and rip apart that bloc at the very least. You are very good with people."

My statement was not the answer she wanted, and a slight narrowing of her eyes was all that she showed before she turned back to her father looking thoughtful.

"What is on your mind, daughter? Planning on how to get back at me for disturbing your toy? It is time to stop playing and start ruling." The Emperor snorted. "He's a human. Once we are done with the naga, we will step over them. Any benefit we could obtain with peace could be taken with force."

I couldn't help but widen my eyes at his assertion.

The Emperor laughed. "What? We are almost an entire ten levels ahead of humanity. Does a level sixty step aside for a level fifty? No. They are nearly twice as strong. Ten levels is a gap as wide as master and servant."

"Father," Elysara snapped. "Stop this. That is exactly the mentality of the naga."

"Of course it is. It should be the mentality of all of us playing in the dungeon's games. Who knows? There might be another race behind the naga. We all greedily push deeper and deeper for more rewards, yet in doing so, we come into conflict with other races trying to snatch up their own resources. It is one giant competition between the races, made to create conflict." The Emperor sneered at me. "That is why there can be no alliances between races. The Nekorian learned that early on, and the dwarves never needed to be taught."

My gut sank as I learned his true beliefs about the dungeon.

And his logic made enough sense that I knew I'd be stewing on his words for days. And the fact that he wasn't even trying to hide his intentions, stating them so blatantly, also did not bode well for my safety.

Elysara was silent beside me. "That is your view, father. I do not share it."

"More performance for him." The Emperor waved his hand as if to dismiss the comment. "When you sit on the throne, you'll understand. Our forefather did not ally with the clans; he absorbed them with force." He made an expression of mock surprise. "Or is that what you were planning with the Trelican here? Playing a deep game daughter?" He nodded as he sat back, continuing to shove a wedge between us.

"Wonderful. You are trying to drive a wedge between us with nebulous speculations and half facts. Congratulations, father, your words were immaculate as always. Yet where is mother?" Elysara tilted her head. "Why is it that she never joins you anymore?"

"Careful." The Emperor's word was clipped.

"No, you should be careful. In your old age, you've become more defensive, more bitter as you grow brittle. That this political bloc has even been able to stand against you should speak as much. Truthfully, father, I could support them. The thought crossed my mind to join them, give them legitimacy and topple you off your throne." Elysara's statements were brutal, and they only backed up the questions lingering in my mind from her father's statements.

"You." The Emperor's face finally left his passive mask.

"Don't even start with me. Your heart has grown cold. If it hadn't, mother wouldn't have pulled away from the political scene. She no longer supports what you've become." Elysara held her head high.

If I had learned one thing tonight, it was that insulting an elf's ability to harmonize with their loved one was among the most dire of insults that they could throw down.

In essence it was to say that you had become unlovable.

"Careful, daughter," the Emperor warned. "I have more patience for you than the other nobles, but you can cross a line."

"Maybe I want to cross a line and be a different type of ruler than you and the elves before you," Elysara challenged back. "All I know is that when I come home at night, my future Adrel will still accept me." She clung tightly to my arm, rooting me in place.

"Your mother has grown too soft. I fear it has rubbed off on you." The Emperor put on his best expression of disappointment and shook his head. "Fine. Go off and pretend, have your fun. The day isn't far away when you'll have to sit here and face the harsh realities."

His attention turned to me. "As for you, Ken Nagato, think about the position you'll put my daughter in if humanity and elves were to come to blows. Could a bond between you two possibly pull two entire peoples together? How will that strain feel when you are caught between the two and how can you be sure that she isn't plotting this whole time?"

"Enough," Elysara snapped. "You've become even crueler, father."

"There is no time for a soft hand." He glanced out at the crowd. "Tell me, daughter, how many align against me? If you take my seat without more support, can you keep it? Duke Selmia's bloc is not the first. And the main branch of the Royal Family has shuffled before." His focus shifted back to me. "If you insist on clinging to my daughter, at least keep her safe."

He waved his hand in a clear dismissal.

Elysara clung to my arm. "You'll stay for the rest of the party, yes?"

"Of course." I could feel the strain in my own smile. The Emperor had certainly placed several weights on my mind. As much as I wanted to go off and be alone to contemplate his words in more detail, walking away from her mid-party would be a huge slap in the face.

I wasn't about to do that to Elysara at that moment. I needed more time to think.

Fayeth squeezed my other arm. "Wow, your dad is a dick."

"Yes, he is," Elysara sighed. "That is why I avoided him until now. We'll have to meet my mother soon to balance things out. She's much better." She gave me a beautiful smile. "You'll like her." There was a hint of hopefulness in her tone and eyes.

"I'm sure she is." A little confused from the talk with the Emperor, I wasn't able to say much with genuine feeling. "Let's put that behind us and finish with the party."

CHAPTER 14

Elysara threw her dress over a chair then whipped off her heels and threw them on top of the material. Stepping over to her dresser, one by one, she angrily placed her jewelry in their proper places.

"Yeah. That's about how I thought the talk with your father would go." Neldra stood by the door, Tish coming through behind her.

"Was it that bad?" Tish asked.

"My father spent the whole conversation driving a wedge between Ken and me. My father is so old-fashioned that it makes me want to topple him out of that stupid chair of his just to see the look on his face." Elysara slipped a sheer nightgown over her head.

Tish let out a breath. "Wow, he really got under your skin."

"He always does." Neldra leaned against the door, casually guarding them and also keeping the conversation private. "Didn't catch any of it, but Ken looked a little lost for the rest of the party."

"Yes, well, my father knows how to break a harmony. He certainly had enough experience with my mother." Elysara took a deep breath and pulled herself together. "He pointed out how well I handled people at the party, and how I came to each with both water and salt ready. Then posed the question of what would happen to Ken if he stepped back. He made Ken wonder if I had my own pressure to apply if I didn't get my way through wooing him."

Elysara took a deep breath, rubbing her forehead. "To make matters worse, Ken is isolated here. After what my father said, he's going to look around and realize the situation he's in. He was supposed to come with Crimson; she would both bolster him and put the two of us on even grounding."

Tish made herself at home, sitting in one of the chairs and putting her boots up over the side. "But you really do like him? I know you talked about trying to fake harmony with a human, but he seems to have harmony with Fayeth."

"Oh no. He's a catch. If his ears were pointed, my father would be throwing me at him or dosing him with an aphrodisiac and sealing us together to lock Ken into something." Elysara rolled her eyes. "That's why I'm so damned upset! I like Ken. Genuinely. I want this to work even more than before he arrived." She held her chin in thought.

"You were outplayed tonight. Now you are on the back foot." Neldra tapped her cheek. "Didn't someone say you should show Ken that half before, so he wouldn't be surprised?"

Elysara sighed. "Fine. You were right."

"She usually is," Tish added on, and it wasn't helping.

"Glad we've established that. So, what do I do, oh wise Neldra?" Elysara turned around with a sweet smile, waiting for her Censor to speak.

"Well. If it were me, I wouldn't be in this situation." Neldra made a face.

"Auntie, are you just going to rub it in or are you going to help?" Elysara changed tactics and gave Neldra big eyes.

"Oh. She called you Auntie. She means business," Tish laughed.

Neldra rolled her eyes, but her expression softened considerably. "Okay."

Elysara scooted her chair forward and turned herself into a diligent student.

"Oh, don't give me that." Neldra pressed the back of her head to the door. "Let's get the full picture of what your father said. Because in the end, we are going to be fighting to counter the thoughts he put in Ken's head. I can't have my niece losing a man that can not only save her, but she's fallen for."

"Auntie." Elysara blushed.

The woman was her second aunt and currently in the buffer that existed between the Royal Family and the nobility to prevent bloody claims to the throne. The term had become one of endearment, and slight manipulation, which Elysara used when she really needed to get her way.

"Oh yeah? When was the last time you threw a fit like this? I'm pretty sure you haven't called me Auntie for at least a few years. Now you've done it twice in the span of a minute to get help with Ken." Neldra raised an eyebrow at her in challenge.

Elysara pouted. "Tish, help me. Auntie is going to bully me because I like a man."

"Oh. Don't drag me into this. You're the one that made it a family matter." Tish held her hands up and leaned back into the chair. "Tell her the whole story."

Elysara made a dramatic sigh and went into detail of her conversation with her father and how he worked to drive a wedge between her and Ken.

"My cousin is an asshole," Neldra snorted. "He's also very stuck in his ways. I have to agree that you weren't exactly wrong about him being more defensive lately. If anything ever comes down to conflict, I'm not sure that he even remembers which end of the sword goes into enemies."

Elysara tried not to laugh and ended up in a coughing fit.

"A big part of this problem will be solved when Crimson comes back. And I would not suggest changing how you treat him. Though, be careful, Crimson is pretty protective of Ken." Neldra paused in thought.

Elysara took notes on her CID. "But will that happen soon enough?" She didn't question if it would happen. From everything Ken had told her and everything she knew about Crimson, Crimson's arrival was an eventuality rather than a possibility.

"In the meantime, you should help him with the deal with the Duchess of Grestain. That deal would give him a modicum of power. Then..." Neldra nearly bounced off the door and pulled it open.

An upset Fayeth was glaring back when the door opened.

"Then you should probably talk to Fayeth," Neldra laughed.

Fayeth, even with her slight frame, dominated the room as she stormed in. "You messed up, Ely."

"That's what we were just discussing. Auntie—"

"She's pulled the Auntie card?" Fayeth asked as Tish brought over a chair for her.

"Yep." Neldra leaned back against the doors.

"Well then, at least you are taking this seriously. You like my Adrel so much?" Fayeth was suitably impressed.

"Yes. It is my father who wants us apart, not me. Tell me." Elysara grabbed Fayeth's hands. "How much damage was truly done?"

Fayeth leaned back in her chair. "I'm not entirely sure. Ken is a little quiet when it comes to these things, but by my impression, a decent amount of damage. I think he's seen some of that part of you when we've been in the dungeon. That is a good place to continue to show it to him."

"Yes." Elysara put that note down in her CID. "What else? Should I come out and just... I don't know... pull back the curtain and let him see all of my plans?"

"It comes off as defensive if you do," Neldra answered, and all the elves in the room knew that she was right.

"My damned father." Elysara fell back into her chair. "I knew he'd oppose the situation, but to so blatantly try to sabotage it was outside my expectations? Auntie, can you get dirt on my father?"

"You already have it all," Neldra chuckled. "Besides, I can't work against him." She mimed having her wrists tied. With how close she was to the royal line, any action she took directly against the Emperor would be met with over-the-top punishment.

"What else, Fayeth?" Elysara switched back to the topic at hand.

"Well. I know that you are being genuine in your affections because I know you well. Give Ken some time to understand you better. I am on your side and will do my best to help. Maybe take charge a little more and show him how you think?" Fayeth was some help, but she did not provide the action plan that Elysara was hoping to receive. So instead, she looked to Neldra.

"Fayeth is right. We are also up here worrying about something that might not even come. A good night's rest might bring some much-needed clarity," Neldra added hopefully. "We can work together as we see him tomorrow during exercises. He always seems to cheer up after those."

"Of course he's happy during those. You two rile him up." Tish had pulled a fruit from her CID and was munching on it.

"Because it's fun." Fayeth grinned.

"Fun for you." Neldra winked, making the younger elf blush. "Maybe by the end of the summer, it can be fun for my little niece, but she's going to have to get a few more things figured out. Even if you do this, you have to figure out how to get one step ahead of your father or he will find the next weak point."

Elysara nodded thoughtfully, "Okay. I'll take your advice and help in spotting them, Auntie. As for Ken, we'll continue like very little has changed, but I think helping him with his concerns about my position within the elves would be a good way along with being more proactive in the dungeon."

"I love it." Fayeth grinned, a far different expression than when she had barged in here.

Fayeth had always been easier to win over.

The assassin who weathered the killing intent of the best the Elven world had to offer didn't seem like someone whose mind was easily changed.

***

I woke up with a groan amid the plush sheets and darkness still in the window, yet a hint of light peeked at the edge of the horizon.

"Shh." Fayeth ran her hand over my face to try to tempt me back to sleep.

I grumbled and settled back in, peeking an eye open to watch my Adrel. She was so lovely in so many ways. Kind-hearted, protective and sweet to a fault. Sleeping here with a slow rhythmic breathing was calming.

My attention caused her to stir, and she opened an eye. "Sleep?"

"Just laying here, admiring you," I told her.

She smiled and wiggled closer, but it was only a hair's breadth if anything. "Love you," she murmured and fell back asleep.

Yesterday had been a trying evening, and I didn't have the heart to wake her. I was vaguely aware that she had left the room after I had settled in. I had a feeling she'd gone to talk to her friend.

Elysara's father had really tried to drive a wedge between the two of us. As someone who lived and breathed politics, it was no wonder that he could find and push on the weakness between us so easily. And he knew his daughter well.

So, on the surface level he wanted to break us up.

But I wondered if there was a secondary level. Did Elysara have a rebellious streak that he was counting on? I would have taken everything at face value, but then he had ended his speech by asking me to protect her.

At first, I hadn't focused on that part, still dwelling on the concern that Elysara had been faking herself in front of me. Yet, the more I thought about the situation, it was obvious that she had to have some skills in wheeling and dealing. Stick and carrot approaches to other political entities was probably as simple as breathing to her.

But it didn't change the fact that she had hidden that part of her life from me. And there was no way to simply wave that fact away.

The Emperor had put me off balance, pushing me away from his daughter, challenging my thoughts should the worst come to happen, then asking me almost flippantly to protect her. Truth be told, I wondered if he was daring me to stay with her given everything she was up against. Almost as if he thought I would rise to the challenge.

The damned old man was impossible to read. My brain kept swirling as I tried to piece together all he had said. But soon I just grew tired of trying to pick apart what was truth and what was a lie.

Wanting to get out of my head, I extracted myself from the sheets, prepared to go exercise and blow off some steam.

"Mmm. Come back." Fayeth tried to pull me back into the bed. The sleepy elf would have us both stay in bed all day if she could. Yet once she got out of bed, she was good to go.

I eyed her, wondering how late she had stayed up the night before.

"Go to sleep. I'm just a little restless." I kissed her forehead and tucked the covers around her again.

She pulled my pillow to her chest and replaced me so easily.

I shook my head and slipped on some loose exercise clothes and peeked my head out of the door.

"Ah. Ken," the censor greeted me.

"Woke up early," I answered. "A little restless. Thought I'd hit the gym and burn that off?" I posed it as a question, asking if she'd guide me.

She nodded and gestured for me to follow while the other Censor remained at her post. "How was the party last night?"

"Eventful," I stated distractedly, my mind still running circles around the topic of the morning.

Some exercise would be good to clear my head and let me focus.

I almost missed a quick hand sign the Censor gave to a passing Censor on the way to the gym, but I was used to them communicating with each other. Ignoring it, I popped into the gym as she turned on all the lights for me.

I ignored her and got ready.

A quick run through my forms in an open space had my heart pumping enough that I worked some dynamic stretching in and moved over to a machine and put some bands up, testing the resistance a moment before starting with some complex lifts. I was going to hit my shoulders and chest to really work them out. They were always a good way to work off a little aggression.

The thoughts that had been running circles in my mind were washed away with the focus and exertion quickly. There wasn't much room in the mind to worry when you have enough resistance to crush your chest if you drop it. Exercise had that effect, making my mind focus on the present.

But when the door opened and a sleepy Elysara in tight, royal blue workout clothes stumbled in still rubbing the sleep out of her eyes, my attention broke.

The distraction caused me to stall mid bench press and dip below the rack.

"Help," I wheezed. The last rep had been hard enough. One more was more than I could do.

Elysara jumped into action, actually calling on her minotaur aspect. She packed on muscle and a pair of cow horns to lift the bar off me. "What are you doing?"

"Getting distracted when you walk in the room, apparently." I rubbed my arms.

She rolled her eyes and shrank back down; the horns disappearing into her messy red hair. "That's what you get for working out alone."

I shrugged as I sat up. "Woke up early and my mind was busy. Besides, I would have just had to do one of those embarrassing wiggles out from under the bar."

She laughed. "Yeah. Those are the absolute worst when other people are in the room. Been a while since I had to worry about them."

Neldra wandered into the room in a tight, gray outfit. "Way to get up early, Ken."

"So, the Censor sent word and had you woken up? What's the secret password to stop that?" I asked, feeling bad that my restlessness had robbed them of sleep.

"You don't want me here?" Elysara nearly recoiled.

I rolled my shoulders, honestly not sure how to answer the question. "You should get a full night's rest. Given all the crap that you have to deal with, you should keep yourself at the top of your game."

That was clearly not the answer the princess had been hoping to hear. Her brows pinched down, and a frown marred her beautiful face.

"But, since you are up, are you going to get your sets in, or should I move on to the next one?" I asked, trying to salvage the situation.

"Give me five to warm up?" Elysara asked.

"That's fine. I'm going to work my rotator cuff a little. Adventuring beats the shit out of your shoulders."

"Sword work in general does," Neldra agreed.

"You know, I was never a resistance band person before. But I think you've sold me on them," I said.

"What do you use?" Elysara asked as she started doing some dynamic stretching and some running in place to loosen up.

Neldra was already chuckling, knowing the answer.

"We have plates made of iron that we attach to similar set ups instead of bands," I told her.

Elysara's jaws dropped. "You mean you have hundreds of pounds of iron just sitting around in rooms like this all over?"

"Yeah. I wasn't joking with the duchess yesterday. We use metal for everything." I knocked on the wooden rack. "We also don't have wood this solid."

"Great Trees need to be strong, those branches extend for miles from the trunk without breaking," Elysara answered instantaneously, almost like she was quoting a textbook. "How do you do dynamic loading without bands?"

I nodded along with her. "That's why I'm becoming a fan of the bands. Hitting the most resistance at the top feels right. Some guys use chains."

She stared at me, her face in a deadpan. "Metal chains?"

"Yeah, big, heavy loops of iron. So at the bottom of the lift, they are resting on the floor, and at the top, they are off the floor, making it heavier."

The look on her face was equivalent to if I'd told her that humans ate kittens.

She burst into laughter. "That's so stupid. You could just put anchors in and use a few bands."

I shrugged. "It is just how we've always done it. Might get Crimson to put some anchors in the school gym."

"Send me some of that iron. I'll melt it down and sell it for a fortune. I'm ready. Do you need another set?"

"Let's get you in first. I'll spot you," I answered and walked back towards the rack. I caught Neldra giving Elysara a thumbs up in a reflection out of the corner of my eye.

I had to hold myself back from rolling my eyes. I wasn't an idiot.

Her guards waking her up when I came to workout was a pretty clear sign. She was concerned about how I'd taken her father's statements and wanted to smooth everything over.

I wasn't against continuing forward. I just needed to be smart and not only think with my heart. In the end, her father might even find that he'd pushed us closer together.

Moving behind her, I prepared to spot her as she lifted a much larger set of bands than anybody would expect given her frame.

CHAPTER 15

"**W**hat?!" Elysara turned on Tish. "They did what?"

We were wrapping up our time in the gym, and Fayeth had joined us for the last part of the session. Currently, I was spotting Fayeth as she threw around five-hundred-pound bench presses like they were nothing.

Fayeth paused and racked the bar to sit up and join the conversation. "No way. The Emperor won't stand for that."

Tish shook her head. "I already brought it to his Censors' attention. They just shrugged, saying that the Emperor hadn't used the dungeon in years. He's aware, and he's not doing anything."

"To seal off the palace's dungeon entrance... the nerve." Elysara's expression darkened, and her eyes narrowed as she no doubt thought about countermeasures.

A moment later, she glanced at me, blushed, and pulled herself out of that focus.

"If I didn't think it was likely someone too high level for me guarding, I'd be sneaking out tonight with my daggers," I half-joked.

Neldra laughed. "Assassination is an easy solution, isn't it?"

"You can't argue with its effectiveness." I grinned and shrugged, drawing a finger around my throat. "Problem solved. Our history is littered with dead kings who got too greedy. Hell, until recently on Earth, that's how humans solved a lot of their problems."

"Still is." Neldra rolled her eyes. "Really, humans are so violent. The rule of leaving what happens in the dungeon in the dungeon is just an invitation."

"With that threat lingering out there, I bet people are a whole lot more polite," Tish chuckled. "Every higher-level adventurer is treated like a Censor."

"Do we know who did this?" Elysara wanted the facts rather than jokes about killing people.

"Rikter was the one who sealed off the stairway between the fifth floor and the safe zone. He's also sitting on the rubble he stuffed into the stairway. Otherwise, the issue would have been cleared instantly. Duke Selmia is making it known that the dungeon entrance is shut down and giving it the pretense of non-violent protest. That tactic is what has made your father dismiss it as not his problem," Neldra reported.

Elysara frowned, glancing at me and then back at Neldra. The older elf nodded and Elysara continued. "I can't just sit there and allow this to pass. If I do, they will assume I'm a soft target."

Neldra nodded again, encouraging her.

I realized from the look a moment ago that Elysara was clearly hesitating to show me this side of her. Wanting to know her more fully, I leaned forward. "Have any solid targets that I could put a dagger in?"

The ruby-haired elf did a double take. "Maybe. I'll have to think about it. Most of these people are pretty buttoned up, but their kids are spoiled and have at least a few buried skeletons. Rather than punching up at level sixty adventurers that have retired to politics, I'm going to fight among my own generation."

"Are they actually worth going after?" I asked.

"Most of them are already being given some public facing duties to prepare them to take over for their parents. It'll do some damage," she assured me.

I actually felt a little better knowing that she could defend herself. "Don't hold back on my account. Also, with all the dukes and duchesses here, where is the younger generation diving into the dungeon?"

"I can't—" She paused and reconsidered her reflexive response. "There are two other entrances under the Holy Great Tree."

"Which one is in a wealthier area?"

"Brisbank?" Elysara asked Tish.

"No competition. It's far nicer and likely where all the younger generation of the nobility will be diving from," Tish agreed.

Fayeth started undoing the bands at her current station. "Do we have time to dive today?"

Elysara was still hesitant. "My secret."

"Who says that the Lady even has to fight?" I smiled. "Pretty sure I can get them to insult me enough that I can step forward and fight anyone."

"You'd do that?" Elysara was genuinely surprised.

"I'd pay you for the opportunity to teach a few of these brats a lesson," I chuckled darkly. "Killing is off the table?"

"Unless we can kill all witnesses, yes." Neldra was stern with me for a moment before relenting. "I'll bring some potions."

"Before we get too far, I have a serious question." I brought up my CID.

Ken Nagato
Class: Emperor
Secondary Class: Demon Lord
Level: 19
Experience: 105183/164000
Strength: 28 (+6)
Agility: 74 (+14)
Stamina: 56 (+2)
Magic: 51 (+4)
Mana: 44 (+4)
Skills:

Dark Strike, Earth Stomp, Charm, Metamorphosis, Sprint, Absorb, Discharge, Dark Blades, Shadow Arm, Camouflage, Shadow Ambush, Elemental Shield, Portal [Special] [Restricted], Blades of Shadow

My stats had gone up a good chunk, but I didn't feel like I had kept up with the standard leveling curve I would have if I hadn't been power-leveled so hard by Neldra on the way to the Elven world.

I would most certainly be level twenty before the end of the summer, which served the elves if I really was to harmonize with Elysara, but wasn't as satisfying to me. I wanted the stats to go with that level of power.

"So, I should have gotten a skill at level fifteen. But I'm disconnected from the UG servers here. My guess is it didn't update, and all the class data isn't actually stored in this small device." I tapped at my CID.

"You've been leveling this whole time without it?" Elysara looked at my CID. "Special and Restricted. That's the portal ability that works between safe zones?" Even she had a little glitter of greed in her eyes.

"Yeah. I was able to close the portal that was opened, but I couldn't get it open again. Actually, when I got the ability, it felt like time froze and the dungeon watched me and intervened personally." I had held back that detail from my recounting of the story.

Elysara turned to Tish. "Get someone researching Restricted abilities. All libraries are open to this."

"Understood." Tish bowed and stepped out of the gym.

"Ever heard of someone experiencing something like what he described with the dungeon?" Elysara asked Neldra.

"Actually... yeah. It's not even uncommon, just not common knowledge," Neldra answered. "Your recent feline admirer could actually tell you a lot about the dungeon. Supposedly, the Nekorians call on the dungeon itself with rituals to show them their people's stats and allow them to modify them. Shamans like her are the ones who do the rituals."

"Feline admirer?" Elysara raised an eyebrow, and I could have sworn a hint of jealousy flashed across her face.

"She thought I smelled interesting." I shrugged.

"Yeah. That was totally all of it." Fayeth rolled her eyes, her voice dripping with sarcasm. "The tigress was all over you and bargained for one of your shirts."

"Their curiosity is legendary," Elysara laughed and covered her mouth. "If your Adrel is doing enough to catch the dungeon's attention, then why is catching the attention of a Nekorian any strange feat? But back to the question at hand. The ability you should have at fifteen." Elysara tapped on her own CID and scrolled through some things before coming to a page where she read slowly. "Mana Burn. Would be the best translation. It requires contact with your opponent, and then you can channel it. Their own mana will burn off, injuring them."

Fayeth let out a soft whistle. "That's intense."

"Level twenty is just as impressive," Elysara stated, blushing a little. "It is also rather iconic for the Trelican. Spell Mirror. It sends back a weakened version of any spell you Absorb."

"Yeah. Getting your fireballs thrown back at you would be pretty memorable." I let out a soft whistle. "So, you wanted me to wait until level twenty so that you could get access to that spell too?"

She couldn't meet my eyes. "If I was to pretend to be a Trelican, that would be the best option. I already have full access to a library of spellbooks to mimic a number of effects. Bluefire Touch looks much like Mana Burn, and Static Shield could pass for Elemental Shield. Pretty much all the low-level lightning abilities look the same because they happen so fast."

"But reflecting the spells would be unique." I nodded.

"Abilities like that are class abilities, ones that define the class." She nodded.

"And the trick to sharing these abilities?" I asked.

She blushed. "When in perfect harmony with your Adrel, you can use Absorb on her. At least from what is stated in the books, it should strike a chord between the two of you and some skills should be shared. Almost every partner for the Trelican wanted the Absorb ability, and falling out of harmony is said to remove the abilities from both." Hurriedly, she added, "I don't want to hold anything over you."

Stepping up to Elysara, I tilted her chin up and kissed her on the lips. She melted into me with relief, and I felt a distant hum of something between us grow louder as the kiss continued.

I broke the kiss with her soft lips. "Thank you. I believe you."

Elysara's smile was so bright.

"You damned better after a kiss like that." Fayeth laughed. "I felt that."

"What? She's going to give me a chance to go kick some butt while we plan to crush our enemies. Now she's speaking my language," I joked with my Adrel.

Elysara let out a sigh. "I had thought after last night..."

I raised an eyebrow. "Do you want to rehash that or move forward?"

"Move forward." She nodded for emphasis. "Absolutely move forward. We have time if we hurry to spend a few hours in the dungeon."

I glanced at Neldra. "Are we going in with you two or are we sneaking in? There is also the chance that if they blocked off the dungeon, it is to create a trap for Elysara."

"Already on it," Neldra answered. "The Brisbank dungeon entrance is being scouted by several of our people. Even then, why shouldn't we stick close to her?"

"I was just thinking that they would expect you to be close. Whatever trap they set would need to account for you two." I used my assassin knowledge to break apart all the possibilities. They were choosing not to come head on, but unfortunately for them, that was my specialty.

"We sneak her in, and then at one of the safe zones, take off the disguise and meet up with you two. You said you already had people checking the dungeon entrance, so it should be safe, right?" I look at the Censors.

"This..."—Neldra glanced between me and Elysara for a moment—"is going to make my hair go gray."

"I hate to break it to you, it already is." I tried to hide a smile.

She rolled her eyes. "It is silver. Not gray."

"Whatever you want to tell yourself," I teased, enjoying that I could rile up the powerful elf.

"Glad you are in a good mood," Neldra sighed. "I'll head through the other dungeon with a few Censors in disguise as you three, see if there isn't any trap I can spring there. Would love to catch a few people and remove a few heads while I'm at it. We'll meet on the fifteenth floor safe zone with Tish, and she'll bring you all out. No need to tempt people too much."

I nodded. "This won't be much of a training session. It will be about sending a message."

"Yes. We will tell Rikter that he can't block me, and that he's wasting his time," Elysara agreed. "Getting into a fight with another noble from my generation will make it spread like wildfire. Then I'll find a punishment for the noble and those who are associated with the bloc."

"Well, then that only leaves one thing." Fayeth looked at me, a big smile on her face. "Which of your abilities do I take?" She gave a little leap of glee.

The group laughed.

"We'll have time for that later. Maybe we should get moving on disguising Elysara and the rest of us."

"Just wear your yoroi and have Ami... Oh! We can make Elysara into another butler! No one will guess it's her."

The princess palmed her face. "Will Ami slit my throat in the night for taking her role as a butler?"

"I will not," Ami spoke from the corner of the room, making Elysara jump.

The princess held her chest. "Damn it. There's a whole family like this?" She turned to Fayeth.

"Yup. The grandparents are pretty loud most of the time, unless they want to kill you. In which case, you're already dead," Fayeth admitted.

I couldn't disagree with that statement. "Still, Fayeth's idea isn't bad at all. Putting you as a servant tends to make people look right over you. Sometimes stealth isn't just about hiding in shadows, it is about hiding in the gaps in people's perceptions."

"Makeover!" Fayeth jumped to her feet and dragged Elysara away.

***

I wore my yoroi while Fayeth wore a ranger's hood that had holes for her ears to stick out. As we got closer to the dungeon entrance, the outfits didn't stick out at all.

Meanwhile, Ami and Elysara were wearing the typical servant outfits that weren't even an uncommon sight. Both of them wore tabards over their clothes, depicting what was apparently Neldra's house.

Ami had her hair pulled back in a way designed to cover her ears while Elysara was completely exposed, her hair pulled back in a tight, utilitarian braid.

We were all acting calm, except Elysara.

Her eyes shifted back and forth through the crowd as we moved. "Did that girl stare at me?" she whispered.

"No. Calm down," I instructed.

"She kind of looks like a new adventurer with jitters." Fayeth walked confidently forward.

"I am not new." Elysara rolled her eyes, and that defiance calmed her nerves a little. A second later she was sniffing the air. "What is that?"

"Grilled vegetables," Fayeth answered, as if it was common knowledge.

Elysara took a few steps as she veered off the direction we were going to the dungeon entrance. "Really? How do they make them smell so good?"

Fayeth suddenly understood. "Come on. Both of you should join the young master and me for the food market." She moved easily through the crowd like she'd done it a thousand times.

The street wound under a root sticking up from the ground, and delicious smells started to punch into my nose. A section of the street was lined with vendors selling all sorts of food.

Elysara sniffed and pointed in a direction. "Why does it smell so good?"

"Because here they aren't serving nobles and emperors. They are trying to attract everyone with the smell and keep them returning with the taste. It's less refined palate and more put as much good shit in it as you can," Fayeth explained as we stepped up to a stall where the owner was pouring a viscous red oil over purple stalk vegetables that sort of looked like asparagus.

"Can we have four servings?" Ami smoothly stepped up and asked the vendor.

"Coming right up." He smiled and slathered the ones in his hand before placing them on the grill and picked up a pan that had ones that must have just come off because they were still steaming.

Ami picked up four sets skewered on wooden picks while Elysara paid with her CID.

"Pleasure doing business with you. Do come back." He dipped his head.

Elysara snatched hers out of Ami's hand and took a tentative bite. "Oh. Wow." She began to snarf down the rest in a very un-princess like manner. "These are so good," she spoke with her mouth full. "So much flavor."

"That's the point. You could see the grains of spice in that oil. They are made to be addictively flavorful." Fayeth took a bite of her own.

I took a nibble, and the intensity of flavor was a little over-whelming for me. My hesitation must have been obvious, because Elysara's eyes dipped down to it and then back up to my face. The question she was asking was clear.

"Sure, I think they are good, but not that good." I handed mine over.

Ami seemed reluctant to remove her mask and handed hers to Elysara as well.

"I'm going to start calling you the piggy princess if you try for mine too." Fayeth held hers away from Elysara.

"No. You wouldn't," the princess said with her mouth full and red streaks from the oil on her face.

"At least no one will mistake her for the princess now," I added.

She rubbed at her face with her sleeve and gasped when she saw just how much of it had been on her face. "This isn't funny."

"It is," I corrected her.

"We'll see if you are still laughing when I don't have to hide." Elysara made a face that had us all laughing.

I was glad she had relaxed; the success of our plan meant she needed to be able to act the part.

"There it is. The dungeon entrance." Fayeth nodded ahead as we walked back the way we had come.

CHAPTER 16

The dungeon entrance we approached was the same one we had exited a little over a week ago when we'd first made our way to the Elven world. Ornate trinkets hung down over the entrance, making the place seem sacred somehow.

An orderly line was formed in front of the entrance, which strategically seemed to weave awaiting adventurers past market stalls.

"There's a line?" Elysara asked.

"You don't get out much?" I teased.

She puffed up her cheeks. "You know the answer to that."

"Hey. You," one of the merchants called to me as we passed. "Get a pretty protective ring to keep your lovely lady safe?" He winked at me.

I snorted. Rings like he described were low level, though they were attractive enough. The bands were made out of a colored crystal to add appeal.

Elysara's eyes were gleaming as she stared at them and then back up to me.

The merchant met my eyes with a giant grin.

Fucker.

"Let's take the blue one." I tapped on one that matched Elysara's eyes.

"Two thousand mana crystals," the man answered happily.

I didn't want to show my CID, so instead I threw down enough mana cores to meet the price. Thankfully, the value of them was the same across the worlds. They were fairly standardized based on which level of the dungeon they were harvested from though.

Yet these rings were exceedingly expensive.

Grabbing the ring, I held it up for Elysara as we continued past the wily merchant.

She just put out her left hand. "Put it on for me."

I hesitated, trying to figure out which finger to use.

Fayeth nudged me past the finger I intended to put it on and instead I put it on her ring finger.

Elysara held it up so that it caught the light; it was a rather pretty ring. "It's lovely. I'll have to change some of my jewelry so that they all match."

"You don't have to wear it all the time," I offered.

"Nonsense. It's the first gift you've gotten me." She held the ring hand close to her chest and gave me a playful bat of her eyelashes.

Her look confirmed my suspicions. They both knew what a ring on that finger meant in the human world. Fayeth still wore the ring I had accidentally proposed to her with.

I decided it would be best to save myself and shifted our focus back to the dungeon as we stood in line. "Ely—" I cut myself off from saying her full name and paused. She was all smiles at it, so I continued. "Ely, do you have something to help us speed through the dungeon?"

She pursed her lips and nodded. "I was looking back through the list of monster types that I have collected. There's a wind elemental that gives me and my party [Wind at Your Back] buff. It's a thirty percent boost to movement. Then I could pick up two more agility-based monsters and keep up with you and Ami, perhaps."

Fayeth sighed. "You just need to be able to keep up with me. So, just do one more agility class, then get a tank for some stamina and maybe a healer in case we need some spot heals along the way?"

Elysara nodded along with her comments. "Sorry, cousin."

"It's fine. I can't be a freak like my Adrel who normally trains with giant metal cuffs on his wrists." Fayeth glanced down. "Are you going to keep slacking?"

"I didn't want to slow anyone down." I shrugged and pulled two heavy cuffs from my inventory and put them on.

"It is a good training method." Ami nodded and rolled up her sleeves to show she had sand filled weight bands on her forearms and then lifted her shirt to show she was wearing a vest with weights on it.

"Is that all necessary?" I asked.

"Yes, because when I take them off..." Her eyes shone. "I go fast."

I was starting to realize that if I wanted to ever give Ami a reward, it might just be best to strap her to a rocket and let her experience that speed.

"Huh." Elysara poked the ones on her wrist. "Iron sand?"

"Yes." Ami covered herself once again. "Normal sand is too light."

"Interesting. Since my ability scales my stats rather than any base additions, I focus quite a bit on the conditioning side. Something like this could be good for me too." She considered the bags.

"Hindering yourself in the dungeon isn't a good idea." A nosy elf ahead of us in line said. "That is how you get yourself killed," he snorted and focused on me. "Your servant should be careful that she doesn't drag you down with her. Just because she might be a wonderful ride doesn't mean anyone can enter the dungeon."

Elysara stood stunned.

I imagined no one had ever talked to her that way. "Mind your own business," I snapped.

"Look at him, getting all protective over his bed servant," another in the group laughed.

Elysara blinked in shock as a little red dusted her cheeks. "They are just jealous that you don't have a bed servant as beautiful as me." She clung to my arm. "Thank you for bringing me into the dungeon so I may work on my stamina, master."

She dialed up her charm to one hundred and ten percent as she blushed and looked up at me with slightly watering eyes. "This bed servant will give you her best when we get back as thanks."

"Damn," one elf ahead of us breathed. "You just wished you had one like that," he teased the first elf to speak.

He scoffed. "Women are nothing but a distraction for an adventurer. He'll be weaker for it."

"I don't know. We've seen great progress on our stamina as a result." Elysara kept her eyes locked on me.

"Oh look. The line is moving." The elf hurried ahead with his group laughing and ribbing him.

Elysara was nearly skipping as we moved forward and into the dungeon. "They didn't suspect a thing!" She giggled.

"No one would suspect you pretended to be a bed servant," Fayeth sighed. "That's only because they don't know you and the mischief you can cause."

"That's on them." Elysara wasn't going to slow down. "Time to get in there and give my master all the support I can."

I let out a deep sigh. "They're gone now. Are we going to do this the whole way?"

"Yep!" all three ladies said at once.

"Thought so," I grumbled.

We moved through the entrance to the dungeon. There was an official that made each group pause as they entered.

"Hold up a moment." He had something like a voice recorder in his hand. "Names and levels please."

"Reese and Flay Gildean, along with two servants. Munch and Dart." Fayeth made up ridiculous names on the spot.

The man didn't even care, just nodded and let us through.

"I'm Dart," Ami spoke up immediately.

"That makes me Munch." Elysara laughed. "Is that because I wanted to eat your food, cousin?"

"Yes. You ate Ken's. And he didn't even get to offer it to me." Fayeth puffed out her cheeks.

"It isn't like we actually have to use those names." I pointed out as we started to jog. The group of elves from before were ahead of us as we moved through a dungeon floor that was some sort of ancient ruin covered in vines with water running through.

Elysara's body was overlaid by a wind elemental, a rabbit, a hydra, and a dryad in quick succession. She now had cute rabbit ears coming out the top of her head instead of horns and a wispy trail that followed her movements.

I felt a gentle breeze push on my back. "Let's go. No sense in taking too long."

The elf in front of us looked over his shoulder, and there was something in his mannerisms that set off my mental alarms. He gave me weird vibes.

We continued through the first five floors, not even stopping for a break at the first safe zone. In the Elven dungeon, there was a path that led adventurers around the edge of the safe zone to skip the little town under the tree.

The landscape changed with the sixth floor, entering a dense jungle. Almost immediately, we lost sight of the group ahead of us.

"One second. I have the map from when we came through before." Fayeth held up her CID. "This way. Ami, can you help us cut a path?"

"Certainly." Ami pulled out a machete and started whacking back the dense jungle for us as quickly as she could.

A low rumble was the only warning we got before a black and gold tiger jumped out on us. I shot forward, my blades crossing and the low-level monster erupting into black smoke.

Elysara clapped. "That was a pretty cool pose."

Blushing, I rejoined the group. "This jungle is so dense; it is hard to see anything coming."

Some vague sense of killing intent made me duck as an arrow sailed past me and into Elysara's chest.

The princess ducked immediately and ripped the arrow out, her chest starting to heal. "I liked this tabard."

"You missed and hit the servant," a familiar voice scolded.

"Don't blame me—he dodged," another voice joined in, and the party from before moved out of the jungle to surround us. "Besides, they are actually cutting their way through. Fucking pampered nobles. Can't let the green things touch you?" he mocked me.

"What is the meaning of this?" Fayeth twirled her spear and stuck the butt in the ground.

"Those two servants of yours." One of the Elven men licked his lips. "The one is a beauty and the other, I'm pretty sure when we rip that mask off her she'll be just as good. You know, you probably got them from daddy and don't know the price, but guys like us could sell them and live nicely for quite a while."

"You think you could sell women under the Holy Great Tree?" Elysara scoffed. "That's one way to lose your head."

"Not here. Out in Galia." He hooked a thumb over her shoulder.

"That's The Selmia Family's new city?" I asked.

"Course." The leader grinned at me. "So, are we going to do this the easy way or the hard way? There's a difference between hardened boys like us and soft nobles like you two." His chipped sword gleamed in the dense forest.

I smiled back, a big grin hidden under my head covering. "So, you have connections to this underground in Galia?" My mind was already jumping to new plans.

The leader blinked. "Oh. Oh, you have something you want?" A different kind of grin came across his features. "I'm sure we could arrange something. Yeah. I could hook you up with any kind of girl you want, for a price. They even have some unique features like Nekorians. Vicious little things, but for a little extra, they'll grind down their teeth and declaw them."

I clenched my jaw to hold back the shudder that was trying to force its way down my spine. It would feel good to bury my daggers into their backs.

Elysara put a hand on mine. She seemed eerily calm all of a sudden as she put a hand on my arm. "Could I say goodbye to my master for a moment?"

"Sure, sure. If we can do this peacefully and get a customer in the process—we'll even give you part of the profits. After we take out a middle-man fee of course." The leader seemed more than happy to do the deal without a big fuss.

Elysara pulled me back a little ways and dropped her voice low. "I would like to hire the Nagato Clan."

Her statement made me switch gears, and all the anger I felt at the situation faded away to a cold ruthlessness. "These four?"

"No." She shook her head. "I would like the Nagato Clan's assistance in collecting evidence of the duke's connection to the kidnapping of Lady Rendral and giving it to the Royal Censors." There was a scheming look in her eyes.

Fuck.

My mind rapidly played out her plan. She wanted to go along with these men and turn it into a trap for the Selmia family. What they were doing was clearly wrong on multiple levels, and Elysara was willing to risk herself to catch them publicly.

There was almost too much to think through at the moment. Even putting aside my own personal feelings, she was the next ruler. She could be recognized and used as leverage.

Think, Ken.

"I accept the job." First steps. Turning back to the group, I continued. "It seems my servant wants to sacrifice herself so that I don't take the blame for losing the other." I held a hand out to Ami. "She's technically a family servant and not mine. I would suffer great harm from losing her."

If I gave Ami over, it would be realized that she wasn't an elf fairly quickly. No, we needed to take this all the way to the sale.

The leader checked something on his CID before he nodded. "Yeah. That's fine. But then you won't get a cut from the sale of this beauty."

"Boss," one of the other elves tried to argue.

"Shut up. No coin is worth your guys' lives. If they are going to give up half the prize without bloodshed, let it happen."

The leader actually cared about his men. Color me surprised.

"Fine." The archer lowered his bow and clicked his tongue. "Let's get moving. Pretty, you keep that wind ability going and we'll move quickly. We have to drop to the 15th floor to make it back over to Galia."

"Of course." Elysara bowed her head.

A few of their eyes lingered over on Ami, and I worried someone might try to take her mask off, because she was a real beauty too.

The whole time, Fayeth was giving me odd looks like I'd just betrayed her. I shook my head, warning her to stop.

The Nagato Clan had taken a mission, and we wouldn't fail. It was now about putting the pieces together as we went. Which meant that I needed to blend in.

"So about these Nekorian that you caught?" I asked.

The elves all chuckled. "Don't worry. Everyone is curious when you learn about them. Best part is they go absolutely nuts when you give them catnip. If you rub a little on yourself, they'll hump you all night long. We'll find you the freshest one so that you can experience it."

I was glad my face covering hid my grimace.

Fayeth grabbed my hand and her brows pressed down like she was trying to read my mind.

"We accepted *a job*." I put the emphasis there to tell two different stories. To the thugs, they'd think I was justifying selling Elysara, while Fayeth would hopefully pick up that this was a job.

She shot a glance back at Elysara, and I nodded with the silent communication.

"This is still a terrible idea. Father won't get you another. She's one of a kind," Fayeth warned me.

"Sounds like your relative doesn't want to lose her either. That bed slave is already used to being passed around?" One of the thugs laughed.

"By the way. What can I call you?" I asked the leader.

"Mishal." He grinned. "And you?"

"Just call me Ken," I answered quickly.

"Odd name. Sounds like a human. Then again, who am I to judge your kinks." He shrugged off the statement and turned his back to me.

I counted down as I stared at his chest, thinking about where his ribs were and picking the perfect place to stick my dagger. But I couldn't do it yet. I had to let go of the anger or he'd pick up on my killing intent and the whole mission would be a failure.

As the head of Clan Nagato, I had just accepted my first mission, and it was from Elven royalty. Part of my sense of honor stopped me from allowing any failure, including indulging in my anger.

Following behind the group, I didn't even dare use my CID to check them, but their combat skills put them slightly ahead of me. Elysara might be a higher level than them, but not by much.

I scribbled a note on a small piece of paper and handed it back to Ami when we went down the stairwell to the safe zone on the 15th floor. She took it professionally, checked the name on the exterior, and pocketed it before we came down into the safe zone.

"Normally, I'd show a new client a good time, but do you mind if we hurry?" Mishal asked me.

"No. Not at all. I'm curious about these Nekorians."

"A man of fine tastes." He grinned. "Come on."

Ami stepped back away from the group for a moment, and for a minute my heart pounded in my ears, worried that they'd realize she was gone.

But my butler was beyond skilled at fading into the background and returned later with a shine in her eyes at what I assumed had been an exercise in speed and stealth that excited her.

"Down this way." Mishal checked over the group to find us all still with him and waved us into a new dungeon path, this one heading back up. He held me back for a moment. "She's doing really well while we are moving fast and traveling. Yet I feel that servant of yours is going to be the tough kind to break, and she's two levels above me. When time comes, can I count on your support?"

I rubbed my chin. "What's it worth?"

"How about an extra five percent?" he bargained.

"Think I'm born yesterday? You haven't even given me a price. Look, you've... wet my roots." I thought I got the right phrase in Elvish. "It isn't about the money. Rather, I'm curious about someone who could offer me more deals than you or a broader selection?"

Mishal rubbed his hands together. "I see you. After the Nekorian you were interested in, I'll introduce you to someone who might have a little more for you to sample. Let me do the introductions, though."

"Deal." I glanced toward the rest of the group. "Let's catch up." I couldn't let them separate us at all, and I wasn't interested in continuing the current conversation. I could only hide my disgust for so long.

CHAPTER 17

Mishal, the man trading in women, took a deep breath as we stepped out of the dungeon. "Galia. Home always smells right to you, you know?" He looked around with a satisfied smile.

The place seemed a little less prosperous than what I had seen of the Elven world so far, and the Great Tree here seemed smaller. Yet it wasn't some big dump. The people bustling about seemed busier, more intent on what they were doing.

That was it. Unlike under the Holy Great Tree, people were too busy to flash a smile or a wave. It made the place feel stifled compared to the other city as everyone hurried about with their heads down.

"This way. This way." Mishal threw me a glance and then looked back at Elysara, quietly telling me to keep an eye on her.

I kept my head on a swivel, taking in the city and our location, memorizing every twist and turn we made in case we needed to escape.

After the third twist, we ended up facing the extensive building built into the bottom of the tree. It was a mimicry of the palace, and I realized he was trying to get me lost. Wherever we were going, he didn't want me to find my way there without him again.

Finally, we ended up at a house that was up against a giant root that ran through the city, and it was clear that Mishal was heading to that home.

Fayeth and Elysara stiffened in some realization that hadn't occurred to me yet.

"In there?" I asked, hesitating as he touched the door.

"Under it." Mishal rolled his eyes and opened the door. The building looked like any other home and the family living there didn't bat an eye at us as Mishal kicked back a rug and pried a few planks up before opening a hatch. "After the ladies."

"Go ahead." I nodded towards the opening.

"Ken." Fayeth glared at me. I could tell the anger in her eyes wasn't for me. "We shouldn't be involved in this. They've built under the roots."

Now I understood what had made both of them stiffen.

Mishal rubbed at his nose. "Nope. In you both go. You can have a spat later. Once you've both dipped into this world, you are on the hook too."

Fayeth set her jaw and went down the ladder, but each step was an angry stomp. I slid down the ladder rather than use the rungs.

The ladder continued down two stories. When I got to the bottom, it was dimly lit with plenty of flashing lights. There was a whole underground city beneath the city. With no light coming from above, it seemed like a perpetual night. Yet to attract customers, every building was trying to defy the darkness with neon lights, each competing to be brighter than their neighbor.

The space covered maybe several city blocks with low squat buildings and ladies trying to entice passersby to enter each establishment.

"Welcome to the Underroot." Mishal gestured to the scene before us. "It can fulfill any desire. If you got a vice, it's got a price down here."

Fayeth snorted. "There's nothing that compares to spending time with your Adrel or the quest of finding them."

"Cute." Mishal rolled his eyes. "Come on. We are going to Madam Root's."

That obviously was not her real name. Naming people after parts of a tree was nearly sacrilege to the elves. That much I knew.

Mishal walked us through the street.

From afar, it seemed brightly lit and beautiful. Yet on closer inspection, the paint was thin enough that I could almost see through it. The ladies wore more makeup than any other elves I had seen, and there was a smoky cloying smell in the air.

"What is that?" I coughed.

"Veinleaf," Elysara answered. "Outlawed because its smoke harms the Great Trees."

"Just this little bit doesn't matter." Mishal waved away her comment. "Besides, it is all contained down here. Most of us have been chasing the high of finding that perfect harmony of an Adrel our whole lives. Just a taste of it is enough for us to keep coming back."

Fayeth glanced up to where roots were above. Little threads hung down from them. "Sure. Let's get this over with."

Mishal moved easily through the crowd, and the rest of his men fanned out behind us, ready to catch us if there was a runner.

It was interesting to see this side of the elves. From the palace, the place almost seemed like a utopia, but I should have guessed there was more hidden in the darkness. There were always those willing to follow desire and profit over anything else.

"Here it is." He gestured towards a structure that was two stories tall. "Madam Root, I have a lovely one for you." He sing-sang the words as he walked in.

"How lovely." A woman in an overly lacy purple dress stepped forward as an overwhelming scent of perfume invaded my nose from the brothel. "Ah another lovely?." She appraised Fayeth, Elysara, and Ami in one gaze. "Do I get to pick?" She licked her red painted lips.

Mishal dipped his head towards the older woman. I didn't need my CID to tell me that she was far more powerful than all of us. "No. Just the red-haired girl is being sold."

"Pity. I could keep them all nice and safe under my roots," Madam Root pouted at all of us, and I got the sense of a cat playing with its catch. "Let's see her," She grabbed Elysara's chin and lifted it high as she jerked the princess around, shifting to see her face in multiple lights before checking her teeth and eyes. "Noble?"

"Noble servant," Mishal added.

Madam Root frowned slightly and checked over Elysara's body, roughly grabbing her breasts and butt. "A little lean. Men like a little softness. I'll have to fatten her up."

"She's premium goods." Mishal pushed.

"No doubt about that." Madam Root easily lifted Elysara to the side, claiming her, and focused on Fayeth, Ami, and me. "Who are these three you've brought in?" Her eyes bored into mine.

"He offered to sell us one of his servants for an introduction. The idea of a Nekorian caught this young noble's eyes." Mishal hurried to introduce me as a customer.

Madam Root's demeanor changed immediately, doing a one-eighty. "Well then! Come on in. I never turn down a paying customer. We'll get you some nip-oil and you'll have the time of your life. There's no harmony with them, but they will physically ache for you as long as the oil lasts. We only sell in four-hour or more blocks because of that. Mana Crystals only, of course." She went right into her typical sales pitch, all smiles.

I glanced at Elysara. "What about her?"

"She's not yours anymore. I thought that was clear. Don't worry, she'll be safe." The Madam put an arm down on the counter, physically blocking me from the princess.

"But I was going to get a cut. So, we should finish that deal first." I held back the repulsion I was feeling at selling Elysara.

If the princess minded, she didn't show it.

Fayeth on the other hand was getting more upset by the minute. My little tank was ready to become a firecracker.

"Oh. Oh." The madam made a noise of understanding.

"Let me haggle out the final amount." Mishal winked at me and stepped aside with the Madam. "Go take a seat. It'll only be a few minutes."

The rest of his men seemed to zero in on keeping Elysara in one place, giving me the chance to sit down with Fayeth and Ami.

Fayeth didn't even give me a chance to speak. "What the fuck," she hissed.

"She asked to hire the Nagato Clan," I tried to quickly explain enough to Fayeth for her to relax. I used harsh whispers that would look like we were arguing.

"This is stupid," Fayeth hissed. "You agreed?" My adrel was pissed.

"In that straight up fight, with no chance for me to ambush, what were our chances to come out with everyone?" I asked her. "We have no way to revive. One mistake and I lose one of you."

Fayeth frowned, but she didn't argue. We both knew that one of us would have paid the cost for being that rash.

Maybe if I had been in a situation to use the element of surprise, I could have done something, but with all of us out in the open like that, it would have been difficult.

I couldn't bear the thought of my bravado getting one of them killed. So, Elysara's plan was sound at least up until the current point.

"The Madam is very high level," Fayeth reminded me.

"Yeah. I didn't exactly expect a brothel Madam to be able to crush us under heel." I rolled my eyes as Fayeth curled her lips to stop from laughing. "Ami got her task done, so we can focus on discovering a connection."

"How do we do that?" Fayeth asked.

"You're going to join me for four hours of Nekorian fun," I told her.

My Adrel grinned, knowing that I wasn't the type to enjoy that, but that doing so would give us more freedom. "I have learned your grandparent's training."

Mishal and the Madam came back, the latter holding a sack and coming my way.

"Well, cutie, is it time to go spend time with a kitty of your liking?" She handed me the sack.

Out of curiosity for what Elysara had been worth, I took a peek.

My jaw went slack.

I had been expecting some purple, maybe blue, mana crystals in the bag. Ones you'd get from the tens or the twenties. I was not expecting yellow and orange crystals. One of the orange crystals was worth a 100,000 Ren, and there were dozens in the bag.

Fuck. Now I understood the temptation that drew people like Mishal into the dark trade, but that didn't make it right. My eyes glanced to Mishal's smaller sack, and I knew it had red mana crystals in it.

"Happy with your sale?" The Madam was acting overly familiar with me and sat down next to me.

"Very." I didn't have to work hard to hide my disgust. Money had a strange way of overpowering that feeling, and this was a lot of money.

"Wonderful. The kitty will be on the house." She produced a small vial of oil. "Rub this wherever you want the girl to pay attention to."

"I would like to see this," Fayeth spoke up.

"Two for one?" The Madam tapped her lips. "Whatever. I expect you not to damage my property." There was intense pressure from the Madam for a moment.

"Never. And after, I'd like to continue to broaden my horizons. Would you be able to help... or?" I left it open for her to fill it in.

She covered her mouth and laughed a little over the top, making her chest bounce in my face. "Nonsense. Madam Root can fulfill your *every* desire. Everything here in the Underroot is for sale."

"Even you?" Fayeth blurted.

Madam Root licked her lips while staring at my Adrel. "The price might be out of your range, but I'm sure we could work something out."

"What about information?" I asked, playing with the sack in my lap.

"Like I said. Ev~er~y~thing," she sang each syllable.

I was growing uncomfortable. "Thanks. We'll go play with a kitty. My remaining assistant can stand watch at the door?" I asked mostly so that she wouldn't be harassed.

"For her safety, she should remain in the room." The Madam winked. "Sometimes people can get handsy with all the ladies they see."

I resisted rolling my eyes and stood up. "Ami, we are moving."

I met Elysara's eyes for a moment. The princess seemed more relaxed than I expected as she calmly stood with the thugs. Neldra was going to lose her mind when she heard that I'd left the princess alone in an underground brothel. I tried to push the thought from my mind. That was a problem for another moment.

"Wonderful. Just go down the hall to the left. Pick from the ladies in the waiting room and they'll show you to an open room." The Madam got up and went to Elysara, grabbing her by the chin. "Mishal, you can leave. I have everything under control."

I had to clench my jaw as I walked away from Elysara, promising myself that we'd finish and get back to her quickly.

In the waiting room, there were a number of Elven ladies lounging about. More than a few looked up with half-lidded eyes as we entered. They lazed about, showing off generous portions of their skin, and my arrival made them start to twist and turn to appeal to me.

Rather than the elves, though, I looked at the two Nekorians. One sat up with tiger stripes, and she reminded me of Felin.

"You." I pointed to the Nekorian. "Show us to a room."

The Nekorian jumped to her feet. "This way, master." Her tail flicked back and forth in interest, but I couldn't get over the situation of just selling Elysara to this place.

"As private a room as possible? Maybe one at the end of the hall?" I asked.

She nodded and continued down the hall to the very end and flipped a placard on the front of the door from 'clean' to 'in use'.

"Do they actually clean the rooms?" Fayeth asked.

"Yes. We aren't savages." The Nekorian frowned.

"You are prostitutes. I'm not sure you even want to be here," I replied.

The Nekorian narrowed her eyes at me, and for a moment, I thought she was about to hiss. "I am lost, but eventually my tribe will find me again. The Madam at least pays me, and I survived what I should not have." She slid onto the bed. "The world is ruled by the strong, and as someone weaker than the Madam, I can only comply. Yet now you are here and my master, thus what do you wish for me to do?"

"Ami, lock the door," I instructed.

As usual, she was quick, darting over to complete the task. There wasn't much else she could do that would stop someone of the Madam's level from coming through the door.

The Nekorian scooted a little up the bed, and I lifted my CID to check her. "Level thirty?" She would be hard to knock out as I had planned.

"Your levels mean little to me. Until a shaman tells me how strong I am, it means nothing," she answered.

"Like Shaman Felin?" I asked, rapidly changing gears for the plan.

The Nekorian's whole body language shifted. Her ears went from a sort of cute droop, to straight up and her tail stuck straight out from her body. "Huh? Who's that?"

"Your body lies. Tell you what, I'll tell you of the last time I met Felin."

"You haven't met Shaman Felin," the Nekorian snapped.

With a thought, I went through my CID for the pair of clothes I had been wearing when we arrived at the Elven world and threw them down in front of the Nekorian.

She sniffed the air and then threw herself into the clothes, huffing in the scent. "You... she marked you?"

"Believe me now?" I asked.

The Nekorian grew meek. "What does someone marked by the next Grand Shaman want with this place and... me?"

Fayeth was already changing her outfit into a dark green yoroi, moving faster than usual. She was done with the brothel.

"Listen to Ami while I'm gone." I was already in my yoroi and went to the window to fiddle with it and see if I couldn't get it open. Remembering at the last minute, I flipped Ami the vial of catnip oil.

"I'll need you to make noise like you are pleasuring my master for a period of time." Ami took the vial in her hand and examined it for a moment before putting it in her pocket.

The Nekorian nodded rapidly and huffed at my old clothes. "Felin sent you?"

"Huh? No. Felin is just a... friend. We are here for another mission," I told her.

The Nekorian's ears were pinned back, her eyes wide in pleading. Damn, they could really pull off some adorable expressions with those ears.

"While we are at it, this place will probably get shut down. I have enough pull with the Elven leadership that we can get you and any other Nekorians sent back to your people," I promised.

She nodded. "I'll help you however I can."

"Listen to Ami. Ami, get some information from her, but prioritize not getting caught." I got the window open and peered around the corner, not seeing anyone that I needed to dodge.

"I will listen to the white-haired one." The Nekorian nodded and sat on the bed. "What do you command?"

Focusing on my task, I activated [Camouflage] and slipped out the window with a camouflaged Fayeth behind me.

A thin layer around my body rippled, mimicking the colors on the other side of me. I wasn't invisible to anyone paying too much attention. With the flickering of the ability to constantly blend in with my surroundings, it would work far better if I was motionless.

"Right behind you," Fayeth told me.

"Let's find Elysara. She's in our party. Does your CID have any tracking for her?" I asked.

Fayeth moved and then continued down the back of the long building. I hurried to follow as my Adrel moved and stopped occasionally to check her CID.

"Here." She stopped and pointed to a window on the second story.

"One second." I hopped against the building and then bounded off the one the other side of the alley to get a look in the window.

Inside, I found Elysara facing the window and grinning at me as my [Camouflage] struggled to hold up with the rapid movement. Another jump had me holding on to the round window as she cracked it open.

Fayeth joined me, hissing. "Ely, this is the stupidest plan ever."

"Fay-fay. Good to hear from you. The mistress put me up here. It sounds like I have to undergo 'training' before she'll put me down with the other girls. But the bad news is that she sent a message to someone about me being a 'look-alike'. If that person is too eager, then we might have a problem."

I rolled my eyes at the idea that there was a market for a princess look-alike. "I wondered why you were worth so much."

She rolled her eyes. "I'm not sure if that is a compliment or an insult."

"Both," Fayeth agreed. "Ken, I don't think I can leave her here alone."

I squeezed my eyes closed and nodded. "I understand. Princess, the Nagato Clan is working as quickly as we can."

"Thank you. I knew I hired the best." Elysara squeezed out a smile. "Now go. I'm safe for the time being. Use that time to get me what I need to crush Duke Selmia." Her smile became genuine and vicious at the same time.

"That's a lovely smile. I'll get it done." Pushing off the building, I flipped back into the alley and looked around before rushing off, ready to fulfill my mission.

CHAPTER 18

Tapping on my CID, I set a timer for three and a half hours. I was on the clock. I didn't want to risk leaving Elysara and Fayeth alone a moment longer. Not to mention someone might check on the Nekorian after that as well.

Slipping over the roof of the building, I stayed away from any of the lights in the district and threw myself to the neighboring roof. Unlike human buildings, there was no flat surface on the Elven roofs. Thankfully, I was an adventurer and had long left the realm of mortal capabilities.

After a small adjustment, I was leaping from top to top of each round building, landing gracefully and quietly. Nobody was alerted to my presence.

The Madam had said she was in charge, but Mishal and his men were moving with a purpose. Once I found them, I kept on them while also observing the Underroot.

From atop the buildings, I could see the ends of the giant cavernous space. There were only eight streets, four going each direction. The whole place was rather organized in how it was laid out, which spoke of planning. Madam Root's building was close to the center, giving credence to her claim that she was the one in charge.

Jumping again to keep up with Mishal and his crew, I lost sight of them for a moment as they went into an alley. Not wanting to lose them, I rushed to the edge in time to see them enter a building, with the hooded ranger staying outside to lean against the back doorway.

The place was a low building, save for a small bump that spoke of a single room on the second story. From the front, the sign had some clever Elven saying that didn't tell me much, but the frothing mug was a symbol that even I understood.

They had entered a bar.

I chewed on my lip, going in was going to be difficult. Taking off my yoroi would mark me as a human on the first step inside. Keeping it on, they would recognize me.

A plan quickly formulated in my mind as my gaze shifted back to the ranger on watch and shifted into position.

Jumping down on the member of Mishal's crew, I got a clean hit as hard as I could behind and below the ear. The hit landed perfectly, and it was like I'd flipped a switch. His body collapsed like a marionette with its strings cut. I caught his body, dragging him further into the alley before I stripped him down and slit his throat over a gutter.

After what they'd done to Elysara, I felt no need to show mercy. He might have been an adventurer, but there were still easy ways to kill someone if they were unconscious.

Taking his cloak, I wrapped the fabric around me and flipped the hood up. I wouldn't do well with scrutiny, but I could at least get close. Stuffing the body into the gutter, I checked myself to make sure that I had no blood on me before I slid into the bar confidently.

My hood was pulled forward to give me as much cover as I could while hindering my ability to use my peripheral vision to watch Mishal and his crew.

Mishal was sitting with three of his men, gathered around a table with one of the first fat elves I had ever seen. By their postures, it was clear that they were deferring to him. One of the others nudged Mishal and pointed to me.

Rather than join them or make excuses, I moved to stand by a window, still keeping watch but from the inside. I could almost feel the angry glare from Mishal, but I ignored it and kept my ears open.

"Good haul," the fat elf spoke. "I told you that there would be some ripe pickings coming out of there. Too much money in the nobility without enough brains."

"Yeah. The guy became a customer for Madam Root even. Went right along with us to save his other servant."

There was a pause. "You let another score like this get away?"

"To avoid bloodshed."

I grinned to myself, realizing that they hadn't quite managed no bloodshed in the end. There was plenty of it in the gutter.

"So what? This is enough to get you new subordinates."

The table broke out in yelling, and I tuned them all out, thinking through the situation.

Four hours wasn't enough to cut my way through the current situation and get to the Selmia family. There would be enough layers that it would take more time.

Rather, my goal should be to get the highest-level person I could and hand them over to Neldra to gather more information. She was probably already pacing around above me in Galia angry that I hadn't contacted her again.

For expediency, my message hadn't been very long.

Footsteps approached me, breaking my contemplation. A quick check in the window's reflection told me Mishal had come over, and the scowl on his face told me that our discussion would not be pleasant.

"You were supposed to wait outside," he growled, and I realized he hadn't recognized me. A slow grin spread across my face and I kept it low to avoid tipping him off.

I dipped my head toward the door and wove around him as he tried to grab me, heading outside for the conversation.

"We aren't done." He followed me out and grabbed my shoulder.

I spun, shaking the cloak off and dipping to the side. In my peripheral, I saw him pivot, working to change directions and punch me. I enjoyed seeing the moment he realized I wasn't his man as I swung my own fist.

My fist met his chin with all the force I could muster, and I followed up with a chop right to his throat.

He caught my wrist even as he stumbled and struggled to breathe. His focus was off, and I pushed my advantage, drawing my dagger and slashing for his throat.

My blade tore through his arm instead as he worked to block the cut and make it too shallow to kill him.

Seamlessly shifting into my next move, I pulled my arm close and pumped the dagger repeatedly in the space between us, filling his chest with holes. His grip on my wrist weakened, and I threw him down on the alley floor, finishing the job.

Cleanup for this kill would not be as smooth as the last. Yet surprise proved incredibly lethal once again. That was the advantage of the assassin, I reminded myself. It would be important that I used it as best as I could given I would be likely to be fighting above my level.

I was splattered with blood. But thankfully, I had buttoned the cloak up to hide myself. After taking Mishal's CID and his magic gear, I stuffed him in the gutter. For an underground city, they actually had an excellent drainage system, like it was built to handle floods.

Glancing around, I thought about the need for those gutters for a moment. Elysara had mentioned that most of the trees had wells or reservoirs under them. I wondered if the space was a reservoir on an official map.

I thanked my lucky stars for the large flood drain and finished kicking Mishal into it.

Next I threw the bloody cloak into my CID before activating [Camouflage] and jumping to the roof, scampering along to the second story over the bar. I assumed the fat elf would live there.

Based on what I saw, I'd put money down on a bet that he owned the bar.

After having played with the other round window, I got the window in front of me unlocked quickly and slipped inside, closing it silently behind me.

The room I'd entered was more like a study. There was no bed, but there were plenty of sheets of paper strewn about. There was no rhyme or reason to them, but I had a feeling the owner still knew where they were all kept.

Sadly, my ability to read Elvish was lacking, so I could only stare at the papers, wondering which would be important based on the headers and their layouts.

Heavy footsteps sounded, signaling somebody coming my way, so I ducked to the side behind the door as it flew open. I dodged before the door hit the wall with a gust and sent papers blowing in every direction.

The large elf stepped in, followed by another lanky fellow with a pair of wicked crescent blades attached on his hips.

I kept as still as I could, adopting a position that I could hold for a longer period of time.

"He left food on the plate because he was trying to make a customer of some noble," the fat one snorted and started to shove papers aside on his desk.

"To gain the loyalty of his followers. That is still important," the lanky one argued.

"He'd do better taking the earnings and equipping just himself so he could push harder into the thirties. He'll stall out as it is."

"He'll still have uses. My bigger problem is that Madam Root continues to hold a vice grip on the Underroot. We can't help but continue to sell to her on top of paying her taxes." The lanky one leaned against the far wall.

"We have that under control. Duke Selmia has assured me that the Madam has out-served her usefulness in keeping this place controlled." The fat one wobbled over to the shelves and pulled out a book with letters sticking out of it. "We'll be fine."

I had to clench my jaw to stop myself from jumping out and grabbing that book. The information in it was exactly what I needed. It was also the kind of thing that would go up in smoke the second Neldra stepped foot down here.

"She's gotten too ambitious. So, he'll replace her with someone else ambitious, but less powerful? You do see that you are putting your own head on the block for the future, yes?" the lanky one warned him.

The fat one put the book down and gave the other elf a droll look. "Do you think I'm an idiot?"

"I think you are possibly too ambitious. Personal power is the surest path forward." The lanky one played with the crescent blades on his hip. The way he moved, I could tell that he didn't wear them as an accessory. He knew how to wield those blades and cut his opponents to ribbons.

My heart pounded, and I did everything I could to breathe quietly. Thankfully, the conversation was ongoing and the bar downstairs provided enough noise for me to remain undetected.

I wanted to use my CID, but that would likely break my cover. I doubted my ability would hide the light from my device. I would have to rely on my intuition to determine their strengths.

"No such thing. Ambition drives us all. Without it, we'd just wallow in the gutters and rot." The fat elf moved things around on his desk, not really looking at them.

"I didn't ask for a philosophy lesson. How are you going to handle the duke going forward?"

"Secondary connections must be made and maintained. Evidence must be kept." The fat one put the book in the lanky man's hand. "Which is why I need you to run this to our safe house."

The lanky elf took the book. "You know, smarter and stronger people than you have had that same idea. Hell, I'm sure Madam Root has too."

"Just because it isn't a new idea, doesn't mean it isn't the best way to manage something. Get lost." He waved the lanky elf away.

I nearly cried seeing the book of letters disappear. It had been an opportunity that was running away.

The lanky elf's footsteps were nearly silent; I had to strain my hearing to even detect the first few past the door.

As the door closed, I was left alone with the fat elf. And I didn't have a lot of options. Unlike the lanky one, he didn't feel dangerous to me, yet he was clearly the one in charge.

That left me with a slight puzzle.

Checking my mana, I felt that it was at about halfway and slowly trickling down even as I sat still with [Camouflage].

The fat elf pulled out a chair and moved a stack of papers in front of him. He settled in, and I cursed to myself. I didn't have the time to wait him out. The door was closed, and he wasn't moving.

But his back was to me, and I could take a chance.

Moving slowly, I eased my weight from one foot to the other and stared at a point above him. People always had a sense when you were staring at their backs. Only once I was in position did I drop my gaze to get my hits as accurate as possible.

He was a valuable source of information. If I could get him to give me the location of their safe house, I could get that book of evidence and give Elysara what she needed.

He flinched as the butt of my dagger slammed onto the back of his neck. His fat gave him enough padding that he didn't drop immediately, but I had expected that to happen. I swung with my other fist for his chin.

The fat elf took the hit and rolled with my hit, fumbling out of his chair.

Neither of the blows managed to knock him out.

"Idiot." He spun his hands, and a ball of fire formed before he threw the ball at me.

Such easy silent casting was already a sign that he was at my level or higher. The heat from the fire told me he was probably at a higher level.

I didn't think too hard, just raised my hand. "Absorb." The air swirled in front of my hand, stalling the fireball for a moment before devouring it.

But the use of that spell led to an unintended consequence.

The fat elf threw himself away from me. "Wha-what? Trelican? Lady Rendral? No. You are clearly a man." He fumbled with the reality after seeing my spell.

I forgot that the elves had more awareness of that class's ability.

I had to think quickly. This was an opportunity to assert myself. He was a higher level and not everything needed to be solved with blood and daggers. "I'm Ken, Lady Rendral's consort." I tried to leverage [Absorb] to give me authority and get him talking.

He backed himself against the bookshelf, a few books falling off. The elf's eyes were darting about, as he rapidly thought of what to do next.

The Trelican was a famous class, but I hadn't expected such a reaction from using [Absorb]. His fireball burned in my system, making it feel like I was bloated with power. He was definitely at a much higher level than me.

"What do you want?" he asked, seeming to decide not to throw more fireballs.

"I had planned on bringing you before the Royal Censors. They are looking for evidence to connect this place to Duke Selmia. He has stepped out of line and needs to be brought back in." I held myself up straight, projecting as much confidence as I could. With the situation as it was, intimidating him might just be the best option.

That and opening up the power scheme above someone as ambitious as him, might just give him ideas on how to move up himself.

The fat elf licked his lips. "Royal Censors?" Then he narrowed his eyes and relaxed. "Sounds like they aren't here with you right now. You bit off more than you can handle."

His smile grew by the second, and his fear lessened as he realized he was in a more advantageous position. My hopes that his ambition would drive him to help us eliminate Duke Selmia dwindled.

"You really want to try someone who has a few hidden Trelican abilities?" I bluffed. "Going against the next Empress isn't a wise move."

Realistically, in the current situation, my options were greatly limited.

"I think I could take someone like you. There might be potential, but you are still young," the fat elf replied. "And currently alone."

"You're going to try this?" I slid my legs apart, ready for a fight. He might be a higher level than me, but he was a mage in a confined space.

"The alternative is to get stuck between Royal Censors and Duke Selmia. One doesn't come out of a situation like that with all their limbs." The fat elf summoned four balls of fire that orbited behind his back. "Die."

A fireball launched over his shoulder, rather than the one I was staring at in his hands.

"Shadow Ambush." I slid out of his shadows, dodging the fireball and sinking a dagger into his back. "Mana Burn." I grabbed onto his shoulder to keep the knife in his back as he lit up with ethereal purple fire.

The fat elf gasped and tried to shake me off, but I held on. When he couldn't shake me, he threw his bulk backwards. I was crushed into the bookshelf by his weight, and he got scorching hot.

"Metamorphosis." I swelled, and my gear sank into my skin as it turned dark and my muscles bulged. My new body had enough strength to ram him into the desk.

Flames built along his body, licking at me and daring me to break contact with my [Mana Burn] ability.

"Discharge," I shouted, slamming him harder into the desk and rocking his body with electricity at the same time.

The ability worked, and the flames vanished from his body.

I used my [Metamorphosis] to dig my claws into him, keeping contact as his mana burnt away. He struggled as I forced him to fight me with brawn rather than magic.

This was messy, but sometimes things didn't go to plan. The mage had to have an absolute ton of stamina to take this abuse.

My horned crown came down on his own as another of the fireballs orbiting him zipped off and missed a direct hit, singeing just one of my shoulders.

"You'll have to do better than that," I growled, picking him up and tackling him against yet another wall. Keeping him in a melee was still my best option, creating any sort of distance would allow him to let loose with spells in a way that I very much would like to avoid.

Our struggle had become a full-on brawl, and his aim was getting worse. Fireballs slashed around the room, catching his office on fire. The elves built everything out of wood, so he must have been desperate to throw around so much fire magic. Everything was catching fire, and it was spreading quickly through the room.

I dragged him through the fire, but he didn't seem to mind one bit, grinning as he grew bolder in the fire.

"Bad move." The fat elf head butted me, leaving me dazed before he kicked me in the knee to separate us.

He stumbled back, looking dizzy. All of his fireballs were gone.

Meanwhile, my head swam, and my knee decided it would not work quite right. I slugged back a healing potion to fix it.

"You know, everyone kind of hates my class. Ember Mages get a terrible reputation that I don't think is entirely deserved." He breathed in the smoke, cracked his neck and rolled his shoulders. "But the reality is that we are a little too strong on the surface. There's too much wood everywhere."

I didn't know the class, but it was clear that amid the flames, he was growing physically stronger.

He threw his hands out, and the entire bar caught fire as he stared down at me. Out the window, I could hear masses running away from the fire, and I cringed. There would be too much attention on our fight soon.

Not to mention he was growing stronger in the fire. At times, an assassin had to know when to strategically retreat.

I glanced out the window, picking someone as far away as I could, and muttered. "Shadow Ambush." I appeared out of their shadow and immediately rushed into an alley. "Sprint." I booked it.

Getting drawn into a large, public fight was about the worst thing I could do for my purposes.

"Get back here!" The elf roared from atop the fire and two jets of flame came from his feet as he launched himself into the air.

Fire surged through the alleys, and I cut down another alley before activating [Camouflage] with the trickle of mana that I had left and sat down, flipping through my CID for a potion.

The fat elf flew right over me as he searched the Underroot.

CHAPTER 19

I let out a sigh of relief and slid down to the ground, holding on to my ability as I sipped a mana potion. Using my other hand, I pulled out a healing potion to wash it down.

Fuck, that had been close.

Another explosion shook the alley, and I decided sitting still wasn't in my best interest. Heading out of the alley, I dropped [Camouflage] and threw the bloody cloak around my shoulders. With everything happening now, it blended in far better and made me look like everyone else rushing about.

People were in various states. Many of them were moving away from the burning bar, but there were also a great number heading towards the bar and trying to stop the flames from spreading.

In all the chaos, I hurried towards the entrance we had used to enter.

"No one leaves!" The fat elf had gotten over to the exit first and had made a wall of fire. "That rat is still here, and I can't risk him getting out." The elf kept casting his eyes back and forth, trying to find me.

Rather than slink away like the one he was looking for, I joined in with the crowd and started shouting with them in a low pitch hoping that mob mentality would win out.

I wasn't so lucky.

"Sirus," Madam Root's voice drifted over the crowd. "Really? What's got you all riled up?" The seductive elf matron sashayed through the crowd that parted around her. "Don't tell me someone ran off with some of your coin?"

"We are both in this together, Root. There was someone snooping around, looking for things that neither of us wants to give away." Sirus' jowls wiggled as he continued to scan the crowd.

Madam Root gasped in mock horror. "You don't say? People snooping about here in our den of hedonistic delight?" She rolled her eyes. "You will remove yourself and allow our customers to come and go freely, or I'll remind you who's in charge here."

She waved her hand and wind picked up, banishing the flames that Sirus had used to block people. It was clear on his face that he knew that he'd lost.

People hurried past him to escape the Underroot. Most would probably be back as soon as their vices came calling. The present conflict was only enough to get them to leave for the moment.

"Oh, and Sirus, clean up the mess you've made or I'll have someone do it and you'll be billed," Madam Root called over her shoulder, walking back through the crowd.

As she moved, she placed a hand on my shoulder and turned me to follow her. "Squeak Squeak," she teased in a low voice. "I thought you were playing with a kitty."

I stiffened.

"Come now. You're my customer, and your session with the Nekorian can't be over yet. Can't believe such a pretty little mouse snuck away from that cat." The Madam was treating everything as completely inconsequential as she herded me forcefully back.

"You said anything was for sale here?" I asked.

"Yep," the Madam answered easily. "Though, cost is another matter."

"How much does discretion cost me?" I asked.

"Nothing. You are already a customer of mine." She smiled and pinched her eyes together. "It is just bad business to hang my customers out to dry."

I honestly didn't understand the woman at all. "How much would the location of Sirus' safe house cost me?"

She pursed her lips together as we reached the door to her establishment. "That's an interesting one. Fairly sure I have the information, and it isn't that valuable to me." She was clearly waiting for more.

"He is working with Duke Selmia to replace you," I told her, curious to see her reaction.

She simply laughed so hard that she had to wipe away a tear from her eye. "It would be funny to watch them try. That is of no concern to me. Why is that information valuable to you? Would it have anything to do with a certain princess that I just bought?" She pressed.

"I'm sorry, what?" I did my best to hide the effect her words had on me.

"You just sold me Lady Rendral, and she is peacefully sitting up in a room while the other noble girl with you keeps her calm. And your assistant is howling in a room with the Nekorian." She tilted her head. "Really, whatever your kink is, no shame."

"If you know all that, why aren't you doing anything about it?" I asked.

"I bought the princess fair and square. You bought time at my establishment. So far, everything is just business. Yet you went and spoiled time with a beautiful Nekorian and went poking around in Sirus' bar. Is Mishal dead?" She leaned against the counter, completely relaxed.

"Does it matter?" I threw the question back at her. Her demeanor was not what I was expecting at all. If she knew that was the real Elysara, then something was very wrong with her reaction, or we vastly underestimated her.

"Nope. Just curious. Knowledge is always valuable. Yet your interest in Duke Selmia, mixed with the presence of Lady Rendral, along with the current strife between the two, could lead me to making certain assumptions." She gave me a predatory smile.

"What do you want?" I asked, realizing she knew far more than she should.

"You see, I have two options before me. One, I try to sweep this under the rug. Kill you, and the other three. After your time is up at my establishment, of course. Good news there is that I get to recoup the price of the princess, so no major loss there. Two, I meet the Royal Censors, risk my neck and likely lose my business. So tell me, why should I take the riskier option? You have until the end of your time here to convince me." Madam Root kept a pleasantly seductive smile on her face as she watched me squirm.

"I have enough sway with the Royal Censors to guarantee your safety, and of course, they could buy back the princess at a reasonable cost." I swallowed. It was a gamble.

Elysara had said that her family didn't actually have a huge stockpile of cash, so I wasn't sure how much they could actually afford. But Neldra would get her back one way or another.

Madam Root must have thought similarly. "Yes, and I'm supposed to believe that? I'm not aware of any prominent men in the Royal Family, at least not one as young as you." She smirked like there was an inside joke in her statement.

I needed to prove to her I could back up my words, and I knew exactly how to appease her.

Holding up my hand, I spoke, "Absorb." The swirl of energy in front of my palm spoke for me.

Madam Root stood up straight. "Again, please."

"Absorb." I held out my hand, and she discharged a minor spell into it, watching the spell get sucked up by my ability.

She narrowed her eyes and was on me in an instant, peeling the mask off my face before I could react. "Ah. You aren't even an elf. How do you have Absorb?"

"I'm Elysara's Adrel," I lied.

"No, you aren't. Because she isn't a Trelican. But you are." Madam Root bit her lip, stepping back as she started to tap at her chin. "You are a Trelican."

I pulled my mask back over my face, in case anyone else stepped in. "Yes. You also shouldn't know that."

"What I know is what I know. There is no should or shouldn't. But yes, this makes a lot of sense for why you are with the princess. But why are you helping her?" Madam Root asked the question, but it seemed more like she was enjoying solving the puzzle herself. "You don't have a stake in the Elven empire, or do you?" She continued to muse. "Wait. Do you just love her?" Her focus shifted to me.

"Nope. It is more simple than all that. She hired me," I answered honestly.

Madam Root's eyes shone like she'd found a kindred spirit. "Yes. Sometimes the simplest solution is the best. You're doing it for money. Money makes the world go round."

"My family are assassins for hire in our world," I explained. "More importantly, I want to know how you know about Elysara's class."

"Simple." Madam Root blinked and held her hand out, palm up. "That'll be five hundred thousand spirit crystals."

"No way." I held my CID closer to myself. "Can I go now? Sirus is probably gone, and I need to get Censor Neldra before she tears this place up."

"Sure. Are you checking out of your room?" she asked.

I looked at my CID. There was still an hour left. "The other two are still using it. I'm heading out, though."

"Fine." Madam Root swayed over to her counter. "Please don't bring trouble back to my business. But I'm happy to pay my troubles away."

This woman would drive me mad. She was letting me go, and I was fairly sure that she would sell the information to either me or the Censors.

Heading out, I kept the cloak over me and hurried towards the exit of the Underroot.

***

Elysara sat by the window. "It's been a while. Is he coming back?" she asked Fay-fay.

"He'll probably cut it close, knowing him," Fayeth grudgingly admitted.

Yet, Elysara couldn't help but wonder how wonderful it would be to know someone that well, to be Adrel.

The door suddenly opened, and Elysara jerked to close the window.

"Don't bother." Madam Root waved away their concern. "In fact, your friend can join us." The Madam moved about the room, pulling out a chair and setting it down in front of the bed. "Don't be shy, little Saintess. I've already had a talk with Ken."

"What happened?" Fayeth pulled herself through the window.

"Well, I might have not seen Lady Rendral here in quite a while, but I doubted that a servant would be so poised as her. And it wouldn't make sense for a servant to be so advanced of a level at this age." Madam Root had her at a disadvantage.

Elysara's mind was a whir as she tried to piece together who was in front of her. Clearly, she'd met the woman at some point. And she had the distinct impression that Madam Root was extremely powerful. Someone powerful that would be down here dealing in shady business...

Hiding.

That's when it clicked. "Fuck," Elysara said. "I'll have your bounty retracted, if that's part of your request."

Madam Root's smile couldn't have gotten bigger. "You are a smart one. You'll sit strong on the throne when your time comes."

"The last time I would have seen you, I was still just a kid. But someone of your caliber, down here? That means you are hiding. Someone of your level that is actively hiding has a bounty from the Royal Family out on them." Elysara spoke her mind, piecing it all together.

"Right you are. Ken just went to fetch Neldra, I believe." The Madam leaned back. "I'm going to sell you back to her."

Elysara rubbed her forehead and tried to think of who there'd be a bounty out on that thought they could force Auntie Neldra to pay. Only one name came to mind. Yet, it gave her something to work with.

The bounty would have been when Elysara was just a toddler, but anything was possible.

"How much are you going to ask for, besides paying down your bounty?" Elysara leaned back. Now that it was clear that Madam Root would not harm her and it was a negotiation, she was far more comfortable.

The Madam pulled out a piece of paper and scribbled down numbers.

Elysara kept her face a mask of calm, but she wished she didn't have to play games with the woman. People like Ken were far better to deal with. Besides, if this was who she thought it was, it wasn't going to be a small amount.

Madam Root threw the paper to her side, and Elysara picked it up to read it and burst out laughing. "You've got to be joking?"

"That cost includes information that Ken asked for. Something about evidence against the Selmia Family?" Madam Root tilted her head, trying to be cute.

Elysara sighed. "Throw in what you also know."

"Wonderful." Madam Root grinned like she'd won.

***

I made it to the exit without a problem and headed up the stairs. As soon as I got to the top, I saw Sirus waiting for me.

"Blow enough smoke and the rat will come scurrying out, eventually." The fat elf puffed himself up and gathered a fireball in each hand.

But he didn't throw the balls.

We both stared at each other, waiting for the first move. From our prior fight, he knew I could teleport behind him and that I had [Absorb]. He was hoping the two fireballs could outmatch me, but he needed me to make the first move.

"You know, I don't like being called a rat," I told him, drawing both of my long daggers and twirling them in my hands.

"What else do you call vermin that huddle in the corners and try to steal your food? Hmm?" Sirus played with the fire in his hand before he threw it on the ground beneath him, setting the floor beneath him ablaze.

It seemed that when there wasn't an obvious target, just bathing himself in flames was the play. After all, he had been growing stronger in the fire before.

The second fireball shot out of the smoke from the first, and I threw my hand up to [Absorb] it. The swirl sucked the fireball in, and I rolled out of the way as multiple streaks of fire sizzled through the air.

Curtains went up in smoke, and the building that held the secret stairs was going to go up in flames with both of us in it. Once again, the flames didn't seem to bother Sirus. Instead, they just strengthened him.

"Die!" He threw fire with abandon, burning all the wood and ensuring the area would go up in a great blaze.

I covered my mouth and rushed through a burst of fire to get to his side. "Dark Strike. Mana Burn." I stabbed into him and dragged my dagger along his back. The cuts all exploded with the purple fire of [Mana Burn].

He shrieked like a pig and burst into orange flames to throw me off. I let it happen, dodging back and using the fire and smoke for cover to once again set up for another attack.

"Come out!" Sirus threw fireballs in every direction.

He did not know where I was, and that made me smile. While he was certainly stronger in the flames, they hindered his vision so much that I could essentially hide and attack with abandon.

"Shadow Ambush. Mana Burn." I raked both daggers across his thighs and danced back as he spun with a backhand that I caught with crossed blades. I let the hit throw me into the burning building around us.

Fireballs chased me, but I was already moving, swinging around the side to come at him again from another angle.

"Discharge." I stunned him briefly while my blades carved into him again. This time, I stayed, swinging several times in quick succession.

He spun to get me again, a giant fireball riding on his hand.

"Shadow Ambush." The words slipped out as the heat became unbearable on my face.

Right before it hit me, I appeared behind him, scored another cut, and jumped out of the way before he came back around. The attack might not have done that much extra damage, but it infuriated him.

Sirus was covered in bloody tracks made by my daggers, and I chugged a healing potion before pouring water over the cloth covering my face. It would be harder to breathe through, but would help with some of the smoke.

Despite my agile fighting, I was constantly taking damage from the surroundings. My yoroi was a patchwork of burns, and red, angry skin underneath. But I'd have to heal later; at the moment, I needed to stay moving.

The pause I'd already taken had given Sirus enough time to pull out his own potions.

I threw two daggers through the smoke, shattering both of the potions. Then I swept through the flames to cut into his stomach while he was recovering from the surprise.

He sputtered and tried to shake the glass off his face as my dagger punched into his thick neck, spurting blood high into the air.

Landing in a crouch, I kicked at his knees and dropped him to the ground.

He caught himself, glass cutting his hands as he rolled to a sitting position. He threw waves of fire around the room trying to ward me off while his other hand tried to keep pressure on the neck wound.

My blades came out of the smoke like two jagged, black specters and took one of his hands from him. As the appendage went flying, I could see the realization that he was going to lose dawn on him.

"No!" Sirus threw fire around everywhere. "You'll burn in here with me!"

I couldn't ease up. Even missing one hand and bleeding from his neck, this guy was still clinging to life and some potions could bring him back from the edge. Such ridiculous stamina for a mage.

"Shadow Ambush." I reappeared behind him, feeling woozy either from the mana usage or the smoke. Probably both. Yet that wouldn't stop me as I brought both daggers down on the back of his neck and tore away the flesh from either side. Enough blood gushed out that I knew he was done for.

He rolled over to the side, and I snatched his CID from him before rushing out of the smoke as quickly as I could. As soon as I got away from the heat, a hand slapped against my chest, stopping me instantly from a dead sprint.

CHAPTER 20

"What are you doing here?" An elf in a uniform stood in front of me with a single hand against my chest. The outfit reminded me of the Royal Censors' uniform, but the colors were all wrong.

I could feel that the place where the hand rested would bruise later, and looked up to meet her eyes.

My head wrap fell away as the cloth was too burnt, and the metal circlet built into it was too heavy. It clinked to the ground as the elf's eyebrows rose.

"A human? A human set fire to our cities!" The elf grabbed me by the throat and lifted me up for others to see.

I paused. I could see how the situation looked, and that did not bode well for me. Even if I wasn't burnt and beat up, it was clear that I couldn't take on this woman.

"Let him go." Neldra had never looked so good as she stepped out of the crowd, her hand lazily on the pommel of her sword.

I didn't notice until now, but her sword matched her armor again.

"This human was burning our city. And you want to protect him?" The elf with me in her hands shouted loud enough for anyone gathered to hear. It was theater, but for what, I couldn't be entirely sure.

I knew Neldra was playing with a politically volatile situation to save me. Yet, I also knew she'd come through for me.

"Fine, then." There was just a glint of steel as Neldra severed the arm holding me, and I fell to my feet. "I don't have time to waste on you. Tish, restrain her and send her somewhere to get that arm fixed."

I pried the severed hand open. "You looked pretty cool right about now."

"Remember that and tell Crimson when she gets here about the time you and Lady Rendral went off on a harebrained scheme and

I saved you from being publicly hanged." Neldra leveled a glare at me.

"I was about to be hanged?" I asked.

"Without a trial," she added to let me know how close I had been to death. "Now, where are we going?" She looked around, confirming quickly that the rest of the party wasn't with me.

"Under the building, there's a passage." I nodded towards the smoldering fire that a water mage had already contained.

Neldra cut through the remains of the smoldering building with several slashes. "Follow me."

I ducked back towards the building, and the crowd behind us was murmuring at the sight of Neldra. "You're pretty famous," I observed.

"Royal Censor to the reclusive next Empress? You don't say." Neldra's humor was dampened at the moment. "Just lead me to Lady Rendral."

I had no trouble heading back down into The Underroot. "This is supposed to be a reservoir, isn't it?"

"Looks like it to me," Neldra agreed, kicking the stone steps. "This might have been an access tunnel to it. Gambling den?" she asked.

"A little more than that." The Underroot came into view as we rounded the bottom of the steps.

Even Neldra seemed a little impressed by the scale of the operation. She let out a soft whistle.

"So, before we get there. You should know that a woman 'bought' Elysara," I fessed up.

Neldra stared at me incredulously. "Hope you got a good price."

"I'm afraid she knows you are coming and still insists on someone buying Ely back." I shrugged and hoped that Neldra would have a little more information to work with.

That news made Neldra's eyebrow tick up. "Interesting. Keep going."

"Oh, and the guy I killed up in the building above was working directly with Duke Selmia, the younger generation. He had a book of letters proving the Duke's involvement with this place," I explained.

Neldra nodded slowly. "I see."

We made it to Madam Roots place. "Up here, dears," Madam Root sang.

I made my way upstairs, opening the door to see Fayeth and Elysara sitting on the bed with Madam Root sitting in a chair.

"Fuck," Neldra spat upon seeing Madam Root. "What the hell are you doing here?"

"Trying to run a business." Madam Root rolled her eyes, still completely relaxed even in Neldra's presence.

"Want to share with the class?" I asked Neldra. Curiosity was gnawing at me, who could this woman be?

"She's a former Royal Censor, but her only loyalty is to money." Neldra narrowed her eyes at the proprietress of the establishment.

Madam Root shrugged. "Money is the only thing that has been loyal to me. Why change? Besides, I'm a wanted woman. There wasn't much for me to do besides come down here and run the place. Really, it is about the best job I could land."

Elysara rubbed at her temples. "So, she's the one from when the Selmia family lost two of their regencies?"

"Yep. Former Royal Censor Miriam Relia. The Censor that was paid to look the other way for years on their tax fraud. She was stripped of her title and disappeared." Neldra frowned.

Miriam did a little curtsy from where she sat in the chair. "Pleasure is all mine. Now, I own your Lady Rendral, and I'd like to negotiate the price, assuming you are going to buy her back." She smiled politely at Neldra.

"Ken, give me what you made from the sale." Neldra held out her hand.

"What?"

"You sold the fucking princess. Now give it to me." Neldra motioned for me to continue.

"Fine," I grumbled and painfully removed the almost two million in mana crystals, giving her both what I got for myself and Mishal's cut. There was no hiding it with the one who paid it in the room.

Neldra let out a soft whistle. "I'll give you double," she told Miriam.

"Nope. The princess is only worth four million? I didn't know you valued her so little," Miriam pouted.

"You promised to remove her bounty?" Neldra asked Elysara, searching for more leverage.

"Yep, and she's going to give us a location that Ken asked to know," Elysara answered.

"I'll do you one better and offer to testify myself for ten million, bounty removal, and cut free of consequences for this little affair," Miriam countered.

"Fifteen million contract for you to sign on for five years under Elysara. You get out of this unscathed, we play it like you've been working for us the whole time. That means full support in sinking Duke Selmia," Neldra countered with a firm tone that even I understood meant it was final.

Miriam jumped to her feet. "Deal." She held out her hand to shake Neldra's.

"We hired her?" I asked, stupefied. For what she'd done she didn't deserve a job.

"Elysara did." Neldra shrugged. "Small price to pay for what she's offering, really."

It wasn't fair in the slightest, but whining about it wasn't going to solve anything. Instead, we'd move forward and get a bigger fish in Duke Selmia. That was what we came here for and her place here would be gone.

"Exactly." Miriam was all smiles. "Now, do I get to keep my establishment?"

Neldra frowned at her.

"Fine." Miriam rolled her eyes. "At least let me sell it."

Neldra held firm. "This is all part of the deal. You work for Elysara now. This place is an illegal establishment that the Empire won't keep. We are going to level it all and get it cleaned up to be a reservoir again."

I sat down next to Elysara and Fayeth as the two bickered like a pair of old lovers. "There's history there."

"A whole bunch," Elysara agreed. "Both of them are around the same age. Miriam used to work for my father. As the story goes, she was bought out by the Selmia family to not look too hard at their dealings."

"Story as old as time. Any concern that she'll just sell herself out again?" I asked, not trusting this sort of person.

"Let Neldra handle that," Fayeth answered, and Elysara nodded in agreement. "Best that way."

"Now, tell me. What did you get yourself into?" Elysara asked, the image of a dryad coming over her before she pressed a hand to my chest. "Regrowth."

Healing magic flooded into me, restoring several aches, and cuts that remained. Not to mention the obvious burns.

"Oh, you know. This and that. Found someone with a book of letters they were holding as evidence in the event that Duke Selmia ever betrayed them. Need to know where his safe house is because he sent away an underling with them." We probably still wanted that to go along with Miriam's testimony.

"What about the guy himself?" she asked. "We could use him too."

I scratched the back of my head, remembering his corpse. "He was a little too high level for me to knock unconscious, and things got a little hairy."

"Looks like things got heated," Fayeth giggled. "But I'm glad you came out okay, my Adrel."

"Oh. I also put Mishal in a ditch," I told her, knowing it would please her.

"Good." Elysara's face turned dark. "People like that don't belong in society."

I glanced over at Miriam, who was still bantering with Neldra. I wasn't convinced she deserved a pass, or that she wouldn't betray us, but I trusted Neldra's judgment. If I had to guess, she was close to Neldra's level of strength. That could be useful or dangerous.

At that level, unfortunately, the rules were different.

"What'll happen to all the people like the ones that Miriam has kept here?" I broke up the conversation and wanting to find some good in all of this.

"The elves will go home. What? Do you think this whole place is filled with slaves?" Madam Root scowled at me. "Once they work off how much I buy them for, they are free and come back of their own accord. Now, the Nekorians... they are a different story. They can't go free as easily."

Neldra was rolling her eyes.

"What if we brought them back to their area of the dungeon?" I asked.

"That would take too much time." Neldra shook her head. "Tish can't take that many."

"Oh darn," I answered sarcastically. "It would have been a perfect opportunity for you to kill everything around me. Might even push me over level twenty pretty quickly." I tempted her.

Neldra paused and glanced at Elysara, who nodded. "Fine, but it'll be after we handle The Duke. We'll take Elysara. And this time, I will be pointedly pushing to kill as much as I can on the way."

"She wasn't trying before?" Fayeth whispered.

I knew the offer would set me back in terms of my comparative growth, but I could accept that for a chance to return the Nekorians to their homes.

"Great. I'm going to go get Ami; she's probably still at it with the Nekorian." I stood up and got an odd look from Neldra. "Pretending. She's pretending so that I could sneak out."

"How'd that go for you?" Miriam rested her chin on her hands and batted her lashes at me.

It was my turn to roll my eyes. "Let's go." I grabbed Fayeth's hand and pulled her along with me. Miriam just got on my nerves.

After the danger we had been in, I wanted to feel my Adrel at my side. Her hands laced perfectly in with mine, like they were meant to be together. I breathed in deep and could smell her even through the perfume of the place.

Heading back downstairs, I found the door and knocked. "Ami, it's me."

The noise in the room stopped, and I could hear the click of the latch before Ami cracked it open to see me. "Ah. Master." She cleared her throat that sounded a little raspy. "Is everything all right? I hadn't expected you to come from this direction."

"Yeah. Neldra is here. The whole Underroot is probably going to get rounded up here shortly." I peered past her to the Nekorian on the bed. "It might be a few days before we can get things wrapped up and the right people to help bring you back, but we'll take you back to Nekorian territory of the dungeon."

The cat girl stood up on the bed with the balance of a dancer and lifted her chin high, exposing her throat. "Thank you."

"You are very welcome. Do me a favor and find the others here. Let them know they will be freed, and you can bring that shirt around if they need to smell Shaman Felin," I added the last bit, not sure if it would make a difference or not.

By the time I headed back out to the main room, the others had come down.

"I am going to clean up this place. Lady Rendral, you are not to leave my side." Neldra's voice was filled with authority. "Miriam, go show Ken the safe house so that he can get what he needs and I can justify what I'm about to do." She started walking out and drew her sword as her voice boomed throughout the entire Underroot. "On behalf of the Royal Family, all of you are under arrest."

I stepped out with Miriam in time to see a few thugs draw their weapons and come running.

"Stupid," Miriam snorted just before Neldra drew her blade a fraction out of her sheath and all the charging men were hit by some ability, suffering gruesome cuts over their bodies, but not dying.

Miriam made a disgusted noise. "She's still so soft."

"What do you mean?" I moved with her, working to keep up.

"You know, some of us called her Neldra the Blunt Blade." Miriam grinned like she knew an inside joke.

"Seems sharp enough to me," I argued, feeling defensive of Neldra.

"Not when you see a real Royal Censor. When I worked for the Emperor, we had free rein to cut people to ribbons for defying us." Miriam gave me a wicked smile. "You and I aren't that different." She tapped at her CID and pulled out the chest piece that matched Neldra's and put it on over her frilly purple dress.

"We are nothing alike." I didn't like the woman next to me one bit.

She raised a manicured eyebrow. "Really? Didn't you just do everything because Elysara hired you? Sounds a lot like me."

"I don't just do everything I've been hired for," I shot back. "I have morals."

"Everyone has their price. Their price is personal. You might have helped Elysara for a single black crystal because you liked her, but you'd help someone else if they dumped enough red crystals on you. Think, maybe the naga even have the color above red. Given that so far they have followed the color pattern, what do you think is beyond red? If I gave you a bag of them, would you do a job for me?" Miriam smiled at me.

"White. I imagine since they start at black, then go through the rainbow, they would go white next," I hazarded, avoiding the question. I didn't want to think about it.

"So, I give you a bag of white mana crystals, you'll do a job for me?" Miriam pushed.

"No. I have morals and I don't much like yours," I spat. "No amount of money would get me to break them."

She only smiled wider at my response. Nothing really seemed to upset her. "I have morals. Mine are simply gold plated."

I rolled my eyes again. "Come on. Show me this safe house." It seemed my final refusal was enough.

We came out of the ruins of the burning building. There was still a crowd gathered and a few elves in a uniform I didn't recognize were controlling the crowd and pushing them back from the ruins of the building.

"Ah. Survivors," one of the guards said. "Come this way."

"No." Miriam dismissed him with a glance, her Royal Censor breast plate gleaming in the daylight made her authority clear.

"I don't think you heard me," the guard spoke again. Several of them were reaching for their weapons.

"I think you are blind." She pointed to her chest and the armor she was wearing. "Royal Censor duty. Get the fuck out of my way."

Another guard stepped up in her path. "This is Galia and Duk—"

He didn't get another word out as Miriam put a hand on each of his shoulders, smiled, and then ripped him in two, spraying blood everywhere. She was fast and flicked her sleeve out. Dark mist shot from her hands into three of the guards that had drawn their swords, and they ballooned before they exploded in showers of gore.

"Kneel," she demanded with a tone that almost felt like it was applying gravity to everyone around her.

The guard that had first spoken dropped to the ground and dipped his head, along with the others present.

Miriam had a disgusted look on her face as she walked up to the one who had spoken and put her foot on his head, pressing him all the way to the ground.

"Make sure you all remember this moment the next time you see someone in this armor." She stomped and turned the guard under her foot to mush. She lifted her gaze and spoke to the rest of the guards. "Because this is the armor of a Royal Censor, and if I say move, you move or die. There are no other options."

Holy fuck. That was intense. They were clearly out there to round up people who came out of the Underroot and keep them quiet. That was just obvious, which I guess made them party of the enemy for Miriam if she was on our side now.

She walked through the gore without another glance. "Come on."

I strode quickly with her through the stunned crowd. "That was a little excessive."

"Was it?" Miriam scowled. "That they stopped me was too much. They even dared draw their blades. I might have been living underground, but what the fuck happened? It's Blunt Blade's fault. Bet she doesn't get out much with Lady Rendral holed up worse than me."

Miriam's scowl faded back to her normal smile as we went and until she stopped at a large four-storied manor. "This is the place. Victor went here with it?"

"Victor?" I asked.

"Skinny elf with curved blades," she offered.

"Yeah. That matches." I agreed remembering the dangerous elf.

"Great." Miriam strode right up to the door and kicked it in with a boom that splintered the door and sent fragments flying. "Housekeeping!"

What kind of excuse was that!

Three elves that had been playing dice at a table in the center of the building looked up like idiots. They didn't even stand a chance as more of that dark smoke rushed into them and ripped them apart.

I couldn't quite tell if she was a caster or a physical fighter. But one thing was for sure. She was noisy as fuck. The three elves had exploded everywhere with the sound of tearing flesh and a loud pop for each skull.

"Who thinks they can make a ruckus in Sirus' place?" The lanky elf I'd seen before stormed down the stairs with those two crescent blades in his hands.

The second he saw Miriam, his eyes lit up. "Madam Root. It seems that you decided to go on the offensive. Too bad for you, we've been preparing to take you on." He spun the blades in his hands and licked his lips.

Miriam stared at him for a moment before she just started laughing.

Victor didn't wait, rushing forward in a blur as his blades criss-crossed all over her body. The blades even moved through her and out her back, raking through her.

Yet, when the blades came out her sides, there was no flesh, no blood, just wisps like he was trying to cut smoke.

Miriam grabbed his head with one palm and because he was taller, she forced his eyes down to her level and stopped his movement. "I've been trying to lie low. That means not showing off my actual strength. You two and your games of trying to usurp me would have been funny to let play out. That the younger Duke Selmia was with you is laughable. The second his father knew who you were going after, it would have all ground to a bloody halt." She grinned, letting him know that he had never ever had a chance with her present strength.

Victor tried to cut her, but the move ended up the same as she continued to push him down to the ground and plucked the blades out of his hands as if he was nothing more than a child to her.

"There's no point making an example when there's no one here to see," I offered and looked down at my CID rather than give her any attention. I used the chance to get a read on her level.

<Elf Level 69>

I cursed. She was a higher level than Neldra and that mustached Rikter. That meant she was one of the top five elves. But that information made hiring the psychopath make more sense. It was probably far easier than trying to fight her.

The sound of someone being ripped apart made me look back up at her in a new light.

"Sometimes I get bored," she admitted and threw Victor's body to the side. "Let's get this book and get back to Blunt Blade before Neldra has a fit that I'm killing people we were going to have to kill, anyway."

CHAPTER 21

After our brief adventure in the Underroot, Neldra kept us under lock and key. It turned out that selling the princess to a brothel had put her in a rather protective mood. By protective, it meant that we basically went from the gym to the dungeon, to dinner and to bed on repeat.

We trained like our lives depended on it, and Tish took us down into the dungeon for a good chunk of the day.

The palace was a swarm of activity as Royal Censors and normal Censors from other cities were brought in. The Selmia Family was held under house arrest. The Underroot and two more like it were dismantled, which was also leading to a growing mound of evidence.

The Selmia Family were operating a number of businesses that weren't paying taxes to the Royal Family. But nothing had happened to the Selmia family just yet.

As for Miriam, the Emperor had come to see her the first day we got back. He had stared at her impassively for a while before leaving without a word.

Given her prior relationship with him, there had to be history. But he wasn't going to air it in front of everybody.

A total of fifteen Nekorians were recovered from Galia, and they were currently living in the palace. The few days stretched into a week before Neldra finally was forced to stop holding us under pseudo house arrest.

"The trial starts today." Neldra leaned on the door frame while I sat, Elysara rubbing my shoulders. "Also, if you need you can have servants do that."

"It's nice to do it myself for my future adrel." Elysara rolled her eyes at Neldra. "Besides, I like it when he makes little moans when I rub his scalp." To make her point, Elysara slipped her fingers into my hair and did just that.

"It feels good." I groaned, Fayeth was dozing in my lap and our conversation hadn't woken the sleepy elf.

"I'm sure it does. But we have things to do both of you." Neldra scowled.

She still hadn't gotten over selling Elysara.

I snapped a lazy salute. "Let's get going then Ely. Is there a part we have to play in all of this?"

"You will have to give a recounting of your trip to the Underroot at most. The evidence is quite clear on this one." Neldra said.

One thing still bothered me. "Why aren't you just taking their heads and calling it a day?" Weren't Royal Censors supposed to be ruthless like Miriam had shown me.

"Because The Emperor wants to make this a public display. To show the populace their crimes and corruption. That way, if any of the high level adventurers still want to support them, they have to do so at the cost of severe negative publicity. Most will probably back off, well the smart ones will.

"The dumb ones or ones who are in far too deep will double down." Neldra sighed. "The point of the trial isn't so much to ascertain if Duke Selmia is guilty or not, it is to prove to the public that he is guilty. So that when the sword drops down on his neck, everyone knows it was well deserved."

I nodded, public sentiment was an important thing for the Emperor to manage.

Neldra pushed off the doorframe. "Come on." She waved over her shoulder.

Ely smoothed down my hair with her fingers for a second. "All good, come on."

I snatched her hand and kissed her fingers. "Let me wake Fayeth." I hoisted the petite elf off my lap.

As usual she was loath to wake up. "Five more~~" She cut off with a great yawn.

"Putting you on your feet. The Royal Censors are summoning us." I did just that and held her shoulders.

She wobbled for a second and let out another great yawn. "Alright. What now?" If she wasn't so cute when she was sleepy like this, I might have been mad.

But as it was, she rubbed her bright blue eyes open and pulled her golden hair back over her shoulders to give me a pleading look as if she wanted to drag me back to being her pillow.

"No. We are going. It's a trial for Duke Selmia." I put my hand on her back to guide her. Elysara slipped in on the other side to make sure she didn't tip over.

"Oh. Well, pretty sure he's fucked." Fayeth wasn't gentle with her words. "Supporting the illegal seedy scene might not get a huge reprisal, but in order to keep those reservoirs dry, they had to be wasting a ton of water and putting that tree at risk. I mean, the tree might not have died, but we have those rules and systems in place for a reason.

"They could cut corners and try to manage things for a while, but eventually they would have killed that Great Tree and destroyed that entire city with it." Fayeth shook her head angrily. "Reckless and selfish."

I found myself agreeing wholeheartedly with her. Understanding just how critical these Great Trees were to the Elven cities, I couldn't really understand what would drive someone to be so reckless.

Then again, it wasn't as if human leaders were that different. They had a history of skimping on essential systems that caused great calamities down the road. Though, our system didn't punish them very well.

Here, Duke Selmia would lose his head.

Neldra turned down several halls of the palace. There was a somber mood in the air as if we were walking to watch a show at the gallows.

"There you are." Tish caught Neldra as we turned another corner. "It's already started."

Neldra moved through the doors as a set of guards opened them up for her.

The room was huge, there were people coming and going in an upper gallery above us that circled a good two-thirds of the room. Up front was a platform three steps above the rest of the room that was divided in four quadrants.

I didn't know which we belonged to and let Neldra lead us to the far left one and towards the front.

Our passage didn't interrupt anything, instead a censor was up front giving a damning testimony. "—That's when I felt I had no option but to follow Duke Selmia's instructions to cordon off several sections of Galia. We were told any disturbances in those areas were to be handled by a special group."

A Royal Censor that served the Emperor was standing nearby. "So, for confirmation, these pictures were some of the members of this group?"

"Yes." The Censor answered quickly with a nod of his head. "I recognize most of them. They were the hand selected group."

"You've previously stated that you felt compelled to follow the instructions to let them handle disturbances there, but you obviously didn't feel that was in the best interest of your city. What did you believe to be happening there?" The Royal Censor continued the narrative.

We sat down, with me in the center holding both Elysara and Fayeth's hands while we watched.

Everything felt familiar even if the setup was wrong, it was court. Though, one thing prickled at my senses. Turning that direction, I found the younger Duke Selmia glaring at me from across the room. He was in the opposite section against the wall on the other side.

His eyes bore into me and then flicked to Elysara with an expression of contempt.

It didn't last long though, the older version of him nudged him hard enough to refocus on what was being said.

"Drugs or some other illicit activity sponsored by Duke Selmia." The Censor answered.

"Never did you believe that they were harming the Great Tree?" The Royal Censor pushed.

The Censor shook his head. "No. Or I would have risked my family's life to ensure the Emperor knew."

That caused gasps in the room.

"That's all." The Royal Censor stepped back and the other Censor wearing Galia colors slinked off the one of the center aisles. "Duke Selmia has the opportunity to defend his actions, though the evidence collected by the Royal Censors has been distributed to public access documents on everyone's CIDs. The Duke endangered the Great Tree of Galia for greed and debauchery. Yet, we follow the rule of law and allow him to plead his case."

The Duke stood, wearing an elven suit with pinched shoulders and no undershirt that was so fine it shone in the light coming through the large windows. "Thank you Royal Censors. I will show you and the world that I am innocent of these crimes and rather than the Royal Family own up to their own issues, I'm being used as a distraction."

"That doesn't sound good." Elysara clenched my hand until her knuckles went white. She cast a glance back at Neldra who shook her head slowly.

"We need to step back to the event that started this whole inquiry." Duke Selmia had a slimy smile on his handsome face as he shifted his attention through the crowd as if looking for someone.

Yet, after two beats, his gaze met mine, and I knew he was timing this all perfectly.

"There you are. Come forward, Ken Nagato." The Duke hooked a finger at me. "For those of you who don't know, Ken Nagato here is the human man sitting next to our future Empress."

I stood up and brushed off my shirt casting Neldra a questioning look.

She shrugged and spoke softly. "Just don't lie. You'll be fine, on my word."

Feeling a little more confident, I strode up to the front. There was nowhere to sit, instead I had to stand and face the Duke. "Pleased to meet you all. I doubt you know me, I'm Ken Nagato." I put a hand to my chest and did a small bow to everyone.

"Ken, you were there weren't you? It was you who alerted the Royal Censors to the place even. Can you tell us briefly how that came to pass?" The Duke asked with faux innocence that wasn't fooling me one bit.

"Sure. I and my party had been attacked by a group of men in the dungeon with the intent of kidnapping the ladies for prostitution. They worked for a man who had direct contact w—"

"Yes. Yes." The Duke interrupted before I connected his family to the scheme.

"Who had direct contact with the Selmia family." I spoke louder before clearing my throat. "Sorry, thought that part was important. There was—" I was hit by some spell and froze mid sentence.

"I'm the one defending himself, not you." Duke Selmia said coldly.

As no one acted to remove the spell on me, I figured this was part of their proceedings. That was fine though, lesson learned, lead with the important bit for me and then follow through with the rest.

"If you'd tell the court how you got out of that situation? I was told that you sold the princess." He barked a laugh and turned to the crowd. "The human here sold our princess. I do wonder what sort of hold he has over her?"

"Not relevant." The Royal Censor who had been leading this spoke out. "You are seeding questions without answering them." She flicked her wrist and the spell over me broke. "Ken, please enlighten the court."

"I hold nothing over Lady Rendral." Now was not the time to flaunt my relationship with her. "She hired me to sell her and investigate the Underroot as it was called." I spoke as quickly as I could clearly enunciate the words in Elvish.

"Then, you must have a receipt for such a risky job that you can submit to the court, no?" Duke Selmia said.

"No, but I'm to understand that someone here can prove if I'm lying." I argued.

The Duke had a gentle smile on his face, like he was merely a victim trying to explain his situation. "Then, she's paid you for services rendered?"

I hadn't actually pressed her for the money yet. "No."

"Then you weren't hired." The Duke said sharply. "Or most of us wouldn't consider it being hired if you weren't paid, unless she paid you in some other way? Her body perhaps?"

"Absolutely not." I snapped at him.

My words were harsh enough that he stepped back raised his hands and looked like the perfect little victim.

Damnit, I was an assassin, not some theater trained politician. Breathing evenly, I remained up there, waiting for the next question.

"The next question comes from rumors around the court. There was a party recently where you were seen being quite familiar with Lady Rendral, are the two of you in any sort of relationship?" The Duke asked.

The crowd murmured, and I got a bad feeling as baleful glares stared at me from around the room.

"We have gone on several dates and are currently diving the dungeon together for training." I answered truthfully.

"Yet, all of this came after you raised the alarm. Given your relationship with Lady Rendral, I could see your desire to assist her and ward off love rivals. Were you aware that my son intended to marry her? That in fact, he was likely the best candidate to marry her. Please answer the question directly." The Duke smiled when he turned away from the crowd.

My mind raced, already seeing where this was going.

"The amount of evidence found is far more than I could have planted if that is your argument here. As for the rest, yes I was vaguely aware." I said.

"You could have planted it?" He twisted my words. "So interesting for you to rush to defend that action. Let's examine that if you will. My understanding is that on earth your family are assassins, elite warriors capable of infiltration, espionage and slitting throats in the middle of the night. Does that skill set include forgery and picking locks?"

The Royal Censor's lips pressed down in a frown but she nodded for me to answer.

I sighed. "Yes."

He was already speaking as soon as that word left my throat. "Then, is it possible that you could have planted this evidence or replaced parts that pointed to the Royal Family?"

I could see his plan, he wanted to turn people against me. Say that the Royal Family was choosing me over his family. That I had motive and the skill to manipulate the evidence.

So, I'd throw a wrench in this. "No." I said firmly.

"Lies." Duke Selmia's face split into a smile. "Censor's check him."

"He's not lying." Said another censor on the other side of the room.

Even the one in front of the Duke's own section shook his head.

The Duke scowled. "Please elaborate."

It was hard not to smile. "I could not have planted the evidence. There simply wasn't the time, I've been under guard even as a guest of Lady Rendral's." My skills aside, I could truthfully say that I couldn't have done it for other reasons than those he had tried to seed in everyone's mind.

The Duke glanced at the censor in front of his own section, and he shook his head again.

He had hoped to trap me, to pressure me and push me off balance before leading me along a verbal trail he'd laid out.

Too bad for him, this pressure was nothing compared to trying to steal Grandpa's cheesecake. Not to mention Grandma Yui's counter interrogation training. I suppressed a shudder.

"I see. Maybe you are just an unwitting pawn in all of this scheme." He still tried to deny his involvement.

Sadly, I couldn't ask him a thousand questions and for whatever damned reason it seemed that they didn't just use the Elven lie detectors and ask him if he was guilty. Then again, that would be very easily corrupted by controlling said elves by giving them so much power.

"That is all of my questions for Ken Nagato. He can return to his spot beside our Lady Rendral." The elf smiled gently at me, continuing his mask of being a pleasant man.

I had to stop myself from rolling my eyes and went to go sit down by Elysara.

She pat my hand as soon as I sat down. "That was well done. Not sure some of the Royal Censors could get ahead of that."

"That's my adrel." Fayeth whispered and snuggled up close to me. "You smoked him."

It didn't quite feel that way, without being able to fight back much as it were, it was a frustrating experience.

Yet, this was their due process, and I had to behave.

***

We were on the twentieth floor, and Elysara was opening a picnic basket full of food for us.

The princess had made them herself. "They aren't anything fancy. Honestly, I haven't spent much time in a kitchen."

"It's important to eat meals made by one's adrel." I said with a smile.

She pulled out some sandwiches, cut into neat triangles and stuffed with juicy looking cut vegetables and a thin slice of meat in each.

"Ooh." Fayeth added her own opinion. "So cute and evenly cut."

"I was half expecting more Elven porridge." I teased Fayeth who wrinkled her nose.

"I do make other things." She pouted and pulled her own sandwiches out.

"Rarely." I teased. She did love her Elven porridge in the morning.

"It reminds me of home when we are on Earth." Fayeth stuck her tongue out and swiped a sandwich.

I picked up one and took a bite while Elysara stared at me while holding her breath. It was mostly sweet with a fresh crunch and finally a salty finish that only made the next bite sweeter. "Very good." I said around a mouthful of the second bite.

Elysara gave me a smile so bright it washed away any weariness from the dungeon. "Perfect. I'll have to practice a few more dishes and maybe figure out how to make a few Human dishes with Elven ingredients."

"No need, this food has been great." I took another bite.

"Good, good." Elysara dug into the basket and pulled out several more. "Because that's all I can make."

I burst out laughing. "All you can make are these sandwiches?"

"Well, I can make other kinds, but... yeah? If it requires heat, I'll make it such that the exterior is burnt to a crisp, and the inside is raw." She laughed.

"At least some of your princess is showing." I teased.

"Hey!" Elysara swatted at me. "I'm feeding you here, be nice."

Fayeth burst out laughing and fell over while still eating her own sandwich.

It was a good day.

Tish had been rather silent in her approach. "Lady, I'm sorry for the interruption, but the trial has finished. Duke Selmia will be executed in three days. You asked to know as soon as possible." She really did seem to regret interrupting our moment.

"Cheers." I raised my sandwich.

Elysara chuckled darkly. "Cheers." I was enjoying Elysara's dark side these past few days. I had joined her on more than a few of her meetings and she could be as gentle as a mother or as wicked as an Empress.

It didn't bother me that she could shift who she needed to be for the moment.

"Cwers." Fayeth said with a mouthful of food and tapped the last corner of her sandwich to the two of ours before swallowing. "To the death of a pest and relief that it may bring the many people of our world."

"Well said." Elysara nodded and nibbled at her sandwich. "The Selmia's have proven they cannot be trusted with responsibility. Thus, they shall not have it again."

Tish clearly had more to say though. "The Younger Duke made a public plea to speak to you one last time. I suspect he'll make a plea to spare him."

Elysara rubbed at her forehead. "Yes, well, we should at least go, publically, so that people can see that I'm not a monster with a frozen heart. After our picnic? I was enjoying myself and though that must happen, it doesn't have to happen now and disturb an enjoyable time with Ken."

"Of course." Tish bowed out.

"Thanks for putting me first." I finished my first sandwich and fished around the basket for another.

"Please have as many as you want. As long as we are eating I don't have to go see him." Elysara took another bite.

I was curious. "History there?"

"Not much." She said, covering her mouth before she swallowed. "The younger duke has been my peer thus we've made plenty of polite conversation at gatherings. But I've never gone out of my way to meet with him." She sighed. "As a younger princess before my relative isolation, I took much of attention boys gave me for granted. Time and other things have given me perspective." She laid a hand on my knee. "I appreciate the time you've taken to be with me here this summer."

The woman was gorgeous, her red hair curled around her face as she looked up into my eyes.

I picked up her hand and kissed the back of it. "You make Fayeth happy, and despite some misadventures we've had it has been a wonderful trip this summer." My mind went to Desmonda, Charlotte and of course Crimson. While this had been fun, I also wanted to return to them.

"You'll have to go soon. Let me monopolize your time a little longer before you return to the others. I hope that I can escape here and visit during this next school year."

"Yes please." Fayeth chirped. "We can show you sushi."

Elysara nodded. "I think I need to see sushi and snow."

I waffled my head. "Not sure those entirely go together, but we can make it work." I teased. On a whim, I put my sandwich aside, suddenly hungry for something else.

Claiming, Elysara's lips I kissed her softly before leaning into her and our passionate kiss turned into a tumble onto the ground. The princess moaned and rubbed herself against me as her hands ran through my hair.

The hum of our souls was so close, I could probably strip her and throw her down here for them to sing as one.

I came up for a breath of air and Fayeth kissed Elysara just as deeply as I had, but with much more softness. The smaller elf woman, laid a hand on my chest and then when she was done with Ely turned her attention to me and I found myself on my back with my familiar adrel grinding against my hips.

"I love you." Kissing Fayeth again deeply, I felt a little jealousy at the moment and knew I couldn't take Elysara now. Soon though. "Let's finish up here and get some annoying business taken care of. Oh, by the way, with the trial over, can we take the Nekorian's back?"

"Yes, that sounds like a pleasant break from the current routine." Elysara nodded firmly in agreement and shared a glance with Fayeth that said the two of them would talk later.

***

Elven prisons were very comfortable. Rather than cold iron and cheap cinderblock construction, the place looked like a nice inn. Probably not the quality that The Duke was used to, but certainly passable.

"Lady Rendral." A Censor stood up straight as we walked in past a crowd that had certainly noticed us and taken pictures.

"We are here to see the younger Duke Selmia. He's requested an audience with me and though he's a criminal, I won't revoke that right." She spoke loudly for the reporters that were still watching from the doorway.

"Right this way." The Censor in the prison gestured.

When I moved with Elysara, they hesitated and gave Neldra one glance before realizing it was best to keep their mouths closed.

Down the hall, the Censor led us to a room and unlocked it.

I had expected a large suite, instead it was a smaller room than the exterior of the building would suggest, that was because it was a buffer.

A guard sat with her head resting on the wall and just nodded at our group before we went through a second door.

Well, Neldra went through first, aggressively to ensure that there was no trap waiting for Elysara.

The younger duke almost fell off a stool he'd been perched on. "What in—Elysara! My love!" He tried to straighten his bright red clothing that had a patch with his actual name. "You've come." Gelid was quite happy and looked ready to rush over and hug her.

Elysara held a hand up and Neldra put out enough pressure to make him stop cold half way to her and instead he snapped into a bow. "Will you marry me?"

We were all stunned with his question.

That was not what I had been expecting.

"No." Elysara's tone was cold. "Did you really waste my time and force me to come all the way here to ask nonsense that you already know the answer to?"

Gelid stood up. "You will marry me and I will become the next emperor." He spoke with such conviction that it would be hard to believe that he was in the middle of prison facing execution.

"I will not." Elysara said with a tone that was final. "You and your father have put your own ambitions above the good of the Elven people for far too long. You've gone too far this time and I have the opportunity to cut the head off the snake in my garden. Gelid, if I didn't have more important matters, I'd sever your head myself, but as it is, I'm going to miss the execution. Shame." Elysara was calm and collected on the surface, but her grip grew tighter on my hand. "This is the man I will marry."

Gelid clutched his chest as if an arrow had struck him. The whole family had a knack for theater. "Impossible. You'd dilute the Royal Lineage with human blood." He spat on the ground. "I won't stand for this, I cannot."

He pointed a finger in my face. "I challenge you for her hand."

"No?" I hesitated, glancing at Elysara making sure there wasn't some rule I was breaking.

"You have no obligation to even answer him. He's delusional." Elysara gave a sad shake of her head. We should go.

Like when his father had me on the stand in the trial and was able to pick the conversation and end it at his own whim, I had the control now.

"Let's go. It kind of stinks in here." I said and turned around, almost hoping he'd come strike at me.

That would give Neldra an excuse to cut him in two and leave the pieces to rot.

But he was at least smart enough to not do that. Shame.

"This isn't the end." The younger duke shouted behind us even as the door closed. "You'll marry me!" He screamed at the top of his lungs.

"Sorry about that." Elysara rubbed at her temples.

"We always knew it would be a waste of time talking to him. The value was in showing the public that we came to talk at all." I shrugged. "Let's go back and pack up for the trip with the Nekorians. When we return, they'll be buried and this'll all be behind us."

Elysara nodded and leaned into me giving me a small kiss on the cheek. "Thank you for being so stable. I think we'll try a restaurant for dinner tonight if you are up for it?"

"Sounds good. We haven't had a chance, though you know Tish is going to empty the place out for you, right?"

Elysara sighed. "I know, but I want to pretend to have a normal date."

CHAPTER 22

Crimson blinked away the red that had filled her vision.

The dry, cracked dirt around her was littered with naga corpses, and blood was everywhere. Their swords were stuck in the ground like morose memorials for the many dead.

She scratched at her side where dried blood was cracking and making her itch.

"Fuck." She clicked her tongue, realizing that most of her red dragon leather armor was gone and the blood was certainly hers. Crimson's mouth was parched, and she reached for her CID on instinct, only to remember that it had been smashed in during one of the fights.

"No sense in going thirsty. They are a fucking aquatic race. They have to have some water on them." She fished around until she found a pouch on a matriarch and upturned it, spilling out far more than should fit in the small sack.

"Jackpot." She grabbed a wineskin and poured it down her throat with a sigh of relief. "Now, what do you all have to eat?"

She sorted through the pile and pulled out more water and wineskins, putting them back in the bag that was larger on the inside before picking through the food. Unsure about some of them, she started a fire amid the corpses and cooked some of the fish, wrapping the fish in pieces of bread.

The savages didn't even have a pot or pan.

While she was stuffing her face, she walked around until she found a warrior with a chain mail skirt and tore the last remnants of her dragon leather suit off, putting the chain mail skirt on and using the last of the suit to bind her chest as tightly as she could so it wouldn't get in the way as she fought.

She shuddered to think what whipping around a sword while [Limit Break] was active would do if her chest wasn't bound.

Crimson looked down. Her shoes were completely gone, and it wasn't like the naga had replacements. But injuring feet was a pretty strong limiter to agility in battle. So, she sat down and tore another skirt off the naga. This one was leather, and she was able to fashion a crude pair of leather coverings. They looked more like leather socks with laces, but they'd have to suffice for the moment. Moving forward, she kicked a sword to see how the coverings would hold up.

They were tough enough that the blade only scratched the leather.

Satisfied enough, Crimson kept moving. She washed some of her face, retied her braid and spent just enough time that she felt human again.

Then she stuffed her face again with more crude fish tacos and even looked at the naga, considering if she should eat more. But she couldn't quite bring herself to cook something that could think for itself.

Ken would hate her for that.

The idea of her little protégé out there without her made her heart sink. She'd be back to him soon. And anybody who had made his life difficult would get to deal with her wrath.

Getting up, she stretched her back and double-checked the skirt to make sure she wouldn't lose it in her next fight. The idea of leaving the red haze and finding herself naked the next time made her giggle.

The laughter bubbled up, the stress of everything causing her to lose it even more. If anybody had come upon her, they'd think she'd gone insane. And at that point, Crimson wasn't sure of much except that she was going to find Ken again.

"I'm coming, Ken." She stepped forward, picking up two swords and putting them over her shoulders as she activated [Eyes of Wisdom]. "Which way is home." Her ability pointed to her right, and she shot off at a blur, passing any monsters and heading right for the exit.

The two giant flamberges in her hands were like two blades of a blender. She spun, twisted and tore through monsters as she passed.

She actually felt very strong.

Even if she didn't have a working CID, it was clear that her stats had made some major progress while she'd been out of her mind slaughtering. But that was to be expected. Part of Crimson was excited at the prospect that she'd had a place where she could unleash without worry of harming somebody she cared about.

When she got to the passage, she got so excited that red lightning crackled over her arms. For the first time, her ability highlighted a stairway going up. She was closer to reaching him.

She cackled like a madwoman. "I'm finally going up."

She didn't really know how long it had been, but it felt like forever. The solitude combined with losing her consciousness to [Limit Break] made it impossible to sense passage of time.

She skipped up the steps with a smile on her face and two giant swords dragging their tips behind her.

Nothing could spoil her mood.

At the top of the steps, she came upon an army of naga arrayed before her. They were in a safe zone. There were many different colors and a big, bald and white matriarch with her six limbs splayed out. They all seemed to turn as one and spot Crimson.

"Oh. I must have taken a wrong turn somewhere," she joked.

The naga hissed in their own tongue. Not that Crimson even cared to learn it.

"Hey. No need to be rude," Crimson scowled at them, at least pretending that they had been rude. Who was she kidding? They probably were being assholes. All the naga so far had been jerks. And at that point, Crimson really just didn't give many shits. There were none left. She'd left them all on the dungeon floor as she'd battled for however many days it had been.

The matriarch charged a spell, and that was all the naga that she needed to understand.

Crimson breathed out, letting it loose in an instant. [Limit Break]. Red lightning poured out of her eyes, and danced along her arms, yet she could still see.

[Dash]. On instinct, she shot straight into the center of the army of naga. [Whirlwind]. She flipped one of her flamberges to a reverse grip before she spun so hard and so fast that the air around her deformed, became white, and an actual tornado appeared around her, sucking naga in as she spun so incredibly fast that she was nothing but a blur.

Flashes of steel covered the tornado.

It was over as quickly as it had started, and dozens of naga corpses fell from the impromptu storm, but Crimson was already gone, appearing behind the white matriarch.

[Sever].

An impossibly thin red line went from ceiling to floor as the naga matriarch crossed her arms in front of her face and was pushed back with blood trickling from her scales.

There was almost a pause in the world before the shockwave of the ability turned all the surrounding naga warriors into red smears.

Crimson was watching the battle, but with her ability active, it was like she was disassociated with her actions. They were all instincts honed from years and years of fighting. She recognized every ability and motion she made.

Floating in the air in front of the matriarch, her two giant flamberges flashed out dozens of times in the span of just two seconds. Each one was intercepted by the hard claws of the matriarch.

Crimson thought she was going to just power through, but then a white tail crushed into her side, sending her flying far from the battle, skipping over pools of water and crashing into muddy ground.

Crimson shot from her spot before a barrage of spells exploded where she had just been and arrived amid the warriors, turning them into a bloody charnel house, staying one step ahead of the powerful white matriarch.

Even with [Limit Break], Crimson wasn't going to fight the matriarch directly. She needed to remove any support.

The white matriarch, however, had other plans. The naga warriors leveled Earth shattering spells that did more damage than Crimson.

She wanted to scream at herself to just run. The battle could wait for another day; getting back to Ken was more important. To her surprise, her body listened and dodged another blast before rocketing towards the exit where the main army of naga had been gathered.

That same exit glowed blue to Crimson.

She shot through it, only to come up in a boss room filled with naga corpses that then sprinkled their way into the rest of the floor. In her current state, she didn't care, rushing past and immediately being blown back by a powerful blast as a rune lit up under her feet.

The area was booby-trapped?

That wasn't good for her current state.

Rather, she tried to use [Eyes of Wisdom] to show her the path through. Home, show me the way home. Scant spaces on the floor of the dungeon were blue, while the rest must be covered with traps.

Crimson looked over her shoulder to see the white matriarch coming behind her, and she knew that the primal part of her that was in charge wanted to fight.

No, dammit. Get through this floor. Get home to Ken.

It listened and rushed through, only stepping on the blue patches and zipping through the dungeon. The aquatic floors blurred past her until she came to another safe zone and burst out next to two elves.

They tweeted like little birds and she ignored them, pushing off the ground hard enough to knock them both back as she shot forward.

She was out of the naga territory and into Elven territory. She couldn't have much further to go. Her instincts knew the way back to Earth and took over.

Woe be to anyone that tried to stop her.

***

I was stretching in the gym when Elysara came in with the good news.

"Neldra is handing off most of the work to my father's Censors now. We'll head into the dungeon after lunch." She came in with her electric blue, tight workout clothes, her arms up behind her hair as she pinned her hair back with a big smile at me for watching her.

She was going more informal now as we worked out in the morning, and I realized she'd been getting extra dolled up before for my benefit. I was glad she felt more comfortable around me.

She joined me in the open area and stretched herself out in front of me. We'd made strides and worked together well, now she was just tempting me. Fighting together in the dungeon formed a bond of trust that was unique both in how fast it formed and how solid it became.

I wasn't shy about letting my eyes rest on her. She was the most eye-catching thing in the room even as the Censors, in similar outfits, filed into the room and started to work out in pairs.

They had relaxed significantly around me. No longer were they posting up in the corners and watching for me to harm their princess. They'd begun doing their own exercises while watching the doors to protect all of us. It was as if I was now part of the Royal Family rather than an outsider in their eyes.

"You guys really have made them eager to improve." Fayeth watched as she came in. "Don't rile him up too much. We have a trip this afternoon."

"Already told him. Sorry if I spoiled it." Elysara stuck her tongue out.

Fayeth shrugged. "As long as he's happy. But I'm more worried that he's grown a thing for cat girls. Back in human society, it's this whole thing. His culture has them very prominently in their fantasy shows."

I sighed. "The Nekorians are not anime cat girls. First off, they only have one set of ears." I had no idea she'd watched anime while she was visiting. Hopefully, it wasn't anything terrible.

Elysara glanced at Fayeth who held her hands up behind her own ears and then moved them to the top of her head to demonstrate the dual ear oddity.

"How would that even work? Two ear canals? Are they connected?" Elysara asked, clearly more concerned with their ears than if I had a thing for cat girls.

I shrugged. "Don't ask me. It's fiction. Besides, I think it is rude to compare them to anime cat girls." The Nekorians were people and might not take too kindly to the comparison.

"Right. They are far cuter." Fayeth nodded, completely missing my point.

I wasn't sure which one she meant, but I was happy to drop the topic before one of the Censors picked up on it. Rumors moved around the palace at unimaginable speeds.

"So, what about this Felin? Are you going to try to see her over all this again? Get her to rub her scent all over you?" Elysara enjoyed teasing me about the Nekorians and clearly wasn't jealous.

I checked up on them often enough, feeling responsible for getting them back after making that promise. "No. We are going to get them back to their territory because I made a promise, and because when we were going through all of that, I couldn't help but sympathize with people who were out of their element."

Elysara's face fell at the mention and she grabbed my hand to support me. "Crimson will still show up."

It had been a month at that point, and she would have to pass through Elven territory on her way back, even if she went straight to Earth. We hadn't heard anything yet.

After seeing some of the strength of the elves, I was starting to wonder if she really could make it back.

"If you let Tish catch you moping like that, she's going to push you on mana training again. She finds your restricted portal spell very interesting." Elysara bobbed her brows. "I even wonder if it would be better than Absorb."

"Huh? You say my name, Lady?" Tish asked from the other side of the gym.

"Don't summon her like that." I kept my head down. Tish's curiosity had been too much. She at least helped me understand the ability and its restrictions.

"We don't have time for you to pass out again. Trip down the dungeon, remember?" Fayeth giggled.

We'd found that I could use my portal ability, but using it didn't make it successful. After researching what the elves had on restricted abilities, Tish put me through a gauntlet of trials.

Her determination was that I actually had the high-level ability portal, along with the special use of it within a dungeon. The use within the dungeon was sealed, so we trialed using it to portal around the surface of the Elven world.

It worked... to a degree.

The spell was too high level for me, and by her best guess, it was not only too high mana cost for me at present but also suffering from a penalty factor due to being under leveled.

The end result was activating the portal and immediately passing out from mana exhaustion.

That was a rather unique scenario from what I'd been told. Most of the dungeon abilities were locked behind requirements to prevent something like that from happening. So Tish and Miriam were interested in pushing me to train to be better with the ability.

But mana exhaustion was no joke. Those headaches were the worst. Just the idea of trying to use the portal ability made me want to go find a toilet in case I hurled.

"He's looking a little ill just talking about it." Fayeth watched me carefully. "Don't worry, we won't sell you out to Tish."

"We'll have to watch Miriam. She might try to buy harmony with him," Elysara laughed as the two teased me.

"What was that, princess?" The newest Royal Censor walked in at an inopportune time.

"Oh, nothing new. Have you gotten everything ready for our trip?" Elysara quickly changed subjects.

"Yes, you've paid me. Consider the job done." She put on a sweet face for Elysara. It was always about money.

None of us really forgave her for her part in the Underroot, but at present, she was a necessity to our plans. And if she got paid, she was happy.

"You know, it makes me think about people back home, like the Harem Queen." I made a face thinking of the woman who had tried to snatch me after Crimson disappeared.

"Hmm? The buxom beauty that wanted to make you hers? What about her?" Elysara asked batting her lashes playfully.

"Well, we've been talking about Trelican power swapping strictly in the sense of elves and my Adrel. But I wonder if the UG back home will settle for that or try to get me to swap this portal power around." I pondered aloud.

Fayeth snorted. "Let them try," she pouted, the look coming off as pure adorable on her face.

I rubbed her head, smiling at my Adrel. While I loved how feisty her reply was, the power of an ability like this couldn't be underestimated.

"Hey, I was trying to be serious. Besides, once you are level twenty I'm going first." She narrowed her eyes, daring me to say otherwise.

I nodded, she wanted [Spell Mirror] which also needed absorb. As a tank, that made the most sense. Of her abilities, the iconic plant armor seemed like the best one I could take from her.

It would be a huge mana drain to use it with [Metamorphosis], but together, the two of them would be a hell of a trump card should I get myself into trouble.

We thought we could switch them up later, but the information that even the Royal Family had was so thin that we couldn't be sure. So, we waited to use [Absorb] during re-harmonizing, not that we weren't doing the latter often enough.

All the stimulation around the two ladies had me happily in Fayeth's arms nearly every night. She happily soaked up my attention.

"Alright, I'm loosened up. Ken, will you spot me?" Elysara stepped over to the squat rack that had just opened up as two of the Censors finished.

Despite her privilege, or maybe because of it, Elysara seemed to be extra considerate. She'd never make it known that she was ready to use a piece of equipment until it was open.

"Yeah. Just don't wiggle your hips at the bottom again; you almost fell last time," I told her.

"Would have fallen into you, so I don't see how that's a bad thing." She had a giant mischievous grin on her face as she hooked up the bands and watched me across the equipment.

CHAPTER 23

Eleven Royal Censors, Elysara, Fayeth, Ami, and I, along with fifteen Nekorians, headed into the dungeon together. Thankfully, we were now able to use the royal entrance. With Duke Selmia imprisoned, Rikter hadn't stuck around. There hadn't been any updates on the mustached elf since. Getting through town would have been interesting with so many non-elves.

"Everyone, stay together." Neldra held a hand up. "We Censors will start heavily clearing the monsters starting around level fifteen. Until then, I think all of us can hustle. Understood?"

A wash of some ability came over me as one of the Censors activated an ability. I suddenly felt like I could run for miles and was as light as a feather.

"Running. Yay." Elysara's tone held zero excitement.

"We can't all be pampered princesses who have someone carry us up and down the dungeon all the time," I teased.

"I mean, we could probably tempt Tish to take us down to where Neldra expects to end up for the night," Fayeth offered. "Bet she'd love to get us some more training."

Groaning, I checked my CID and did some quick math. "We are just a little above average for total stats at level twenty."

"Average is fine at this point. It sounds like it won't hinder our progression," Fayeth offered. "Besides, it's almost ten percent over, and we need some gear replacements. We are still plenty ahead."

Elysara was waffling her head back and forth as we followed the Censors through the dungeon, quickly going through the levels. "Neither of you are really wrong. Staying up to par with the stats for each level is important. Yet you could catch up, and you certainly aren't at a point where you'd have to fight lower-level monsters to make any progress yourself."

Wrinkling my nose, I nodded. "I'd rather be exceptional. We were very far ahead before this."

"You got a nice boost from your trip." Elysara squeezed her eyes together when she smiled. "Not to mention, you've been doing plenty of exercising." She winked at Fayeth who laughed.

Sex seemed to be a common topic among the Elven culture, and the two elves weren't shy.

So far, Elysara and I had only spent about a month together. Yet after spending most of every day with her while she was actively pursuing me, my walls weren't just down, they were springing back up with her inside.

I wrestled with the fact that she could be manipulating me, but the harmony between our souls didn't lie. She was genuine in her desire for me and did what she could to step down from being a princess to spend as much intimate time with the two of us as she could.

Given the pressures on her, it wasn't an insignificant effort she was making for me. I knew that my status as a Trelican played into her attraction for me, yet the same could be said for any other relationship. We were who we were and if a woman found something you had attractive, then all the better. Because a relationship was about fulfilling each other's needs in as many ways as possible.

We went through the first five floors quickly and hit the first safe zone. Rubble was off to the side where the blockade had been removed. After the Selmia family had been put under house arrest, the high-level adventurer hadn't kept up the pressure.

Elves that were in the dungeon stopped what they were doing as we moved through, staring. Many spotted Elysara between the Censors and shouted at the princess. Some of them were confused as to why she was with so many Nekorians.

The cat people kept up with us easily. Most of them were higher level than our small party, and they seemed physically very capable.

"Actually." Tish slipped in next to us, the nosey Censor having overheard us. "I'd be happy to carry you guys forward. I think the Nekorians could handle a higher pace, and not using Elysara's abilities is a current limitation."

"I'm not holding us back, am I?" Elysara's head whipped back and forth to find someone slower than herself.

"Take them to the forty-fifth floor. I think we can make that with the Nekorians before we need a break." Neldra hopped on the idea. "Miriam, your job is to just smash anything and everyone who gets close to them."

The newest Censor's eyes flashed. "Can do, Blunty."

"Why is everyone so concerned with the state of my blade?" Neldra threw her a glare. "Tish, take the four of them. We'll catch up with you at the safe zone for the night."

Tish was in the middle of Elysara, Fayeth, Ami, and I in an instant before darkness enveloped us and Miriam shot forward faster than a bullet.

While we were in the bubble of darkness, nothing happened for a while. I floated weightless amid the ability. I jumped a little as a first set of hands wandered over my body, soon joined by a second pair. The touches were almost immediately followed by a set of giggling laughs from my elven women.

I couldn't be quite sure who each set belonged to, and they were both overly familiar with me. Given the situation, I felt for both of them but almost as soon as I did; the darkness disappeared, and we reappeared in the dungeon.

My left hand was on Elysara's breasts and the other on Fayeth's ass.

Tish raised an eyebrow. "All we've had to do this whole time was put him in a dark room?"

"This... is exactly what it looks like." I hesitated and then gave up.

Both of the ladies had stopped touching me as the ability dissipated, and it looked like I'd been groping them the whole time.

Elysara giggled.

"I see," Ami spoke monotone. "I will have to be careful entering dark rooms with my master."

A large rock monster appeared a moment later, and Miriam flashed in front of us, punching the monster so hard it just exploded into dust. "Tish, we have about eight hours to do as much damage as we can manage to this floor."

"Maybe use that mountain as a center point?" Tish pointed to a snow-capped peak.

The dungeon floor was so large that I would have almost called it a world upon itself. Scholars theorized that every floor was cumulatively the same size. And that meant that the forty-fifth floor was absolutely massive. Several smaller countries could fit within it.

"Put a big sign on it that says Princess Training here?" Miriam joked. "No, that's fine. We'll pick a point halfway up and let them exercise, or fuck, or something."

"I'll stay near them to keep the princess safe. Let loose." Tish started moving, and we followed her as Miriam darted off only to rock the floor as she started crushing giant rock monsters.

I let out a soft whistle. "By the way, what's her class?"

"Fierce Merchant." Elysara shook her head. "Yeah, she's a fucking merchant."

"Merchant of Death," I muttered. Miriam was quite the oddity, but many adventurers got stranger as they reached the top. It was often unique combinations that allowed adventurers to push that far down into the dungeon.

"She would love that one," Tish chuckled. "No, it isn't even Fierce Merchant, but she tells everyone that. It is a merchant class. To my knowledge, a lot of her strength comes from actually having a purpose. Giving her a contract multiplies her strength by a percentage of what she's earning. A lot of her abilities have to do with cost. Don't ask for the specifics. At her level, it's a secret an adventurer would kill over."

"Such an odd skill," I muttered watching the merchant crush monsters. "Still, can't fault her efficiency."

"The dungeon provides all sorts of things. I don't think it meant for her skill to be used the way she does. Miriam is basically a giant money funnel, though. If she has to go all out for something, I think it actually eats her mana crystals she has stored," Tish explained.

I shook my head. "That explains some of her personality."

"It really does," Ami agreed. "But I would pay to be faster."

Tish pointed to Ami as if the taciturn butler had made a very good point. "Many would, especially when they hit training walls. But you all have so much training to do." Tish's eyes gleamed. "Start jogging. We'll see what sort of heavy armor we can put on you while you jog. If you are last, Ken, we'll see if we can't train your mana and magic until you can use that portal ability of yours."

Elysara shot forward, followed quickly by Ami.

"Wait up, I can't be last." I hurried after them with Fayeth pushing as hard as she could with Tish urging her on. I didn't want to experience mana exhaustion again and pushed myself as hard as I could.

* * *

Crimson stepped out of the dungeon. Without her CID, she hadn't known the exact route, but she was clearly on Earth. She recognized the familiar UG logo on a building nearby.

The UG employees were staring, questions in their eyes.

But Crimson couldn't blame them. Her weapons were coated in blood, as was her body. She was wearing scaled clothing like the naga, and it was more tactical than meant to cover the less decent pieces of her body.

Luckily for them, they were staring more at her face.

Crimson tried to smile, and it felt brittle. "Can you help me?"

"Chi è quel barbaro? Pensi che mangi le persone?" one of the counter ladies spoke in a way that Crimson just knew was ugly gossip.

Not having patience left, Crimson quickly identified a target for her feelings. Crimson appeared before the woman and smashed the paltry barrier that stood between them. It was far more decorative than functional. At least to Crimson.

Lifting the woman off the ground by the collar, Crimson put her face right up in the other woman's.

Shouting ensued in a language that Crimson thought was Italian all around her. It was a lot of noise and a lot of talking after being alone for who knows how long.

Crimson blinked away the slight disorientation and shook the woman in her grip. "Shut up." Crimson held up her smashed CID that was barely clinging to her wrist. "I need a new one." She enunciated each word clearly.

The woman blinked and started shouting something at someone else nearby.

Crimson ignored everybody else as she spotted a bag of chips on a neighboring desk. She dropped the woman on her ass and just tore through more of the divider to grab the bag of chips. They all started screaming like she was going to slaughter them.

She hefted and shook the bag, finding it at least half empty. But she knew it had probably started half full of air, anyway. She decided not to punish the person that had eaten some of her chips.

She picked one up and took a bite with a big smile. "Fuck. Someone, go get me more chips," she groaned.

After eating dungeon meat for weeks, the chips felt like home.

More noise sounded around the corner as several men and women in UG security uniforms turned the corner, their weapons drawn and their armor on.

Crimson slashed out negligently with her chip, destroying their weapons and armor. "Don't bother me while I'm eating." She ate another chip before she looked at the mess she'd made and shrugged.

She grabbed a nearby hunk of a low stone divider wall and ripped it out, moving it to the center of the room and stabbing it into the floor to make herself a seat while she waited.

"Come on, people. Chop chop." Crimson motioned to the room of dumbfounded UG workers and the line of adventurers that had stalled, not wanting to enter the room. "I need a new CID. And if I have to wait, you are going to get me more chips."

"Excuse me," a man spoke in a thick accent. "Can I help?"

"Yes. Finally. I need a new CID and potato chips. Lots of them. Oh, and if you could unlock the inventory on this one and get it in the new one, that would be absolutely fantastic." Crimson handed the man the broken CID.

The man turned to someone and started speaking quickly.

This one had come out from the back and was mostly concerned with the CID, lifting it up. They turned it over and looked at it for a moment before turning to Crimson with their whole body shaking and their face pale.

"Cremisi. Questa è Mistress Crimson, idiota. Sbrigati adesso, dalle tutto quello che vuole." The one concerned with the CID turned back to her. "Scusa scusa. Le mie più sentite scuse."

She had no idea what he was saying, but it almost sounded like he was begging her.

The one translating was now sweating profusely. "We are very sorry for not..." He looked her over. "...recognizing you. You need a new CID, and this one's inventory transferred?"

"Yes, please." Crimson smiled, pleased she was finally getting somewhere. "I know that'll take an hour or so, please get me some junk food. I feel like I could just eat the world."

"Eh." He struggled a little with her statement.

"Potato Chips. As many as you can bring me." She tapped the bag that was now empty.

"Yes!" He quickly mumbled something to the man with the CID and then hurried off, apologizing to everyone and asking for something.

The adventurers in line started to hand over some bags of chips that the man quickly put on the ground in front of Crimson as if they were offerings of worship.

Crimson clicked her tongue, and he shot off, likely to get more. "Go on. Don't mind me." She waved to the line.

That gesture seemed to break the frozen adventurers. After a few tentatively were able to make their way past her without being slaughtered, the others seemed to grow more comfortable. A slow trickle ran its way around Crimson's current position, making sure to stay as far away from her and as close to the walls as possible.

"He better hurry." She ripped open a new bag and munched on a chip. "Only thing better than this is when I'll be reunited with Ken." Crimson did a little jig on her makeshift seat as she ate chips and thought about how close she was to reuniting with Ken.

***

I lay on Fayeth's lap. "It's like a switch, and when she flips it, Tish is a nightmare. Crimson would get along well with her." The Royal Censor had worked us hard today.

Fayeth laughed. "Yes, she would... I wonder how Crimson is doing?" Fayeth ran a soft finger along my forearm absently.

"Lots of people of any race are probably quaking in their boots." I answered before a sneezing fit overcame me.

"Bless you." Fayeth gently brushed her fingertips over my face and tapped at my nose.

The group had wanted to push a little further into the dungeon when they met up with us, so we had pushed to the fifty-second floor before pausing and setting up a campsite. There were four fires. Ours was a little away from the others, a little bit of privacy.

Elysara walked over and sat down next to Fayeth where she could absently start running her fingers through my hair.

I closed my eyes, enjoying the touches. The two ladies were doing their best to spoil me at every opportunity.

"You know, I never get to do the whole camping in the dungeon thing." Elysara looked around like an excited little girl.

"It's great." Fayeth beamed. "Really great when you meet other groups and sit around a campfire swapping old stories."

"Especially when people make great food." I glanced over at Ami, who had somehow set up an entire mobile kitchen. The kitchen had an opening in the center that sat over the fire and heated the top where she was now cooking a gourmet dungeon camping dish using some ingredients from the past few floors.

"It smells good." Elysara's nose wiggled. "Thank you, Ami, for cooking."

"A butler's duty is never done." Ami nodded and kept chopping some vegetables with blinding speed. "Unfortunately, my master would not allow me to make the tents."

"No. I like my tent a certain way." I made a face. Having her do everything would have been too much. There was no special way to do a tent.

"I notice that you didn't make a tent for yourself, Ely." Fayeth raised an eyebrow at the other woman.

"Huh?" Elysara tried to sound innocent, but had clearly over-done it. "Oh. I thought parties slept together. That's what your stories sounded like." She batted her lashes at me.

"Sure. As long as you don't snore," I answered, happy to agree to anything if it kept those fingers running through my hair. Besides, I'd long run out of reason to push her away.

She gave me a slight drag with her nails. "Wonderful. And no, I don't snore. I sleep daintily, though. Too often, I'm woken with news and need to be ready to go quickly."

"Then I'll have to be careful if I rise early," I murmured with two ladies' soft touches.

The smell and sound of the crackling fire added to the moment as I melted into Fayeth's thighs and let myself relax.

"Well, there are some things you can feel free to wake me up for," Elysara teased.

Too relaxed to think through her statement, I asked. "What would that be?"

"To stick your dick in me," Elysara answered quickly, and I realized her tone was different.

Tilting my head so that I could look into her eyes, I saw no small amount of vulnerability there along with a little bit of cunning. Her statement wasn't just teasing; it was a blank check.

"I'll keep that in mind. But since the Censors are going to take care of watch, we'd probably get that out of the way before we go to sleep." I winked and then, as casually as I could, went back to enjoying relaxing on Fayeth's lap.

Elysara paused running her fingers through my hair for only a moment before she resumed with a little more nail. "Fay-fay, can we trade places?" The fiery-haired elf had a hint of mischief in her eyes.

Yet, she didn't have time to get herself in any trouble.

"Dinner is ready." Ami finished, throwing a cloth over her shoulder and laying out four shallow bowls. "It is roasted phoenix with rock salt and some mushroom cream to temper the spice." It smelled absolutely incredible.

"Later," Fayeth answered Elysara's question. "I have never had phoenix before."

Ami sat down with us. "It was really fast." Her eyes shone once again talking about speed.

"It spooked all the Nekorians with how quickly it appeared above us," I agreed. "Note to self. Do not try to scare the cat people. They respond with violence." The Nekorian's had over reacted when surprised.

"Lots of violence," Fayeth agreed. "But then again, we are in the dungeon. Violence solves most problems." She stabbed into her meal.

"Not all problems." Elysara looked down at her crotch, her mind still in the gutter.

"Sex and combat aren't that different, really. It's kind of like sparring," Ami spoke up, seeing her distraction.

We all looked at the butler who was cutting into her dish like she'd grown a second head.

"What? It is. You start slow, then it grows in intensity and you start pulling out your special moves until one of you is defeated. Then you go another round." She went back to eating after explaining it so clearly.

"I can see it." Fayeth blew on her first piece that was heavily coated in the mushroom cream. "Spicy," she mumbled around the piece.

I took my own first bite. The phoenix tasted like spicy chicken, cooked very well.

CHAPTER 24

Elysara and I didn't end up tumbling in our tent. After a heavy make-out session that included Fayeth, we all had to agree that we were just too tired to make it memorable.

Even in that conversation, it was clear we were beginning to experience harmony as we instead moved to sleep together in a small pile.

We continued through the dungeon floors for two more days before we finally began to see Nekorians in the forties. We slowed down to let word get back to their people, and we didn't have to wait long. When we reached the safe zone on the fortieth floor, there was a small army of Nekorians arrayed loosely within the space.

The Censors shifted a little anxiously, and I realized it was the first time I'd really seen them get nervous. They were currently out numbered and while many of them were powerful, so were the Nekorians.

"Miriam, stay up front," Neldra ordered.

The strong elf rolled her eyes, but she moved to the front of their formation. "I hope there's a big, strong lion of a man here."

Elysara rolled her eyes.

The Nekorians in the safe zone shifted and opened up to a small group that walked forward.

I spotted Felin among them immediately. "Actually, mind if I step forward?"

Neldra spotted Felin as well, letting out a sigh. "Fine. Lady, go with him. This is an Elven group, and we don't want to be represented entirely by a human."

Elysara happily grabbed my hand, and we walked out of the group with smiles on our faces.

"Hello." I waved with my free hand. "Felin, I hope you haven't forgotten about me."

Felin's ears perked up immediately, her nose going higher into the air as she breathed in and turned, her eyes locking onto mine.

A fanged grin spread across her face. "Ah. It's Ken." She skipped out of the group without a sense of propriety.

The one at the front of their group made a prolonged growl that undulated, clearly their language.

Felin turned and grimaced at the speaker with her own growling before whipping back to me and closing the distance. She wrapped me in a hug before she started to rub her face on my neck.

"Good to see you too, Felin." I rubbed her back.

When I pulled away, Elysara had a faint pout leaking into her smile. The woman was jealous, despite how she had previously teased me about the Nekorians.

Part of me wanted to prod further and see what the jealous woman would do, but the other half won out, and I squeezed her hand to reassure her.

"Felin, you can meet another of my Adrel. This is Elysara, the future leader of the elves," I made the introductions.

Elysara caught my introduction and did a double take at me.

"What? Are we not in harmony? Feels like it," I teased. "Or would you prefer Fieore at this point?"

Elysara blushed slightly. "Pleasure to meet you, Felin. I have heard a little about you from my Adrel."

"Smelled me too." Felin let out a little soft meow that was most certainly a laugh. "But I'm afraid I do have to ask why you have Nekorian prisoners?" Her eyes lit with a bit of fire.

"Not prisoners," I corrected her. "There was a faction of elves that recently were found to be keeping people against their will, including these Nekorians. We have freed them."

"It would be best if you let them reunite with their people," Felin advised me with a cautious look over her shoulder. "Otherwise, there will be a contest of strength."

I figured easing the tension would come first, but that was Elysara's gesture to make not mine. Raising an eyebrow at her, she nodded, in sync with me.

"Neldra, please allow our guests to return to their people," Elysara spoke up.

The invitation was apparently all they needed. The nervous Nekorians behind us practically sprang into action and threw themselves into the arrayed Nekorians. A cacophony of growling filled the area as they quickly reunited.

"Thank you." Felin bowed.

Several of the other, clearly important, Nekorians joined Felin, approaching us.

"You have my thanks as well." The Nekorian that spoke was another woman, though older with silver strands in her hair.

"Actually, I doubt I could have done it without Felin." I pointed at the tigress, getting a cute, surprised expression out of her in return. "When we met previously, she found me curious. I used those clothes with her scent on them to convince these Nekorians that I was an ally. Without that, I don't know if they would have been compliant enough to make the journey."

The older woman glanced at Felin briefly. "So I see. It must be fate for such a thing to lead to the return of our people. Maybe I should give you more freedom."

Felin gave a big toothy grin to the older woman. "I am a grown Nekorian. It is time to stop coddling me so that I may gain my own strength and expand the strength of our tribe."

The woman nodded slowly and sniffed. I got the feeling she was scenting me, much like Felin had, only without being all over me. "You reek of potential."

"Thank you," I answered. "It is partially due to this woman." I held Elysara closer, feeling her being a little left out.

"She has power, but you have the greater potential. You will make a good pair in time." The old woman spoke like she was prophesying. She sniffed again. "For your two's assistance, would you allow us to honor you?"

"Absolutely," Elysara jumped in. "The elves and the humans have only just begun to work together, but both parties have been very interested in the Nekorians for quite some time."

"Our ways are not casually shared." The old Nekorian glanced at Felin, whose tail flitted back and forth nervously. "Little Felin, would you be interested in drawing out their power?"

Felin's tail went rigid, and she stuttered, "T-truly, Elder?"

"Yes. I think we should invite them for a meal here in this safe zone, and then you may prove to me that your heart is in the right place. For these people have aided ours and it would only be right to offer something in turn."

Felin suddenly seemed like a bundle of barely contained kitten energy. "Of course. We should hold a feast for those returned."

"Yes." The older Nekorian nodded and stepped back, growling at the gathered Nekorians.

The surroundings suddenly erupted into deafening roars that sounded more than a little intimidating, but at the same time, none of the noise seemed to be directed at me.

"They are happy. Those are cheers of victory and thanks to The Great One." Felin smiled, but the fangs in her mouth always made the smile seem predatory.

"The Great One?" I asked.

Felin pointed around them. "The one who provides all the beasts to hunt and the power to hunt them."

"The dungeon?" I asked.

Felin scowled. "Do not use that word. In your language, it is... a prison. A place you keep the unwanted."

I wanted to argue. But that was one use of the word. I hadn't actually tied the two together in my head, but I could see her confusion. "Ah. I meant no disrespect."

Elysara bowed her head. "He did not. So, the Nekorians worship The Great One?"

"Yes. It has several names depending on how it is interacting with us, but why wouldn't we worship it? It is a powerful being beyond our comprehension. The Great One saved our people." Felin smiled. "Come with me, and bring the rest of your group, we'll set our fire, and hunters will come back with food quickly."

Already, there were Nekorians racing away.

"Should my people hunt?" Elysara asked.

"No. You are guests. Our people will roam as deep as they can to come back with the meat of powerful beasts and then share it. I'll be your host." Felin smiled again and pulled at a little pouch around her waist before removing some sticks and starting a fire.

Elysara motioned to the remainder of our group, now just Censors, Ami and Fayeth. Fayeth was at my side in a hurry.

"Ah. Fayeth." Felin smiled at her. "I had thought for a moment that he traded out elves."

"Fat chance." Fayeth held my other arm. "Though he is dangerously expanding past his ability to hold a party." She narrowed her eyes on me.

I rubbed my nose. "I don't know what you are talking about. Ely is going to stay in her world; she can't just come to Earth."

"Uh huh," Fayeth said and glanced at Felin. "It is good to see you again, Felin. Can I trade some of his dirty clothes for a spellbook?"

The Nekorian blushed and folded her ears. "I'm not sure what you are talking about. No self-respecting Nekorian would steal dirty clothes." She glanced over her shoulder to find the older Nekorian further away before turning back.

Ami was there staring at the Nekorian, a silent conversation passing between them.

"Well met again, Ami." Felin nodded to her. "Would you join us for a fire and meal?"

"It would be our pleasure." Ami bowed at the waist.

I pulled a set of camping chairs out of my CID and sat down to talk with the Nekorian to swap stories. This time, she was much more open about her people. Having freed some of her people had lowered their caution.

"You were in the important group, care to share?" I asked.

"Ah. I am a shaman of my people. That means that I carry one of the spatial pouches." She tapped her hip. "It also means that I help empower our people after a vigorous hunt, calling on The Great One to assist their growth."

"Like what you'll do to us tonight?" Elysara was quite curious.

"Yes and no. You've never had it done before, and I should mark you as a friend to the Nekorian. Beyond that, The Great One will acknowledge you. Well, the two elves." Felin sniffed. "Ken has already met The Great One, and it has personally assisted his growth."

I was now staring at Felin with wide eyes. "Wait, you can tell that?"

"Yep. You are marked by The Great One. It pays attention to you. What did it give you?" Felin asked.

"An ability. But I don't fully understand it yet," I told her.

Felin gave me another toothy grin. "I can assist with that. This must truly be fate." Her head picked up and her ears swiveled before the crowd of Nekorians returned from their hunt. They held mostly meat over their shoulders and were doing a sort of dance as they returned.

The Nekorians growled with their arrival.

Fayeth cleared her throat and tried to join them in growling.

Felin laughed. "Deeper, like this." She growled, picking up into a low roar.

Fayeth and Elysara joined her, and I shook my head, doing my best to growl with them.

The hunters came back and started to show off their meats. Felin turned her head away at the first few and started to show interest at the others. It was an interesting ritual. We enjoyed ourselves, observing and working to not do anything to mess up the ceremony.

Eventually, Felin picked out several pieces, and they were quickly skewered before Felin seasoned them to barbecue next to the fire.

I pulled Fayeth tight to my side and watched everything with a big smile. "Think we are the first to receive this?"

"Maybe. It doesn't matter, though. This is pretty awesome." Fayeth just watched as the hunters celebrated and congratulated some of their numbers while the other Nekorians were all split up into campfires and enjoying themselves.

The Censors had made their own space and campfire and were being served by a Nekorian.

"A celebration just does something." Felin smiled. "We were all meant to enjoy life, and when the spark for an event like this is formed, it grows into a great blaze. We'll have to get you all good and drunk before we do the tattoos."

"They are going to hurt, aren't they?" Elysara asked.

"Don't worry. With enough alcohol in your system, it's not that bad." Felin's smile seemed a little extra predatory. "We'll need a private space for it though."

"Shall I set up a tent?" Ami asked from the side.

"Please." I nodded to her, still not used to having someone on hand to help me so often.

Ami moved quickly, getting to work.

***

I put down my dish. I was completely stuffed, and unfortunately still quite sober. As were the two elves.

Ami had set up the tent and a massage table that Felin would use for the tattoo. I was picked to go first.

"This is so cool." Fayeth grinned like a loon while rubbing her stomach that stuck out like it was pregnant. She was currently exaggerating it after all she'd eaten.

Elysara had reined herself in better, but still held her stomach and leaned back in her seat. "To be the first humans or elves to see this is an honor."

Felin wobbled a little, the alcohol having affected her far more. "Don't worry. I got this."

"For the record, that does not make me feel more comfortable," I muttered into the massage table. My shirt was cast aside and promptly stolen by Felin.

I had a feeling I was not going to get that piece of clothing back.

Felin rubbed something over my shoulder blade with a little wooden spoon before it went back in a small jar. Ami stood nearby, holding a tray of items for Felin, who picked up a sharpened bone needle and a little mallet.

"It's going to hurt a little," Felin told me, pressing the needle to my back before tapping lightly over my shoulder blade. I could certainly feel the pain, but it was manageable.

"I've had worse." I put up a little bravado, it just couldn't be helped. There was something ingrained in me to deny that there was any pain.

"Oh good. I can go a little faster." Felin started moving the needle quickly to new spots and did a few small double taps along my back.

When she got right over the bone of the shoulder blade, I had to bite down on the cloth of the massage table. That hurt like getting stung by dozens of bees without pause. The worst part was that I couldn't do anything about it. I had to remain still. The inaction was almost the worst part.

An itch like ants crawling under my skin turned into a faint burning.

I hissed. "Felin. Is it supposed to burn?"

"Hmm?" The woman looked up from her work. "Yeah, there's some acid in the ink; otherwise, it doesn't set in adventurers very deeply."

"Maybe I'll pass," Fayeth murmured.

"No. We'll do this together," I growled through the growing pain.

Felin worked quickly as I twitched under the needle and mallet. Soon, the pain began to build and become nearly unbearable.

"Alright. Almost done. Ami, you can burn the incense now." Felin started tapping quicker and humming a tune under her breath. "O' Great One. We call for you, seek your guidance and guiding hand towards our strength and a better future." It sounded a little strange, but that was probably the translation's doing.

"Yes. Great One, gaze upon us, give me insight unto the ability you bestowed on this one. He doesn't understand the tool he's been given." As she spoke, she started to stomp her feet and wipe off my back.

Felin growled in her strange Nekorian language.

I felt something, far less intense than last time, but a feeling that prickled the hairs on the back of my neck like someone, or something, was staring at me.

Felin swirled her fingers over my back, and magic danced off of me, pouring over my side and down to the floor.

"Come see his back." Felin waved to the two elves. "Ami, I'm unsure which language it will be in, so please come and help interpret if needed."

"Language?" I asked and felt a strange sensation starting at my shoulder where the tattoo had been made.

"Whoa." Fayeth gasped.

The cool sensation flowed down to my spine and then scattered along my back.

"What's happening?" I asked.

"The tattoo just melted and flowed down your back, and a bunch of words are showing up on it now," Elysara told me.

"Wait? Really?" I craned my neck, and Ami held up a mirror for me. There were words in English written all over my back. "Ami, can you take pictures?"

"Already on it." She put the mirror down.

Felin ran her fingers along my back. "Show us the skill you've given him."

"Portal," I added.

"Show us Portal, Great One," Felin chanted, and once again, I felt the sensation of ink moving through my skin.

"Pictures taken," Ami confirmed.

"Now bless him." Felin stomped her feet and poured more magic over my back.

I felt the ink crawl back up to my shoulder, wiggling through my skin. It felt like a thousand little droplets of cold water racing along my back, all gathering back up at one point.

"Oh. A dagger, very cool," Fayeth squealed.

"It's a dagger?" I asked.

"With lots of detail and scroll work along the blade and hilt," Elysara explained. "Pretty fitting with your magical assassin style."

"I like it." Everything settled down and I looked to Felin, who nodded.

Getting up, I stretched my arm. "Doesn't hurt. I expected more pain afterwards."

"You've been blessed by The Great One. Why would that be painful? We merely needed to give it the ink to work with. The hilt of the blade also contains Nekorian writing. If you show that to any you meet, you'll not need my scent to convince them you are a friend." Felin bowed. "Now, who wants to go next?"

Fayeth practically hid behind Elysara.

"Alright, princess, come and lay down." I got off the massage table and Ami tapped at her CID before bumping it to mine.

I glanced down at the photo in shock.

[Portal] [Restricted] [Special] - The ability to create a magical portal from one location to another. The target location must have previously been visited. [Restricted] The mana cost of the ability is greatly increased because of a level deficiency and its special properties. Without the total requisite mana, the spell will fail. [Special] This ability now functions within the dungeon. This property greatly increases the mana cost of the ability.

Well, that couldn't have spelled it out better, unless it would have given me a target mana to be able to use it. For now, the spell was nothing more than a training tool. Sometime in the future, I knew it would be precious.

CHAPTER 25

E lysara's tattoo went well. The woman barely made a peep through the whole process. The fiery-haired princess had just gotten her dress back on after. It had all been in Elvish, and she didn't need information about her class like I did.

Fayeth, who was currently getting her tattoo, was another story.

"Stop! It tickles so much," Fayeth giggled and held on to the table with enough strength that it creaked.

"You are going to break the table," Elysara chided the ticklish elf.

"It tickles!" Fayeth squirmed enough that Felin had to lift the needle away.

"Yes, you are certainly the tank of the group." Felin smirked. "I wonder if Ken can do anything to take your mind off of this?"

I came around to the front where Fayeth had her head propped up and kissed my giggling Adrel. Her lips pushed back, and she breathed out a low moan as our tongues played.

Felin took that moment to hammer away at Fayeth's back, but her focus was away from that and on my lips.

I ran my hands through Fayeth's hair and lightly touched her ears, making my Adrel melt into the massage table like a little puddle. I was learning special touches that she liked.

"Done." Felin wiped at her brow. "Okay, let's see what we can't do for you. Great One, share with us her strengths and help guide her." She rushed the incantation.

Fayeth's tattoo melted along her back and shared her stats and abilities in Elvish.

Elysara took notes just as Fayeth had done for her. "This is remarkable."

"This is the dungeon," I answered, shaking my head and checked my own CID.

There was a new ability now, and this one was a passive ability in my list. [Blessing of The Dungeon]. The ability was quite simple. It led to a flat five percent increase in stats. At that moment, the lift wasn't considerable. But percentage-based buffs could stack in truly remarkable ways.

"Do you want any of your abilities examined?" Felin asked.

"No. I want to drag my Adrel off to bed after kissing me that much," Fayeth admitted.

Felin let out a low growl. "Well, then I only have Ami to finish."

"I'm in your care." Ami bowed.

Elysara's hand slid into mine and intertwined our fingers. "I do apologize, but I think Ken needs to take care of Fayeth."

"Of course." Ami bowed. "I am content to talk with Felin tonight."

The two of them shared a look, and Felin nodded. I made a mental note to check my inventory later to see if I was missing any other sets of clothes.

But that thought fled from my mind as Fayeth slung her dress over herself, not bothering to get the straps right and dragged Elysara and me out of the tent and into another smaller one that had been set up earlier for sleep.

I had a feeling the tent was going to get less sleep than originally intended as the two Elven beauties blushed.

Elysara was wearing a thick, royal blue dress, one with plenty of cutouts to not restrict her movements. And it pinched in at her waist beautifully. Her hair had been carefully coiffed atop her head, but the day had undone it, making it a little more messy and adding a few extra strands that hung down around to frame her face and her deep blue eyes.

Fayeth was wearing what she normally wore, the green and gold strappy dresses that she so loved to show off her sun-kissed skin. Her blonde hair hung down, loose and flowing over her shoulders.

"Yes? My Adrel?" I spoke to both of them and ignited beautiful smiles in the ladies as they worked to push me down on a large bed roll.

Elysara hummed and leaned over me, kissing me tenderly, savoring my lips as we gently brushed them together. "My Adrel, do you feel our harmony?" She kissed me again.

I felt it and had been feeling it. We both sang, nearly the same note. And as we kissed, our whole being seemed to waver slightly, falling in and out of tune, touching on harmony every time our lips passed. It was a soft caress that ignited a passion in me.

We were so damned close, and we both knew how to take that final step.

"Ken." Fayeth pulled out a strip of silk. "We are going to play a game."

I raised an eyebrow as Elysara slid off of me and took my pants away, causing my cock to stick straight up into the air. "And what would that game be?"

She hung over me, her chest in my face for a moment before my eyesight was taken from me by the strip of cloth. "You see, this isn't uncommon in larger Adrels. We want to make sure we are in harmony, work towards it. So you'll need to be able to tell who is who, without your sight."

Elysara let out a low moan, and a hand caressed my shaft. Yet, I didn't think it was her. I was fairly certain that it was Fayeth touching me.

"So, how does the game work?" A second hand wrapped higher on my shaft and both of them coaxed me together, but slightly off beat.

The touch alone was enough to make me twitch and let out a sigh.

"You have to figure out who's pleasuring you at any moment, while we try to be each other so well that you can't tell." Elysara's voice shifted, trying to mimic Fayeth.

Then I wondered if it was Fayeth trying to mimic Elysara? Taking away my sight for this game had made me second guess myself. Yet it had also made me pay far more attention to each touch. Their skin on mine felt electric as they teased me.

"We'll begin," one of them said, and I felt two pairs of lips kissing along my shaft. Their wet kisses leaving warmth with each peck.

"Both of you, that's not fair," I groaned as their petal soft lips left warm, wet patches as they worked to cover me entirely with their love.

Nails dragged along my inner thigh, making my hair rise and doing wonderful things to me.

"You like that?" Fayeth asked, taking a break from kissing for a moment.

She returned, and I felt her tongue roll over my head. I imagined the two of them, both kissing with me in between. Yet, I continued to focus on the feeling, losing my sight had heightened the pleasure.

Then they both moved to the head. Both of their soft lips were divine as their tongues slithered over my sensitive skin only for soft kisses to make me twitch and want to thrust up into one of them.

I wanted them, and they wanted me, making our souls vibrate together.

"Wonderful," Fayeth murmured as Elysara swallowed me with a small sputter, but she relaxed her throat and worked me deeper while Fayeth ran her fingers along my stomach and twirled loops down my leg. I forgot about guessing and just enjoyed the two of them.

She kissed at my hips while Elysara bobbed on me.

After a moment, I could feel her pull back and lap at the tip, sucking off any precum and pass me to Fayeth who didn't hesitate to go all the way down on me.

"You two. I want both of you," I growled.

Elysara didn't speak, but I could almost see her in my mind as she moved up to cradle my head and start kissing me. Her lips were only a slight distraction from the motion of Fayeth going down on me.

I put a hand on the back of Fayeth's head, looping her hair around my fingers and started to push and pull her. She didn't need the direction, but I liked to participate.

Elysara pushed my hand to her breasts, and I was surprised to find exposed nipples. It took me a moment to make the realization, but then I leaned forward and brushed them again more eagerly.

She moaned into my mouth and tilted her head, pressing her kiss deeper, with more passion.

I wanted to take care of her. My hand slipped down her toned stomach to between her legs. My fingers only probed for a moment before they sank into the warm, wet heat of her sex.

I could feel her clit just inside, swollen such that I knew once we started we weren't going to stop. Stroking it gently, she shuddered against me.

Fayeth came off of me and crawled up to press her chest to my other shoulder.

Elysara freed my lips and tilted my chin to Fayeth for her to claim my lips as my fingers walked down her back, around her side and in between her legs. My first Adrel let out a happy chirp as I found her clit and started stroking them both at the same time.

"That feels so good," the princess moaned in my ear, her lips brushing against it, and I could feel her hot breath wash over my neck. "Don't stop," she pleaded.

If anything, I sped up on both of them. Eager to hear pleasure on their lips.

Both of them moaned in an ear promising me sweet nothings.

The three of us were each cords vibrating in perfect harmony. My whole body felt like it had been hit by a tuning fork and the ladies shuddered, orgasming over my fingers together.

"Oh no. We left him out," Elysara whispered in a light, playful tone.

"That needs to be corrected," Fayeth agreed. "Why don't I help you, Adrel." Rather than speaking to me, I felt Elysara lift up and there was a brush of soft cloth against me that ignited my imagination.

A moment later, I felt Elysara sink down into my lap, her swollen clit providing some resistance before I slipped in.

"Oh yes," Elysara sighed and rode me.

Fayeth's hand ran across my body until she got to my head, and I felt her lips press down on mine. I cupped the swell of her breasts, fondling them as Elysara pleasured herself on me.

From their teasing earlier, I was already feeling quite ready, and it didn't take long between Fayeth's pampering and Elysara's hard riding of me to erupt into my newest Adrel.

That moment was like being struck by a tuning fork again, and I gasped in Fayeth's mouth as Elysara cried out and ground herself against me a little more to have her second orgasm.

"That was lovely," Fayeth hummed and pulled away as Elysara slid off of me and came down to my other side, curling against me.

I ran my fingers through Elysara's hair, feeling that it had come loose from its styling and cupped the back of her head to bring her lips to mine.

"Knees up," Fayeth told me, and I could feel her tight little butt rest on my pelvis as she mounted me in reverse, using my knees to give her balance and leverage to do as much as she wanted.

I kissed Elysara once more. "Oh, I'm done being passive."

"Wait, you can't see," Fayeth playfully scolded.

Ignoring her, I quickly flipped the two of us so that she was face first on the bed and ripped off the blindfold. "Kiss her and play with her breasts while I remind my Adrel of who's in charge."

Elysara's eyes gleamed a little at the idea and cupped Fayeth's face before she wiggled under and the two of them made out while I rammed myself into Fayeth's tight, wet pussy.

She was a small woman, and her sex squeezed all around me. It felt incredible to be back inside of her.

I pushed my hips down, rubbing hard against her clit until she came. As soon as she did, I slipped myself out and angled down just a few inches before thrusting into Elysara.

The redhead gasped at the surprise, but both of them were fondling each other and kissing as I satisfied myself with them. The sight of the two of them did something to me, making me feel like I was a steel rod pistoning into them.

I needed no rest as I went between the two several more times before pushing Elysara down and knowing that she needed to feel like she wasn't above us.

I knew exactly how to do that. "Absorb." I held both of them down as I felt something transfer between us. "Now you are all mine, Ely. Get on your hands and knees."

***

Crimson swayed her foot back and forth, starting to get impatient. The president of the UG was on his way and she'd just had a shower.

She had a working CID again, and she was wearing a spare red dragon leather suit. It wasn't as nice as the first one, and honestly, she'd probably have to go farm something stronger soon.

Crimson paused, wondering if she should change up the color. She had a certain style, but maybe with her return, she should do a big change up. She certainly felt like a slightly different woman than when she'd left. With gaining some control over [Limit Break] she was feeling like a new woman.

That idea swirled in her head, but red had always been a part of her brand as an adventurer. Hell, it was her name. So, she'd have to see if there were any other high-level dragons, or maybe she'd get a suit made out of naga scales.

Those bastards.

Another chip broke between her teeth while she waited. Finishing the bag, she crumpled it up and added it to the pile.

The President of the UG came in panting. "You waited."

"Yeah. For two whole hours. My time is precious, so let's get on with this." Crimson's foot tapped back and forth.

"What do you know?" he asked.

"Nothing?" Crimson raised a manicured eyebrow. "I've spent the last... I don't know how long, honestly, killing naga. You don't look like you've gone gray since I've been gone, so you tell me how long." She pulled another bag of chips out of her CID and carefully controlled her strength while she opened the bag.

"Just over a month," he told her.

Crimson let out a heavy breath. "That could have gone worse. I'll just go get Ken and do some rough training to get him ready for next year."

The President of the UG winced and Crimson's gaze sharpened.

"What happened to Ken?" Potato chips went flying everywhere as the bag exploded from her pulling too hard.

"Uh. Nothing too bad," the President backpedaled.

'Too bad' was still bad. "Tell me. Quickly." Crimson's eyes flashed death. The President was a pushover, and that was all she needed to do.

"You see, after you went through the portal, Ken seems to have learned the artificial spellbook that made the portal. He was able to close the portal."

Crimson blinked, shocked. "You mean he has a portal ability that works in the dungeon?"

"He tried and failed to make another one. I am unsure of the details of the ability. Yet it was tempting enough for several of the adventurers who had been down in the dungeon for the demonstration to become overcome with greed."

The armrest on Crimson's chair cracked in half. "Go on. Names would be nice."

"The Harem Queen," the President admitted. "But she didn't get him. Neldra took him and the ambassador's daughter. They fled to the Elven world, or so the Nagato Clan has claimed."

Crimson leaned back, her chair frame creaking and a little looser than before. "That bitch was never satisfied with what she had and hates that she could never beat me. Hmm." Crimson pondered the new information for a second. It seemed confirming with Ken's grandparents would be her next stop.

"Yes. Well, can you tell us more about what you've experienced?" He glanced at something on a tablet. "Your level and stats..."

"Honestly, it was a lot of red." Crimson smiled and nodded. "Lots of red paint splatter really, and some flashes of steel. I killed a... lot of naga."

"So it seems." The President was staring at the tablet with a little sweat beading on his forehead. "You've made significant progress. And after that display with the matriarch, you were quite strong before you left."

Crimson tilted her head. "Point?" They'd done this song and dance before. He poked at asking for more about how she had gotten to the level that she had and she vaguely threatened to stop helping the UG. Then he'd just give her the same support. After all, at her level as an adventurer she was pushing into new territory for all of humanity anytime she dove the dungeon. Information she could share was valuable and only cost the UG their full support of her dives and situations like this where she came back covered in naga blood without a working CID.

"Fine then. The UG will still support you wholeheartedly. Though we'd ask for your assistance if we ever needed it." The President of the UG dipped his head.

Oh Goodie, he skipped the dance. Now she can get on with it.

"Sure. You still have it. Though Ken and his family take precedence. You clash with them, and I'm sorry, but I like Ken better."

Crimson was tapping her foot on the air now hard enough to make a rhythmic woosh with every tap. She was getting impatient.

The President of the UG gave her a stiff smile and swiped on the tablet. "I've sent you a report of everything that might interest you since you've been gone, and our investigation from the naga attack. Oh, and most of your students are at the Silver Fang Guild, including most of their parents. I would ask, as a favor, not to kill the Harem Queen. She might not compare to you, but given rising conflicts, I would like to keep every ounce of strength we have as a collective."

Despite the Harem Queen only being the second strongest woman, she was still the top of humanity and thus in a year or two could be vital to fighting off the naga or any other threat. Just because Crimson could crush her now, didn't mean that she couldn't be useful tomorrow.

Crimson let out a put-upon sigh. "Fine. Thank you for the report. I'll be going now if there's nothing else." She started to tap at her CID, having already programmed a route through the dungeon back up through the Nagato Estate and what sounded like a budding Silver Fang's guild.

"N—o…" Before he even finished the word, Crimson was gone.

The UG President looked back down at the tablet and shook his head. "Absolutely terrifying. And she thinks one day that Ken will be her match?" He rubbed at his chin. "Maybe we should expend some UG resources and see if the Nagato Clan needs any additional assistance."

CHAPTER 26

I had woken up with the biggest smile on my face. We were now almost halfway through our day, and that smile still remained.

We moved through the dungeon, headed back towards the Elven world, while Neldra and the Censors did their best to annihilate entire floors of monsters as we moved.

"I mean at this point, you can just admit you are power-leveling us," I sighed. We were hurrying, but not using Tish's ability to return. More of an excuse for them to power-level us all.

"Lady Rendral doesn't get as much time as she should in the dungeon." Neldra winked. "This is an opportunity to help her along. After all, her stats are way ahead of her levels."

I rolled my eyes.

We were currently on our way down. It wasn't until the level thirties that we slowed down for them to start slaughtering and dumping the experience into our party since this was the most optimum level to do it for us. Anything higher and we'd get a penalty.

"Neldra." One censor had broken off at the top of the dungeon path we took to go scout ahead. "Message from the guards on the sixtieth floor." She cast a glance at me and then showed Neldra something on her CID.

The Royal Censor burst into laughter. "Fuck. Crimson is back, and they did her some real justice with their description. I guess, even for her, a month among the naga must have been fraying."

"Huh?" I perked up at the mention of Crimson, my heart skipping a beat.

"They say she was nearly naked, wearing a leather skirt and torn red leather around her chest. They called her a human barbarian. Lots of blood and two big flamberges," Neldra read over the description again. "But insanely strong. They lost track of her fairly quickly."

"When?" I asked in a hurry, anticipation building inside of me.

"Not quite two days. I'll bet she zips down to Earth and then pings back over to the Elven world." Neldra glanced at all the Censors. "No more farting around. The last thing any of us need is for Crimson to reach the Elven world before us and tear through it in search of Ken."

The other Censor continued with another part of the report that made Neldra's brow pinch down in a frown.

"There's more?" Elysara asked.

"Some minor trouble with the naga. It sounds like the whites made a big push through two of the trapped floors." Neldra smirked. "I bet they were chasing Crimson after she slaughtered her way through them."

There was a slight intake of breath from the Censors that were escorting us. "The whites?"

"They are different from the red ones?" I asked, genuinely curious.

"It's sort of a tribal thing as far as we can tell. Colors don't mix. And from what we can tell, the white ones are on top. So, yeah, a white matriarch is a real problem. But we've repelled them before. I can only imagine that the Emperor is going to prepare to deal with them again," Neldra answered. "The good news is that every floor of the dungeon is a bottleneck and can be turned into a minefield. We've done it before, and they couldn't weather the losses even with a white matriarch in the lead."

Elysara nodded. "Though, many argued with my father's action. By having those buffer floors, we've likely saved many, many lives that would have been lost before we got a force up to stop the naga."

Miriam grunted. "Still, they grow stronger, and our strongest have become hobbled. It certainly isn't a long-term solution." It seemed she didn't entirely agree with the emperor's actions.

"Will your father go up for the fight?" I asked, curious if he would oversee it personally. He was a seasoned adventurer in his own right, though that was well in his past.

"Absolutely." Elysara nodded. "It's a show of strength, one that he could really use right about now. He'll take it. So hopefully, we won't have much problems with him on our return."

Neldra clapped her hands. "That's enough. Tish, take them out of the dungeon. The rest of you, top speed. Let's get out of here."

Darkness enveloped me, and I felt two ladies grab onto me. In the void, feeling them pressed against me was comforting.

***

The darkness pulled back, and a whoosh ripped through the air before Tish cried out in surprise, "Down!"

I grabbed both of my Adrel and pulled them close, before kicking off the ground and getting clear of whatever trouble we had stumbled into.

We were on the first floor of the dungeon, just at the palace entrance, but we weren't alone. Rolling grassy plains spread out with small clusters of trees. And out of one cluster came a group of elves that looked less than friendly.

Leading the group at the front was our old friend, the mustached elf, Rikter.

My heart dropped seeing him coming, something was very wrong. Was it an attempted revenge for Duke Selmia and his son?

Tish had been attacked. Her right arm was bleeding badly and hanging limp while she drew her sword backhanded and flipped it around with her left hand.

For drawing the sword with the wrong hand, it was a cool move.

I had my daggers out, staring at the group behind Rikter. I could tell immediately that they were higher leveled, and they'd been waiting for us. My favorite advantage was gone. I'd not have the ability to sneak and surprise them.

"Rikter, you've gone too far. The rest of the Censors are right behind me," Tish growled like a cornered animal and kept herself between Elysara and the stronger elf.

"But they aren't here now, are they?" The man's smile grew. "Capture them. We need the hostages." He flashed towards Tish, pulling out an absolutely giant sword that was more like swinging around a car on a stick.

But as Rikter charged forward, it was clear Tish wasn't his target. He threw himself directly at Elysara. Tish's smaller sword seemed like a toothpick as she was forced to protect the princess against Rikter's massive sword.

I braced myself against the explosive force of their exchange, the wind whipping and pulling at my clothes.

Four other elves surrounded us in an instant. They weren't using any spells; they were all powerful agility type fighters.

Fayeth's chest wrapped up in the root armor, only to crack at the first blow. She spun, trying to force them off, but they were too fast for her, disappearing and reappearing behind her to knock her forward.

Rapidly, they blurred around the tank, knocking her about.

Elysara screamed and swung wildly with her trident to ward off her attacker; she couldn't use her abilities in the open, and I could tell how frustrated that made her through our harmony.

Ami tried to match her opponent, but was still outclassed in speed.

"Metamorphosis. Sprint. Hydra," I growled, putting every buff I could use on myself at the same time. This would be my first real use of Elysara's ability.

In a flash, I was taller than my opponent, and my hands blurred forward in a rapid exchange with the elf, suddenly finding himself with someone stronger than he expected.

We matched each other for a moment, and my head snapped forward, smashing my horns into the elf's face. The elf stumbled back, and I pressed in, scoring two strikes before they sped up considerably, and a huge gash opened up in my back, my legs and chest.

Blood splashed out on them and they staggered back, feeling the acidic blood. They had done a solid amount of damage to me with their hits.

"We have healers on standby. Go all out!" Rikter shouted as he kept Tish away.

"We don't have to win," I coughed at my group. "Just last however long you can." I pushed my back to Fayeth's fighting together was our best option.

Fayeth stomped on the ground, roots growing out of her calves and connecting to the ground before she withdrew her spear and crouched with her shield, making herself as small of a target as she could. "Come get me."

Her opponent was far faster, but she wasn't getting knocked around anymore. She weathered the blows as best she could.

Elysara threw her back to ours, finding safety in each other and covering our backs.

Ami's eyes flashed. "I am speed." Rather than try to match her higher-level opponent, the butler kicked off the ground and activated multiple abilities. She shot forward like a bullet.

Their goal wasn't to kill us, and we each had our own ways to protect ourselves. "Ely, don't worry about what they see."

The princess was probably in the worst situation. There was blood dribbling out of the corner of her mouth. "Minotaur, Hydra, Dragonturtle, Gargoyle," she shouted as the creatures overlayed her one after the other.

She swelled, growing scales and a hardened layer over herself before a pair of wings snapped over her and she crouched as she turned to stone. Her opponent stopped after their blade skittered off the stone wings.

Elysara came out of the crouch, with a heavy swing of her trident. She was far slower, but it seemed much more durable.

I stared back at my own opponent, the wounds on my leg closing as the hydra form's healing ability kicked in. Listening to my own advice, I entered a defensive posture and waited. With each of us in the adrel covering for one another, it was not my style of fighting. Yet, it was the best thing for all three of us.

Their blades came quickly. I stopped trying to block each hit and instead took on the ones that I was able to anticipate, blocking and dodging where I could.

Cuts opened up along my arm and chest, but I was avoiding over half of the attacks and managing to decrease the damage of the actual hits to shallower cuts.

The three of us in the adrel were holding out together, each of us suffering from blows, but by putting our backs together we had prevented the agility based fighters from out maneuvering us.

I had to chug mana potions to keep on my feet with these abilities active, but it was worth it to protect the two behind me.

"Hurry up!" Rikter shouted and hit Tish with an ability to knock her back against the dungeon entrance. "We need the hostages."

In Tish's moment of being blown away, he reappeared next to Elysara and grabbed her by the collar before slamming her against the ground. He stunned the princess before dragging her up and holding her like a bad kitten.

His attack had left her limp and broke our defensive formation.

"Unhand her." Tish leveled her sword at their people's eighth strongest adventurer.

"We are leaving." Rikter moved towards the entrance, taking Elysara with him.

My opponent tried to break off from me and rush towards Rikter. Tish tried to stop him, but he used Ely like a shield. And he was effective. Tish couldn't risk her attack injuring the princess.

A thunderous boom sounded behind us as someone landed hard enough to send dirt and grass exploding everywhere.

Miriam stood up amid the crater in front of the entrance with a casual stance. "Sorry, dearie, but you are going to have to give my employer back." She beckoned at Rikter.

I let out a sigh of relief, that meant that Neldra and the others weren't far behind. We had held out long enough.

Rikter took a step back, using Ely as a shield. He suddenly looked far less sure of himself. His entire team had paused their rush towards the entrance with Miriam's appearance.

"Twenty Million for you to step aside," Rikter spoke quickly.

"Alright, hand it over." Miriam held out her hand with a beckoning gesture.

"Miriam!" Tish shouted angrily.

"I don't have it on me. Bu—"

Miriam shot forward like a cannonball. "Sorry. No deals on credit!"

Rikter threw himself back and met her attack with his blade, using it to make more space between him and the monstrous Censor.

I surged forward for my own opponent. They were a higher level, but I could stall them for the moment that Tish needed. They couldn't turn and run with me right on top of them.

Sure enough, with Rikter occupied, Tish appeared behind my target a few heartbeats later. Her blade had no mercy as it severed both of their legs in a single flash before she disappeared again.

I panted and released the abilities I was holding before my mana dipped dangerously low. My wounds were catching up to me as I staggered.

"Fayeth." I rushed to her side. She had been beaten black and blue and was standing from sheer willpower alone.

But she was still connected to her roots. Holding her upright, I could keep her connected to the roots working to heal her.

Neldra appeared next, moving behind Rikter as he tried to escape with Elysara. One by one, the rest of the Censors joined the fight. One stopped by us and held out a hand, enveloping both of us in a golden light as they wiped all our injuries away like chalk on a chalkboard.

"Ami led one of them on a chase," I reported as soon as I was strong enough to speak.

She nodded. "She's fine. We caught them by the second floor stairs."

I let out a sigh of relief and glanced back towards the main fight. Rikter had his blade to Elysara's head and was shouting at them.

"Get over there and make sure that Ely survives," I told her and pulled Fayeth out of her roots, still holding her close.

"That was close," Fayeth grunted and despite the healing, let me support her weight. "But I'm healed."

"Yeah, but that was exhausting. At least let us lean on each other," I encouraged her knowing that even if she was healed, getting beat like that took a toll on you.

My Adrel didn't argue, shifting her weight onto me as we walked forward to get a better view of what was happening with Ely. Neither of us could walk away while she was in danger.

"—too late," Rikter shouted at the surrounding Censors. "The King left this morning to repel the naga. Emperor Selmia now sits on the throne."

My approach was noticed by Tish, who had switched her sword back to her dominant hand after being healed.

"Seems that there were more supporters of Selmia than we expected. With both of us and the King away, they revolted and now hold the palace." Tish rubbed at her brow, catching us up.

"Do you—" I started to ask.

"No, Ken. This is above your level," Tish cut me off. "Besides, the princess is perfectly safe. The healer on hand can bring her back no matter what Rikter does."

I let out a sigh of relief. They had this under control.

"Rikter, put her down." Neldra was standing. She seemed far more relaxed than I would have expected of the situation. "Miriam will put you down, regardless. I'd just rather not see Lady Rendral's insides before our healer does her job. Elysara is walking out of here. You are not."

"So what? You all already lost," Rikter growled. "I'm trying to make that clear to you. Put down your weapons and maybe Emperor Selmia will spare you or let you join his son's Censors."

One Censor spat on the ground. "We'd all kill him and hide his body rather than serve him. Lady Rendral is our only charge."

The group that had encircled Rikter all slammed a single fist to their chest, except Miriam who looked like a beast ready to pounce.

"You are fools, all of you." Rikter continued to hold his oversized blade against Elysara. "You've lost. Even if you save Elysara here, there's no throne for her. Emperor Selmia sits there and has taken full control of the palace. You would have to slaughter all of your own people in order to stop him."

"So?" Miriam grinned. "I have no problem with that as long as I get paid."

"You'll cut off all resources going to the King." Rikter's mustache was quivering. "You slaughter your way to the throne, and you'll lose enough people that you'll cut the supply lines to Duke Rendral."

I snorted at him already changing everyone's titles.

Elysara shifted enough that it was clear she was awake. "Destroy him." Her expression was hard. She knew what those words meant for herself.

Miriam didn't hesitate. She was next to Rikter in a flash with an explosive punch that mangled Elysara and sent her flying while throwing Rikter onto his back.

The healer was on Elysara in an instant, golden light was fixing her arms and putting her back to rights as I rushed up to comfort her.

The circle of Royal Censors closed in to keep Elysara out of the fight as Miriam went all out on Rikter, shaking the ground with each punch as she drove him into the dirt.

A great flash of an ability met with the smoke of Miriam's own abilities, sending out great shockwaves. But the impact of the battle was all contained by the circle of Censors.

I picked up Elysara and cradled her in my arms.

"Fine," she groaned and peeked out of her eyes. "Don't want to experience that again. Would much prefer another drunk Nekorian tattoo session than that."

I snorted, she was well enough to make a joke.

The healer stood over us, shifting her focus to the fight. "The problem with adventurers when they get that high level is that sometimes keeping them from running away is harder than actually killing them."

I nodded. "Anyone who has survived that far into the dungeon is full of tricks."

Miriam kept going at Rikter. She expanded her hands, filling a stack of gold coins between them before she pressed them into her right hand, which immediately glowed like it held a sun inside of it.

Her next attack was like there was a bomb going off as she punched. Rikter's massive sword shattered before the rough Censor sent him flying upwards to smash against the ceiling of the first dungeon floor.

He stuck there for a moment, and Miriam appeared before him before her fists blurred, each one shaking the roof and making chunks of stone fall down all over the floor.

"Sometimes you need a woman like her. Just one in any organization." Elysara watched and leaned on me. "Someone who's willing to crush someone under heel. Not a whole organization of such people, but just one slightly unhinged woman you can let off their leash from time to time."

Miriam finished up her whaling on Rikter, who was now deeply embedded into the ceiling, before spinning and activating an ability to smash him back down into the ground.

There was a sense of finality with that last blow, and Miriam floated down slowly with a big smile.

"Yes. Best not to have a whole group of people like that," I agreed. "She's enough. The bigger question right now is what are we going to do? Given what Rikter said, it seems that your home is currently under someone else's control."

Elysara frowned. "Neldra, make sure Rikter is dead, and then we need to gather up and strategize."

Neldra nodded and jogged to the crater where Rikter lay to check on him.

"Also, any concerns about Miriam taking payment and bailing on us?" I glanced warily at the elf as she finished floating down.

"I think it was just an act," Fayeth added. "Even if he could have paid her more, I don't think she would have worked for Rikter."

I grunted, not so sure. But I had to give her credit. She had saved us all, even with her 'gold-plated morals'.

CHAPTER 27

Crimson breezed through the dungeon out to the Nagato Clan Estate, stopping in the inner courtyard.

"I saw that, you stinky rabbit! Come back here!" The old man shouted.

Bun-bun shot out of Hemi's garden with a carrot in his mouth. He was hurrying, but not quickly enough. Ken's grandfather was chasing after Bun-bun, his sword out and flashing, ready to sever the rabbit's fluffy little head.

But he paused at the last second and sheathed his sword, stopping in front of Crimson with a goofy look on his face. "Hah! You're back! Between you and me, you are the best granddaughter." He gave her a conspiratorial wink.

Crimson couldn't help but smile. She'd been so lonely in the naga's territory with nobody to talk to. Something about returning to the estate felt like returning home.

"Aww. I'm just a filial granddaughter." She did a slight bow, falling into the role. "But I'm afraid I'm going to need to cut to the chase and find Ken."

"Crimson?!" Charlotte bounded over.

The girl somehow looked older after just a month. Some of the shyness had been filed away, as if by a course stone. It still existed, but it was backed by a stronger woman.

Crimson activated [Eyes of Wisdom] and saw that Charlotte was now level twenty-one, and her stamina, mana and magic had gone through some serious improvements.

To raise her stamina like that in such a short time, her students might have pushed themselves harder than she would have in her absence.

"Hello, Charlotte." Crimson paused and then moved forward to wrap an arm around her before stepping back. "I just got back and am looking for Ken." She got to the point.

"Neldra took him away for his safety," Charlotte answered quickly. "After the Harem Queen tried to catch him, that is. She's here by the way. The Harem Queen."

"She joined the Silver Fangs?" Crimson asked incredulously.

"No. Helen did and refused to go home with her, so she's lurking about trying to train her daughter." Charlotte pointed off in a direction.

The cute druid had certainly hardened herself to so brazenly point Crimson in the direction of Ken's harasser.

Even Grandpa was chuckling. "Well, remember not to destroy everything."

Crimson, now with her CID back, pulled out a heavy chain. "Oh. I'm just going to go play with her." She crouched before shooting over the roofline.

***

Charlotte started running to catch up with Crimson, who had charged off.

"Bun-bun. Growth!" she shouted, and the rabbit shot out from under a bush he'd been hiding in and turned into the size of a small horse, still nibbling on a carrot.

Charlotte threw herself onto his back in a smooth motion.

"There you were, you long-eared rat!" Grandpa shouted.

"Sorry, Grandpa! I need him for now." Charlotte clung onto Bun-bun as he shot around several buildings before clearing the wall between the inner and central courtyards.

She passed by a group of Silver Fangs coming back from the dungeon. Des was among them. "Des! Crimson is back and going for the Harem Queen." She slowed Bun-bun down for just a second.

The purple-haired woman whipped her hands down, and with a blast of magic, shot herself over to catch up to Charlotte, flipping and landing on Bun-bun. "Go. I want to see this!"

While Charlotte had been doing intensive training with her mother, Des had been off for a few weeks with her own parents, having come back with a little more devilishness to her looks.

Though Charlotte didn't think it possible, Des had become even more lovely. There was something about staring into Des' eyes now, though. They made many people uncomfortable, but they were mesmerizing to Charlotte.

"If she's back, that means that she's going to go get Ken and Fayeth, right?" Des asked, excitement filling her voice.

"Dunno. We spoke for less than a minute before I told her the Harem Queen was here."

Before Charlotte could say more, there was a sharp cracking noise and then a very feminine scream.

"Hurry, Bun-bun, or I won't hide you next time you steal a carrot!" Des flicked the rabbit's side, and he responded, swallowing the current carrot whole and bounding forward faster.

Helen's front door was blown in and there was screaming inside.

"Stop." Charlotte pulled at Bun-bun's fur, and the rabbit slid sideways, to a quick stop.

Des started laughing behind her.

Crimson dropped a man to the side and was finishing up using a heavy anchor chain to tie up Helen's mother.

Charlotte let out a soft whistle. "That was fast. Really puts Crimson in perspective."

"I know. The Harem Queen is a bitch, but she's strong as hell." Des watched as Crimson strung up the Harem Queen in the doorway.

Throughout the entire event, Crimson was whistling a small tune to herself. "You went after my protégé. There has to be a punishment or it'll keep happening. Right?"

The Harem Queen said something, and Crimson slapped a few teeth out.

"Wrong answer." Crimson yanked on the chains and hoisted the buxom redhead in front of the doorway. "Okay, I'll let you know that the President of the UG already offered me a ton to not kill you. So, congratulations, you get to live. But I need to make you pay..." Crimson tapped her foot as she pondered her new masterpiece.

"You fucking bitch. One of these days, I'll be stronger than you, and then you'll regret this!" The Harem Queen squawked and struggled against the chains.

Crimson laughed, waving away the comment as she continued to ponder what she should do next.

Charlotte watched it all play out and realized that Crimson was antagonizing the Harem Queen on purpose. There was some hidden bitterness there. But there was also a little relief.

"You should make her give up some of her charming skills," Des shouted over Charlotte's shoulders. "Think of how Ken would love them?"

Crimson's eyes went wide. "Yeah. Des has a really good point." She looked back at the two on the rabbit with glowing blue eyes. "You two have done remarkably well. Seems that you got some assistance without me being here. So, you get bonus points. Okay, both of you come here. It appears that I'm going to have to settle a few things before I go get Ken. Harem Queen, these two are part of Ken's harem and want to raid your skillbooks, as well as get some copies of the ones you've used in the past."

Crimson shook the chains until the Harem Queen got dizzy. "But first, a little punishment." She pulled the Harem Queen down and stepped down on the woman's thigh with one of her heels.

***

"So." Elysara and the rest of our group sat down in the dungeon. "What did you find?"

One censor had just returned from a probe of the palace.

"The place is orderly. Too orderly if you ask me." The Censor's face shifted back to the one she had left with and she swapped herself out from a servant's uniform with Selmia's tabard to the Royal Censor armor. She moved quickly, like she was trying to scrub filth off herself.

"He's fully seated in the throne, isn't he? This was too quick to not have been in the works for quite some time." Elysara held her chin. "Meaning that this was going to happen sooner or later whenever the chance came." She shook her head. "My father has been far too lenient with them." There was a dark anger lurking underneath her expression.

Not that I blamed her. These people had started an internal fight while her father was off fighting for their people and she had been returning people they had enslaved.

"Good. So we can rush in, crush them all, and then wash the palace floors afterwards. I have a great recipe to remove blood from wood flooring. Just a little baking soda and vinegar is all we'll need... well probably a lot of it if we are honest." Miriam chuckled darkly to herself.

"I'd rather not have to replace everyone. There are probably many of them that are just going with the tide to survive. And we are seeing increased forces on the naga side." Elysara rolled her eyes. "If we rush in and fight, we'd have to disable as many as we could."

Miriam let out a huff. "Whatever, as long as I'm getting paid."

"I noticed that there were more high-level elves than I expected," the Censor that went to scout reported. "A lot more than I'd expect from the political bloc, especially after your father went to war."

I pressed my eyes together. "Either they were hidden or they refused to help your father?" They had been hiding Miriam under

Galia, there could be other places like that spread across the cities that the bloc controlled. That meant that the measure of their strength was hidden for now.

"Only more reason to preserve what strength we have. Hell, I'd maroon them between our people and the oncoming naga as punishment. At least they'd be valuable there." Elysara's expression was one of a brutal ruler at the moment.

"How deep inside were you able to go?" Neldra asked.

"Not as deep as I'd like." The reporting Censor clicked her tongue. "I can't hide my level, and they were scanning people. Lower levels were being admitted without a problem into the main building of the palace."

I glanced at Elysara. We were in harmony, and she knew exactly where my mind was going.

"No," Neldra refused, seeing the two of us.

"It's not a bad option," Fayeth suggested.

"For those of us that aren't Adrel with you, can you spell it out?" Tish asked.

Elysara looked to me to explain.

"Lower levels aren't being held back. That means I could sneak in and maybe do some damage. Honestly, it sounds like we might get that chance to go after those of our generation." I glanced meaningfully at Elysara. "At the very least, it would make a wonderful distraction. That's what you all need, right? A distraction? Then you all spearhead straight for the throne, kill Duke Selmia, plant Elysara there, and watch as everyone folds. Like you said Ely, a lot of these people are just doing their job regardless of who's in charge."

"The snake still twitches after you cut the head off," Ami spoke for the first time.

I nodded. "That's true. There will probably be some holdouts that still try to fight this. But it doesn't mean this approach is wrong. We need to move quickly. It's already late enough into the evening that this is our chance."

"Speed matters," Neldra grudgingly agreed with me. "The longer we wait, the more entrenched Duke Selmia becomes. And the greater the risk to your father, Lady."

Elysara nibbled at her lip while she thought.

"Ken is very capable," Tish threw in.

"Of course he is. But it's risky. I have reason to worry about the plan and consider options, especially because I am going with him," Elysara spoke casually, as if she hadn't just said a statement that made every single Censors' focus turn laser focused on her.

"No, you aren't," Neldra snapped.

Elysara slowly lifted an eyebrow at Neldra's tone. "Want to try that again?"

Neldra crossed her arms, and there was almost a physical tension between the two of them. "You have no training or skills for this. It is best to leave it to Ken and who he brings with him."

"He's my Adrel. I'm going with him. We'll pick out an appropriate set of monsters to use," Elysara shot back. "We are in harmony. Even if I don't have the skills, I can pick up what he wants me to do easily."

"You need to walk silently. That is not one of your best skill sets when you are shifted," Neldra was almost yelling.

Elysara narrowed her eyes. "When people talk of this in the future, they'll either say that I sat back and had my people handle it, or they'll cheer and clap for me knowing that I stepped forward when the station demanded it."

"We could lie," Miriam added, which earned a very 'unhelpful' glare from Elysara.

"Ken, what do you think?" Neldra turned to me. "She'll be an inconvenience for you on this mission, won't she?"

"Not at all." I was already thinking, planning out the operation. "She can wear a uniform, right?" I could leave her behind, but we would be stronger together. More than once, I had tried to go alone and every time I came to realize that running off on my own wasn't the answer.

Neldra scowled at me, but Elysara jumped to my side and gave me a big hug.

"Don't worry. I'll follow your and Fayeth's leads. Then we'll kill those bastards." Elysara was all smiles.

Neldra's jaw flexed. "We go through together. We will silence anyone around the dungeon entrance. Then, Lyn, you are going to go as far as you can with them and stay close at hand if something happens. You relay to me and kill everyone between you and Lady Rendral."

Elysara pouted. "Neldra, you—"

Neldra reached forward, grabbing Elysara by the point of her ear and pulling. "Don't you sass me. Your Auntie is looking out for you."

"Yes, Auntie," Elysara parroted quickly.

"Good girl. Now, get ready. We don't have time to waste. We will begin the plan as soon as possible." Neldra winked and stepped up to the dungeon exit along with several of the Censors.

I turned to Elysara. "Chances are that they'll be staying in the Royal Quarters, so you'll need to be our guide."

"Leave it to me." Elysara thumped her chest. "What sort of monsters should I take on?"

I thought for a second. "You need to still look Elven, so hiding anything secondary is good. After that, speed is king, followed by anything you have to blend in better. You have that servant uniform from before, and I hope you have several tabards from your own family."

She rolled her eyes and threw an extra tabard at me. "Of course I do. Now, get dressed so we can go. You too, Fay-fay and Ami." She threw out two more tabards.

Ami looked at the material with a wrinkled nose, but she got dressed back into servant attire the same as the rest of us. It wasn't anything fancy. It seemed made to be as plain as possible.

Elysara finished, and two humanoid forms melded into her.

I raised an eyebrow in question.

"Vampire," Elysara answered before a spaded tail flicked out the back of her dress and pretended to be a belt. "And demon."

I nodded. Only once she started talking did I realize her canines were a little extra long and her skin might be a shade or two paler. "I really should have gotten a better list of all of them before I used Absorb on you the other night."

"We'll change it up a few times before you leave." She winked. The beautiful woman wasn't letting up just because we'd harmonized.

I realized she was just that forward, and I would not ask her to stop. It was kind of fun being desired so much. "Let's go. Keep the chatter to a minimum, even if I do love to hear you talk."

The smile I got in return was worth the flattery.

"Alright. Lyn, go through. Clear the room. We are going to set up." Neldra walked over, spotting that we were ready.

Lyn had changed her face again. This time, she'd changed it to Rikter's and put on clothes similar to the other elf before moving through. She wasn't the right level, which would cause questions at any of the checkpoints where they scanned for level, but the disguise could probably move through the palace with ease.

We waited only a few seconds before Neldra led a charge through the dungeon exit. The room leading to the dungeon only had one way out.

Neldra waved, and one Censor moved to position themself behind the door while the rest of them moved to be less obvious should someone enter.

"It's getting late." Neldra held up her CID. "They might be up celebrating, or they might be in bed. Move quickly."

I waved Elysara forward and pulled out some cloth from my CID and pretended to carry it. "Let's go." It was time to play the part of a servant following Rikter.

Elysara gave Neldra one last smile before hurrying to lead us.

"Look forward. You know where you are going. Go with a purpose," I whispered to Elysara.

Ami and Fayeth were doing just fine, but they'd also had some training from my grandparents.

Lyn walked in the back of our group wearing Rikter's face and that ugly mustache. "Can't you all hurry up?" she grunted just before an intersection, playing the part of a surly elf to perfection.

We passed by a patrol a moment later. The group flashed Rikter a glance and then ducked their head and kept moving.

Even if Elysara wasn't actually under threat, she still moved faster with Lyn's words.

"Thank you," I whispered.

"Of course, that's why I'm here." Lyn gave me a smile that looked more like a grimace. "Small things like that can get you to avoid questions. Stay busy."

"Left," Elysara whispered, turning down one hall and heading up the stairs. "We just need to get past the safety curtain."

"Safety curtain?" I asked.

"Royal Quarters have one entrance and exit. Unless you count the windows. There's a curtain made to keep intruders out. I figure we get in there, drop it, and then we can run amok in the Royal Quarters. I'm going to kill anyone who stole my room," Elysara spoke with a vengeful tone.

I chuckled. "Is the room pink and fluffy?"

"No, it's quite stately," Lyn answered. "She is a princess."

I rolled my eyes, and we hastened through the halls, passing several groups that were also moving about the palace while chatting. Our conversation helped us blend in. We kept the tone light and the topic benign as we moved.

"Right and then..." Elysara dragged the word out as we rounded the corner to a passage that had two guards at the end.

They were checking two servants that were entering ahead of us.

Only two of them, that might change things. "Can you take them?" I asked Lyn. "Replace them with yourself?"

She paused, reconsidering the new plan. "Maybe. Can you stop one from shouting?"

If we replaced the guards, pulling down that curtain and having Lyn outside turning anyone away would buy us far more time.

The real question then, was if it would benefit us to take Lyn with us into the royal quarters. That was a question for after though.

"Left," I indicated my target.

Lyn nodded and picked up an extra swagger to her stride, looking much like the cocky Rikter. "Aye." She nodded at the two guards as we approached.

"Sorry, please halt for us to check your group over." The guard on the right held his hand up for us to stop.

"Split up." The woman on the left motioned for my group to step up.

Elysara and Fayeth went first with no problem.

Lyn gave me a glance, and I knew what was about to happen. I jumped into the guard on the left, grabbing her mouth with one hand and trying to flip myself around onto her back.

Unfortunately, she was stronger than me and reacted quickly, slamming me against the wall hard enough to make my bones creak.

"Charm," I wheezed.

The pink heart hit her in the face, and there was just the briefest moment of disorientation before her scowl returned.

Fayeth and Elysara jumped on her back with me, wrapping their arms around the woman's throat and squeezing with all of their strength to keep her quiet.

Lyn moved quickly towards her target, and her dagger buried itself in the guard's side, stunning the guard for a moment as Lyn then pushed something in the woman's open mouth. The next moment, the pommel of her dagger smashed into the woman's temple twice.

The guard slumped to the floor unconscious.

Fayeth and Elysara coughed as we lowered the other guard to the ground after she'd passed out.

"Good job." Lyn picked up both guards and dragged their bodies just inside. "They might survive. Didn't want to make too much blood. But they won't be awake for a while."

I thought about slitting their throats for safety, but I trusted Lyn. "Okay. Post up here?"

She hesitated. "It might be best for me to join you in there."

I thought about it, "No. Stay here and turn anyone away. We'll scout the place out and do what damage we can. If we need you, we'll send Ami back."

Lyn hesitated for only a second to check with Elysara before she nodded and quickly donned armor that looked much more like a guard's. "Drop the curtain," she told Elysara. "I'll buy you as much time as I can."

Eventually that time would run out as we launched our distraction, but we'd have to sweep the place before we could do that safely.

CHAPTER 28

Elysara quickly worked with the doorway until panels of wood came down from the top, but on the backside of the panels were irregular shafts that ran horizontally across the back with strange chains holding them all together.

It took me a second to realize what they were. "High level spears?"

"Yeah. They take hits from the strongest of adventurers and monsters. They've been modified by smiths, but why craft something else when they already have incredible durability." She moved down to the ground and locked the curtain in place. "Won't completely stop a determined intruder, but the goal was always to slow them down rather than stop them entirely."

I glanced at her in a new light. She probably had a checklist in her mind somewhere and was clearly drilled on what to do in the event of an intruder.

"Okay, let's go scout this place out and kill some people. The Royal Quarters are bigger than they need to be. There are fifteen rooms." Elysara moved to the side and started off at a soft jog, trying to keep her feet silent.

"Ami, scout ahead, Camouflage and Silent Paws," I ordered.

The butler needed no excuse to use her abilities and speed up ahead of us. She moved quickly, and her [Camouflage] struggled to keep her blended in, a slight flickering of her shape as she moved.

Ami dropped her [Camouflage] ahead and motioned at the room. She held up two fingers and then twirled them before using [Camouflage] again and moving on.

I knew the signal well enough and rounded the door for that room, picking out the two targets instantly and rushing towards them. Fayeth was behind me, but Elysara was faster and zipped around her, reaching her target seconds after me.

There was a slight squeak of surprise from my maid before I knocked her out.

"Tie them up and put them in the closet." I pulled out some flexible metal zip ties and handed them to Elysara before giving her some cloth to gag them.

"I feel bad tying them up."

It was cute that she was reluctant, but it needed to be done.

"Can't risk it." Fayeth had stopped and was now keeping watch. "We don't have time to question them and learn their loyalties. But them getting the room ready means there are more people supposed to sleep in this wing. We need to hurry before they come and find they can't get in."

"I'd guess some of the bloc is staying up, waiting for Rikter's good news," I added. "That, or they are celebrating."

We left the room, and Ami motioned to the next room. She lifted two fingers and then she made a swift x by slashing in the air twice.

I nodded, and she moved along.

"Kill?" Elysara asked quietly, trepidation entering her voice.

"Yes." I heard them before I could see them.

The wet slapping of flesh made their activity quite obvious.

"—take it, bitch," a male voice grunted as a woman let out muffled moans.

"But she's..." Elysara tried to argue.

I pointed in the door as we got there. Guards' armor was piled up at the foot of the bed. He might be rough with her, but she was on his side.

Two daggers appeared in my hands and I nodded to Fayeth. She pushed the door open slowly, and I prowled in with [Camouflage] active. Elysara was right behind me, but she remained by the door.

The two were going at it so hard, that they hadn't even noticed us enter. Fayeth pulled the door closed with a soft click.

The noise was a foreign enough sound that the woman jerked. "What was that?"

Elysara came around the other side of the bed, the butt of her trident connecting with the man's head and knocking him off the woman. I moved forward, my dagger plunging twice into the woman's chest as I covered her mouth with the other hand.

She let out a muffled yell and caught my dagger before I could plunge it down again in a vise grip that slowly inched me away, despite me having the leverage.

Fayeth came around my side, a heavy blade in her hand, swinging down and cutting deep into her neck. The woman gurgled on her own blood as it rapidly drained from her.

I glanced at the man and hissed at Elysara, "Kill him." There would be a problem if she was hesitant to kill.

"He's a duke. He might have information," she shot back.

I tongued the inside of my cheek for a second before nodding. "Be ready for him to scream."

She nodded and pulled out a healing potion before pouring it down his throat. The second he blinked his eyes open, Elysara activated an ability.

She'd never looked so beautiful, so perfect before. I wanted to push her down and worship her.

Elysara flashed me a smile before focusing back at the young duke in her hands. "Dear, are you okay?"

"I am now," he answered in a half-dazed, half dream-like tone, a big smile blooming on his face.

Elysara giggled and blushed. "I need you to tell me some things."

"Anything." He looked like a love-struck fool.

I couldn't blame him. Elysara was drop-dead gorgeous before she activated whatever magnetic effect she had at the moment. My eyes couldn't help but rove over her, wanting to devour and remember every inch.

"Where is everyone? Who's staying here?" Elysara asked with a sweet tone.

A little jealousy was building in me as she talked to him in such a sweet, seductive tone. I was feeling incredibly possessive of her at the moment. Even though I knew it was part of the ability drawing me.

"I'll tell you if you marry me," the fool spoke with a love-struck stupor.

"Aww. That's so sweet. But we haven't even had a conversation yet. I just wanted to know who's all staying in the Royal Quarters with a big man like you? Any young duchesses that I have to worry about?" Elysara batted her lashes, and her eyes were rimmed with a little pink glow.

"None of them compare to you. We kicked everyone out. The leaders are all here in the Royal Quarters. We won—we'll all rule," he answered with a big grin.

Elysara struggled to keep her smile soft, but I could see just how much she wanted to put a knife in the man. "What about the Empress?"

"Imprisoned with the rest of those wastes. The Emperor has abandoned the throne and they wouldn't listen," the man scoffed.

Even I wanted to end him now.

"What about the new Emperor and his men?" Elysara's tone was like silken honey.

"Celebrating. A few of us headed back early for some." He cleared his throat and looked towards the woman, his eyes growing wide as he saw her blood.

We all reacted, ready to jump on him as the spell lost its hold.

"I see. Thank you." Elysara grabbed either side of the man's face and then jerked with her adventurer strength.

His neck cracked, and she stood. The aura she was putting out dissipated.

It seemed she wasn't reluctant to kill and had just wanted the information; I had read her wrong earlier.

"Brutal. I've heard of getting your heart broken, but that went all the way up to his neck," Fayeth chuckled, not at all bothered by the brutal deaths of both of them. "You had him on a leash."

Elysara clenched and unclenched her jaw, before casting a glance my way with a burning blush. "Sorry about that."

"No. We should explore how that works. You know, really test it out," I teased.

She stuck her tongue out at me and changed the topic. "Sounds like they really did take over the Royal Quarters to feel high and mighty. Though we need to hurry before more return from his celebration. They won't be the only ones wanting to take a pretty guard to bed."

"We'll work our way through, but we won't be this lucky each time," I warned her, leading her back out into the hall.

Ami was moving back down the hall and made a motion for us to follow. Then she pointed at several rooms before making zero with her pointer finger and thumb.

They were empty.

Instead, she continued down to what felt like the main rooms and pointed, held up three fingers and three slashes.

Elysara licked her lips. "That's my room."

Ami held her hands up for us to halt. She flashed two fingers and made a fist while straightening her back.

Two guards.

There was a rhythm in the room. I could hear a bed smacking the wall.

I frowned at Ami and flashed three fingers with a frown, and then two for the guards, and then two before making a lewd gesture. Ami's shoulders sank, and she shook her head, motioning for me to come by where the seam of the door was to peek through.

What I saw made me clamp my hand over my mouth to stop from laughing.

I'd recognize the younger Duke Selmia anywhere. He was atop Elysara's bed, humping a pillow. Elysara crept up next to me to see as well and let out a snort before she could suppress her laughter.

"What was that?" a voice from the corner of the room, shouted and there was a thud as they swung a mace from their belt. "I'm checking the door."

We were running short on time.

Fayeth pointed to herself, motioned at the doors, and then pointed at me. She motioned deeper into the room before pointing at Elysara and the direction of the other guard.

There were nods all around, and we stepped back from the doors, readying ourselves. This attack was going to be louder than I'd like, but if we could get the young duke, then I'd be happy. It was time for our distraction to go off.

The doors opened up as they came to investigate, and we had no more time to prepare.

Fayeth threw herself forward, her root armor branching out and wrapping around her shoulders. A shield formed on her arm as she rammed into the guard with the full weight of her charge.

The man shouted in surprise, meeting her with a swing of his mace.

Elysara shot in and her trident clashed with an elf holding a staff studded with crystals. "Absorb," she shouted, drawing in before shouting "Spell Mirror" and reversing a barrage of ice shards right back at him.

My job was simple, darting in and tackling the younger Duke, ripping him off the bed and slamming him against the wall.

"None of you move, or I'll kill the pillow fucker." Even with the serious moment, I couldn't help stifling a laugh at the statement.

"Get off me." He struggled, but I had him pinned before pressing a knife against his spine.

"That includes you. Don't talk unless spoken to." I pressed him hard against the wall again. It would be nice to just slit his throat here and now, but those two guards were a problem. I needed to stall them for a moment.

Ami materialized behind the caster and shoved two daggers into his throat before opening it up like a fleshy butterfly.

Good girl.

"They are going to kill us! FIGHT!" the younger duke shouted. There was something extra in his voice that bounced off the wall and slammed into me like a physical force, driving me off of him.

He spun, pulling his pants up with one hand as he now held a sword in the other. "Elysara. I'm so glad that you came to me. Adrat, crush them and get me the princess."

Only now did I glance back at Fayeth. A portion of her root armor was cracked and a third of her shield was missing from her short fight with the remaining guard.

I didn't have to tell my Adrel what I was thinking. We were in harmony, and Elysara's forms rapidly overlayed her. A wreath of flowers wrapped around her and her hands glowed green as she rushed to heal Fayeth.

My focus shifted back to the younger duke.

"You're the human that she wanted to be with? A rat dreaming of the swan." He glared. "Don't worry. Last time I promised I'd marry her and I've come to make good on that."

"At least I'm not so pent up that I go wild on her pillows." I laughed and danced in with my blades.

For a cocky young duke, I knew he was also well trained. He parried me expertly and spun around with a hand that thrust forward with a spell that came out as three expanding rings.

"Absorb." I threw my hand into the rings, draining the spell and reflecting it back on him with "Spell Mirror". The air shook as the sound attack flew back at him, shattering glass on the nightstand and making him wince.

That ability was loud enough that people would come running. We were officially on the clock.

He chuckled once, and then it kept going like he'd lost his damned mind. "You... you have her Absorb?! Princess, tell me you haven't harmonized and soiled yourself with this man." I guess he wasn't paying much attention or was so blind he didn't see anyone but Elysara.

"He's a fantastic lover," Elysara shouted with a laugh before catching Fayeth as she was knocked backwards.

"A really good one," Fayeth grunted in agreement.

The two of them just had to egg him on. Then again, he'd make mistakes when he was angry.

Ami dashed behind the guard, keeping him busy for a moment as the two elves healed back up. The guard quickly realized that Ami was just a distraction and came swinging for the other two again with a strike that blew through the wall.

"You!" Duke Selmia screamed and pierced right through my ears, making me stumble backwards.

Warm blood trickled out of my ears. I needed to stop him from casting whatever ability he was using. Even if I could [Absorb] them, they were so fast that, without warning, I had no time to even get my [Absorb] up.

Pressing him with my blades, I struck out several times in succession before I activated [Hydra]. Scales dotted my skin and my ears rang as they tried to repair themselves.

Duke Selmia kept me at an angle, circling as we fought and focusing on staying at the end of his longsword's range. He was certainly a brawler, and I needed to pull him out of his element and into mine.

[Shadow Ambush]. I melted out of his shadow. "Dark Strike, Mana Burn." I cut him, leaving a wound flickering with blue flames. Rapid slashes scored his back in his moment of disorientation.

He screamed out in pain, once again his voice amplified painfully. I staggered back, my ears were healing themselves, but it was slow. The hit ripped right through me and my balance faltered as my vision swam. It was a truly powerful class for fighting another adventurer.

The other room was filled with loud booms and crashes as the rest of the group fought off the higher-level guard, while also getting the remnants of Duke Selmia's sound-based attacks.

There was no way that someone wasn't trying to bust their way through the protective curtain that Elysara had put down. Even if Lyn was guarding it, our time was limited.

"Metamorphosis." My body swelled, my muscles absorbing my gear and my skin darkening. Shooting forward, I knew I needed to finish the battle soon before guards come to help.

"Sonic Barrier." The air rippled in front of the duke in a semicircle.

I palmed the spell. "Absorb." Even though I tore through the spell quickly, it still robbed my momentum.

"Sonic Slash." The duke was ready. As soon as the barrier disappeared, he exploded from the point he was standing, his sword vibrating so quickly that it was a blur.

A moment later, the sword came crashing into a barrier that appeared in front of me 'Spell Mirror'. [Spell Mirror] even copied something like a barrier spell.

His blade shattered the barrier and the look of surprise on his face was priceless as he came up short, but my fist was more than happy to make up the distance.

My demonic knuckles smashed against his face hard enough to deform it and send him flying back against the wall.

"Shadow Arm." I rushed him, my dark limb stretching out and grabbing hold of the duke. "Mana Burn."

A blue fire spread from the [Shadow Arm] to where it connected to the duke and kept burning. As long as I kept contact with him, I could drain his mana. [Shadow Arm] was far better at keeping contact than many of my other combat skills.

He cut through the arm, and it wavered but stabilized after draining more of my mana. Not giving him time to recover, I charged forward, my long claws forcing him to focus on saving his skin rather than stopping the mana burn.

Yeah, this combination was fantastic, I wondered briefly if Elysara and Neldra thought of this combination when they gave me the spellbook.

With the wall behind him, he had lost his maneuverability and struggled to keep me at a range that his sword would favor. Now that I was up in his face, he was just barely deflecting my claws and more often than not he was forced to sacrifice his forearms and shoulders to save his vitals.

"Absorb." After even our short exchange, I was getting better at reading his movements. I could predict what he would try next.

His mouth opened up and my [Absorb] ripped the sonic attack right out of his throat only to hurl it back on him with [Spell Mirror], hammering him into the wall once again.

I pinned his sword arm, sinking my claws into it and holding him there while my other arm cocked back and hammered down on his chest until it caved in and blood gushed out of his mouth.

"Dark Strike." My clawed hands made one final swish and his head rolled along the floor before his body slumped.

I stumbled back, panting as I let go of [Metamorphosis]. I held on to [Hydra], loving the self-healing. Now I understood why Neldra said I needed something like it, eventually.

Brawling like this wasn't ideal, and I'd paid the price.

My own blood from the fight dribbled down on the duke, sizzling at his boots. As I caught my breath, a crash from the room next door reminded me that the battle wasn't over.

Taking off, I rushed through the hole in the wall to see the three ladies working in nearly perfect concert. Fayeth was holding on, with Elysara backing her up and providing healing. Ami was doing all she could to distract and disable their opponent.

Yet, he still soldiered on, smashing through Fayeth's defenses.

I liked the combination that I had used with the duke, so I used it again. "Shadow Arm. Mana Burn." I attached the shadow limb to his back, breathing blue fire down it and burning away at his mana.

It was a battle of mana at that point between us, and I needed to make sure he ran out of steam first.

My attack got his attention, and he turned, swinging his mace at the same time. I blocked with both of my blades, letting his force drive me back rather than try to take it all.

"Fuck. He's strong," I grunted. "Why does he have to be a tank?"

"But slow." Ami appeared behind him and cut twice at exposures in the joints of his armor.

Fayeth rammed into him with her shield, trying to topple the guard.

Even with the momentum of his spin, the elf held himself up and just switched to a backhanded swing that glowed briefly before it sped up and around Fayeth's shield to catch her in the shoulder.

She went flying backwards as Elysara caught her and infused her with green glowing magic. Ami's blades raced over his armor, clanging as they tried to find purchase in the gaps.

"Brats!" He wobbled and his eyes blinked as my [Mana Burn] flickered out.

I stepped in and grabbed the arm holding the mace, shoving my hip against his. Then I used his own strength to lift him off the ground and slam him back down. Sometimes simple martial arts was the solution rather than abilities. "Mana Burn."

It lit up for a moment before burning out again as he ran out of mana again. His eyes had trouble focusing.

Elysara, now sporting her badass horns, a big tail, and heavy metal plates on her shoulders, body-slammed herself on top of him. "Kill him. I'll hold him down!"

Fayeth came running over with a spear over her head. She screamed and let out her frustration in a savage blow to his head.

Ami let out a whistle and moved to the joints in his armored legs, punching her daggers between them and spilling out crimson blood with each thrust.

I stepped up and used [Mana Burn] again to keep him weak while my other hand sought the soft part of his armor at his armpit and shoved my dagger as deep as it would go before I twisted and tore it back out.

Life flooded from his eyes in short order after a few more whacks from Fayeth.

"Well. We got him." Fayeth wiped at her brow as a loud crash preceded the pounding of feet into the Royal Quarters.

"That doesn't sound good." Elysara shrank back to her normal size, but the vampire fangs still protruded from her mouth as she spoke.

CHAPTER 29

G uards poured into the Royal Quarters. Dozens of elves, all of which were likely level fifty or higher, filled the hallway and blocked every room. Shouting filled the hall as they reported up and down the column.

"What do we do?" Fayeth looked to me, then to Elysara.

"I think we get caught," Elysara answered, her head held high. "Even if we jumped out the window, there's no way that we can get away from all of these guards. Hopefully, Neldra and Miriam did their part and we'll be released once everything is sorted out."

I didn't disagree with her as the guards came pouring in, our odds of making it out of here dwindles and starting a fight would not end well for any of us.

Sometimes, you followed the plan. I put my daggers away and put my hands up.

There were already multiple guards filling the doorway to the room. One lifted her hand, and the window was instantly encased in ice.

"Healers! Here. Get in here and start reviving my son!" came shouts from the room next door.

I could hear his heavy breathing as an older elf resembling the dead younger duke stalked into the room.

My heart fell into my stomach, he should be dead. Not good.

His eyes were full of rage as he looked upon us. "Send word down the line and to those pesky Royal Censors. We have Lady Rendral, and we won't be too kind if they continue." He moved across the room in a single stride and grabbed Elysara by the throat before backhanding me and sending me flying into the foot of the bed.

"Sir. Your son was revived. He's a little disoriented, but fine." An elf poked his head through.

The older Duke let out a sigh, and some of the fire left his eyes as he held Elysara aloft. "Gather them, and we'll head to the throne room where several decrees will need to be made."

"I won't—" Elysara choked mid-sentence as he squeezed harder.

"You will do exactly as I say, and I'll be entirely clear here. You will marry my son, or you will marry me." The duke held her tightly and pulled her along as the guards filled in around me, Fayeth and Ami, keeping us moving.

Her face wrinkled at the prospect.

The Duke's eyes were darting about as he thought.

"You see. Nothing would make me happier than for you to marry into my family, publicly, before your father returns. But rest assured, he'll allow it to happen too. Because our people are far too battered to go to war with each other, when he could just hand you away and solve it all." The Duke sneered and shook his head. "This is what is best for our people to come together under one banner and push back the naga."

I snorted, he was the one causing the division, bold words.

"I'll ne—" Elysara was cut off again, this time with a slap to her face.

I wanted to jump forward and shank the duke. My killing intent spilled out, and a guard jabbed me with a spear in warning.

"You'll do exactly what I want." The duke held her tightly, and we were all led out of the Royal Quarter to the throne room.

The procession was slow with dozens of guards packing around us. Yet, I was separated from Elysara who the Duke kept at his side.

"He survived." I hissed to Fayeth.

She shook her head. "We'll figure this out."

Just outside of the room, there was a ring of dead bodies and several high-level guards still fighting. Neldra was alive, along with the rest of the Royal Censors. They were packed together tightly in the hallway and it seemed they had done their half of the plan if it were not for Duke Selmia leading the group.

Plenty of dead, important looking elves in fine clothes lined the hall. Either by luck or some divine miracle it seemed that they hadn't found Duke Selmia with the rest of his political bloc celebrating.

"Lady!" Neldra shouted, her sword drawn and pointed at the mass of guards around us.

"Uh uh." The Duke tutted as he held a knife to Elysara's throat. "Don't even think about it. You might be fast, but I have enough time to kill her. Can your healers get to her while we all fight? You might have killed many of my allies tonight, but that wasn't enough." The Duke gloated while Neldra and the rest of the Censor's slowly lowered their weapons. "Strip them of weapons and armor."

The remaining guards around them rushed in to remove the censors' weapons and CIDs. They were rough with the Royal Censors, yet their eyes spoke of fear.

"Father." The younger duke came out of the crowd behind us with new clothing on. There was a haunted look on his face. "She's not a Trelican. Harmony doesn't matter with her, just that she is obedient. Don't feel terrible about roughing her up."

"Vicious bastard," I muttered.

The younger duke turned to me and sneered. "Thought you won? Too bad. It looks like I won our fight. I'll be the one to marry her as I won."

Elysara chuckled before it split into full on laughter that didn't sound entirely sane.

"What's so funny?" the younger duke snapped.

"He fucking killed you, and you think you won." Elysara laughed even as the older duke hit her hard enough to silence her.

"Heal her," the Duke ordered, and white light washed over Elysara. "There's no escape, not even in death." He shifted his focus to the Censors. "She'll be publicly married to my son in the morning. The victors write history, I think my son won her in a valiant duel." The Duke smiled before he glanced at the hallway and it died on his lips.

Even if he survived tonight, he had lost much of his support. I could only hope it was enough.

The younger duke gave me a vicious smile. "Thought you could steal from the elves? You'll get a front-row seat to this."

"Take them away. Keep everyone separate. I want a dozen guards on each of the Censors. Tonight, no one sleeps." The duke's face split into a large fatherly smile. "I'm so happy to receive a new daughter. Son, you should do your best to make her pregnant as soon as you can. That way we won't need her anymore."

Elysara struggled but received a fist into her stomach for her efforts.

"Son, you should handle your betrothed tonight." The duke handed her off to a high-level guard. "Neldra, will you turn over your blade?"

"I'd rather salt my roots." Neldra spat on the ground in front of her. She was the last Censor with a weapon still in her hand.

"Shame. Miriam, I'll double whatever they were paying you," Duke Selmia said to the Royal Censor.

Her eyes lit up like two giant coins and she slipped out of the Royal Censor ranks and came up to the duke. She put a hand on his chest while she purred. "I knew you were the wealthiest. Happily.

Is there anything this poor lady can do in return?" She clung to him like a lover.

The duke laughed, feeling on top of the world with Miriam's attention. "Take Neldra's weapon."

"Miriam," I growled before a guard hit me across the face.

"I have my morals." She shrugged and stepped up to Neldra, Miriam ripped the sword out of her hand. "You all shouldn't be so brutal with the boy. His master recently came back from battling the naga. She's likely to emerge soon."

The duke snorted. "The famed Crimson? She's not as strong as they all make her seem or she'd be here and none of this would have been a problem. She's just another powerful adventurer. She's not some shadow that lurks in the dark to gobble up bad children. Let's go. Break everyone apart and do not let them out of your sight."

I was pulled away from Fayeth and Ami, dragged off by half a dozen level fifty guards.

"This feels right to you all?" I grumbled to the men keeping hold on me.

My guards were silent, not engaging even as I grumbled a few other comments. Their answer finally came in a rough punch to the gut followed by a healing and another punch.

Message received.

When they got me back to what was going to be my room for the night, I tried a Hail Mary and used [Portal].

It didn't work. Instead, darkness embraced me and sent me to sleep. But at least they couldn't force me to stay awake.

***

"My love." The Younger Duke threw open her bedroom door. "It's time. Let her go, I can handle her."

Elysara jerked her arms out of the guards that had been hauling her around. "Like shit you can." She snorted and put the bed between her and the duke.

"You're going to regret challenging me." The Duke lept over the bed and grabbed her arm to pull her close with puckered lips.

Elysara called on a ram monster, a pair of heavy curled horns sprouted from her hairline before she activated an ability and slammed them into The Duke's face.

There was a solid thwack echoed by the crack of bones in his face.

The Duke screamed and fell back with blood spurting out of a broken nose. "Heal me!" He shouted as he tried to stop the blood from flowing.

Elysara stood there with a smug smile on her face. He wasn't going to fucking touch her.

A guard stepped forward and put her hands on The Duke before green light sprouted from her hand, running through the duke and correcting his nose.

"Do you have any idea the situation you've created? Your Censors slaughtered all of my father's allies. You might think that a good thing, but now there's no one to argue with. He can quickly and swiftly enact anything he wants without debates. You've handed him the Empire on a leaf of The Holy Great Tree. The sooner you realize that it's over and accept your fate the easier I'll make this." The Duke prowled forward with a smug confidence that Elysara was more than happy to shatter.

"Alright. I understand." Elysara slinked forward, doing her best to hide her smile, cocky people were the easiest.

"I knew you'd come around." The Duke was confident and grabbed her hand to pull her close.

A cobra monster came over her and the skin around her neck extended and thinned into what she thought was an ugly hood before she spat venom in his eyes.

He screamed so loud that it threw Elysara back, but she didn't mind.

Instead, she just laughed and let both monster forms fade away as he cried out.

"Someone, fucking heal me you idiots! Why aren't you all preventing this?" The Duke clutched his eyes. The same healer was quick to restore his eyes.

Yet, Elysara could see the fear in them when he looked at her this time. "I have dozens of tricks up my sleeve. Come on, I could go all night." She said the last slowly with faux seduction before she burst into laughter again. There was no way she'd let this man touch her.

Crimson had been seen coming out of the naga's territory. Elysara might have to even go through with the wedding, but if she kept herself and her people alive long enough. Then she could get out of this and keep herself to her adrel.

So, she needed the younger duke to be terrified of her, too terrified to push things tonight.

"You fucking woman." The younger duke scowled.

The healer put a hand on his shoulder. "Maybe it would be best for you to let her come to terms with things tonight and try after the wedding?" The female elf shot Elysara a sad smile.

"She will know me as her husband tomorrow. Maybe after her father writes her telling of his agreement she'll understand her situation. Elysara, I love you, but I won't forget this and you will pay." The Duke threw down that last comment and stormed out shouting at the guards.

Elysara sighed and grabbed a blanket before finding a corner to lean against, she knew she wouldn't sleep tonight. Instead, she'd get comfortable and figure out what to do tomorrow.

***

"Wow, not how I expected to find you." Crimson's voice woke me as she poured a potion down my throat.

I blinked my eyes awake, my mind still tired and tried to rationalize not only where I was, but Crimson's presence. "Crimson, is that you?"

"Oh, you are in a bad sort. How many of these people should I crush for you?" She tilted her head with a smile, picking me up and putting me in a sitting position before pulling out a bag of chips. "Chips?"

"Thank you," I reached inside and grabbed a handful to shove in my mouth. Alright, not a dream. But Crimson is actually sharing her chips, so something is very wrong.

"So, if this is Elven hospitality. Why shouldn't I just, you know, kill everyone?" Crimson looked in the bag and grabbed a chip for herself.

"It was going real well up until tonight." I said, working at my jaw and realizing it didn't feel as stiff as I expected it to be. "There was a coup and as a guest of the princess, I'm here now." I went with the simplest explanation.

"Oooh." Crimson dragged the word out. "Sounds rough."

"There's supposed to be a wedding tomorrow. Shit. Can you check on Elysara for me?" I asked, more concerned with her than myself.

Crimson's eyes glowed blue. "Someone by that name is just fine, she's dozing on the other side of the palace." She popped another chip. "Your wedding, or hers?"

"Hers." I said. "To the people that led the coup."

"But she's yours." Crimson could read the situation, for that I was very thankful. "Got it. So, do we want to fuck things up now, or...?" She hesitated, waiting for my opinion.

I grabbed her and wrapped her in a big hug, pressing my teacher to me. "Thank you for coming. I'm thrilled that you are here."

Crimson tentatively wrapped her arms around me and squeezed gently while breathing deeply, her nose buried in the side of my head. "I'll always come for you Ken. Right now I'm having a little trouble holding things together. All of these elves should die." Red lightning crackled at the edge of my vision.

But that wasn't what I wanted right now. Instead, I pet her head with one hand while holding her to me with the other.

The red lightning disappeared and Crimson scooted closer. "That feels nice." She said, her chips being crushed without a thought as she hugged me tighter and one of her hands wandered down to squeeze my butt.

I just held her for a moment before I kissed her cheek and pulled back.

She had a pout that was one half reluctance to release me, the other half happy for the kiss.

"Hey, you aren't bursting into red lighting." I commented, just now realizing I had been playing with fire.

Crimson beamed at me, her eyes almost uncomfortably fixed on me. "I've had some progress there. But I can tell you about it later."

I shook my head. "No, tell me everything Crimson." I pulled her into my lap and smiled at how she let me. She might be the most terrifying adventurer ever, but with me she was growing softer.

That she wasn't crackling up a storm right now spoke volumes and let me be a little bolder.

I ran my hands over her thighs and seated her firmly in my lap on the floor. "Okay, let's get comfortable, because you have a story to tell and then we need to make a plan for tomorrow."

"Wedding crashing?" Crimson grinned. "Let your enemies throw your own wedding."

I laughed. "Wonderful idea indeed. First, your story. Then my plan."

Crimson pulled out another bag of chips. "Where do I begin? So, I went through the portal and crushed some naga skulls, or I think I did..."

***

I woke up the next morning, not feeling rested at all, but feeling oddly refreshed. Talking to Crimson all night had perked me up in a way nothing else could.

Guards shoved me around, and I got the message, getting off the floor and getting my nicest Elven suits on. I let the silent guards lead me around and out into the hall.

It appeared I wasn't the only one they were preparing. Guards were swarming the palace. More than a few groups had a large number of elves with one of the Royal Censors at the center. It seemed they were going to make a showing of this wedding.

That made me smile. Crimson had left in the early dawn, just enough time for me to get a wink of sleep before they came and got me.

They quickly shuffled me out of the palace only to see blue and red streamers everywhere. A big balcony at the front of the palace was ornately decorated with swooping sheer streamers of white cloth. Flowers and large leaves decorated each column of the balcony. Given that there was less than a day since the wedding was scheduled, a lot of work had happened between then and now. I wondered how happy the staff was with him.

The duke had a big smile on his face, greeting me and several of the Censors being dragged out to watch. Miriam still clung to his side. He was paying attention to every detail.

He saw me and picked me to come pester. "Ah. There you are. So, how does it feel?" The duke had bags under his eyes, but he looked happy. One night of forgoing sleep was a small price to pay for joining the Royal Family.

I didn't speak to him. He wasn't worth my time. I stood quietly, vowing in my head to rip his throat out if I got the opportunity. Chances were, Crimson would turn him into a smear on the ground before I got there.

"Speechless? Yes, I wouldn't want to talk before my Adrel got married away. Last night, she used Absorb, and given that we know she's not the Trelican and you are, it was easy to see." The duke touched his nose with a smirk. "See, that made me think about some things. Your Absorb is a potent tool, one that we could use to share around the Elven royalty. Of course, you'd have to be in harmony with everyone."

I sneered. That would never happen. Besides, there was no point in speaking to a dead man.

"Oh. Feeling like my plan is futile? You'd be surprised. There have been instances of even the strongest people breaking under extreme stress. While harmony can be difficult to achieve, it is still a matter of the mind. The mind can be reformed into whatever you want once broken."

My sneer fell from my face. It would be better for Crimson to keep him alive long enough to regret this.

The Duke leaned back roaring with laughter. "Yes. That's the face I was looking for."

Part of me couldn't understand why he would do what he was doing, but I was realizing that there was a similarity between elves and humans. For some reason, those that rose to power never were satisfied with what they had.

I wasn't sure which came first, the power or the desire to claw for ever more. Yet, they often went hand in hand.

The Duke was clawing for every scrap of power, and even now that he'd made himself Emperor for all of a day, he wanted more power over people, to push them down in a sense of raising himself up.

"Go take your seat." The duke smiled. "You'll get a front row view of the whole affair." He gestured off where seats were lined up all over the lawn in front of the balcony.

I spotted the seats and was already figuring out angles and distances for when it would be my time to make a grand entrance. The duke had no idea what was coming.

Meanwhile, the guards were out in force. Hundreds of them lined the space. And they were likely needed. Neldra was in heavy chains, but she was still a force.

The duke, even with Miriam now on his side, was terrified of the leader of Elysara's Royal Censors.

I would be too if I were him. The way Neldra was staring at him felt like she was trying to kill him with her gaze alone.

"Alright." The duke clapped his hands loudly with a light chuckle. "Let's not waste any time. No need to delay this. Bring the bride and groom out for the world to see."

The celebration had already attracted quite the crowd, and there were hundreds of thousands of elves stacked up on their roofs and all along the street watching. This was going to be a spectacle that they would not soon forget. In fact, I hoped it would go down in the history books.

Elysara was dragged out in a stunning red dress. From how close I was, I could see that there was some blood mixed with the fabric's dye. Based on how the younger duke kept a nice arm's length from her and had fear in his eyes, I could put together the pieces.

I laughed for the first time this morning.

She wasn't one to give up and that would only make what was to come that much sweeter.

Quickly, she found me in the crowd and begged me with her eyes to do something.

I nodded at her and smiled to tell her it would all be okay.

She seemed to buoy up, her shoulders squaring, and she lifted her chin defiantly.

Trumpets blared all around, and people threw leaves into the air. The leaves caught and twirled all around. It would have made a magical scene if it weren't a hostage situation and not a wedding.

"Everyone!" the duke shouted with deafening force. "Today we hold a wedding between Lady Rendral of The Former Royal Family and Prince Selmia of the current Royal Family. We do this to heal our people! Please join us in the celebration of their wedding and of our people's future!"

The crowd gave him a thunderous applause that shook my seat.

A good wedding was always worth celebrating I guessed. It wasn't like the general populace really understood the resentment that Elysara held right now.

But before he could go much further, there was a boom as something exploded at the back of all the seats.

"Oh, a party for me?" Crimson's voice was like water for a man dying in the desert.

"Crimson!" I shouted out, "Make him suffer."

A nearby guard threw a punch straight for my face in response, but it was stopped short.

A red leather-clad hand held the fist. Then red sparks jumped over the arm into the elf, who then exploded in a splatter of red gore that was so powerful it blew back and killed the guards near him.

"Ken!" Crimson squealed and grabbed me, lifting me up and squeezing me. "Oh Ken! Your wedding is so beautiful." Crimson twirled with me.

"What is the meaning of this?" the duke shouted. "Stop her." He pointed down at Crimson.

She tilted her head and playfully glanced at Neldra. "Broken Blade, why is the reception so poor? And why are you in chains?"

Neldra threw her head back and laughed like a madwoman. "These people were going to torture your favorite protégé." She didn't know Crimson already knew the details, just wanted to rile her up and watch the gory fireworks.

There were already murmurs among all the nobility present in front of the balcony, and the murmurs were rippling back through the crowd beyond them.

One word was present on everyone's lips. 'Crimson.'

I chuckled to myself at the horror stories they would come up with after she was done.

"That's no good." Crimson's whip cracked as it uncoiled into a full circle. Suddenly, the wedding was a shower of crimson.

"Let me go. I have someone to save." I pulled out of Crimson's arms and raced towards Elysara.

"Yes. Deal with your own problems. Say 'hi' to the Lady for me." Crimson nodded, and with an errant flick of her wrists, shattered Neldra's chains. "Broken Blade, you should really help warm up the reception for me."

"Miriam!" Neldra shouted, and the woman clinging to Duke Selmia didn't even shift her smile as she broke both of his legs and forced him down to his knees.

Miriam winked at me. "See? I have *some* morals."

"Keep him alive long enough to see his son die, for good this time." I leapt against the building several times to get up onto the balcony.

But Elysara wasn't waiting like some damsel to be saved. She already had a bloody dagger in her hand and her other arm outstretched. "Absorb."

In front of the entire Elven populace, she caught the younger duke's ability and reflected it back on him with another shout of "Spell Mirror!". The blast sent him through the railing and he tumbled down four stories.

I couldn't help but grin at the display. Nobody would doubt that she was a Trelican after watching that display.

Guards rushed out from behind the curtains to recapture her.

I slammed my back against hers and drew out two daggers as she traded hers out for a trident. The guards rushed us, and I didn't have time to think, just act. My blades parried the first blade to come in my range. I ran it back over his opponents to tangle up their weapons.

The slight turn of my waist was mirrored by Elysara, whose hips stayed flat against mine. She covered my open side with a twirl of her trident before cleaving into the crowd in front of her.

I swayed back with her. "Elemental Shield." The barrier crackled into place along her now open side, catching a guard's weapon as I fanned my hand behind it.

I used the ability that had been a gift from Elysara to defend her. "Blades of Shadow." Over a dozen dark daggers shot out from my hand and dove into the crowd of guards.

The current guards attacking weren't nearly as strong as the ones that had been holding me before. They must have put the strongest guards on the Censors.

Back to back, Elysara and I fought, knocking guards off the balcony and whittling down those too stubborn to fall off. We were in perfect harmony as we protected each other.

A giant of an elf came charging through the curtains with a mace held high. I recognized him as the guard from the night before.

With nothing more than a glance, we broke apart. I went left and high, using my blades and going for his eyes. Meanwhile, Elysara went low using her trident to stab into his foot.

He was far too distracted with my daggers going for his eyes. He didn't even see it as his foot stuck to the ground and he stumbled.

I cut his forehead as he fell forward to try to reach his foot. We both gathered behind him for a moment and kicked as hard as we could, sending the large guard tumbling off the balcony.

The younger duke had been getting up only to have the large guard tumble down and slam him to the ground once again.

I jumped down, wanting to see the younger Duke's end, Elysara followed me, a special kind of hate in her eyes as she shoved her trident into his stomach and twirled it like a fork in spaghetti.

"Damn." I hissed.

"He fucking deserved it. But fear not, he didn't touch me last night. He tried and got a broken skull and venom in his eyes for it." A dark smile ghosted over Elysara's lips.

I stepped up and kissed her. "Never doubted you for a second. What do you say we make this our wedding?"

"That's enough." Tish appeared on the balcony with her sword out, threatening all the guards. "Lady, please address the people in this time of confusion."

Elysara smirked and grabbed my hand tightly, not letting me get away as we jumped to the front of the balcony that was missing most of its railing.

"My people!" she turned and shouted at the top of her lungs, still holding my hand tight. "Duke Selmia has attempted a coup. He, along with his family and his supporters, will be sentenced to death."

The crowd exploded into a cacophony of noise.

Elysara squeezed my hand tighter. "However!"

The voices calmed down when it was clear she was going to continue.

"However, let's not let this wedding go to waste! I, Elysara Rendral, do pledge myself to the man I've found harmony with. The Human Trelican, Ken Nagato!" she shouted loud enough that there was no mistaking her words.

I felt myself blush a little, but the current moment was a time to be bold. Through our harmony, I could feel her agree whole heartedly. It was all so fast and so sudden, but equally as right.

I grabbed Elysara and pulled her into a kiss that was anything but chaste. She kissed me back deeply, pushing her tongue past my lips and letting the kiss linger long enough that people were whistling and cheering.

She pulled back with a faint blush on her face. "They wanted a wedding. So, I gave them a wedding. You don't think me too rushed do you?"

"You are trouble. Besides, I told you to," I chuckled and held her hand before looking out at the sea of elves.

"You like a little trouble." She leaned against me.

Crimson came up to us, carrying Fayeth who joined the two of us with a giant smile.

Fayeth kissed Elysara quickly, before kissing me deeply and trilling excitedly.

"Ken. I hope you haven't been slacking on your training." Crimson clicked her tongue, a little jealousy painted on her face. "Getting kidnapped nor getting married will spare you from training. You need to get stronger."

I reached back and grabbed Crimson's hand, pulling her closer so that I could speak over the roaring sea of elves. "I know. Thank you, I need to get stronger or how else will I chain you up, pull you down, and make you mine?"

I was feeling particularly bold with all the cheering around us and the fact that we'd just escaped an awful situation. Crimson smashed her lips to mine, kissing me even as red lighting danced out of her closed eyes.

My tongue pushed into her mouth and she battled it for just a second before pulling back with slow, measured breaths.

"Promise." There was vulnerability in her eyes.

"Yeah, push me as hard as you like. I'm going to catch up," I told her.

The last few sparks danced out from her eyes. "Enjoy this time. We start training after."

CHAPTER 30

A part of me wanted to stay on the balcony with Elysara and Fayeth, but we had a lot we needed to get done.

Elysara dragged Fayeth and I down to do a quick greeting of the nobility.

Having Crimson with us was handy. She parted the crowd like the Red Sea wherever she went. There were going to be some very fun stories coming out of the slaughter that had just been witnessed by quite the crowd.

But the celebration was brief; our work was not done.

Elysara threw open the doors to the throne room and walked up the dais to sit on the throne. "Alright, we have much to do."

The room was largely empty with a large audience of empty chairs and seats for nobility to sit at, and one massive throne on the other end. Everything was carved and polished wood with flowers blooming along the edges.

I wasn't sure what the proper thing for me to do was, so I hung back with the Censors and Crimson as nobility filed into the room.

"Ken, don't be silly. Come sit on the bench up here." Elysara motioned to a plush bench that sat behind the throne.

I pulled Fayeth and Crimson with me. Neldra and Miriam came up behind me and stood to the side.

Leaning over, I met Miriam's eyes. "Gold-plated morals?"

She rolled her eyes. "I never betrayed Lady Rendral. I was simply biding my time."

"There's a clause in her contract. She got a bonus for that," Neldra added with a roll of her eyes.

"Ah," I sighed and leaned back, understanding the situation.

"Sometimes you just have to know how to manage certain people," Neldra muttered and then nodded for us to be quiet as Elysara started.

"While my father is out, I will be acting regent for The Great Holy Tree as well as temporarily holding the Emperor's throne." Her voice was clear as she spoke out across the gathered group.

"Several members of nobility have made a move attempting to counter mine and my father's wishes. Bring in Duke Selmia."

Two guards held the duke between them as they moved forward. The man looked worse for the wear and had to be dragged; no one had bothered to fix his legs.

"Bucket please." Elysara made a gesture, and the guards produced a bucket and placed it before the duke. "To disrupt our people in a time of war when we need to be united the most is a disgrace, a dishonor, and only serves our enemies."

Her expression was stone cold as she sat on the throne in her wedding dress and motioned for Neldra to step forward.

It was kind of hot to watch her assert her authority.

"For this, in the time of war, I sentence Duke Selmia to death." Elysara was short about it, clearly showing her dislike for both the Duke and needing to do this.

Yet, it needed to be done.

Neldra didn't hesitate and cleaved the Duke's head into the bucket while the two guards tipped him forward to control the splatter as best as they could.

The mess wasn't entirely contained; there was still blood on the floor.

Elysara leaned against her hand like she was bored and focused on the back of the room where a crowd was guarded heavily. "Leave it. Now, for the rest of you that were caught up in this treason, there will be an escort to bring you to the front lines of the current conflict with the naga. There, you will prove to myself and to my father that you still hold the best interest of our people in your hearts. If that proves true, I look forward to seeing you in the future."

The throne room was silent, and everyone was staring at Elysara with wide eyes.

"Dismissed." She waved her hand. "Bring them to my father for support immediately. Ensure that they are at the very front of the oncoming conflicts."

Crimson chuckled in the otherwise silent room, causing elves to turn and stare at her. "What? She is a pretty little thing, but I see she's got some barbs hidden after all. I like her."

"Thank you, Crimson." Elysara put on a blinding smile. "Given how much Ken talks about you, I was worried you'd not like me."

Crimson crushed me to her side. Somehow over her adventures, she'd gotten much more touchy feely, and I was just hoping she continued to remember that she could still break me.

"Ken talks about me?" Crimson asked, ignoring any effect she was having on me.

Elysara gave me a soft apologetic smile. "Yes. We should discuss that later. For now, I have to do some rather dull business." She cleared her throat. "Eight Trees will be changing regents. Please put in your bids by the end of the day. Discussion is now open."

Nobles started talking over one another, only to be organized by two of the attending Censors.

I zoned out, no longer interested, and shifted my attention to Crimson who was staring at me much like a cat would with a mouse it just caught.

"We were preoccupied earlier. Thank you for your help today." I dipped my head.

She scooted a little closer. "Oh, you know. Cut up a few elves here and a few elves there. Did my best to not kill all of them." She shrugged off what I had a feeling was a grand feat for anyone else.

She had been gone for a little over a month, stuck among a powerful race that would likely attack her on sight. If it were me, my nerves would be fraying, and I'd be twitchy while looking over my shoulder at every turn. Then I had asked her to dive right into battle to help me.

I rubbed at her back. "It must have been difficult." I meant more than just today.

Crimson stiffened for a moment before she relaxed and leaned on me. "Wasn't that bad," she muttered.

"No. You are just that strong," I told her. "We talked all night, but I still feel like we only scratched the surface. How long were you out of it in Limit Break?"

"Week... weeks?" She hesitated. "A lot of it is a blur," Crimson pouted. "I can see what happens now, though. And..." She stopped, clearly changing what she was going to say. "It's like driving something that is going too fast for you to react properly with."

"That's wonderful." I squeezed her in a side hug.

"It really is," Fayeth spoke from nearby, stars in her eyes. "Maybe then it wouldn't be too dangerous for Ken to get Limit Break one of these days."

"Get Limit Break?" Crimson asked.

"Yeah. You two could harmonize, and then he could use Absorb on you during sex." She smiled, genuinely meaning the offer.

Red sparks danced over Crimson's eyes before she covered them.

"Careful, Fayeth," I teased my Adrel. "Did you see any improvement in your stats?" I asked Crimson.

"Oh. Yeah." She held out her CID and showed me her stats, skills, everything as if I'd asked for the weather.

For someone of Crimson's level, the information she was showing me was vital. If it got out in the open, it could put her at a serious disadvantage.

"Holy fuck," I blurted and then covered my mouth. "You have over five thousand agility," I lowered my voice.

"It more than doubles with Limit Break." Crimson smirked. "That's just also how stats work. With exercises, levels and then gear. It resembles more of an exponential curve than a linear one. There's probably a better math term for it, but I teach people how to kill things, not math."

Crimson waved away my shock. "Speaking of killing things, I stopped at your family's estate. Everyone is fine and working hard. Even Harley is working hard, which was a surprise. She's got her own little group that she's been running with this summer," Crimson added.

"Good for her." I nodded along. "And I'm aware you are still avoiding the conversation about your trip to the naga, but we can talk about that later."

"Sure, we can see how much energy you have to chat in between our training sessions." Crimson's eyes glowed blue. "I need you as high a level as possible as soon as possible. By your current level, my guess is that you've let the elves power-level you." She clicked her tongue. "So lazy. We'll be correcting that."

I felt a cold sweat go down my back.

"Yay. That's the Crimson I remember," Fayeth giggled.

"You still owe me some one-on-one training for the summer. I haven't forgotten," I pointed out.

Crimson's eyes sparked. "Perfect."

***

Court ended, and the Duchess of Grestain didn't hesitate to seek me out.

"What a pleasure to see you again, Ken." She was all smiles. I caught it when her eyes flitted over to Crimson before returning to mine. She was definitely aware of Crimson's presence. All the elves were after the wedding. She had made quite the impression.

"The pleasure is all mine, duchess. A shame we missed our meeting. The situation got a little more complicated than I expected." I dipped my head.

"Well, you've been busy. Some things must take priority. I was actually coming to talk to you about that." The duchess moved a younger version of herself to stand in front of her. "This is my daughter. She's here to get a little experience."

"Silvie, pleasure to see you." Elysara came up and leaned on my shoulder. "That's right. We did miss the meeting with the trial of Duke Selmia." She clicked her tongue. "The rest of my day is actually rather free, but I don't know if that would be a bother for you?"

The duchess dipped her head. "Of course not. I'm happy to bend to your schedule. After all, even Great Trees must grow towards the sun."

"An apt comparison to Ken." Elysara squeezed herself to me and changed the meaning of her words. "Let's speak further in one of my rooms." She looked around for Tish and motioned for her to lead us.

The Royal Censor seemed to be in a much better mood than she'd been just a few hours ago. Though, they were still quite busy. Order had been restored, but there was still a hunt for the squeaky wheels.

It was almost startling how quickly the guards and the servants switched to the next leader. Then again, that was probably the best way for all of them to keep their heads. Sometimes people were forced to make choices against their wills for the sake of their survival.

Elysara walked with her arm in mine. "Crimson, I wanted to thank you again for your intervention today. You stopped a disaster."

Crimson shrugged off the comment. "I was just coming for Ken. Everything else was just a barrier between me and him." Her eyes dipped to where Elysara was holding my arm.

I held out my other arm for her. "Where's Fayeth?" I asked, having lost my other half.

"She went to check on her mother," Elysara answered. "Before you ask, she's fine. But give the two of them a little time alone. We'll go check on them after."

"Speaking of mothers, I still need to meet yours," I pointed out.

Elysara wiggled her nose in thought before nodding decisively. "Dinner with her tonight then."

"I'd love to," I answered.

Crimson had taken my arm, and the three of us walking abreast made it difficult for the duchess and her daughter to strike up conversation. They seemed to be waiting until we got to the room anyway.

"You're not going to get out of training for whatever this is," Crimson reminded me.

"We'll do exercises in the morning and then go diving in the early afternoon," Elysara agreed. "With my father out, I'm going to become a little busier."

"I'll make sure Ken is getting plenty of training." Crimson squeezed my arm possessively.

"There's no doubt about that," Elysara giggled and pushed some of her hair back. Letting it be clear that she welcomed Crimson in to do whatever she liked.

"I like your hair," Crimson commented. "Given the name, I always think about dyeing mine red, but then with my normal outfit. It feels like a little too much red." Crimson glanced down at her red dragon leather suit and then pulled at her long, black hair.

"Do you have like a dozen of those?" I pointed at the suit.

Elysara glanced at the outfit. "That's made from material from the raid on the fifty-sixth floor, isn't it?"

Crimson nodded. "Good eye."

"To get multiple whole-body suits of it... impressive," Elysara spoke with awe.

Crimson grinned. "When I was having difficulties with one of my skills, letting loose in a sealed raid was where I did some testing."

"You farmed it solo?" Elysara gasped in disbelief.

"Yep. Though, you have a point. Maybe I should find a raid in the sixties and see if there isn't a new outfit I can get materials for. Might even be a chance for that outfit change..." Crimson looked herself over.

Elysara had her CID up and was looking through something, leaning into me so that she didn't have to take her arm out of mine while she swiped at her CID.

"There's a raid with lizards that drop hide on the sixty-second floor," she answered. "That's pretty close to the fighting, though. I believe my father has set up a defense on the sixty-third floor at the moment."

"Oh?" Crimson tilted her head. "They are fighting the naga again?"

"A white matriarch pushed through around the same time that you came back. We were guessing that she chased you?"

Crimson gave an awkward laugh. "Might have destroyed her army."

"She found a new one. Those warriors are just fodder," Elysara explained with one of her eyes twitching at the absurdity of the concept.

Yet neither of us doubted that Crimson was capable of taking on the army.

"Ah. There sure were a lot of naga. Their world is kind of bleak," Crimson answered.

It was my turn to blink. "You saw their world?"

"Yeah. There's not really much to see, though. It's pretty wet. Some females and matriarchs, but mostly it was just eggs everywhere. It's like their world has been reduced to simply being a nest," Crimson explained. "The ground was littered with eggshells."

"Interesting." Elysara leaned forward, clearly interested. "We don't really know much about them."

"Do you need to know much about their lives? They are your enemies and to make it worse, they are the aggressors." Crimson had a grim view of it all.

I didn't disagree. There was no reason to even attempt to humanize them as long as they were constantly trying to invade the elves.

"We know they reach maturity pretty quickly and spend quite a bit of their lives in the dungeon," Elysara confirmed. "But some information might be important for war as well."

Crimson just grunted. "Sadly, until Ken is able to make portals, I don't think we are going to find an easy way to get there."

"Another reason that Ken needs to become stronger." Elysara looked at me out of the corner of her eyes.

"Too much to do. After this summer, I'm going back to Haylon. While the interests of the other races are fascinating, it is above my paygrade as a student."

My comment made Elysara roll her eyes. "Sure. Make sure you stay on top of your studies."

"The good news is that Crimson is allergic to slacking." I gestured to the woman on my other arm. "No chance I get to slow down."

Tish opened a door in the hallway and gestured us into the room, slowing down our idle chatter and bringing the Duchess of Grestain and her daughter, Silvie, into focus for the conversation.

"You are able to make portals?" Silvie asked. She was much like her mother, with deep blue hair and sharp hawkish features.

"No, just close them," Crimson scoffed. "He trapped me in the naga's territory."

"Don't say it like that." Guilt surged through me, and I had trouble looking Crimson in the eyes. I shifted my focus to her lips, which quirked up as she noticed my discomfort.

"He did. There was an invasion with naga coming into a fifth-floor safe zone next to our world. They've somehow contacted a group of humans and have been working with them to sabotage us. Our scientists were trying to connect safe zones with portals," Crimson explained.

"That would be quite the achievement," the duchess gasped.

"Well, the scientist working on it is now dead and Ken here absorbed her synthetic spellbook. I'm sure losing both will put them behind years." Crimson hooked a thumb at me.

I scratched the back of my head. "That's for the best. Otherwise, I think they'd try to study me."

"Fair." Crimson waffled her head. "But now Ken has the ability. He might just be able to use it one of these days. Or maybe he'll try to absorb more synthetic spellbooks."

I shuddered at the memory. "Having the dungeon focus on me like that was a lot. I don't want to know what would have happened if it made a different decision. It isn't worth the risk." The Dungeon felt like it could squish me on a whim.

"No, you aren't worth the risk." Elysara put a hand on my lap. "But for now, travel in the dungeon will have to remain the old-fashioned way. Which will make importing metals from Earth more difficult. We know shipping will be the hardest part." She brought us back to the topic at hand.

The duchess perked up as we shifted to business. "Yes. Sending an adventurer on such a route would be tedious."

"Thankfully, with a new alliance brewing between our two people. We can expect more regular travel from my Royal Censors, if you wouldn't mind cutting me into the deal." Elysara gave the Duchess a wide smile.

"Of course not, Empre— I mean, Lady Rendral." Her mistake was obvious, even to me.

Yet, the mistake still made Elysara smile wider. "Perfect. Neldra will continue to be a liaison. Miriam may take her place from time to time." Elysara turned to me as she crossed her legs and leaned back into the seat. "We could ship as much metal as you can back with each trip they make. The Royal Family will hold the metal for you until it needs to go to Grestain to fulfill your obligations that you set here today."

"You'll function as a buffer between the Nagato Clan and Grestain," I stated.

She nodded. "I'm far from a neutral party, but I also think that this could be beneficial for all of us."

"We'd want a rather large amount contracted up front," Silvie spoke up.

"How much?" Crimson asked, tapping at her CID.

Silvie looked at her mother and the two communicated silently for a moment before the duchess nodded having made the conversion beforehand. "At least a million metric tons."

"What do you need all that metal for?" Elysara asked with a slight frown.

"Infrastructure mostly," the duchess admitted. "Grestain is an old tree, and much of the sewers are only still running by the grace of the tree's roots. It would also allow us to update our farmland. The metal holds up far better for the newer automations, but it is in short supply and quite expensive. We haven't been able to justify it at open market prices."

Elysara nodded. "Alright then, let's get down to numbers and mana crystals."

CHAPTER 31

E lysara was in her full hostess mode as we prepared for dinner with her mother.

"Ken can sit here at the head." Elysara tapped on the chair, "Then I'll sit to the left and Fayeth to the right. Is it okay if you sit next to Fayeth and not Ken?" Elysara was doing her best to include Crimson, but she was fumbling about slightly.

Crimson pulled out the indicated chair and sat down with a chuckle. "Thank you for your consideration. I might be out of arm's reach from him, but he can't escape me."

"That makes sense." Elysara nodded to herself while Fayeth rubbed at her back. "Okay. I think Neldra went to get my mother and Fay." Elysara straightened the silverware and plates for the third time.

"Sit down." I pointed at her chair.

The dining room was immaculate. Soft blue walls made it feel very open, while polished wood trim made it ornate. The wood stain matched perfectly with the table to the extent that I wouldn't be shocked if they were a set. The table was set for six with what I could only assume was Elysara's nicest flatware.

"It's fine. I just need to..." She tried to continue 'fixing' everything.

[Shadow Arm] shot out from beneath me, grabbed her shoulder and gently turned her away from adjusting the tablecloth.

"Need to sit down and breathe," I finished the sentence for her.

"I want it to be perfect so that my mother likes you." Elysara continued to fidget but relented and sat down next to me.

"Thank you. I appreciate it." Taking her hand in mine, I ran a thumb over her hand to relax her.

The door opened, and if it wasn't for my adventurer reflexes, I wouldn't have caught Elysara's chair that she launched backwards with how quickly she stood.

"Mother." Elysara moved to greet the woman who entered.

I stood up too with a more relaxed smile. "Hello, both of you. Good to see you again, Fay. Great to see you, Selie." I called them both by their names rather than try to call them mother.

Elysara's mother, Selie, was a thin woman with a hard-set jaw and hair that was darker than Elysara and her father's. More the color of rust, her hair was only lightened by the strands of gray staining it.

"Ely, it's so good to see you. Fay-fay, you are as lovely as ever." The woman cordially greeted both before her eyes rested on me.

There was a tension in the air between us that she let settle into place long enough for Elysara to fidget again.

"And you," she spoke slowly, "have my thanks for the assistance you've provided for my daughter." She was being firm, but at least acknowledged that.

"Mother," Elysara whined. "This is my Adrel, Ken Nagato."

Her mother pursed her lips. "Yes, the man you married before even letting me meet him." She wasn't happy.

"The situation escalated quickly. It was the right move." Elysara was clearly uncomfortable as she shifted her body weight back and forth. It was cute to see her nervous before her mother.

I stepped around the table and wrapped my arms behind Ely, pulling her back to my chest. "Frankly, I think we rushed that a bit, don't you?" I said mostly for her mother's benefit. The two of us were in harmony.

Her mother nodded. "You did, but I also understand the situation my daughter was placed into."

"Then let's do our best to move forward?" I offered, extending an olive branch to my mother-in-law.

Her mother nodded her agreement, but couldn't help getting the last word in. "Your father will be quite upset when he returns," she warned.

"Actually, I think he would be happy. In his own way, he blessed this," I told her.

Both ladies looked at me like I'd grown a second head.

"No, really. The last thing he asked of me was that if we insisted on being together, that I would protect her." I kissed the top of Elysara's head. "So, I'll hold to that commitment."

That statement seemed to crack the ice with her mother, and the older Rendral smiled. "Remember that."

I turned away from the two ladies to see how the other mother-daughter pair was doing.

Fay was frozen still, staring at Crimson with no small amount of trepidation. Crimson was completely oblivious to the fear that the older elf was staring at her as she grabbed an appetizer off the table and popped it into her mouth.

"Fay, this is Crimson, my teacher and in all likelihood, a woman who'll join us as Adrel." I went around the table and put my hand on Fay's shoulder to guide her to the table. Unfortunately, we had laid out the table such that she'd be sitting right next to Crimson.

"Hello, mother." Crimson turned up the charm like she'd done with my grandparents. "Fayeth is a wonderful woman. She and I have a lot in common with our interest in Ken."

Crimson was still much more smiley than usual, and it was slightly creeping me out. But I wasn't about to challenge her.

"That's a lovely outfit." Fay struggled to do anything but stare.

"Thanks. It's kind of my signature." Crimson beamed. "Though, I'm thinking about changing it up."

"Oh?" Selie gracefully sat in her chair and engaged Crimson.

"You see." Crimson held up her long, black braid. "Some hear 'Crimson' and just assume everything is red. So, if I changed my outfit, maybe I could dye my hair red. As it is right now, that would be too much red."

"Red is a good color. Some might call it the best, but maybe Ken likes variety." Elysara gave Crimson a sly smile.

"What do you think?" Selie put the pressure on me.

I shrugged. "I'm surrounded by beautiful women. There's no need for me to ask for any changes." That was the truth. Though, Crimson could probably pull off a pretty hot red head.

"We aren't asking for a change, just your opinion." Crimson leaned on the table. "Maybe I'll have to get some new outfits and then just play with the colors? There are potions to change your hair now. Maybe I can find an ability to do it so I can refresh it whenever I want..."

"That could be fun." Selie glanced at Fay who still seemed frozen next to Crimson. "Fay, you might have heard, but Crimson saved our daughters today."

"She turned a small band of guards into a stain on the palace lawn," Fay agreed, still scared of Crimson.

"It wasn't that bad, mother, I just poked them all a few times." Crimson pouted. "Besides, I only did it because one of them had the audacity to punch Ken in front of me."

"Yes, quite the protective teacher you are," Selie commented and glanced over as an elf came in and poured wine for the table.

"Well, Ken is special," Crimson admitted. "One day, I'm certain he'll have the ability to join me in diving the dungeon. At my current level, I've outstripped humanity, and probably the elves too. It's lonely at the top, and so I'm eager for him to join me."

"Ah. Yes, he's a Trelican. A very powerful class." Selie nodded along. "Have you truly outstripped the elves?"

Crimson sipped at her wine. "This white matriarch that you are all so worried about, I fought her and her army single-handedly. Though, I ran from her because it was going to be a very drawn-out fight, but I don't think I would have lost."

"That's a bold claim." Selie narrowed her eyes.

Crimson shrugged and didn't bother with trying to prove it, instead she shifted her focus to Elysara. "So. How'd that throne feel? Getting comfortable with it?"

"Quite the contrary. It felt stifling. I'd like my father to return as quickly as possible so that I can spend more time with my Adrel. There's only a month before he has to go back, and I'm afraid that I'll be stuck here for some time," Ely pouted. "Are you sure you'd not like to govern, mother?"

"I set politics aside," Selie brushed the comment off.

"The weight of being an Empress must be heavy," Fay added in. "I remember when my parents pushed for me to take a man to raise my station, but I've seen too many dukes go gray early."

"You'd look great with gray hair," Fayeth tried to be helpful.

"Quiet you. I love my hair. Your father called it golden, and I wouldn't be a fool and trade gold for silver any day." Fay huffed and looked over her shoulder as two elves brought in dishes. "Oh, this looks lovely."

***

Dinner had become quiet as a full four courses, each with a pairing of wine, was laid out for us. Each dish was better than the last. It was truly a lavish meal that had me leaning back into my chair feeling stuffed.

Crimson pulled out a bag of chips as soon as we finished, and the squeak of the bag opening made Selie's face twitch.

"Don't like potato chips?" Crimson asked.

"Just an interesting option after everything we've eaten," the older elf commented dryly.

Fay was still quiet in her seat, but I could tell that the spark of conflict between Crimson and Selie had her once again worried.

"I like them," was all the explanation Crimson offered before popping another chip into her mouth.

"On that note." I cleared my throat. "What do you do now that you are done with politics, Selie?" I tried to go for light conversation now that dinner was done, but the wine was still flowing.

"Mostly teaching." The older elf was quiet.

"Teaching?" I asked. "What do you teach?"

"My mother is a little shy about it, but she does some outreach in which she funds and teaches those who come from poverty. It started as a PR thing, but she's grown fond of it," Elysara explained, eager to show off what her mother was spending her time on.

"It sounds so cliche... am I using that word right?" Selie turned to me.

"I think so. It's as cliche as a photo op for us. Yet, if you enjoy it, why should you care?" I smiled at her.

"Just so." Selie beamed back at me. "I felt it provided more fruits and deeper roots than governing."

Fayeth nodded at that. "To be fair, someone has to govern. It isn't that different from a party. Someone has to tank and lead the group. Someone else has to heal and keep everyone ready to keep on fighting."

Elysara tipped her wine glass back. "Does that make me a tank?"

"I think so." I lifted my glass as the server came back and poured us more. "You are keeping everything running. Maybe when your father comes back, you can sink back into damage dealing. Everyone knows that's the best role." I smirked and picked up my refilled wine.

"Not biased at all." Fayeth rolled her eyes. "Some people like to heal or be a tank." She gestured at Selie and bringing the conversation back to the woman's teaching and outreach.

"She's right. Going out and supporting the communities is a luxury, though. I know not everyone could remotely afford to spend the time, not to mention the cost." Selie held her hands out palms up. "Yet it is also self-serving, I enjoy when the students make achievements."

"I understand the sentiment." Crimson broke off part of a chip. "But what about your own goals? Don't you still have those, or are you going to claim that those are long gone?"

Selie grunted in a very un-empress-like manner. "You boxed me in with that statement."

Crimson crunched another chip loudly, but it didn't hide the corner of her lips curling up.

"My Adrel leads the empire, not me. Yet, I wish to do what I can for my people given the wealth of resources I have on hand." Selie gave a very political answer that didn't satisfy Crimson at all.

"Ever think about going back into the dungeon?" Crimson prodded. "You know, find three other beautiful ladies and tell your husband you just need one more to help?"

"Crimson," Elysara scolded her.

In response, Selie threw her head back, laughing. "That just might be the best suggestion someone has ever given me. Though he is dedicated to his people in his own way, it might soften him up. But I doubt he'll leave before Elysara is ready to step up. He wants her to have a life before she gets too tied down by the throne."

Ely dipped her head. "I know. He was quite rude to Ken, though."

"I'd have been ruder if you hadn't already proclaimed him your Adrel in front of all of our people." Selie rolled her eyes. "Really, what were you thinking?"

"That Father pushed hard to drive a wedge and break the harmony between Ken and me. I wanted to cement our harmony," Elysara pouted a little at her mother.

"If you two are truly in harmony, then there is no reason to rush anything," Selie chided her daughter.

"Ken is a catch," Crimson added. "Good on her for locking him down. From what I understand, there's even a Nekorian Grand Shaman trying to get closer to Ken. And back home, there are dozens of ladies at his dungeon college interested in him. Hell, that doesn't even include myself or a buxom redhead that goes by 'The Harem Queen', who would probably kill to get him alone."

Selie gave me an odd look. "You intend to become Adrel with this many? That would be the largest Adrel... since... since the founding emperor."

"It fits," Elysara answered with a smile. "He's also a Trelican."

I waved my hands in the air for them to stop. "Don't start shipping me off to dozens of ladies. I want a close party."

"You'll need a raid, eventually. First one is in the thirties..." Crimson tilted her head to the side for a moment. "That would be an interesting exercise next year."

"By the time we are doing raids, Harley might step out in search of her healer harem," Fayeth added.

"That would almost be like throwing Ken to the sharks," Crimson mock gasped.

"Well, if the rest of the class has kept up with us, which I doubt," I added. "It might not be something we touch until the third year."

"You'd be surprised. I think while you are having fancy dinner parties and sitting around in political drama, the rest of your class is working harder than you. Des is already level twenty-five. Meanwhile, Charlotte was level twenty one, but her stats are way ahead of her level," Crimson added. "Your little harem is blossoming this summer."

"Sounds like it." I leaned back, smiling and happy for the update that they were doing well. "Charlotte really pushed herself that much?"

"You'll have to see for yourself. By the time you get back, she's going to feel different, that's for sure. That mother of hers is a brutal but effective teacher."

"Huh. I guess I'll have to train a little harder these last few weeks." I grabbed Elysara's hand. "After all, I'm still a little behind you. While you are off handling matters, I can't stop training."

"I understand." Elysara patted my hand. "I already knew you were a dungeonhead."

"As long as you two are in harmony. Now that you've gone and announced it, you'll both have to put the effort in." Selie watched us carefully.

"We are committed," I promised her. "I guess part of me is quite greedy since I don't like to let things go."

That statement made Elysara smile. "Me as well. We'll make the long-distance work."

"Good." Selie dabbed at her lips with a tablecloth. "Then tonight is your wedding night, and we should all leave the wedding couple to enjoy their time together."

Elysara's cheeks turned as red as her hair, and she glanced at me out of the corner of her eye. "My bedroom should be cleaned and repaired by now. Miriam was supposed to make sure it happened."

"Then, if you'll all excuse me." I didn't let go of her hand as I stood up and pulled her along with me. "I have a part of my Adrel that needs to be in perfect harmony. Not to mention, I want to play with some of her other abilities."

Elysara's eyes widened slightly as she dipped her head at her mother. "Thank you for tonight, mother. Thank you for your daughter, Fay, and your tutelage of Ken, Crimson."

"Enjoy your night tonight. Tomorrow starts your training, Ken." Crimson wiggled her fingers at me with a big smirk on her face.

Elysara practically pulled me out of the room, biting her lip as a Censor cleared the hall ahead of us. "Thank you for being cordial with my mother even if she was a little aggressive with you at the start."

"She was just concerned for you like any mother should be." I stopped letting her take the lead and swept her off her feet. "Enough about your mother. I don't want to think about her right now. Just you. So, what combinations do you want to play with tonight?"

"Think it's sexy to get bitten?" A vampire settled over her form and a pair of fangs flashed at me. "Or maybe a little danger of becoming addicted?" A demon settled over her and a pair of horns jutted out of her hair while an aura of magnetism drew my eyes to hers.

"Finally. I've seen you look at those Nekorians." She let both of those fade before she overlayed herself with three different monsters, one of which had been a big tiger.

Elysara was now a red-haired Nekorian, or at least quite close. "Meow." She batted at my face.

"Pretty sure they'd be insulted if they saw you like that," I teased.

"Some things are more fun to pretend than they are in real life. Now, take me to the bedroom and show me which you like better." Elysara kissed me deeply, and I had to be careful where I was walking because even when I freed my lips, she wouldn't stop necking me and smothering me in kisses.

It wasn't until I threw her down on her bed that her body left mine for even a moment, and the second she hit the bed, she hooked her legs behind me to drag me closer.

CHAPTER 32

C rimson had several of the weights that I'd seen Neldra use wrapped over her shoulders while she deadlifted with the maximum weight on the bar. But even with all that added weight, it looked like she was just bending over to pick up some trash.

"This isn't that bad. I think I can feel it." Crimson teased Neldra as she worked through a set of twenty.

"We can't all be freaks of nature." The Elven censor leaned against the equipment; No one was bothering to spot Crimson.

Realistically, she just had to tap into [Limit Break] if required, and she wasn't actually exercising hard considering what that would do to her heartbeat.

I was fairly sure that she'd come down to the workout area to walk around in the workout clothes she'd clearly borrowed. They were the same Elven style that all the others wore, except Crimson's were a neon red.

"Ken, can you spot me?" Crimson asked.

"No." I deadpanned. "You aren't even working up a sweat."

Her eyes flashed dangerously, and she racked the weights with one hand, entirely proving my point, but that wasn't the problem right now.

"Your turn." She smiled sweetly. "Elysara, you can heal, right?"

"Yes! I can." Elysara replied a little too quickly for my liking.

"Great, we are going to do some intensive training for Ken." Crimson stepped away from the weights and changed the straps out.

"That's my one rep max." I stared at the weights.

"Uh huh." Crimson agreed. "I thought we'd really confuse the crap out of your muscles and let you do sets of twenty with enough healing to make it through." The smile Crimson gave me sent chills through my spine.

I had to admit her plan was feasible but sounded awful.

But I had to admit to myself that Crimson hadn't led me wrong yet, even if her methods were questionably brutal. "Alright. Ely, I'm in your hands."

Flowers bloomed around Elysara in a wreath. "I'll keep you going."

"Yes, we need to speed up Ken's training. He really is going to fall behind otherwise." Crimson lamented with a sad shake of her head.

I got under the bar and lifted it off, going for my first squat. As expected, I struggled through the single rep. Yet the feeling of accomplishment was washed out by the reality as healing swept through me. Crimson smiled until I dipped back down for a second.

The process continued for several reps. I was expecting Crimson to do something ridiculous as I finally reached the last of twenty reps.

Sure enough, she stepped up, putting her hands on my shoulders and stopped me dead about halfway up and put pressure on me.

"Keep going, Ken. You got this. Just finish this one." She eased up a little, letting me slowly come back to the top.

I grunted. It felt like I had a mountain on my shoulders until I finally finished with an enormous sigh.

"Great set." Crimson made sure the bar was secure. "First of five."

I glanced at Ely, who gave me a helpless shrug.

***

After our workout, I used taking a shower as an excuse to escape and hadn't returned.

"Ken, what are you doing?" Tish spotted me and my camouflage outside the palace.

"Hiding." I muttered from the bushes.

"Yeah. That was pretty brutal. I've never seen someone force the flight or fight response to increase your weight lifting before. When she strapped you in with enough weight over your head to crush you, I was a little worried. But you made some wonderful records." Tish gave me a stiff smile.

I deadpanned at Tish. "That's not the point. I need a break. She's going to push me again and again."

"It's how she shows her love." Tish shrugged. "It is very tough love."

"The fighting training was different. This is her just trying to crush me. I know she means best, but that was a little much." I looked around. Thankfully, she still hadn't found me.

"Well, you are going to have to make a decision. Because when she wants to come find you, she probably will find you. So, what are you going to do?" Tish asked, leaning against the wall.

I let out a breath. "I've handled monsters, thugs and assassins. Crimson's training isn't so bad."

"Glad you think so." Crimson spoke up behind me.

Jumping, I turned and glared at her. "You pushed it too far this morning. I understand the need to push me and I don't mind that, but this morning you kept stretching the finish line out ahead of me. It was demoralizing."

Crimson's smile dropped, and she kicked at the ground. "Maybe I was compensating."

"For?" I urged her on.

"For not being here all summer." Crimson's face scrunched up in anger. "I was off playing with naga for a month, and then when I got back it was clearly almost too late for something terrible to happen. Normally, I play it all off as casual, but that was cutting it really close. But!" Her face lit up. "If I get you as strong as possible as soon as possible, then I don't have to worry if I get pulled away again."

"First off, you weren't 'playing' with the naga. You got stuck there because you were once again defending me, and frankly, the entire earthen population." I clapped my hands against my sides and did a full bow to Crimson. "You've saved me several times now. It is on me to get stronger so that I can return the favor. And you are willing to help me get there, which I appreciate. But don't crush me like a tin can."

Crimson crossed her arms and shifted her weight. "Glad you've seen some sense. Alright, no crushing like a tin can. But I want those heavy cuffs back on your wrists. We'll do some training with Fayeth this afternoon while Miss Pretty Red Hair is busy with politics. You can have some fun with them after."

"You have a thing about the red hair, don't you?" I straightened up.

"I told you. People keep expecting me to have red hair. It's a thing." Crimson waved the comment off. "Now, as punishment for trying to hide and run away, I expect fifteen laps around the palace. Let's go."

I eyed Crimson. With the slight side comments, I would have sworn she was a little jealous of Elysara.

Tish flashed me a weak smile as I put on my cuffs and started a brisk jog around the palace. I found out pretty quickly that we were in fact not out for a simple jog.

Crimson decided to attack me at random throughout the run, making me be on edge with every step that I took.

***

After almost two weeks of training, I wished that I could have just lived life as a training montage rather than go through every aching and strained muscle.

But I had to give Crimson credit. My stats were racing upwards under her constant oversight and training.

I took [Hydra] from Elysara to use throughout, letting me self-heal as needed.

Today was different. I was getting ready, strapping on my dungeon gear.

Crimson, Tish, and I were going to go check out the front lines of the war with the naga.

Then Crimson and I were going camping in the raid on the 62nd floor. I would be in charge for that portion of the trip, and then we'd head back and Crimson was going to push me in combat to ensure I was acclimated to my new stats.

After that, I knew that I would only have a few days with Elysara before it was time for Fayeth and I to return to our world and continue our studies. I knew leaving Elysara would be tough, but I was excited at the idea of being back with Des and Charlotte.

"Alright." Tish had her armor polished to a mirror shine, and she had Miriam with her. It would just be the four of us in front of the palace dungeon entrance.

Crimson nodded and Tish's ability enveloped us in darkness, but the darkness struggled.

Crimson held a hand on my shoulder, and the ability had trouble curling around us.

Tish made an awkward sound. "If you'd please let it work, I can carry us to the sixty-third floor easily enough."

"Fine." Crimson stopped whatever she was doing and darkness carried us away.

I felt her hand on my shoulder the entire time. Though, the way her body moved, it seemed like she was looking around.

"Can you see in here?" I asked.

"Yup." Crimson turned to me, two glowing blue irises in the dark void. "I don't take chances with transport skills like these."

"Why's that?" I was curious if there was history there.

"Ever wonder why there aren't a dozen services offering to take you up and down the dungeon?" Crimson asked.

Now that she mentioned it, that would be pretty easy money for someone with an ability like Tish or my grandmother. Yet, I hadn't seen something like that yet. "Call me curious."

"Okay, Curious." Crimson's eyes crinkled in the dark. "People did them in the past, but they got a poor reputation. Not everyone who goes down the dungeon comes back up. So when people died, at first the taxis were blamed."

"But people dying in the dungeon is normalized, so they blamed it on those who needed a taxi to get to certain floors?" I asked filling in where this was going.

"Something like that, but the deaths continued until some governments pressured the UG to start guaranteeing these taxis. They looked into them. Lo-and-behold, a good twenty percent of them were actually killing their riders. Essentially, they were ferrying around these adventurers that were walking bank vaults." Crimson's callous laugh was eerie in the darkness.

"Well, that's just stupid. Killing off your clientèle?" I snorted.

"A few deaths and they could go buy a place in the Bahamas." Crimson explained. "A level forty plus adventurer is a walking hunk of cash. Strip him down and clean out his CID, then rinse and repeat a few times. It is fast money."

I grudgingly admitted that she was right, not that I liked the sound of people always looking for such short-term results. "Then what happened?"

"The market imploded. A few companies running the taxis went under and the UG cracked down. Now when you visit those high level safe zones, most of those are run by places that have transport on staff. They are vetted, and most likely threatened with death if they or their people go missing." Crimson chuckled. "It's a retiree's job now."

"So, they still needed people to transport, but they can't just do cheap third party all the time? Doesn't sound like such a bad end result." It wasn't like the third party workers really ever worked out well in the long run.

She just grunted. "I spent a long time wishing they were still a thing in the early 30's. It's a pain to go up and down that far and you don't have that much to make it better yourself. I actually found a shady group still doing them; got my ass robbed once."

"How are they now?" I asked, feeling like I already knew the answer.

"I painted the wall with them a few years later. They didn't remember me. I took a ride with them to the forties and then poof. Anyway, that's when I learned the history and why I watch out when I'm taking them now. So, be careful about accepting them yourself." Crimson finished her lesson.

"This isn't going to be a class lesson is it?" I teased.

"Fuck no. I killed the ones who did me wrong so that no one would ever hear the story again." Crimson chuckled. "But I trust you."

The dark void peeled away, and we were standing amid a dungeon floor that was occupied by thousands of elves. So many were around that nothing was spawning in the surroundings.

"Tish." An elf jogged forward and snapped a respectful nod of their head at the Royal Censor. "Are you here to bring a message?"

"Yep. Crimson and her protégé are here as well." Tish gestured to me.

The elf scowled at Crimson, but said nothing else as they gestured for us to follow and jogged back to a large tent set up in the middle of the camp.

I guessed that Crimson's reputation from the wedding hadn't spread here or they didn't believe it. Otherwise, they'd treat her with more respect.

Through it all, I could see where the exit from this floor to the next was located. Or at least, where I guessed it was through the wall of elves that stood around.

"They can only fit maybe two abreast through the stairs." Tish explained. "A hundred ranged damage dealers firing constantly into the stairs at the first sign of naga."

"There's a lot more than that here." I looked around at the elves gathered.

"Yeah. Every now and then they'll make a big push with a matriarch at the front. They'll try to establish a beachhead at the stairs. If they can get that set up, then it becomes a more formal battle." Tish moved through with the elf leading us and stopped when she entered the big tent and gave a full bow at her waist as we approached the Emperor.

Miriam did the same, and I quickly did a bow of my own.

Crimson grabbed my shoulder and straightened me up. "He's your father now. Don't bow to him."

Her words caught the emperor's attention, and his eyes flashed angrily to her and me.

He dismissed the elves that had been surrounding him. "A message from my daughter and... Crimson?" He spoke her name like a question.

"Back from playing with the naga." Crimson ignored his tone. "By the way, your palace was a mess. I had to clean it up to get to my protégé. Don't let it happen again." It was immediately awkward.

Tish cleared her throat and passed the Emperor a message with her CID.

The Emperor held up a finger to stop Crimson.

Crimson snorted, not caring. "We'll go check out the setup."

"You don't get to wander our camp on your own." The Emperor stopped her.

Crimson did a slow turn. Her eyes met the Emperors, and he sat back with a twitch of his face. "You'll have to stop me if you want to control me. I would advise against trying. Could be bad for diplomacy, and all that. Read the message. We'll be back."

Whatever the Emperor saw in her eyes made him struggle with his authority and hesitate.

She pressed on my shoulder and turned me, guiding me out of the tent.

The Emperor didn't try to stop her again, nor did he give her his express permission to leave.

I guess that was the best we were going to get.

Tish had a raised eyebrow, as if asking me if this was the wisest course of action.

But I knew that Crimson would be Crimson. There was very little I could do.

"Really?" I asked as soon as we were out of the way.

"He challenged me. Damn pushover needs to be taught a lesson if he does that again. Think he has someone who can revive him nearby?" Crimson asked with a far too casual tone.

I pressed my fingertip to my brow. "You aren't killing the Emperor. The man is far too proud to let that stand, and I don't want them sending all the Royal Censors to die at your hands."

"Aww. You think they'd all die." Crimson gushed.

"Not the point." I kept my head up as Crimson drew plenty of attention from all the surrounding elves. They weren't openly hostile, but more than a few were watching us warily. "Don't antagonize them. They are allies."

Crimson crossed her arms and walked with me to see closer to the stairs that they were guarding. "Didn't feel like the Emperor was one."

Like Tish had described, there were dozens of ranged DPS sitting around watching the stairs. Three of what seemed like tanks were standing not far away, ready to seal the stairs as well.

As we stood, a naga rushed out.

A powerful arrow, more like a ballista bolt pinned the naga down as a dozen magic spells crashed over the naga, obliterating it and sending more down the stairs it had come from.

I flinched at the sudden and brutal explosive nature of it all.

Crimson whistled. "Stupid slow ass naga."

"None of them seem to be particularly fast." I agreed and picked at my ringing ears.

The spells stopped, and then naga poured out from the smoke cloud.

Elves were yelling orders up and down the line as spells, and arrows started flying once again.

A white matriarch led the naga, throwing up shields to hold off the barrage of fire from a hundred and counting elves.

All six of her scaled arms were hurling up shields, buying time, as smaller female naga slithered out and threw their magic into the formation, creating great walls of light that held off the spells.

Even the warriors with their twisted flamberges came forward, using skills that created great blue shields in front of them with their swords in the ground.

As an army, they built up enough protections to shield the stairs so more could pour out onto this floor of the dungeon.

"Crimson..." I turned to her. We were being given a chance to help the elves and possibly improve relations with the elves.

"The Emperor was just rude to me." She crossed her arms. "Besides, it's just a few scaly bitches. I killed more when I sneezed."

"What if I asked you?" I tried another tactic, knowing Crimson's weakness

The Elven tanks moved forward, with powerful abilities that cut into the shields, shattering them.

Yet, even as they moved quickly, the shields were multiplying faster and faster as more naga emerged.

It was a situation that needed a swift blow of overwhelming power.

"If you asked me, then I would go." Crimson stated plainly. "I would kill them all and come back just fine."

I nodded. "Then I would like to ask for your help."

"Say it." Crimson's voice was a little funny. "Tell me to go kill them and come back."

"Fine." I shook my head. "Crimson, my lovely Crimson. For me, will you go kill all of these naga and then come back here to me?"

A big grin filled her face as red lightning crackled over her eyes. A moment later, the lightning flooded out from her eyes to subsume her entire body, crackling in and out of her skin.

I'd seen the ability before, but that was when it was simply crackling over her eyes or over a single arm. I'd never seen it reach the intensity in front of me, and I had to admit it was a little terrifying.

But something about the way she stood told me she had garnered at least a level of control over the ability.

Red lightning covered her entire body crackling. I took a step back, a little nervous being in such close proximity would draw one of the bolts to me.

But my step ended up being pointless. While I moved, Crimson also moved, exploding forward like a giant cannon as she headed straight on for the naga.

CHAPTER 33

I could barely breathe as I watched Crimson fight an army on her own. She was incredible; she was at what felt like an unreachable height.

Crimson slammed into the wall of magical barriers. Her fists blurred as she pounded into them as fast as they could come up. Yet, the explosions from her fists were able to blast past the shields, affecting the naga behind them.

Her sudden entrance gave the elves pause, and the barrage of spells petered out as they all stopped to watch the one woman army.

"Sever." Crimson drew her whip. The whip stretched unnaturally to its full length in a straight line as the skill turned it into a giant sword. She swept the weapon horizontally through the entire mass of naga.

A thin red line that seemed to devour all light around it cut right through the mass of naga.

Dozens of magical barriers exploded as the entire left and right wing of the expanding naga army was cut in half.

The only naga remaining was a holdout of the matriarch and the smaller female naga that were clustered in the center.

Crimson disappeared after the hit, only to reappear above them, striking down with the stiletto of her heels. Red magic ringed around her foot and became a powerful drill as she shot down like a meteor.

Any remaining barriers were shattered like glass underneath her heel before she crashed amid the few remaining naga.

I couldn't even see what happened next as dust from the impact blasted out. I had to shield my face to protect myself from the intensity of the wind.

When I could look back up, Crimson's whip was going wild and tearing into the dust cloud before it went taut.

On the other end, the naga had been annihilated down to the white matriarch.

Crimson glowed as the elves threw buff after buff onto her. Meanwhile, other elves started throwing debuffs onto the matriarch. Soon, the matriarch had glowing cracks and dark splotches all over her white scales.

The naga matriarch turned to run, throwing Crimson's whip down. Apparently, the difference that the buffs were making was too much for the matriarch to stay.

Crimson smiled, clearly not planning to let her opponent slink off. Crimson's whip wrapped around the tail of the matriarch, and with a jerk of her arm, she pulled the matriarch back in range and unsheathed her short sword.

The resulting clash blew back the elves, and I slid on the ground, leaning into the gust.

Miriam appeared at my side to help me steady myself. "Damn."

"That's Crimson for you." I shook my head. The battle was mostly hidden at that point, but I could hear the explosive ring as she traded blows with the naga matriarch.

"She should really sell her services." Miriam offered. "I bet she'd get paid better than me."

"Think you could take her?" I asked.

"Not a chance. I'm more concerned if I could survive a confrontation with her." Miriam watched the battle with interest, rooting herself in the ground in front of me. "She certainly makes an impression though."

Crimson came out of the cloud of the conflict, once again using her ability as she slammed her heel down on the matriarch.

There was a finality to the blow, silence descending as the battle was completed.

A Crimson crackling with red lightning as she reappeared before me.

Miriam took a step back; the lightning was reaching and stretching, trying to crush her.

I didn't know what to do for a moment as I stared at Crimson. There was no reason to believe she was in control and wouldn't crush me, but somehow, I trusted her.

"Booooop." Crimson poked my nose and [Limit Break] disappeared as she made a long tone. "What are you looking all worried for?" She blew a raspberry at me. "You look like I was about to go on a murder spree or something."

"Glad to have you back Crimson." I moved her finger off my nose.

I paused, suddenly feeling all the eyes that were on me. Every elf in the area was staring at me like they needed to memorize what I looked like.

Crimson, they already had ingrained in their memory. But now they were taking notice that I was important to her. And therefore it was vital to their own survival and wellbeing that they didn't harm me.

Even the Emperor had come out of his tent to watch the battle and was staring at us.

"I think he'll treat you better now if we go back." I offered.

Crimson grunted and pulled out a bag of potato chips. "He'd better. I just helped him with his little snake problem." She crunched loudly as she shoved a whole fistful of chips into her mouth.

I glanced at her.

"Wha?" She said with a mouthful of chips. "'As 'ungry work." She swallowed a big lump of chips.

I nodded to Miriam and headed back towards the Emperor's tent.

The older man seemed far happier to see me as we approached, though he beat me back inside and resumed his seat on the throne.

"Hello again." I waved as Crimson came along behind me, trying to lighten the mood.

Crimson had finished the first bag of chips and had started in on her second. "Hi Emperor. Did you read the message?"

He cleared his throat. "I did. It seems that you aided my daughter in some difficult times." It was an indirect thank you, but it appeared to be as close as he would go for the moment.

Crimson chewed on a chip for a moment, thinking over his words, before she swallowed. "Got your wife out of prison. She was probably going to die in it, too." She added pressure.

"That too." The Emperor agreed, a little sweat beginning to accumulate on his forehead.

"Saved your new son-in-law. Saved a bunch of your nobles and some of the fighting power that is here now." Crimson continued to stare him down and bit off another chip with a little extra bite.

Even I could see that she wasn't happy with his response and was just going to keep piling on.

"Thank you." The Emperor acquiesced.

"Don't mention it. It was for Ken here. He was the one that asked me to go play with the scaly visitors too." She smiled, intensity filling her eyes as she immediately dismissed the thank you she had pressured out of him.

I was glad that she'd done the recent display of power. Otherwise, the words she was choosing likely would have led to far more conflict.

"Then thank you too, Ken." The Emperor nodded.

Only once he thanked me did Crimson smile.

"You are welcome. I'm guessing the letter included news of our wedding?" I asked.

"Yes." The Emperor leaned back and steepled his fingers, his eyes drifting to Crimson. "I was considering what to do about that."

Based on the look he was wearing, his opinion had changed in the last few minutes after seeing Crimson in action.

"Well, if I may be so bold, Elysara has made her wishes clear." Tish butted in.

"So she has." The Emperor waved Tish away. "It seems that you will be involved in my life for some time to come." The Emperor didn't seem too happy about that involvement, but that was his problem not mine.

"Are you returning to The Great Holy Tree?" I asked, somewhat hoping that he'd free up Elysara.

"No. We will stay here for a time until we can reclaim up to the 65th floor. It is vital that we hold a blockade between us and the aggressors." The Emperor sucked in a breath and sighed. "However, it would seem that there may be more value to relations with the humans than I expected."

Crimson loudly broke a chip in response.

It was impressive how she used a basic food item as verbal and actual weapons.

"As adrel with your daughter, it would be my pleasure to return to my world with that news." I dipped my head, knowing Crimson would stop me from doing more.

"Wonderful. Ah... Crimson, what are your thoughts?" The Emperor shifted his gaze.

She finished chewing her current chip before she spoke. "I just get to sit in the room when the important people talk. As long as I keep training Ken and killing shit. I don't care much for politics."

The Emperor was at a momentary loss of words. "I... uh... understand. What will you be doing now?"

"The raid on the 62nd floor. Ken and I are going camping." Crimson answered. "For a few days, I'm all his."

Tish snorted at the implication.

"Well, I look forward to forging new alliances between our two people." The Emperor gave us both a soft smile and a clear dismissal.

"Thank you. For what it is worth, I protected Ely." I grabbed Crimson and ushered her out before she could upset the Emperor. If I had to guess, he was struggling with his thoughts at the moment. An agreement to negotiate later gave him time to get those thoughts in order.

He had likely read the message and been about to throw a fit, but now he'd seen Crimson in action and was of two very different minds.

"Your father-in-law doesn't like you much." Crimson muttered.

"No. No, he does not." I sighed. "So. Want to tell me more about raids?"

Crimson frowned. "Later, when we get back to Haylon. I think next year will have plenty to do with raids. All you need to know for now is to hold on tight." She wrapped an arm around my waist and shot off while holding me.

***

The raid on the 62nd floor was not full of lizards.

There was a very clear misunderstanding between Elvish and English when the raid zone had been described to Crimson.

Of course, that wasn't my primary concern.

"Mush!" Crimson shouted as she rode atop a giant T-rex, cracking her whip and making it chase me. "Keep running, Ken! This one is really slow." To be more accurate, the raid was full of dinosaurs.

My heart pounded in my chest as my feet beat across the hard packed path, trying to outrun the dinosaur. "Crimson, I thought you were farming these for their leather!"

"I killed all the others. This one's name is Fred because if he catches you, it rhymes with dead." She cackled and urged the T-rex on.

I didn't care what she had said. Fred was not slow. It might be slow for a level sixty two, but it was not slow.

If it got close enough, Fred's jaws would assuredly crush me in a swift single blow, if it didn't just run over me and kill me with the massive claws on its feet.

"There's camp!" I pointed up ahead.

"Fine." Crimson jumped off Fred, and with a flick of her wrist, her whip wrapped all around him and cut him to ribbons before it puffed into black smoke and she landed on the ground. "Oh. Some more leather. We should really play with colors."

"Play with colors?" I dashed back to the campsite that Crimson had set up and grabbed a bottle of water before pouring it down my throat. We had been training for the last two days.

"Yeah. You have me all to yourself and you haven't done anything fun. Just training." Crimson's eyes held a challenge. "I even told you that you'd get a kiss if you could outrun Fred."

I stepped up to Crimson until she was backed to a wall and put a hand against the wall behind her so that I was leaning into her. "That's right. Close your eyes."

She closed her eyes and swayed back and forth patiently.

"Crimson." I whispered. "Thank you for what you've done for me. I'm going to work my ass off to catch up to you."

She tilted her head up and waited patiently.

My other hand grabbed her chin, and I slowly pressed my lips to hers.

Red sparks poured out from her closed eyes, but she didn't move except to open her lips slightly and suck on mine.

It was a slow, searching kiss as we both braced for [Limit Break] to interrupt us.

"Tell it to stop." Crimson breathed. "You are in charge today. Tell me to turn it off."

"Crimson, stop using limit break." I breathed against her ear.

Like I had flipped a switch, the red lightning cut off.

I kissed her again, this time with less tenderness and more heat.

Crimson mirrored my passion and moaned.

The kiss lasted only about thirty seconds before [Limit Break] sprang back to life, blasting me a foot away.

"Stop." I panted, my clothes seared from the lightning.

The ability turned off again.

"Fuck. Fuckity Fuck!" Crimson let out a string of curses. "I thought we had this under control!"

I chuckled. "Far better than before. Maybe we can figure this out a little slower though."

"Fine." Crimson grumbled. "I'm taking out the hair dye potions and you are going to make me drink them. Give me a kiss with each and see which you like better."

"We can do that." I nodded and picked at my collar where there were a few burns and activated [Hydra]. I'd used that ability many times during the day already.

Crimson laid out a dozen vials, each a vivid color and arranged them from dark to light. "These were all I could get from the elves. They seem to have dazzling hair color choices."

I stared at them. "Do you want to go in order or...?" I hesitated.

"If there's one you like best, we'll do it last. They'll last a few days if I don't take them back to back." Crimson played with one that was a dark blue, almost a blue velvet. "Yep, we'll do this one first. I always liked the expression 'so black it was blue'." She popped the top off and slugged it back like a shot.

It took a few moments, but the dark blue color rippled out from her scalp to dye her entire hair. "What do you think?" She did a little twirl.

"I think you need to be pressed up against a wall." It was clear she was trying to come up with excuses for me to get physical with her.

Given the way her ability worked with her heart rate, I wondered if she'd been able to even relieve herself in years.

We kissed, and I pulled away just in time for red lightning to spark across her. "Turn it off." I demanded.

Her ability fizzled out again and Crimson pouted. "I don't know. You didn't seem all that hot and bothered about blue. We'll have to go down the line. Test each one thoroughly."

I nodded along. "Don't do the next one yet. Maybe we should do a small fashion show. Can we really be sure if it works if we don't try multiple clothing sets with it?"

We couldn't do more than kiss, but there were other ways to be intimate.

Crimson beamed. "I do have a lot stuffed away in here." She pulled at her CID and out came first one, then a second rack of clothing. "We can either let you use me like a dress up doll or..."

"Or you could just try them all on for me one at a time." I suggested.

Crimson blurred and her red dragon leather was replaced with an obscenely tight white blouse and black pencil skirt along with glasses and a ruler. "Someone has detention." She smacked the ruler against my chest.

I pulled her close for another brief kiss, and she blurred again into another outfit.

I was happy to spend the rest of the day playing with her and giving her some attention. It was a hell of a lot more enjoyable than being chased down by Fred.

***

I woke up and rolled out of the bed with Elysara.

It was the last night we'd have together before I headed back to my world.

She peeked open her eyes and propped herself up on one arm. "That time already?"

"Afraid so. Time for me to head home." I glanced down at her and the still sleeping Fayeth, along with the mess we'd made of the sheets.

"Don't worry, someone will straighten them. I slept with a tag on this corner." She held up the offending tag. "It was over there at the beginning of the night." She pointed to the opposite corner. "I have no idea how we rotated them all the way around."

"We were having too much fun." I kissed Elysara, a long lingering kiss that neither of us wanted to break.

That kiss went on for minutes until someone knocked on the door.

"Lady, breakfast is served, and this is your wake up." Neldra spoke from the other side of the door.

Elysara held the kiss for another moment before breaking it. "Fine. We'll get you going. But the second my father is done with the war, I'm chasing you down."

"Promise." I teased her. "Don't be too late, or you heard Crimson, I just have dozens and dozens of ladies after me."

Elysara rolled her eyes and slid out of bed, putting her feet in a pair of slippers and covering her delicious nudity with a fine robe. "Are you going to get Fay-fay up?"

I nudged the sleeping elf, who was still fast asleep. "Care to do it together?"

Ely came around the side and took Fayeth's arms and I lifted her legs and dragged the other elf out of bed.

"Huh?" Fayeth mumbled halfway out.

Ely kissed her upside down. "Good Morning. You have to go today, and I'll need a dozen promises that you'll take care of our adrel while I'm not there."

"Promise. Now sleep." Fayeth tried to pull Ely back to sleep.

"No, you don't." Elysara was strong enough to lift the other elf out of bed and set her on her wobbling feet.

The trick to getting Fayeth up was removing her from the bed. Nothing else was effective.

Fayeth blinked several times, and like a miracle she was now wide awake. "Oh, did I sleep in?"

"Yes, you did. Breakfast now. Then we are heading out, otherwise we'll be late for our second year at Haylon. Who knows what the Headmistress would do to us if we were late?" I said, before realizing she'd been late last year and missed the whole 'I'll kick you out spiel'. In fact, tardiness probably would have no effect on her given that the Headmistress didn't follow through for her.

"Oh. Okay. I wonder what Charlotte and Desmonda have been up to. Do you think they've changed at all?"

"Have we changed?" I asked.

"Certainly. It was a big summer." Fayeth nodded and started dealing with the straps of her dress. "Next up, breakfast. Then our second year." She beamed at me.

AFTERWORD

Hey Everyone,

I hope that you enjoyed DD104. We stepped away from the school life and got a little serious for summer break. Don't worry, we'll be back to the school and lighter storyline for the next book in the series. This was a necessary pitstop along the way.

Otherwise, I'm happily churning away on Ard's Oath 2. My wife thinks some of Ard is spilling over into how I talk, which is one hundred percent appreciated, I'm sure.

After AO2, I have a month 'off'. My second kid is coming and I am going to chip away at a non-harem book as a side project. Or maybe I'll just play with a few side projects. There's a reincarnation, the non-harem and a scifi that I've been fiddling with when I need to step away from my current projects. All of which have about 1/4 to a 1/3 of a book written. Many of my book ones go through something similar where they get fiddled with every now and then, reread and expanded multiple times. The ideas of those books just age a little longer.

Anywho, thanks for reading I'll be back with the next book in the series, I already have a solid idea for it.

Please, if you enjoyed the book, leave a review.

Review Dungeon Diving 104

I have a few places you can stay up to date on my latest.

Monthly Newsletter

Facebook Page

Patreon

Made in the USA
Monee, IL
12 January 2024